Praise for Leslie Tentler's
MIDNIGHT CALLER

"A smooth prose style and an authentic
Big Easy vibe distinguish Tentler's debut...
the shivers are worthy of a Lisa Jackson."
—*Publishers Weekly*

"Tentler's novel is filled with suspense and
mystery and centered around a compelling plot
with a terrifying villain, and two main characters
readers will come to care deeply about.
This is one riveting read."
—*RT Book Reviews*

"A romantic thriller that continually
keeps you on the edge of your seat."
—*Fresh Fiction*

"With twists and turns around every corner,
Tentler has crafted a dark, contemporary
romantic thriller that will enthrall readers.
The Vampire-like killings will strike a
resonating chord with thriller fans, and
her sensual romance between Trevor and Rain
will thrill romance fans."
—*Night Owl Romance*

"Leslie Tentler shows what she is capable of...
producing a first-class suspense/mystery novel."
—*Manic Readers*

"Readers will relish this well-written,
tense thriller...the taut tale means
leaving the lights on after midnight."
—*Genre Go Round Reviews*

Also by Leslie Tentler

MIDNIGHT CALLER

Look for Leslie Tentler's next novel
EDGE OF MIDNIGHT
coming soon from MIRA Books

leslie TENTLER

midnight FEAR

MIRA®

MIRA®

Recycling programs
for this product may
not exist in your area.

ISBN-13: 978-0-7783-1246-8

MIDNIGHT FEAR

For questions and comments about the quality of this book please contact us at Customer_eCare@Harlequin.ca.

www.MIRABooks.com

Printed in U.S.A.

In memory of my father,
who told me to "go for it."

I did, Dad.

Prologue

Southwest Washington, D.C.

The muffled cry meant the woman was still alive. Reid Novak tightened his grip on the Glock braced in front of him and moved cautiously forward, his eyes searching the shadows of the abandoned factory. Above him, anemic moonlight filtered through grime-streaked windows set in crumbling brick.

Another distorted sob. They were close. His adrenaline soared and he felt his heart pound.

He sensed more than heard his partner's presence behind him. Although FBI agent Mitch Tierney looked like defensive line material for the Washington Redskins, he possessed a surprising stealthy grace. He moved into Reid's line of vision, the barrel of his powerful firearm leading his stride.

"Blood splatter," Mitch noted in a rough whisper. He jerked his jaw downward to point out the trail of drops. "Party's already started."

Together they inched to the blackened doorway,

acutely aware of the rotted wood floor beneath them. Reid looked at Mitch in the tide of darkness, a voiceless communication occurring between them. Then he removed his left hand from the Glock and raised three fingers, giving the count.

One. Two. Three.

He turned the corner, Mitch covering him as he burst into the room.

"FBI!" Reid made a sweeping arc with the gun, his eyes straining to find human form. His breath clouded in the biting cold. The cavernous industrial space held the rusty odor of mildew.

"Jesus. There," Mitch growled.

Faint light from a far window barely illuminated the victim. Her mouth had been covered with duct tape and her hands were bound together as if in prayer. The large knife being pressed against her throat glinted silver. Already, the woman's white blouse was torn and streaked with blood. Joshua Edward Cahill stood behind her, the planes of his face submerged in shadow. He clutched her against his chest.

"Drop the knife, Joshua." Reid kept his voice calm, moving closer.

"I'll cut her throat!"

The woman made a mewling sound as he pressed the knife harder. Her eyes grew large and rolled back in fear. A thin line of crimson appeared on her pale throat. Despite the frigid air, Reid felt a drop of perspiration roll down his back.

"Damn it," Mitch snapped, lurching forward. Reid halted him.

"Look at me, Joshua."

"Go away!"

"You know I can't do that. Step back and let her go."

"So you can send me to prison? Someone told you wrong, Agent Novak. I'm a *paranoid schizophrenic with poor control of impulsive behavior*." His derisive tone sounded as if he were quoting from a psychiatrist's notepad. "I'm not a moron."

"No one has to die."

"Right." Joshua's voice cracked as he took a step toward the floor-to-ceiling window, dragging his captive with him. She struggled until another nick with the knife made her freeze. Reid knew that three stories below lay the icy Potomac, snaking along the ground like a black ribbon edged in snowdrifts. He stood about ten yards away now, his gun still trained on the shadow that was a U.S. senator's son.

"We can take you to Dr. Lauderbach," he bartered. "You trust him, right?"

"Lauderbach's an asshole."

As he dipped his head into the wash of moonlight, Joshua's dark eyes appeared beneath a shock of ebony hair. He glared at Reid and tightened his hold on his hostage. The woman was in her early thirties, blonde, with legs clad in dark tights beneath a plaid skirt. She'd lost one shoe somewhere in her nightmare. Panting, her cheeks puffed in and out behind the gunmetal-gray tape concealing the lower part of her face. Reid looked into her tear-filled eyes and tried not to look there again. To do so would be to lose his objectivity, something he couldn't afford.

"So what do you want, Joshua?"

"I want to see my sister! I want to see Caitlyn!"

"We'll get her for you, man," Mitch offered, the sagging hardwood planking emitting a groan beneath him. Reid feared his partner might go crashing through to the next floor.

"You're lying—"

Mitch advanced a step. "We'll send a unit for her. Have her here in fifteen minutes. But you've got to give us something. Give us the woman—"

Joshua's voice rose, steeped in panic. "You step back! I'll slit her goddamn throat!"

Mitch did as ordered—no easy task, Reid realized. His partner was wired, his big shoulders hunched under the navy Bureau jacket like a cat ready to spring on its prey.

"Caitlyn took my journal, didn't she?" Joshua cut his gaze to Reid. Betrayal burned in his eyes. "She gave it to you."

"That doesn't matter—"

"It does to me!"

Reid tensed as Joshua dragged his captive closer to the window, coming to a stop only when his back met the filthy glass. Where were the sharpshooters? There should be a helicopter overhead by now. The trickle of blood pooled in the collar of the woman's blouse. Reid's mouth went dry. Joshua's hostility was escalating. They were running out of time.

"Caitlyn gave me the journal," he acknowledged. "She cares about you. She wants you to get help."

Hearing this, Joshua's face crumpled. He sniveled and scrubbed a hand over his eyes but didn't remove the one that held the knife to the woman's throat. Reid's index finger remained poised on the Glock's trigger. Could he get off a clear shot? The woman made an effective shield. If his bullet missed its mark by even an inch...

Joshua muttered under his breath, his words rippling with vulgarity and promises of violence. In his peripheral vision, Reid saw Mitch closing in again. His partner apparently sensed the same build of energy around them, hinting at the growing doom.

"You said nobody has to die." Joshua's dark eyes glittered.

"Nobody does—"

"What if I want to?" He let out a high-pitched sob. "What if I want to end it right now?"

"Joshua...listen to me. Don't."

The crack of rotting wood filled the room.

"Fuck!"

Reid saw Mitch fall through, his legs disappearing into the hole that had opened up in the floor. His gun skittered away as his arms flailed to gain purchase on the remaining planks.

Joshua struck. The knife's cold metal flashed across the pale throat in a fierce move, with Reid's gun discharging a fraction of a second later. He barely noticed the weapon's kick that flared pain into his wrist. Struck in the shoulder, Joshua fell backward into the window, crashing through it in a burst of shattered glass.

The woman dropped to the floor like a broken doll. Blood rushed from the gash in her throat. Reid landed on his knees beside her, already knowing it was too late. Her body convulsed as he leaned over her, trying to apply pressure to the wound with his hands. Arterial spray covered his jacket. Behind him, Mitch had hauled himself from the splintered wood. He now hung half-way out the window, looking down into the Potomac where Cahill had disappeared. He barked orders over his radio to the team below.

"Find him! Find that little son of a bitch!"

Reid's attempts to control the bleeding were useless. He looked into the woman's eyes, all need for objectivity gone. Her fear faded as her gaze became fixed, the pupils dilated. A feeble last rattle of air left her body. He felt her fluttering pulse stop. "No. No!"

Mitch laid a hand on Reid's shoulder. He shook it off, anger and helplessness choking him. There was no point in CPR. His throat burned. The air around him smelled of gunpowder and blood.

"Carotid's severed—she's gone," Mitch stated, voice flat. "Let it go."

Reid sat back on his heels, his palms slick with blood. Above them, a helicopter roared over the building, its spotlight searching the river. The gaping hole where the window had been let in a glacial blast of January wind. He shuddered, the icy air seeping into his chest and making it hard to breathe. Already, he could hear the mechanical crank and rattle inside the ancient elevator shaft, telling him paramedics were on their way. But there was no hurry now. He continued to hold the woman's still-bound, lifeless hand.

For two weeks, Joshua Cahill had been a suspect in the serial murders case. His father had done everything possible to keep the joint police and FBI investigation away from his son. But in the end, Reid had been right. Whether Senator Braden Cahill was worried about his own reputation or was in serious denial about Joshua's mental illness was up for speculation.

"Damn near fell through to the next floor." Mitch had returned to the window to scan the black water. "You think he's dead?"

"Maybe," Reid answered softly. "I don't know."

He closed his eyes against the scene. Pain bloomed inside his brain, the beginning of another migraine. He'd desperately wanted to end Cahill's spree at five victims. But tonight, one more woman had been added to the gruesome, senseless list. Should he have taken his chance? Fired in that instant before the weakened floor gave in? Before Joshua had made his choice?

Rising from the floor, he prepared himself for the onslaught of questions that would be launched at him. Questions that would start with SAC Johnston and no doubt travel all the way down from Capitol Hill.

1

Two Years Later
Near Middleburg, Virginia

I trusted you, Caity.

Caitlyn Cahill jerked awake, her heart racing. It took a second to realize she'd been dreaming again. Still, her brother's face—his voice—had been as clear as if he'd been standing next to her bed. In her dream-image of Joshua, he gripped a large kitchen knife and his eyes were black with hatred.

She had the nightmare at least once a week.

With a slow release of breath, she sat up and looked at the clock on the nightstand. Outside her bedroom window, she heard only familiar morning sounds. Although it wasn't quite light yet, a meadowlark chirped from a branch in the stately orange-leafed oak, and a horse's whinny drifted up from the stables. Caitlyn had taken refuge in the rolling horse country of Northern

Virginia, using her trust fund to purchase the rambling, two-story farmhouse with stables and acreage.

She'd had to get away.

After Joshua's capture, after her father's fatal stroke, there had been little left in Washington to keep her there. The high-society lifestyle she'd been raised in had come to an abrupt end. *Ostracized* was the more specific description of her treatment. At times, she admitted only to herself that she wished Joshua had died from his gunshot wound, or drowned after his fall into the Potomac, instead of law enforcement fishing him from its icy depths. But then she felt guilty, then guilty again for thinking of her brother instead of the six innocent lives he had taken.

He was sick. But was that an excuse?

Nothing could ever explain what he had done.

When Joshua's trial was over—a three-week maelstrom involving forensic evidence and psychological testimony—Caitlyn had quietly packed and left without a word to those who had once been her family's supporters and friends. She understood anyone with the last name Cahill was a pariah now, and that it was best for others to disassociate lest they carry residual dishonor.

Her father, Senator Braden Cahill, hadn't been able to bear the weight of Joshua's sins. He'd collapsed during a press conference announcing his resignation, and died a week later. Then her mother, Caroline, had lost what was left of her mind.

The Rambling Rose stables and farm had provided the distraction Caitlyn needed, had given her a purpose that made it possible to go on living despite the notoriety and shame. She'd transformed the stables into a therapeutic equine center that helped disabled and disadvantaged children by allowing them to groom, care for and ride horses. Caitlyn had given her time, energies and funds to create the nonprofit, animal-assisted therapy program. In her mind, Rambling Rose was a way to somehow try to make up for the evil her brother had done.

It was late October, and the crisp early morning air made the old house chilly. Caitlyn pulled a roomy cable-knit sweater on over her pajamas, then padded downstairs to make coffee and prepare for the day. A bus full of special needs children from D.C. was expected in a few hours, and she needed to arrange for box lunches—turkey sandwiches, yogurt, apples and oatmeal-raisin cookies—from one of the quaint restaurants in nearby Middleburg. Caitlyn also planned to lead the afternoon program herself, taking the more advanced children out for a ride along the forested path. On top of that, Eli Burton, one of the area's large-animal vets, was coming out to check on a weanling.

The coffeemaker had just begun its steamy drip into the carafe when the telephone rang. Caitlyn picked up the handset, settling it between her right shoulder and ear as she rummaged in the stainless steel refrigerator looking for the last carrot muffin.

"Ms. Cahill?"

"Yes?"

"This is Hal Feingold."

She closed the fridge door. The reporter's name caused a churning sensation inside her stomach.

"I apologize for the early hour. You may remember me. I covered the Capital Killer investigation for the *Washington Post,* but I'm out on my own now."

"I know who you are, Mr. Feingold," she said.

"I wanted you to know that I'm working on a book."

"About my brother?"

"About your family, actually. About their role in the murder investigation."

Caitlyn hated the faint tremor in her voice. "I won't give you authorization."

"I don't need it, Ms. Cahill," he replied in a calm tone. "It's a matter of public record. Not to mention your father was a public figure. One could argue *you* are, as well. You played a key role in your brother's arrest. You took his journal to the FBI after the judge—a friend of Senator Cahill's—refused to sign the search-and-seizure warrant on the Logan Circle property. A very brave decision. I know what it did to your family—"

Caitlyn's words were clipped. "Goodbye, Mr. Feingold."

"The book is happening with or without your co-operation. I'm offering you the opportunity to present your side of the story. You should consider it."

Caitlyn stared at her image in the window over the deep farmhouse sink. The glass created a mirrorlike reflection, and she ran a hand through her sleep-mussed, honey-blond hair. She didn't want the book in print, didn't want it to create any renewed interest two years later. She couldn't live through it again.

"Ms. Cahill? I'd like to come out and speak with you in person. Perhaps we could talk about you writing a preface—"

"Please don't," she whispered, and disconnected the phone. It actually didn't surprise her that someone wanted to write her family's story; it had all the characteristics of a bestseller. Two foster children brought into a loving, prominent family and given everything they needed to succeed. Only one of the children couldn't fight his internal demons and became one himself. Caitlyn had been adopted as a newborn, but Joshua had been years older when he was taken from his abusive, drug-addicted mother. According to psychologists, the damage had already been done. But it had taken years for the evil to seep out. The fact that D.C. had no capital punishment was the only thing that had kept Joshua off death row.

Thinking of him, a mixture of anger and bittersweet nostalgia built inside her. He wasn't her biological brother, but there had been a strong connection between them, up until Joshua's schizophrenia had progressed in his early twenties. She wanted to remember him like he was in their childhood—shy, intensely intelligent yet withdrawn—but somehow she couldn't. All she saw was the face of a killer. Caitlyn left the muffin on the distressed butcher-block counter, the coffee equally forgotten. But she hadn't yet exited the kitchen when the phone rang again. Expecting the pushy journalist, she answered tersely.

"Mr. Feingold—"

"Caitlyn, it's Manny Ruiz."

"Manny," she said on a sigh, relief threading through her. The big, raw-boned foreman managed the day-to-day tactical activities on the working ranch, including the stables. "I'm sorry. I thought you were someone else."

"I've got some bad news." Sorrow roughened his voice. "It's about Aggie. One of the stable hands found her this morning. She was about fifty yards off the trail…she's dead."

His words stunned her, tightening her throat. Aggie was a gentle, fifteen-year-old dappled mare and a particular favorite of Caitlyn's. She had been missing from the Rambling Rose stables for several days. Aggie was known to occasionally wander away in search of sweet clover, and Caitlyn herself had taken out another horse looking for her, to no avail. "What happened?"

A long beat of silence. "Someone killed her, Caitlyn. Her, um…her throat's cut…among other things. It's a pretty big mess. I'd say it happened days ago."

She felt the blood drain from her face. Finding her voice, she said, "I'll be right there."

"Maybe you shouldn't—I'm not sure you want to see it."

"I'm coming down," she repeated. "Have you called the police?"

"They said they'd be by later this morning."

After she said goodbye and replaced the phone on its console, Caitlyn stood, immobile, shock still coursing through her. She wrapped her arms around her slender frame and slowly shook her head in disbelief. She'd loved Aggie. Her heart twisted at the thought that someone could kill such a beautiful, living creature. And for what? The senselessness of it rocked her and made her realize that violence could reach far beyond the urban sprawl.

Even out here, nothing was safe.

2

The cell phone woke him, a Justin Timberlake ring tone one of his nieces must have downloaded as a joke. Reid Novak squinted against the morning sunlight angling through the window blinds. He lay on the couch in his apartment in D.C.'s Adams Morgan neighborhood, the television on and turned to CNN. Running his hands over his face, he reached for the phone, desperate to shut off its electronic wail.

"Novak," he muttered.

"Agent Novak, it's SAC Johnston—"

Reid sat up, caught off guard by the SAC's deep baritone. He hadn't heard it in months, at least not in any official capacity.

"Sorry to be calling so early. I realize you're still on medical leave for another three weeks. How are you feeling, Agent?"

He squeezed the bridge of his nose. "I'm fine."

"Good. We've been keeping up with your recovery at

the Bureau. If you're up to it, there's something I'd like to discuss with you. I need your professional analysis."

Reid picked up his wristwatch, which rested on a stack of *Sports Illustrated* magazines. He looked at its face—7:32 a.m. "What is it?"

"A homicide investigation. The District police have referred it to us. Agents Tierney and Morehouse are at the scene now," Johnston said, referring to Reid's partner and the rookie agent he'd been paired with in his absence.

"What's the reason for the referral?"

Johnston took a deliberate pause. "There are some notable similarities to the Cahill murders. I thought you should have a look."

Reid felt his shoulders tense. The Capital Killer investigation had been particularly high profile, which was why the FBI's Violent Crimes Unit had gotten involved. "How similar?"

"I'd like you to get over there."

He located a pen and notepad. Listening, he jotted down the street address in the city's Columbia Heights neighborhood where the body had been found.

"You aren't yet cleared for duty," Johnston reminded. "I'm authorizing you to go to the scene and determine the threat level. See what stands out to you. I'm sure Agent Tierney will appreciate the assistance."

"Yes, sir." The SAC didn't have to elaborate. He wanted to know if the specifics of the crime scene were merely coincidental, or if it indeed suggested a copycat looking to emulate Cahill's work. The only certainty was that it wasn't Joshua Cahill himself—he was incarcerated, serving a life sentence without any possibility of parole. That fate had come about only after a roster of high-paid attorneys failed to have him declared mentally unable to stand trial. Reid's own deposition had seen to that. Cahill was psychotic, yes—but he was also highly intelligent and an ordered, methodical killer as opposed to a disordered one. Those facts made him culpable for his crimes.

"Three weeks left on your leave isn't very long," Johnston noted. "Have you been to the firing range?"

"Not yet," Reid admitted. "Soon."

"See that you do. You'll have to re-certify on firearms, as well as use of deadly force. No more blurred vision, I hope?"

He felt his face grow hot. "No."

"That's excellent news. You're one of our best profilers." He sounded sincere. "You've been missed by the VCU."

After the call ended, Reid scrubbed a hand through his dark hair, grown back to its previous thickness after surgery for a benign but critically located glioma some six months earlier. At what point last night had he stumbled out of the bedroom and ended up on the couch? He didn't often use the prescription sleeping pills Dr. Isrelsen had given him, but last night he'd been particularly restless.

I'm fine now. The tumor was gone, and so were the

headaches and double vision that had been the first signs of his illness. He was working out at the gym regularly and felt back to his old self. His last two MRI scans were clean. Reid knew he was one of the lucky ones. But the health scare had changed him. For the first time since graduating top of his class at Quantico nine years ago and starting work for the FBI, his life hadn't revolved around criminal violence. Instead, he'd had more personal problems to deal with, confronted with the very real possibility of his own death or incapacitation. Reid thought it ironic that with the dangers his job entailed, it wasn't a homicidal maniac but his body's own rebellion that had nearly killed him.

Without warning, an image of the woman in the abandoned factory—Cahill's last victim—flashed inside his head in Technicolor clarity. He saw her terrified eyes and the glinting knife Cahill held to her throat. Then the bright spray of blood, the prim white blouse turning red and her body shuddering as she bled out in front of him. Reid's bullet had been a half-second too late, his hesitation costing Julianne Hunter her life. She had been the wife of an up-and-coming prosecutor in the federal courts, with two small children who were now without a mother. His failure in stopping her death had cut him particularly deep.

His hand traveled over the sofa's leather as he shook away the brutal recollection. Only to himself, Reid admitted that the one small benefit of his illness had been the temporary distance he'd gained from all that—the victims' haunting faces, the shocking cruelty he'd been witness to, his self-recrimination for not stopping the madness sooner.

Sometimes he wasn't completely sure he wanted to go back there.

The row houses were being converted into condos in a newly revitalized area of Columbia Heights, an urban neighborhood just a few miles from the White House. Although the area still had a reputation for gang activity and drug-related crimes, it was slowly giving way to gentrification, evidenced by the smattering of upscale coffee shops and restaurants.

Reid pulled his Ford Explorer next to a semicircle of police cruisers blocking the end of the street. *Just like riding a bicycle,* he thought with a slow release of breath as he opened the door and climbed from the SUV. He pulled his shield from the pocket of his leather jacket and flashed it at the uniforms congregated outside the last unit. Then he ducked under the crisscrossed crime scene tape, went up the short flight of stairs that led to the stoop and entered the building.

Inside, the hardwood floors were battered and gang symbols had been spray-painted on dingy walls. A rickety staircase missing sections of its banister snaked up to the second floor. Just inside the front door, a barrel-chested cop with silver hair and a guard-dog expression stood sentry.

"What do you know, a fibby in jeans," he mused, examining Reid's shield. "Thought you boys had a dress code."

"Sorry to disappoint you."

He shrugged. "This 187's getting its share of Fed attention. There's two of your kind already back there."

"Were you the first responder?"

The cop grunted in acknowledgment. "Carpenters arrived early this morning to start construction—this is the only building that isn't pre-sold. They found the body and called 911."

"You took their statement?"

"Tried to. So did the Ward One detectives. The workmen are Hispanic—big surprise—'no speaky English,'" he said in a mimicked accent. "They're still in the kitchen if you want to give it a go."

He looked Reid over with a quizzical expression, his bushy eyebrows lifting. "You headed up that serial murder case a couple of years ago, right? The Capital Killer? Senator's son turned Ted Bundy? I recognize you from the TV."

Reid didn't reply, instead heading down the dreary, windowless hallway. As he neared the back room, he heard Mitch Tierney's booming voice.

"Hey, Reid. Johnston said he was sending you out here."

His partner stood in what appeared to have once been a dining room, directing a forensics photographer on a series of shots being taken of a bloody footprint. Mitch was dressed in a navy suit that made his coarse, sandy hair stand out in contrast. He stepped forward and clapped Reid's back with a large, latex-gloved hand. "You should've told him you were still on vacation."

"Medical leave."

"Whatever." Mitch gave a goading grin. "Want to meet your replacement?"

"*Temporary* replacement," agent Jimmy Morehouse emphasized, shaking hands with Reid. Blond and fresh-faced, he looked to be straight out of the academy. "SAC Johnston says I'm being reassigned once you're ready for duty. You can have your old partner back."

"You don't want him?"

"Like you'd let me go," Mitch wisecracked. "Novak and me are like Batman and Robin. Giving me up would be tantamount to losing his superpowers."

He introduced Reid to the two D.C. homicide detectives also on the scene. Then, sending Morehouse in search of the crime scene log, Mitch grumbled privately. "Seriously? Johnston thinks I can't handle this on my own? I worked the Cahill case right beside you."

"I know," Reid agreed.

"He forgets because the cameras preferred your pretty face over my Irish mug."

"I think he just wants to ease me back into the job."

"Or maybe he thinks I can't walk and chew gum at the same time." Mitch blew out a breath, his hand disappearing into his nape as he rubbed his muscular neck. "You know what? Forget it. My massive ego aside, it's good to see you, Reid. I'm getting tired of wiping rookie ass. Morehouse can barely holster his gun. I keep threatening to take his bullets away from him."

He punched Reid's arm. "You look good. A hell of a lot better than when you were lying in the hospital six months ago. And Johnston's right about one thing. I'm going to need some *adult* assistance. Especially if we're dealing with what I think we are."

Dread knotted Reid's gut. "Where's the body?"

"Basement. You're not going to like this."

Reid waited in somber silence as Forensics finished its job, bagging the corpse's hands so it could be moved to the M.E.'s office without disturbing evidence that might have been captured under the fingernails or in the hands clenched with rigor mortis. The basement was the secondary crime scene; lividity and the relative absence of blood indicated the body had been dumped there postmortem. The fetid odor of death permeated the space, causing Morehouse to excuse himself and escape back up the stairwell as soon as he could think of a reason.

"Forensics estimates she's been dead twenty-four to twenty-eight hours." Crossing his arms over his chest, Mitch leaned against the cinder block wall. "So what do you think? You're the crack profiler—Johnston wants your opinion. Do we have a copycat on our hands?"

Reid's gaze traveled again over the victim. Bruising was evident on the wrists and ankles, indicating that she'd been bound during the torture evident on her nude body. While the blackened ligature marks around the neck revealed strangulation, knife incisions were visible on the breasts, abdomen and thighs.

"There're similarities," he acknowledged quietly. "The use of restraints and pattern of mutilation."

"Those are generalities. That's not an answer."

Reid looked at Mitch. "I think the pawn is your answer."

Now in a cellophane evidence Baggie, the Staunton chess piece, a pawn, had been inserted into the mouth of the corpse. To Reid, it simply said *your move,* and its very presence made him feel as if a razor blade had slid over his nerves. Joshua Cahill had been a rated chess master.

"Anyone checked on Cahill at Springdale recently?" he asked.

"I called there an hour ago. Snug as a bug in a maximum security cell."

Kneeling next to the corpse, Reid examined the small, circular marks on the pale skin of the right forearm. Joshua Cahill had claimed in testimony that his birth mother had burned him with cigarettes as a child, before he'd been remanded into foster care. It was an act he had repeated on his victims. "Sexual penetration?"

"Preliminary forensics suggests it. We'll know postautopsy. There might be DNA."

"No condom? That wouldn't match Cahill's MO."

"No," Mitch conceded.

Reid studied the woman's face. She had been attractive, that much he could tell despite the ravages of death. Her long hair was blond and well maintained. She might have been in her early to mid-thirties. Her bare feet appeared to have had a recent pedicure, her toenails painted with a tasteful neutral polish. She belonged to somebody, Reid thought, a mix of anger and helplessness tightening his throat. They always did. There was a roommate, a husband, a mother, children somewhere—she hadn't come home to. He tamped down his emotions.

"How did the unsub get the body inside?"

"There's a service door in back," Mitch said. "The direction of the footprints indicates it was the entrance point. The perp likely carried or dragged the body to the basement. Blood smears on the floor indicate the latter."

"And no one saw anything?"

"Uniforms are conducting a door-to-door, but so far, nothing. This last unit's been undisturbed for months."

A dreadlocked member of the M.E.'s office interrupted them, asking if his team could start the process for removing the body. Reid left Mitch to attend to matters and went back up the stairs, feeling the need for daylight and fresh air.

A solarium was positioned to the right of the stairwell, although its windows had been boarded to discourage vagrants. Reid walked to the room's far corner, the aged linoleum creaking under his feet. Cool autumn air seeped through a crack in the plywood covering the windows. Through the two-inch vertical slit he glimpsed a burst of bright yellow, a sugar maple in the house's side yard. Morning sunlight worked its way through the crack, causing something to glint on the worn flooring. He bent to retrieve it.

"What's that?" Mitch asked, entering the room.

"A horseshoe."

"What?"

"A charm." Using his gloved hand, Reid carefully picked up the U-shaped pendant by its edges. It was white gold or platinum, with a small diamond embedded in its arch. *Tiffany & Co.* was engraved on its back in small print.

"Was the victim wearing any jewelry? A charm bracelet?"

Mitch shook his head. "He probably dragged the vic through here on the way to the basement. The charm got torn off whatever he ended up taking as a souvenir. That or the Mexicans pocketed it before calling 911."

Withdrawing an evidence bag from his suit jacket, Mitch opened it so Reid could drop the object inside. Then he examined the charm more closely. "Tiffany, huh? And fancy horse crap to boot. Cahill liked the ones with money, too."

Reid didn't answer, lost in his own thoughts. But he wasn't thinking of the current crime scene or of the victim. Instead, another honeyed blonde appeared in his mind. One with a direct connection to Joshua Cahill and an affinity for horses.

The last time he'd seen Caitlyn Cahill, her world had been collapsing around her. In many ways, Reid knew he was to blame. He'd appealed to her—pressured her—and torn between family loyalty and a need to do what was right, Caitlyn had given in. She'd delivered what Reid needed to harden the case against Joshua Cahill and finally put him away.

And then he had walked out of her life. Reid had

placed FBI protocol ahead of any feelings he might have had for her, or that he suspected she felt for him. He had maintained the professionalism his job required, but he hadn't forgotten her. He'd thought of Caitlyn, in fact, as he lay in the sterile confines of a hospital room, waiting to see if the tumor pressing on his optic nerve was operable.

The team from the M.E.'s office moved past, carrying the black body bag. Reid looked away, trying to dismiss the grim proceedings from his mind. But he couldn't shake the heavy, troubling feeling of déjà vu.

It was as if somehow Joshua Cahill had managed to strike again.

3

Caitlyn watched as the backhoe operator filled the hole in the wooded hillside where Aggie's remains had been laid to rest. Her heart heavy, she shivered as the afternoon sun failed to warm her. When the task was finally completed, she climbed onto her white-socked bay and began the trek back to the stables, unable to stop thinking about the horse's gruesome death. The sight and odor of the carcass, deteriorating, buzzing with flies, would remain etched in her mind forever.

As she left the trail and came into the clearing near the equestrian schooling ring, she spotted Manny outside the stables, still talking with Ed Malcolm, the Middleburg chief of police. A third man had joined them. Tall and broad-shouldered, he had dark hair and wore jeans with a leather jacket. Only as Caitlyn climbed from the horse did she realize who it was.

Reid Novak's cool gray eyes met hers.

He gave her a small nod. Caitlyn remained frozen. One of the stable hands took the horse's reins from her and led the bay into the stalls. As Reid approached, she took inventory of him. He looked thinner, different in some way, but he was as handsome as she remembered. She tried to sort through the tangle of emotions she felt.

"Caitlyn," he said in greeting, his voice rough.

She took the hand he offered, aware of the chill to her fingers despite her recent ride. Children's laughter came from the stable's tack room. Caitlyn hadn't wanted to disappoint, so the therapy program had gone on as planned despite the discovery of Aggie's body.

"Agent Novak."

"Reid," he corrected. "I thought we were beyond formalities, Caitlyn."

"I haven't seen you since the trial." She lifted her chin, a faint defensiveness in her words. "Why are you here?"

If her abruptness bothered him, he didn't show it. Instead, he squinted toward the range of smoky Blue Ridge Mountains behind her. She could see his mind working and wondered what he was preparing to let her in on. The visit was one of necessity, not pleasure, she knew, and that worried her. The possibility that something had happened to Joshua in prison, and that Reid had come to tell her himself, crossed her mind.

"The police chief says there was a horse mutilation on your property?"

"Manny found her this morning," Caitlyn replied solemnly. "Chief Malcolm thinks it was some local teenagers. There've been rumors about them being part of a satanic cult."

"Do you believe that?"

Uneasiness washed through her. "I really don't know what to think. It's hard to imagine that anyone—especially teenagers—could do something like this."

But she had mulled it over. If Chief Malcolm's guess was accurate, Caitlyn wondered if her farm had been selected at random, or whether she'd been targeted because of Joshua's notoriety. The thought of a bunch of kids attacking Aggie in some sort of twisted homage to her brother made her stomach turn. Caitlyn ran her hands over the thighs of her riding pants, brushing away a thin layer of dust from the trail. Pride forced her to keep her tone impassive. "Surely you didn't come all the way out here about a dead horse, Agent. Or is the FBI's Violent Crimes Unit now dabbling in agricultural matters?"

He didn't reply, but the seriousness she saw in his eyes made apprehension tingle along her skin.

"Is there somewhere we can talk in private?"

"My office," she said, and began walking efficiently toward the stables, self-conscious about the messy ponytail her hair had been hastily pulled into that morning. Although Caitlyn didn't look back, she heard the thud of Reid's hiking boots on the packed dirt as he followed her inside. Once they were seated in the modest office—a small, sparsely furnished room with Rambling Rose Equine Therapy printed on its door—Caitlyn's gaze again met his.

"You're doing a good thing out here, Caitlyn."

"You're familiar with the program?"

"I saw the article about it in the *Washington Post* last spring."

Caitlyn felt inexplicably pleased he'd kept up with her, and proud of her achievement in equine-assisted learning. She had put her heart as well as her bank account into the stables. "I have four instructors now, all part-time but they're certified. I received my EAL training this past summer so I also teach some of the courses myself."

"If I recall, your background is in social work?"

Caitlyn nodded. She had chosen that field of study to give something back to the system that—at least in her case—had worked. After being abandoned by her birth mother when she was only a few weeks old, Caitlyn had lived in the care of a foster family until her adoption by Braden and Caroline Cahill. Prior to Joshua's arrest, she had also served as director at one of the District's urban centers for at-risk children, and held seats on the boards of several nonprofits, positions of prestige that being Senator Cahill's daughter provided. The equine therapy program allowed her to continue her work while staying out of the D.C. spotlight.

"How's your mother?" Reid asked, pulling her from her thoughts.

"I had to move her to a full-time care facility. I'm putting the house in Georgetown up for sale."

"I'm sorry." He sounded sincere.

A horse whickered from one of the interior stalls, reminding her why they'd gone inside to her office.

Caitlyn straightened the papers on her desk, her posture rigid. "You wanted to talk in private, Agent Novak?"

He didn't comment on her continued formality. "Have you spoken with Joshua recently?"

"No, I…" She shook her head. "We haven't talked since before the trial."

"Has he attempted to contact you?"

"Joshua believes I betrayed him. I don't expect to hear from him, nor do I want to."

"I understand."

"Do you?" she asked softly, an irrational dart of resentment sailing through her.

"I know what your role in the investigation cost you, Caitlyn," he said. "And no matter what Joshua did, I understand he is still your brother."

"He's a murderer," she whispered. Her face felt hot. "What he did—"

"Wasn't your fault." Reid reached across the desk and covered her hand with his, an unexpected, consoling gesture. Caitlyn didn't look at him, afraid her eyes would reveal the loneliness and pain she'd felt since her family's unraveling. Reid was a specialist in behavioral psychology with an advanced degree—surely he could sense such things. When he withdrew his hand after a brief moment, she released a breath and slowly repeated the question she'd asked earlier.

"Why are you here?"

"I was at a homicide scene this morning. A female victim. The signature was similar to Joshua's." A tense beat of silence fell between them. "It's being viewed as a possible copycat."

What felt like a cold stone sat in the pit of Caitlyn's stomach. "You think someone's emulating Joshua? Why?"

"There are a couple of theories." Reid templed his fingers on the desk as he spoke. "It's believed copycats have the same impulses as regular killers, but lack the originality to go their own path so they mimic the style of someone they admire. They may also view it as a bonding ritual with the original killer."

"You said *regular* killers. I'd consider that an oxymoron."

He gave a small nod. "That's true."

"How was the murder similar to…" Caitlyn's voice trailed off, but she forced herself to finish. "To the ones Joshua committed?"

"The victim's physical description is similar to the women he chose—mid-twenties to mid-thirties, blonde, attractive. There's also a similar pattern of wounds to the body. The COD—" realizing his use of law enforcement lingo, Reid checked himself "—the cause of death appears to be strangulation."

"What about the cigarette burns?"

"They were present, as well."

Caitlyn swallowed, thinking of the crime scene details brought out during Joshua's trial. "But those things could be purely coincidental, couldn't they? It isn't enough to know for certain."

"There's something else. A chess piece, a pawn, was inserted into the victim's mouth."

She felt a chill. Joshua's mastery of the game had been widely discussed in the press reports surrounding his arrest and trial, since it pointed to his high intellect and was symbolic of the privilege and culture in which he'd been raised. One journalist had even used the game as a metaphor for describing Senator Cahill's strategy for thwarting the FBI investigation into his son. It was a game her father had been winning until Reid Novak approached Caitlyn and convinced her Joshua was responsible, asking for her help.

Her arms folded over her white turtleneck sweater, Caitlyn stood and walked the short length of the office, until she reached the window that provided a view into the equestrian ring. Sarah, her newest instructor, was on foot and leading a brown gelding by the reins. A boy of about ten, his face and anatomy bearing the physical characteristics of Down's syndrome, sat in the horse's saddle. His expression was one of pure delight. Above them, the sky was bright blue with only a few wispy clouds.

Caitlyn sensed Reid's presence behind her. She turned slowly, tilting her head upward to stare into his face. She'd been right. There was a new leanness to him and his dark hair was shorter, making his strong, clean-cut features more pronounced.

"I wanted you to know about this. If there are other murders, it could create renewed media interest in your brother."

Her throat felt tight. "You think there could be... others?"

"I hope not. But the chess pawn indicates the perpetrator wanted to be sure we made the connection. It's not a good sign. Just be prepared, Caitlyn."

She did her best to sound calm and nonchalant. "I appreciate your concern—"

"I also want you to be on alert."

She blinked. "Why?"

"A charm was found at the crime scene. Most likely, it fell off a bracelet the victim was wearing. It had a Tiffany logo, so the Bureau's checking the store registry to see if they can trace it to the owner in order to ID the victim." When he saw her puzzled expression, he added, "The charm was a horseshoe."

She understood where he was headed. "Virginia *is* horse country. That doesn't mean anything."

"Maybe not. At least that's what I kept telling myself until I came up here and found out about your mutilated horse. What if it isn't coincidental?"

An image of Aggie's bloated corpse filled her mind. "What are you suggesting? That I knew the woman? Or that I'm a possible target?"

He sighed tiredly, rubbing his forehead with two fingers of his right hand. "I don't know what I'm saying. I just felt the need to come up here and see you, that's all."

They stared at one another for several seconds, a meaningful silence filling the space between them.

Then she asked, "Did you mention any of this to Chief Malcolm?"

"He didn't see any connection between the D.C. murder and your horse, either. 'Barking up the wrong tree, son,' is how he put it. I hope he's right."

Looking into those flint-gray eyes, Caitlyn wondered how one man could conjure up such feelings of physical desire and pain in her simultaneously. She thought of the spark they seemed to have shared even as Reid had urged her to search for evidence that could prove Joshua's guilt. Afterward, she wondered if she'd only imagined the magnetic pull between them, or if Reid had simply charmed her in order to close his case, to get what he'd wanted.

"I brought a Polaroid snapshot from the crime scene." Reid sounded hesitant. "I know it's a long shot, but would you be willing to take a look at it? Make sure you don't know the victim?"

She took a small breath, preparing herself. Reid withdrew the photo from his jeans pocket and handed it to her. Caitlyn felt her stomach clench. The victim's skin was blue-tinged and waxy, her eyes sunken and corneas clouded. She didn't look real.

"No," she said in a soft voice, shaking her head. "I can't be sure, but...no."

He retrieved the photo. "Thank you for looking."

She nodded without speaking.

"I *am* sorry for what you went through. For what happened to your life." Reid's voice was a low rasp. "I should have told you that sooner."

He appeared as if he wanted to say something more, but instead he broke their gaze and walked to her desk. Picking up a pen, he wrote on a small notepad she kept there.

"That's my cell number. If anything unusual happens, don't hesitate to call me."

"I still have your card from before—"

"This is my personal number. I'm currently on leave from the VCU."

The announcement surprised her. She didn't see Reid as someone who took time off for an extended vacation. "But you said you were at the crime scene—"

"As a consult only, due to the similarities to the previous murders." He offered no further explanation. Reid retrieved his leather jacket, which had been folded over the back of his chair, and put it on. She noticed its soft, distressed leather and realized that until now she had seen him only in the dress suit and tie that his job with the FBI required. The casual clothes on him—the faded jeans and hiking boots, the long-sleeved T-shirt—made him somehow more appealing.

"Take care, Caitlyn."

She watched from the window of her office as Reid went back to his vehicle. Several moments later, the Explorer kicked up a cloud of dust as it traveled down the dirt-and-gravel road and disappeared from view.

4

Caitlyn rinsed her dinner plate under the stream of water in the kitchen sink as she talked to Sophie Treadwell on the phone. Sophie and her husband, Rob, were the nearest neighbors to the Rambling Rose stables, which in the Northern Virginia countryside was still a good three miles away. Apparently, word of the horse killing on her farm had spread quickly through the rural township.

"Who would do such a horrible thing, and all the way out here?" Sophie fretted. "The poor thing's head was nearly severed. Honestly, we left D.C. to get away from all the crime." She paused, then added awkwardly, "Sorry, Caitlyn. I didn't mean—"

"It's okay," Caitlyn assured her. Since her arrival some eighteen months earlier, Sophie was the closest thing she had to a friend. Nearly a decade older than Caitlyn, she and her husband were childless and closely integrated into the local horse community. Rob was a successful architect who worked mostly from their large, country estate home, and Sophie wrote children's books. The couple knew about Joshua, of course, and had asked questions, but it hadn't kept them from welcoming her into their home and wide circle of acquaintances. Caitlyn was grateful for their acceptance.

"Are you sure you want to be all alone out there tonight? Ed Malcolm thinks it was some kind of cult—"

"A cult comprised of *teenagers,*" Caitlyn pointed out, not wanting the rumors that were flying around to get any worse. Still, the fact remained that someone had committed the brutal act.

"Teenagers or not, the very idea of something like this is frightening. Rob wants to come get you. He *insists,* actually. You can stay in one of the guest rooms."

Wiping her hands on a dish towel, Caitlyn politely refused the offer, but not before agreeing to meet the couple the following evening in Middleburg for dinner. After saying goodbye, she replaced the receiver on the console and rubbed her hands over her upper arms to ward off the night chill. Although the radiators were on, the farmhouse was old and not blessed with the thick insulation installed in newer homes. A fire in the stacked-stone fireplace would be nice but Caitlyn didn't have the energy or interest in bringing in kindling from the back porch. Instead, she poured a glass of merlot, went into the large living room and turned on the television.

But her thoughts remained on seeing Reid Novak again.

Two years ago, when he had first come to her asking for her assistance in proving her brother's involvement in the murders, Caitlyn had been angry. But a part of her had also worried his suspicions were correct.

"Joshua's behind this, Caitlyn," Reid had warned, the intensity of his conviction unnerving. *"We've been able to link him to two of the five victims. That's no coincidence, no matter how much your family would like it to be."*

Caitlyn picked at the tassel of the throw pillow she held in her lap, the recollection enveloping her like a cold fog. Joshua's connection to the two women was loose—one had taken a college course with him, and another had belonged to his gym, a large facility with hundreds of members. Still, considering his mental history, the revelation had been troubling. The FBI had interviewed him, the discussion setting off something that had put Joshua in their sights. But they had little else to go on, and not enough for a warrant.

Help me look into him, Caitlyn. Before anyone else dies.

In the end, Reid had gotten through to her. She'd used the key Joshua had given her to slip inside his Logan Circle loft apartment at a time she knew he wouldn't be home. Her all-out search had ended when she came upon the spiral-bound composition book under a pile of clothes in the bedroom closet.

What she read inside the notebook repulsed and terrified her. She'd been physically ill—vomiting in the bathroom sink, her stomach convulsing and her bones numbed by the handwritten journal detailing Joshua's dark secrets, including some of the names of the dead women. The crude drawings accompanying the passages were worse, with nude female figures bound and gagged as they were degraded and tortured. Mutilated. Distraught, Caitlyn had removed the evidence. After an hour driving aimlessly around the city, she had met Reid at FBI headquarters and turned over the notebook.

It was the right thing to do, Reid had assured her. He'd taken her into a private conference room and allowed her to cry against his shoulder. They had barely known one another and yet the bond between them seemed instant. Later that evening, under Reid's guidance, Caitlyn made a televised appeal to Joshua when another woman went missing, urging him to turn himself in.

In the end, however, Joshua claimed one last victim before the FBI could stop him.

Caitlyn had always known about Joshua's sickness—the schizophrenia and borderline personality disorder he had been diagnosed with, the antipsychotic medications he took—but never had she imagined him a killer. At twenty-eight, still dabbling in graduate school but in and out of psychiatric treatment centers, Joshua would seem normal for weeks at a stretch, then suddenly turn secretive and morose. Often during those times, Caitlyn, his older sibling by three years, was the only person he would talk to.

Joshua's psychiatry records were confidential and her parents rarely spoke of his condition, instead shielding him from the public eye as much as possible. When the FBI had first taken interest in Joshua due to his connection to the murdered women, Senator Cahill had done everything he could—calling in favors all over the District to get the investigation directed elsewhere. And Caitlyn had been instructed to speak to no one.

What her father had done was wrong, she conceded. But it was out of love and a staunch denial that Joshua could be capable of something so heinous. Even though they weren't his biological children, Braden had been devoted to his adopted son and daughter. Defending them to a fault. In the end, Caitlyn had managed what he could not—she'd turned Joshua in to the FBI. But she had been too late to halt the death of another woman and equally powerless to stop her family's very public unraveling.

Her father had died, disgraced by Joshua's crimes and hating her for what she had done.

Stop this, she thought, sitting with her feet tucked under her on the camelback sofa. *Stop dwelling on the past and things out of your control.* Caitlyn continued to stare at the television screen, the sound turned too low to hear. She tried to take the worrisome feelings off her chest—and her mind off Reid Novak—but without much success.

Reid had been professional, aloof at Joshua's trial—a change from the man who had come to her and appealed for her help in capturing a killer. From the man who had comforted her. Then he had simply disappeared, all connection broken between them. What had she expected?

And now there was the possibility of a copycat killer on the loose. Outside, Caitlyn heard a dog barking somewhere in the distance. The room's picture window was a large black square, the rural darkness outside opaque and all consuming. Maybe she should have taken Sophie and Rob up on their offer. Finishing the wine, she sat the balloon goblet on the end table and stood, letting the soft cashmere throw she had wrapped around her shoulders slip to the couch. Caitlyn closed the curtains, then went to the front door to double-check the lock and make sure the security system was activated. But as she stood in the foyer, her eyes fell on the small, white rectangle that lay on the hardwood floor. Had she walked over it earlier without noticing? She bent and picked up the business card.

Harold Feingold, True-Crime Author.

The card included his contact information. A handwritten note on its back said simply, *we need to talk*. She felt a spiraling sense of anxiety. He had been here today at some point, still trying to get an interview for his tell-all book despite her adamant refusal. Apparently, he'd shoved his card under the front door when no one answered his knock. Caitlyn had the distinct impression he wouldn't give up.

Especially not if Reid was **on target** and there was someone out there looking to repeat her brother's crimes.

* * *

"So let me get this straight. You went all the way out to see Cahill's sister, just because of the damn charm?" Mitch drained his whiskey and signaled the bartender to pour him another.

"I had a hunch."

Mitch let out a sardonic laugh. "Makes sense. Cahill likes horses. The vic likes horses. They have to know each other, right?"

Reid took a sip from his beer bottle. He'd met Mitch at the Lucky Irishman, a pub near the VCU offices in Judiciary Square that was a popular hangout for law enforcement. The place was dark, noisy and tonight filled to overflowing.

"What if I told you a horse on her property was mutilated?"

The information gave Mitch pause. He took a sip from his newly filled glass, then shrugged. "I doubt it's related. There are freaks running around everywhere these days. The District doesn't have a monopoly on them. Did she call the local police?"

"They think it was a bunch of teenagers turned Satan worshippers."

"They might be right."

"Still, I'd like to run a criminal history check on her employees, both for the farm and stables. I can get the names and socials from her."

Mitch shook his head in disbelief. "You've got three weeks left on your leave, remember? Why don't you take a vacation? If I were you, I'd be soaking up the sun on a beach somewhere, preferably one of those nude ones in Miami."

"Just run the CHC for me."

"Whatever you want, partner." Mitch gave the once-over to an attractive redhead who had seated herself at the opposite end of the bar. Then he offered, "But if you ask me, I think you're just looking for an excuse to sniff around Caitlyn Cahill."

Reid didn't respond, instead nursed his beer. He *had* taken the opportunity to drive all the way out to the Rambling Rose stables, instead of just contacting her by phone. He'd wanted to see her, he admitted to himself.

"I'm assuming as long as you went out there, you showed her the vic's photo?"

Reid nodded. "She didn't recognize her."

"I'm shocked."

"Any word from Tiffany's?"

"The charm was discontinued two years ago. We should have a registry list, including purchases made in the D.C. area, by tomorrow," Mitch said. "The horseshoe is platinum and the diamond is a quarter-carat, VS1 quality, which, judging by the way the guy said it, is a big freaking deal."

Reid considered that the pricey jewelry also made it likely the victim was in a similar socioeconomic status as Joshua Cahill's preferred targets. "Do we know how many were sold?"

"Less than a thousand nationally—no idea how many

locally at this point. Hey, another round," Mitch called to the bartender as he passed by. "And white wine for the redhead at the end of the bar." He glanced at Reid. "You want another brewski?"

"No, thanks." He held up his bottle, indicating it was still half-full.

"Lightweight."

Reid had never been much of a drinker—and certainly not able to keep up with Mitch, who still went at it like a frat boy. They'd been partnered since shortly after Reid joined the FBI following graduate school at the age of twenty-five. Nine years later, he acknowledged that Mitch hadn't changed much...except for the fact that he'd packed on twenty pounds, gotten more cynical and gone through a recent, ugly divorce—his second. The woman accepted the wine the bartender took over to her. Flipping her hair over one shoulder, she smiled coolly at Mitch, who gave her a little salute with his whiskey glass.

"Probably a real ice queen, but worth a shot, right?" His mouth quirked up. "Speaking of ice queen, how *is* Ms. Cahill?"

"She's fine...considering," Reid answered, ignoring his barb. "She's running an equine therapy program for disabled and disadvantaged kids."

"Big farm?"

"About ninety acres, I think. It looks like an English countryside out there."

Mitch grunted. "Money will buy that."

Reid knew Mitch had his own share of money troubles related to his latest divorce. "How are things going with the house? Are you going to be able to keep it?"

"Probably, if I can refinance." Mitch scowled in thought. "Eileen would like to see me lose it. It's about the only thing she didn't get handed to her in the settlement."

After another twenty minutes, Reid left Mitch to pursue the redhead, who had accepted a second drink and gotten a little friendlier. Shouldering his way toward the front of the bar through the packed crowd, he tried to disregard the faint throb that had started in his temples a few minutes earlier. *It's only a headache.* Anyone could get one in a packed bar buzzing with loud music and too much conversation.

It was nothing to worry about.

Reaching the exit, he welcomed the rush of cool night air onto his face and headed left toward the side street where he had parked his SUV. But as he clicked the key fob to open the door, the pain inside his skull suddenly became sharper and more insistent. Reid closed his eyes and raised the fingers of his right hand to his forehead, leaning against the vehicle to steady himself.

A minute later, the dizzying pain subsided. He felt a momentary anxiety that the tumor was back—that it had somehow regrown or the surgery had failed to remove all of it.

He shrugged off the irrational thoughts. His last MRI was one hundred percent clean.

Reid opened the door to the SUV and slid onto its leather seat. He felt fine now. The headache had come and gone like a summer storm. Still, he sat inside the vehicle for several more moments, staring out through the windshield and contemplating his lengthy recuperation. Although the tumor hadn't been malignant, its location had been in a vital region, making its removal necessary. The surgery had been complex and invasive, and it had taken months to get his life back. He'd been weak, fragile, two things he had no intention of ever being again.

The crime scene photo—the one he'd shown to Caitlyn—lay on the passenger seat. Seeking a new direction for his thoughts, Reid allowed his gaze to settle on it. The victim in the row-house basement eerily mirrored the dead women Cahill had left behind. Frowning, he picked up the photo and studied it more closely. For him, the chess pawn removed any possibility of coincidence.

He wondered how long it would be before a second body turned up.

5

The snapshots were stored in a cardboard box, in back of the closet shelf almost out of reach. He had placed them there after the funeral, unable to bear seeing her beautiful face in the photos that marked the ridiculously short time they'd had together. Someday, he would give the photos to his daughters, who had been too young to remember much about her. But he needed no reminders.

Her image was burned into his mind.

Sometimes, he imagined seeing her—in the throngs of shoppers at the Georgetown mall during the holidays, or among the businesspeople headed to work on a busy Tuesday morning. His heart would lift until reality grabbed him by the collar.

She's gone. Let her go.

Once, he had followed a woman for five city blocks, mesmerized by the sway of her blond hair in the morning sunlight. She had worn a navy peacoat that looked achingly familiar. Winded, he had caught up with her, his throat tight and his heart beating in hopeful anticipation. He'd reached for her, whirling her around to face him. But the eyes, nose, the tilt of the chin were all wrong. Not even close to her beauty.

Startled, the woman had backed away as he offered a broken apology, his face red and eyes tearing with another foolish disappointment.

He knew better—knew that sick son of a bitch had killed her—and yet he continued searching. His children were being raised mostly by nannies now, and his in-laws were seeking custody. *Of their children.* They were the only things he had left of her. His hand closed more tightly around the perspiring tumbler he held, half-full of gin and tonic, mostly gin.

She had suffered a brutal death. Afraid. Cold. He realized some time ago that he'd died right along with her in that dilapidated building. The bastard had destroyed them both. Sometimes he believed his pain and anger were the only things tethering him to this world.

Leaving the tumbler on the dresser, he reached onto the shelf, his hands touching the solid presence that represented what his life used to be. For a moment he considered a walk through memory lane, but he didn't take the box down. He didn't want to open it. Not yet. The cardboard felt like a coffin to him. The flat, static photos of her were dead. He wanted warm skin against his body, the feel of silken hair slipping through his fingers. When he closed his eyes he could almost hear the husky sound of her laugh. What he wanted was answers.

He wanted to keep looking for her.

6

Caitlyn drove on the two-lane rural highway toward her home. The night out with Sophie and Rob had been relaxing, although she'd stayed longer than intended. After dinner at a local bistro, they had gone to an outdoor symphony concert that was part of the Middleburg Fall Arts Festival. The digital clock on the BMW's dashboard indicated it was already after 9:00 p.m. Overhead, an obsidian blackness had set in that not even the occasional streetlight could penetrate. Growing up in the District, Caitlyn hadn't realized how dark nighttime could be without the endless cityscape surrounding her.

At the stacked-stone and wood sign announcing the Rambling Rose stables, she took a left onto the long, private road that led to her house. The car's headlights illuminated tall oaks and maples, their branches moving in the breeze that had picked up. Fall leaves rustled in the air and crunched under her tires.

Something on the road suddenly darted in front of her, two large shapes in the darkness. Caitlyn gasped and slammed on her brakes. The tires slipped on the canvas of leaves, causing the car to fishtail slightly before coming to a screeching stop. Two white-tailed deer froze in her beams before leaping gracefully back into the woods.

Breathe, Caitlyn, she chided herself as the deer vanished. She accelerated and continued along the drive, albeit more slowly. But the ease she'd felt during the evening ebbed away. If she had lost control of the car, skidded into the forest and crashed into a tree, would anyone even notice she was missing?

She had come to the countryside seeking privacy and refuge from her family's very public drama, but there were times the isolation out here was unnerving.

I'm still a young woman, thirty-three, and living alone in an old farmhouse like a spinster. Instead of cats, I have horses, Caitlyn thought glumly. At the concert, as she sat on the wool blanket Sophie had brought and sipped Chardonnay, a man had come by and asked her to dance. He had been good-looking enough, she supposed, but Caitlyn politely refused. Later, Sophie had scolded her and Rob insisted she dance with *him,* if only to bring her out of her shell. She'd let him lead her into the swaying crowd as Sophie watched. She'd felt out of place, like a third wheel.

Would she always punish herself for Joshua's crimes, closing herself off from others and retreating from any opportunity to have a normal life? Lost in thought, Caitlyn gripped the steering wheel harder as she exited the wood-lined drive and the farmhouse came into view.

The main floor of the house, with its wide, wrap-around porch and black-painted shutters, was dark. But on the second floor, a pale light emanated from her bedroom. Caitlyn slowed the car. She had turned the light off after getting ready to go out that evening. She was certain of it.

The fine hairs on the nape of her neck rose as a shadow passed behind the room's closed curtains.

For several seconds, she stared up at the window, unsure of what she had just seen. The deer had already spooked her—was it only her overactive imagination? Still, the image of Aggie's bloated corpse filled her mind.

Ed Malcolm thinks it was a cult....

Caitlyn turned off her headlights and backed the car slowly away from the house, until it was hidden in the dense shadow of trees.

She made an instinctive decision. Her fingers clumsy with nerves, she opened her purse, searching for her cell phone and the piece of paper on which Reid Novak had written his number.

"Are you all right?"

Reid looked at his sister, Megan, who sat across from him at the kitchen table in her home in the D.C. suburb of Silver Spring. Two years his junior, her dark hair and slate-gray eyes mirrored his own.

"I can always tell when you have something on your mind," she added, tapping a spot on her forehead. "You get this line right...here."

"I'm fine. Just a little preoccupied," he admitted. "There's a case—"

"Honestly, Reid. You're not even back to work yet. Are you?"

He stared at the remnants of the apple cobbler on the plate in front of him, then took a sip from the coffee mug he held cradled between his palms. Over the past six months, he and his sister had grown even closer as she helped him to recover from his surgery. For the first twelve weeks, he hadn't even been allowed to drive. Reid didn't know what he would have done without her.

"Oh, God. You *are* back to work—"

"I've been called in as a consult, that's all," he said, downplaying things with a small shrug. "The crime scene had similarities to an investigation I handled a couple of years ago."

"It's too soon."

"It's not. I'd be going back in another few weeks officially, anyway."

"Couldn't stay away any longer, could you?" Reid's brother-in-law, Cooper, quipped as he passed through the kitchen, grabbing a bag of potato chips on his way to the den. He grinned at his wife. "Meg, you owe me fifty bucks."

"Shut up, Cooper."

Reid raised his eyebrows. "You had a bet on me?"

"He was sure you wouldn't make it all the way through your leave. Cooper's been saying as soon as you got half a chance, you'd be back on the job." Megan gave him a pointed stare. "I guess he was right."

"Cooper just thinks everyone loves their job as much as he does."

"It's football. What's not to love?" he called from the comfort of his leather recliner in the den. A former player at the University of Virginia, Cooper now headed up the football program for one of the suburb's largest high schools. "Hey, are we going to watch the game or not? Halftime's almost over."

"Let me know when it's back on—"

"Reid," Megan said quietly as he stood from the table to take his plate and mug to the sink. "You *are* okay, right?"

"Are you going to keep asking me that?"

"It's just that your illness…it scared all of us. Especially Dad. And you've been so quiet tonight."

Reid paused as his two nieces, Maddie and Isabelle, ages nine and seven, strolled into the kitchen wearing their pajamas and carrying a board game.

"Don't worry about me," he assured her. "And as long as we're on the subject of Dad, where is he? Missing one of your family nights doesn't fit his M.O."

"He had a retired police officers' meeting."

"So he's drinking beer in a pub somewhere, arguing about politics and playing pool?"

"You got it." Megan laughed softly, then her eyes grew serious again. "I guess I've just gotten used to having you around without the crazy schedule and a gun attached to your hip. You know what it was like with Dad when we were young. I always worried he might get hurt on the job and not make it back to us."

"But he always did," Reid reminded.

She sighed. "You're right. Girls, thirty minutes and then off to bed."

He leaned against the counter, watching as Megan cleared the remaining dessert dishes from the table and wiped it down so the girls could use it for their game. He thought back to his own childhood. For so many years, it had been just the three of them—their father, Ben, a vice detective with the D.C. police—Megan and himself. Their mother had died at the young age of thirty-five, the victim of a fatal brain tumor. Reid had been twelve and Megan, ten. Ben Novak never remarried. But they'd had a solid family life, thanks to grandparents, uncles and aunts who filled in the gaps.

Reid was helping Maddie set up the game when his cell phone went off. Both his nieces giggled at the ring tone that still hadn't been changed.

"Novak."

He walked to the far end of the kitchen at the sound of Caitlyn Cahill's voice, trying to hear her above the conversation in the room. He listened as she explained what she thought she had seen inside her house.

"I want you to call the local police. Drive to a public location and tell them where to meet you. Don't go back home until they give you the okay. I'll be there as soon as I can."

Closing the phone, he caught Megan's gaze.

"The case you were talking about?"

"Yeah." He kissed her cheek and mussed the hair of each child as he moved toward the door. "Thanks for dinner. Tell Coop I'll have to take a rain check on the second half."

Outside, he started up the SUV. Middleburg was nearly an hour away, but he felt the need to go up there. Caitlyn had been unsure of what she'd seen, but he didn't want her taking any chances. And she'd called *him,* asking for help. That meant something to him.

Despite her attempt to hide it, Reid had heard the slight tremor in her voice. And it was possible things were about to get worse. What he hadn't yet told her was that, thanks to the Tiffany charm, they had just gotten an ID on the dead woman in the Columbia Heights row house. She and Caitlyn *did* share a connection beyond horses.

The victim was a resident of Middleburg.

7

Caitlyn waited tensely in the living room as Reid spoke with Chief Malcolm on the front porch. Around her, much of the wood furniture, as well as the light switches and door frames, carried a sooty dusting of carbon fingerprinting powder. Although the conversation outside was mostly inaudible to her, she already had the gist of what Reid was probably being told. Someone had gained entrance into her home through the kitchen door, shattering the window and reaching inside to unlock it. The phone line wired into the standard house-grade security system had also been cut, rendering the alarm ineffective.

As far as any theft or vandalism, however, there were no indications. While the filing cabinet in her home office and the drawers in her bedroom were rifled through, it appeared nothing had been taken.

Two uniformed officers nodded to Caitlyn as they walked past. One of them carried a dusting kit.

"Did you find any prints?" she asked.

"Quite a few, but based on ridge size and density they appear to be female. They're probably yours," the younger officer said. He was the same one who had waited with Caitlyn at a nearby gas station until she'd been given the okay to return home. "The chief wants you to come by tomorrow to have your fingerprints rolled. We'll know more then, ma'am."

The men disappeared through the front door. It was several more minutes before Reid wrapped up his conversation and came inside.

"Well, at least you know you weren't imagining things," he commented.

"What does Chief Malcolm think?" Caitlyn stood and smoothed her hands over her gray wool skirt, still dressed in the clothing she'd worn to dinner. Outside, the remaining patrol cars were starting up their engines and leaving the property. "Does his theory of rampaging teenagers still hold out?"

"Apparently, there's been a rash of burglaries in the area. He thinks the units that arrived scared off the perpetrator—or perpetrators—before anything was taken."

"Is that what *you* think?"

His gray eyes locked with hers. She felt her throat go dry.

"I'm not big on coincidences, Caitlyn. First the horse on your property, and now the random break-in?"

She took a breath, trying to sound calm. "I'll have someone in tomorrow to repair the window and security system."

"And in the meantime?"

Her chin lifted fractionally. "My father was a card-carrying member of the NRA. I know how to use a gun."

"I don't doubt it. I saw the gun safe in your office. But you need to understand—"

"Thank you for coming." Caitlyn knew she sounded dismissive, but despite her claims, she felt vulnerable and defenseless. Frightened. It wasn't a part of herself she wanted to reveal, especially not to him, not now. She shook her head, regretting her earlier decision. "I shouldn't have called you. I'm sorry—I guess I panicked. I've been a little spooked since what happened to Aggie. But whatever's going on, it's something the local authorities can handle."

"I'm glad you called me, Caitlyn. Because I think you might be in over your head."

She searched his face, realizing that he had more to tell her.

"You got an ID on the victim," she guessed, dread filling her. "The one from the crime scene in the District."

"Her name is Allison Murrell. She lived in Middleburg."

The name didn't ring any bells. "What was she doing in the city?"

"We don't know," Reid said. "She was last seen several days ago. Her elderly mother reported her missing. There's a possibility she might have been abducted locally. I got a call on the drive up tonight. Her car was found in a parking lot behind a wine bar here in town. A place called Bellavino?"

Caitlyn's stomach did a small somersault. The bistro she'd had dinner at that night with Sophie and Rob sat right across the street.

"You look a little pale. Caitlyn?"

Reid took a step closer, lightly touching her upper arm to recapture her attention. She'd removed her herringbone blazer earlier and she could feel the heat of his palm through her silk blouse. "I…I'm fine."

"Do you ever go to Bellavino?"

"I've been a couple of times, with friends," she admitted. "I'm not a regular."

"I'd like to stay here tonight," he told her, his voice low. "Your security system's knocked out and the break-in must've been unnerving."

Caitlyn felt surprise at his offer. "You don't have to. It's already after midnight—"

"You'll be doing me a favor, then. I won't have to drive back to the District so late."

The set of his jaw told her that he wouldn't take no for an answer. The thought of Reid Novak spending the night in her home was both comforting and unsettling. Caitlyn looked into his eyes and saw his concern. He obviously had no ulterior motive beyond her protection. Finally, she gave a small nod of agreement.

"Are you tired?" he asked.

"Not really." The truth was, she couldn't imagine sleeping tonight.

"Then maybe we can start a fire in the fireplace and have some decaf? I saw kindling on the porch."

He went outside for the wood as Caitlyn moved to the large, country-style kitchen to make coffee. Someone had swept up the broken glass from the window and stuffed cardboard into its open pane to help block out the cold air. But more than the broken window caused the chill she felt. She tried not to think about what might have happened if she had gone into the house while the intruder was still inside.

Working around the fingerprint powder residue, she made the requested coffee, returning to the living room a few minutes later with a wicker tray bearing two earthenware mugs and a sugar-and-cream set. Reid had removed his leather jacket and laid it over the arm of the couch. Dressed in jeans and an untucked button-down shirt, he knelt next to the fireplace, arranging the kindling with an iron poker. Already, flames were licking greedily at the seasoned wood.

When he was done, he rose and dusted his hands on the thighs of his jeans, then accepted the mug before sitting on the opposite side of the couch from Caitlyn.

"Other than the horse, has anything unusual happened around the house or stables recently?" he asked, stirring cream into his coffee.

Caitlyn took a sip from her cup before speaking. She thought of the journalist. "I'm not sure if it's worth mentioning, but there's a reporter who called. He covered the investigation and Joshua's trial for the *Washington Post*. He's out on his own now and writing a book on my family, apparently. After I refused to talk to him on the telephone, he came out yesterday. I didn't see him, but he put a business card under the front door."

"What's his name?"

"Hal Feingold. Do you remember him?"

Reid nodded. "We had a few run-ins during the investigation. Is there any chance he might be the one who broke in here tonight? Maybe he was looking for information for his book?"

"I don't know. I get the feeling he's pretty tenacious, but breaking into my home…that's going a bit far."

"I'll look into it."

"You sound like you're getting involved beyond a consultative role, Agent," Caitlyn observed quietly.

"It's *Reid*," he emphasized. The room's soft lighting revealed the lean, masculine planes of his face. Caitlyn studied his features as he sipped his coffee. The contrast of his gray eyes and short, dark hair was striking to her. Despite the events of the evening, she felt the same undeniable attraction.

"Reid…" she asked tentatively. "Why *are* you on leave?"

She thought she saw a flicker of shadow appear in his eyes. But after a moment, he shrugged. "I needed a break, I guess. Some time away."

Caitlyn considered this. "The things you deal with at the Violent Crimes Unit must be difficult, to say the least. The work has to take its toll."

"You sound like my sister."

She hadn't considered that a man like Reid Novak

had family or much of a life outside of the FBI, Caitlyn now realized. In fact, she'd taken it for granted he was single, based on the absence of a wedding band. Not to mention the intensity that emanated from him led her to assume he was singularly career-focused.

"You have a family?"

He chuckled faintly at her question. "Does that surprise you?"

"I…didn't mean," she stammered.

"My sister, Megan, is a first-grade teacher in Silver Spring. She's married with two kids. I also have a father who's a retired vice detective with the D.C. Police."

Caitlyn found that interesting. "So law enforcement runs in your blood."

"I'm the third generation of Novaks to serve and protect. My grandfather was a cop, too." His eyes appeared smoky under dark lashes, his gray irises ringed with black. *Bedroom eyes*. Caitlyn had heard the phrase before, but only now did she truly understand its meaning.

They continued talking for nearly an hour, until the coffee was gone and the deep chime of the grandfather clock reminded them of the time that had passed.

"You should go to bed," Reid told her when she stifled a yawn. "I'll make sure the fire's out. And I'll clean up some of the mess Forensics left behind. It's everywhere."

Caitlyn touched his wrist as he attempted to step past her. "I'll take care of it tomorrow. You must be tired, too. You can take one of the guest rooms upstairs. The first room on the right has a larger bed."

She felt her face heat at the realization of just how close he would be sleeping to her. Done up in shades of yellow and periwinkle-blue, the bedroom was adjacent to hers and offered a morning view of the stables and equestrian ring. "There's an attached guest bath. It should have everything you…"

Her words halted as he reached up to brush an errant strand of hair from her face, settling it behind her ear. Reid frowned as he studied her.

"I know tonight's been upsetting…"

"I really am fine," she promised. For a moment, she thought he might say something else, but he simply continued staring at her, as if measuring the truth to her words. Behind them, the dying fire crackled.

"Thank you again for staying. Good night, Reid," she murmured.

Caitlyn withdrew her gaze from his. She went up the stairs.

Sitting on the edge of the bed, Reid scrubbed a hand over his face in frustration. *He'd touched her.* In that split second, his male instincts had gotten the better of him. Her pale, tousled hair had spilled into those vivid green eyes and he had momentarily lost control of the situation.

He wasn't officially assigned to the investigation into the D.C. murder, and at least so far, Caitlyn hadn't been linked. But the dark history between them was complicated, and she was fragile. As strong as she appeared to be, he suspected she was barely holding herself together.

Reid lay down on the bed again, chasing sleep. He had so much on his mind—Caitlyn, his pending return to active duty. He had brought the pain reliever Dr. Isrelsen had prescribed him in the early days, when he'd first begun having severe headaches but the tumor hadn't yet been diagnosed. He'd been carrying it around with him since the incident outside the bar, just in case. But Reid reminded himself he hadn't experienced another dizzying headache. The first one had been a fluke.

With the knowledge that sleep would not be coming easily to him, he opened his eyes and took in his surroundings. Although he had turned out the lamp, there was enough moonlight to make out the bed's carved-wood posters and the antique, claw-footed dresser. Blue curtains with creamy sheers framed the double windows. He didn't know if Caitlyn had decorated herself or hired a professional, but the home managed to be elegant and cozy at the same time.

He considered the facts of the case so far. Allison Murrell was from Middleburg, and it now appeared she might have been abducted nearby. Mitch had told him that he and Morehouse had spent the afternoon in the quaint town, talking to the bar staff to see if anyone recalled the victim and whether she had been with someone. They hadn't learned much of use. Reid felt a knot in his stomach. The abduction was too close for comfort where Caitlyn was concerned, especially considering the recent events on her property. Earlier, he had told her the truth when he'd said that he didn't believe in co-incidence. After several interminable minutes, he got up and walked to the window, his arms crossed over his bare chest. Through the glass he could feel the night-time air. It put a chill upon his skin.

The sound he heard was at first weak, distant. Caitlyn was calling out...pleading?

Taking the time to pull on his jeans, he went into the hallway.

"Caitlyn?"

He could hear her, talking and sobbing.

Reid pushed open her bedroom door. A nightlight was on, casting the room in a soft haze. She lay on her side, her knees curled up against her stomach. Her slender body was a small mound under the floral coverlet.

"Caitlyn," he whispered, touching her. She woke with a start, nearly scrambling from the bed until he caught her by the shoulders and steadied her. "It's okay. Look at me."

She stared at him, bleary-eyed. "Reid?"

"You were having a nightmare. That's all."

She slowly shook her head, appearing bewildered and embarrassed. "I woke you... I'm so sorry."

"I wasn't asleep anyway." He lowered himself to the edge of the mattress, so that he was sitting next to her. Reid waited for her breathing to return to normal. He laid his hand on her back in a soothing manner and felt the dampness of her skin through her cotton pajamas.

"Want to tell me about it?" he asked softly, offering an ear but not wanting to push too hard.

Caitlyn paused for a long moment. She drew in a weak breath. "I dream about Joshua. At least once or twice a week. Sometimes he's standing over my bed, holding a knife and asking me why I betrayed him. Other times, I'm tied up and he's...hurting me."

She looked at Reid, her eyes haunted. "He's my own brother. And the things he's doing to me..."

Reid drew her against him then, holding her. She didn't resist and instead laid her head against his bare chest, causing his heart to beat harder. All of Joshua Cahill's victims had been blondes, about the same age as Caitlyn and with similar pedigrees. Reid had often wondered if Joshua's preference in victims had anything to do with his pretty, adopted sister. Apparently, Caitlyn had wondered the same thing, even if subconsciously.

"He can't hurt you," he whispered against her hair. "He's never getting out of prison."

But a single, troubling notion filled his mind. He thought of Allison Murrell and wondered if there was another killer out there looking to finish Joshua's work.

Looking to come after Caitlyn.

8

The aroma of sizzling bacon woke her. Caitlyn sat up in bed, trying to get her bearings. The recollection of being held in Reid's arms was intense, as if it were part of a dream so vivid her mind was confusing it with reality. But he was here, and most likely making breakfast in her kitchen, based on the tantalizing scent wafting up to the second floor. The sticky fingerprint powder residue on her bureau and bedroom door frame gave further evidence that last night had been all too real.

Caitlyn dressed quickly in jeans, a scooped T-shirt and soft yellow cashmere cardigan. As she ran a brush through her tangle of hair, she was aware of the flush to her skin. The thought of her face pressed against Reid's bare chest as he spoke comforting words to her—the intimacy of him in her bed—embarrassed her. Still, she gathered her courage and went downstairs.

His eyes met hers as she entered the kitchen. He handed her a mug of steaming coffee.

"This time it's the real thing. No decaf."

"Thanks," she murmured, as grateful for his casual demeanor as the coffee. She looked at the skillet on the gas burner, which contained a large, fluffy omelet. Two thick slices of bacon drained on a paper towel. "You cook?"

He gave her a look. "It's just eggs. You learn skills or you starve."

"Or eat takeout."

He smiled at her comment, the grooves in his dimples deepening. "Actually, my sister and I learned to cook when we were young. Dad had a crazy work schedule."

"What about your mother?"

"She died when I was twelve."

He handed her a plate containing the omelet, bacon and toast. Behind him, Caitlyn noticed that the maple cabinets and butcher-block countertops were now print-free. He must have been up for a while, she realized. The truth was, she had no idea if he had gone back to the guest room or stayed in her bed. The last thing she remembered was reveling in the feel of his strong hands stroking her hair. It was the first time she'd felt safe and protected in as long as she could remember. She must have fallen asleep in his embrace, although this morning she'd awakened alone. Taking a sip of coffee, Caitlyn wondered what he must think of her weakness.

"Aren't you going to eat, too?" she asked.

"I already did." He sat down on a stool on the other side of the island, his own mug in hand. Reid wore the same clothes from the previous evening, and she noticed the bluish hint of stubble on his jaw.

"About last night…" she began hesitantly, not meeting his gaze.

"It's all right, Caitlyn."

She shook her head. "It's not."

Reid reached across the table, laying his fingers over the back of her hand.

"I want you to get your security system repaired and upgraded. Today." The seriousness of his words sent a chill through her. "Promise me that. I think—"

The shrill of his cell phone interrupted. He reached into his shirt pocket for the device.

"Novak." His eyes fell on Caitlyn as he listened to the caller. She moved the omelet around on her plate with the fork, unable to eat more than a few bites. Whoever was talking to Reid had his rapt attention. He paced the kitchen floor, then went into the hallway to continue the conversation. When he returned, his expression was tight. "I've got to go."

"It's another murder, isn't it?"

His eyes told her all she needed to know.

"I'll be on guard," Caitlyn assured him from the porch. Reid had donned his leather jacket, and he stared out over the front lawn into the autumn woods that concealed the drive leading back to the road. He had told her little about the second murder, other than that another body had been discovered in D.C., far away from her quiet township.

"I don't like you being out here. It's too remote."

"Maybe not as remote as you think." They heard the

sound of a car coming up the drive. Rob and Sophie's black Mercedes station wagon emerged from the orange-and-gold canopy of leaves and pulled in front of the house.

"They're friends of mine," she said.

"I should go, then." Their eyes held for another second, and then he went down the porch steps. Reid nodded a curt greeting to Sophie and Rob as they exited their vehicle. He got into his SUV and drove away.

"We ran into Ed Malcolm at the Breakfast Nook," Rob called as they came across the driveway and onto the porch. He was tall and heavyset, with prematurely graying hair. His wire-rimmed spectacles caught the sunlight. "He said you had a break-in last night. You should have called us, honey. Are you okay?"

"Everything's fine. The police came by and dusted for prints. Nothing was taken, as far as I can tell."

"Who was that?" Sophie wanted to know, her head still turned in the direction the SUV had taken.

What should she say? *The FBI agent who captured my serial killer brother. The same one who now thinks there's a copycat with me in his sights.* Instead, Caitlyn said simply, "He's with law enforcement."

"I haven't seen him around. Is he with the Middleburg Police?" Rob asked, curious.

"Not exactly. You guys really didn't need to come over."

"You're our friend." Sophie was petite, with auburn hair that she wore in a stylish, chin-length bob. "Of course we're going to check on you, Caity."

Caitlyn nearly flinched at the nickname. No one ever called her that except Joshua, and he'd used it last night in her dream. In it Caitlyn had been tied up like the women in Joshua's grotesque drawings. Naked. Spread-eagle. He'd started to torture her with the hot, burning end of a cigarette when Reid had woken her, pulling her from her nightmare.

Rob looked around the porch. "How'd they get in?"

"The kitchen door. They broke the window. The phone lines were cut, too. The security system was tied into them."

"You sure you don't want to use our guest room for a while?" Rob asked. He gave a small bow. "Our *casa es su casa.*"

When Caitlyn smiled faintly but declined, he grew more serious.

"A pretty, single woman like you out here all alone. Burglars probably saw you as an easy mark. Let's hope stealing was all they had in mind."

He took his cell phone from his pocket and scrolled through his contacts. "I can give you the name of a local repairman for the window. I also have some pull with the Middleburg phone company. They're typically slower than Christmas, but I might be able to get you back up and running today. Need me to stick around and supervise things?"

"I'm sure you're too busy. I can handle it," Caitlyn said.

"The Garwoods' summer house was broken into just last month," Sophie noted worriedly. "Ed Malcolm says the trouble is spreading up from the District. I don't think there's really anyplace safe anymore."

Biting her lip, Caitlyn looked at the porch's wide, whitewashed planks.

Sophie had no idea.

As it turned out, a repairman for the broken window wasn't required. Soon after Rob and Sophie's departure, Manny had come up from the stables once he'd learned of the break-in and offered his assistance as a jack-of-all-trades. By 10:00 a.m. he was back from the hardware store with a new glass pane and the proper supplies.

Caitlyn left Manny in the kitchen and went upstairs while she waited for the telephone technician to arrive. It was hard not to think that just last night, an intruder had been inside her home, invading her privacy and planning to do who knew what before the police sirens chased him away. She stopped in the threshold of the guest bedroom. Reid had made the bed. The striped duvet was in place, and the pile of matching pillows at the headboard had been carefully arranged. Caitlyn ran her hand over the duvet's smooth fabric, thinking of him sleeping there under the goose down comforter.

In the guest bathroom, she noted the slight disarray of towels, the only remaining sign of his presence. She picked up a damp towel from the vanity to take to the laundry, then stopped as a plastic pill bottle rolled from under it and fell to the tiled floor. Caitlyn picked it up, hearing the rattle of tablets inside it. The prescription was in Reid's name.

Sudamitrix. 10 mg. Take as needed.

The prescribing physician was someone Caitlyn recognized from her board work on several D.C. charities. Dr. Rahm Isrelsen was a neurologist, a prominent specialist in his field. He had been a key contributor to an urban youth program Caitlyn had chaired several years earlier.

She thought of Reid's mysterious leave from the Bureau. The amber bottle with its neatly typed label sent an arrow of worry spiraling through her.

9

"Let him through," Mitch called to the officers at the cordoned-off crime scene. The victim lay in dense shrub, just off the concrete biking path at Hains Point, overlooking the Potomac.

Reid shouldered his way through, stopping when he reached the nude body of the woman concealed from onlookers by a raised plastic tarp. An ugly, blackened ligature mark was evident around her neck, with similar bruising on the ankles and wrists. Knife wounds marred her small breasts. Decaying leaves and twigs were tangled in the blond hair spread out on the damp ground behind her head.

"Johnston called and said you were on your way. It took you long enough. We've been holding the body." Mitch tossed him a pair of latex gloves. "Where the hell were you?"

"Out of town."

"Where? Middleburg?" Mitch's eyes bugged when

he realized his guess was on target. "That's a slippery slope, brother."

Reid didn't want to talk about Caitlyn. Not while another woman lay dead at his feet. Pulling on the gloves, he knelt beside the body. Circular welts—cigarette burns—stood out on the inside of one forearm. Rigor mortis hadn't fully developed, indicating the time of death was relatively recent. His stomach turned as an insect crawled from the nasal cavity. He looked away briefly, focusing on the river's rough, gray waters.

"Is there a chess piece?"

"Stuffed into the mouth. Forensics already bagged it."

"A biker found the body around eight this morning," Morehouse, Mitch's partner, said as he ducked behind the tarp to join them. He had been talking to some bystanders being kept back from the scene, but he'd worked his way over when he saw Reid. "Looks like the unsub tried to conceal the body with leaves and branches, but it was too windy to keep it hidden long. The guy who found her is still here if you want to talk to him."

Reid stood, glancing at the overweight, middle-aged biker who had packed himself into spandex for his morning ride. The harsh breeze rushing in from the river felt like a slap across his face. The tips of his ears were cold, and he noticed Mitch's nose was red from the time he'd spent outside.

"Morehouse, tell the photographer to take shots of the crowd—just in case the perp came back to watch the circus." Mitch turned to Reid. "The uni's conducted a grid search of the area an hour ago. There's tire tracks that indicate a vehicle pulled off-road, probably to dump the body. I know it was in the dark of night, but this guy's got some big, brass ones to put her here in a public park."

Reid scanned the broad perimeter of shoreline. A few bikers and inline skaters were getting their exercise on the promenade, moving along with their routines as if nothing unusual had happened. *Just another murder,* he thought. Leafless trees lined the path that ran along the peninsula, their bare arms stretched upward to a pale blue sky.

"The placement was important to him," Reid noted quietly. "It was symbolic."

It was also another direct challenge.

"Johnston figured you'd think that, which is why he wanted you down here," Mitch said, his eyes following Reid's to the other side of the Potomac. A steel-and-glass high-rise stood at the water's edge, housing pricey loft apartments. Two years ago, it had been the site of an abandoned, rundown factory.

Although the dilapidated structure had been torn down to make way for progress, it was where Joshua Cahill had taken his last victim.

The VCU offices were located in Judiciary Square, in a redbrick building off Pennsylvania Avenue that was in proximity to federal and municipal courthouses. Afternoon sunlight spilled through the plate-glass window in the fifth-floor space Reid had previously shared with Mitch. He'd spent most of the day there, pouring through the Cahill case files with the other two agents.

"We need to know who Joshua Cahill's been in touch with," Reid said, rubbing his strained eyes with the thumb and forefinger of one hand. Cahill had worked alone—was a loner by all accounts—but there was always the chance the copycat had reached out to him. He would want to get to know the killer he was emulating as personally as possible.

Mitch directed Morehouse, who took notes on a yellow steno pad. "Call the penitentiary and have them send me the visitor list—if Cahill's had any. And get a monitor put on his mail. He's probably got pen pals."

"Aren't those usually women?" Morehouse asked.

"Just do it."

"He's your partner, not your secretary," Reid pointed out once Morehouse had left the office. He'd gotten up from behind the stacks of files on the conference table to sit on the edge of the credenza.

With a snort, Mitch swiveled his desk chair in Reid's direction. "He's a rookie. Lucky to be in the VCU. Apparently his high scores at Quantico and a well-placed word from one of the Washington pencil pushers got him in here. You remember your rookie days, right? He should be glad I don't send him to pick up my dry cleaning."

"Remind me why I *liked* being your partner?"

"My charm?" Mitch grinned. "Or maybe it's because I've always had your back under fire."

That much was true. Reid studied Mitch, who'd undone his tie and rolled his shirtsleeves up to his elbows. Crime scene photos from the Cahill investigation were interspersed with the recent ones and spread out on his desk, along with the preliminary forensics report on the first victim. The report indicated there was no semen inside the body, no latent prints or other physical DNA evidence left behind on the skin. The killer had been careful.

"Tell me about the first victim—Allison Murrell," Reid said. "The one from Middleburg."

Mitch stretched and cracked his knuckles. "Like I told you over the phone last night, Morehouse and I went up there yesterday when the car was found. We'd had an APB out on it ever since we got the jewelry registry list and cross-referenced it against missing persons. We talked to the staff at the wine bar and showed the vic's photo around. The bartender thought he recognized her, but didn't recall seeing her with anyone. All he remembered was that she'd been drinking cosmopolitans alone. Lots of them. And no, there were no surveillance cameras on the parking lot or premises."

"What's her background?"

"Divorcée, a wealthy one. No kids. Closest relative is her mother. We talked to her but didn't get much information—she was too upset." Mitch shook his head. "She's elderly and had to make the ID through a photo from the morgue since she was unable to come down in person."

"What about the ex-husband?"

"He lives in Portland now. He's also got a solid alibi."

"Did you talk to the Middleburg police chief?" Reid asked. "Ed Malcolm?"

"He's been apprised of the local abduction, but the discussion went no further than that. At that point we had one vic—I didn't see a need to sound the alarm on a serial murderer that might or might not exist."

Reid thought of the second victim. Another Jane Doe. "But that's changed now."

"Yeah," Mitch agreed, looking serious for once. "By the way, I have the background check you wanted on Caitlyn Cahill's employees. It came through this morning."

He shuffled through the unwieldy, dog-eared pile of papers in his in-box. Finding the paper-clipped documents, he slid them toward Reid. "I haven't had a chance to get all the way through it yet. But there's one you might want to take a look at."

Reid paced the office as he looked through the papers. He stopped when he came to the section Mitch had underlined in red. "I'd like to bring him in for questioning. Today."

"So I guess that means I have to schlep back out to the sticks?"

"It's your case," Reid reminded.

"Why do I feel like it's not anymore?" Mitch grabbed his suit jacket from a hook on the back of the door and shoved his muscular arms into its sleeves. "Just so you know, I was joking earlier when I asked if you'd been out to Middleburg. Who knew I was on the money?

When I called you last night about the Murrell woman's car being found, why didn't you tell me you were on your way to see Caitlyn Cahill again?"

"There was a break-in at her home last night. She got scared."

"And she called you?" Mitch opened the door and Reid followed him out. "Like I said, that's a slippery slope."

"Nothing happened."

"Disappointed?"

He ignored the comment. "I think she's at risk."

A half-dozen inner-city youths were gathered around the white-faced quarter horse named Gemini. Caitlyn was instructing them on how to curry the animal, in order to loosen up the dirt that had accumulated on the trail ride. It was late afternoon, the last session for the day, and she allowed each one to take a turn stroking the animal with the nubbed paddle. Although some equestrians skipped currying and went straight to stiff brushing, Caitlyn explained that the horse benefited from the invigorating massage the currycomb provided.

She'd just retrieved the water hose with the wide, gentle showerhead when a dark sedan rolled into the open dirt space in front of the stables.

Three men climbed from the vehicle, including Reid. In the presence of the others, he looked somehow different to her than he had that morning. His lean features seemed harder, his physical presence more aloof. Caitlyn felt a knot settle in her stomach. She had an unsettling recollection. These men were official—just as they had been when they'd arrived at her place of work two years ago, wanting to talk to her about Joshua.

"Can you take over for me?" Caitlyn handed the hose to one of the stable hands. She waited until he had stepped in and picked up her discussion with the teenagers. Then brushing her hands on the back pockets of her jeans, she walked over to meet the men.

"What's going on?" she asked.

"Caitlyn, you remember Agent Tierney?"

She took heed of the formality in Reid's voice. He indicated his partner, who was dressed in the standard FBI uniform of a dark suit and heavily tinted sunglasses. Agent Tierney looked as unfriendly and imposing as he had during the Capital Killer investigation and Joshua's trial.

"Ms. Cahill." Tierney gave her a sharp nod, then gestured to the other man and added, "This is Agent Morehouse."

"Ma'am," the younger man, also in a suit, said politely.

"What's going on?" she repeated.

Reid spoke. "Could we go into your office?"

Without a word, Caitlyn turned on her heel and traveled back through the stables with the men behind her. Her mind kicked out several reasons for their appearance, including the possibility that the second victim—the one Reid had mentioned that morning—was someone Caitlyn knew. Preparing herself for whatever news she was about to receive, she led them into her office and closed the door.

"What's this about, gentlemen?"

"We ran the background check on your employees," Reid informed her. "How long has Manny Ruiz worked for you?"

Caitlyn's throat tightened. "He's been here since we opened. Over a year—"

"Is he here now?"

"I sent him to the feed store." Her heart began to beat faster. Manny? What could they want with him? He was a hard worker and had proved himself to be trustworthy and reliable, which is why she had put him in charge of the stables and farm. "Whatever you're thinking about Mr. Ruiz, I can assure you that you're mistaken. I checked his references—"

"Then you know he's a former inmate at Springdale Penitentiary," Agent Tierney supplied. It was the same federal penal facility where Joshua was serving a life sentence. Surprise must have registered on her face, because he added, "I'm guessing that little nugget didn't make it onto his employment application."

"What…what did he do?"

He pulled his sunglasses from his broad nose and stuffed them into the inside pocket of his suit coat. His eyes were a pale blue. "Kidnapping and battery. You still want to vouch for this guy?"

Caitlyn was speechless. She thought of Manny's gentle manner with the horses, and the patience he had with the stable workers and field hands. It was unimaginable that he had lied to her. That he'd done the things they claimed. She looked between the men. "You can't be serious. You're sure about this?"

"Caitlyn." Reid's voice was low. "Some of his time at Springdale overlapped with Joshua's. We want to talk to him."

She took a wavering breath. Despite her best efforts she was trembling.

"Please excuse me for a minute," she whispered.

"Caitlyn—"

She walked back toward the stalls. Several workers lapsed into awkward silence when she appeared, and she guessed they'd been speculating about what was going on. Normally the smell of horses and hay had a calming effect on her, but at that moment she felt slightly nauseous. She concentrated on the sound of the teenagers talking and laughing while they wet Gemini down with the hose, oblivious to the encroaching tension.

"Start at the feet and work your way up," she heard Dennis, one of the equine instructors, tell them from the wash stalls. "The water's cold—let him get used to it."

"Caitlyn." Reid loomed beside her. He caught her elbow. "Where are you going?"

"I…don't want to be part of your investigation again." Caitlyn pulled from his grasp, unable to control the slightly panicked tone of her voice. She knew she sounded unreasonable, but couldn't help herself. "I don't want people around me getting arrested. I don't want to be a part of this."

Reid frowned, his gray eyes darkening. He moved closer, ensuring their words were a private exchange. "You didn't want to know this guy has a record? What if he's the one who was in your house last night? Whether you like it or not, things are going on here."

She stared at him, trying to reconcile the man in front of her with the one who had comforted her last night. But all she could see at that moment was the FBI agent who'd torn her life apart two years earlier.

It was happening again.

The rumble of an approaching vehicle filled her ears. Her heart sank as a cherry-red pickup truck bearing the Rambling Rose logo pulled up outside the stables, its bed loaded with burlap bags of feed and supplies. Agents Tierney and Morehouse appeared from her office.

"That's him," Reid said. Caitlyn pressed her hand against her stomach.

"Manny Ruiz?" Tierney called as he and the other agent strode toward the idling truck. Both held up their badges. Manny froze, and for several long seconds Caitlyn believed he might put the truck back into gear and make a run for it.

"Mr. Ruiz, step out of the vehicle."

Manny hung his head, the premature lines in his face appearing deeper. His shoulders slumped and he released a long breath before turning off the engine.

"Put your hands where I can see them!"

Manny's eyes met Caitlyn's. She felt a mixture of pity, anger and confusion overtake her. He slowly got out of the car. Her vision was blocked by Tierney's broad back as Manny spoke with the agents.

"Whatever he did, he isn't involved in the murders," Caitlyn appealed to Reid, who still stood beside her.

"You can't be sure of that—"

"Why? Because I didn't know my own brother was a killer?" Her eyes clung to his, and her face felt hot. He placed his hands on his hips and looked at the ground.

"Where are you taking him?"

"To the Middleburg police station for questioning. Like I said, we just want to talk to him for now."

A horse snorted from one of the stalls, its hooves stamping the ground. Caitlyn thought of the prescription pill bottle she'd found in the bathroom that morning. She wondered if Reid needed the medication, if he was looking for it. But now didn't seem the time to bring it up. At the moment, he appeared strong and resolute. Invincible.

Tierney motioned for Reid as the younger agent led Manny to the back passenger side of the sedan. Manny climbed inside and the door closed behind him.

"I've got to go," Reid said. She nodded blankly.

He didn't look back. Caitlyn watched as the sedan drove away, feeling more isolated than ever.

10

This wasn't Reid's fault, Caitlyn told herself. She couldn't blame him if Manny had lied about his past, if the secrets he'd been keeping were now coming back to haunt him. But Manny wasn't responsible for Aggie's death or the break-in to her home. Certainly, he'd had nothing to do with the murders.

She *was* sure of it...wasn't she?

A thread of doubt traveled through her, making her question her own judgment. Kidnapping and battery were serious offenses—felony convictions Manny had failed to inform her about. In any case, falsifying information on his employment application was grounds for termination. She would have to begin an active search for his replacement, and soon. His responsibilities at the stables and farm were too large to be left unhandled for long.

She had already gone to bed when the phone rang on her nightstand. Glancing at the glowing numbers on the digital alarm clock, she saw it was nearly midnight.

Not that it mattered since she'd been too wired to sleep and had instead been tossing and turning.

"Hello?"

"Caitlyn, it's Reid."

Holding the handset against her ear, she pushed herself up against the bed's antique, ironwork headboard.

"I'm sorry for calling so late."

"Where are you?"

"Back in D.C."

"What about Manny?"

"He was released a few hours ago."

Caitlyn reached to the nightstand and turned on the lamp. "Meaning the FBI doesn't have anything to charge him with."

"There's nothing substantial enough for an arrest," he conceded. "In particular, Ruiz has an alibi that checks out for last night when someone broke into your home. But he lied to you, Caitlyn. He never told you about his prison term. Isn't that something you want to know about a man you're entrusting your stables to?"

Caitlyn rubbed her forehead. She knew Reid was right, but she was still upset about the disruption at the stables that afternoon. Even more, seeing him with the other two agents had brought back bad memories of the investigation into her brother—memories she'd worked hard to push aside.

"Did he…" She closed her eyes. "Did he know Joshua in prison?"

"He denies it. We also checked Ruiz's prison records and there's nothing to indicate their paths crossed through work detail, especially since your brother's in maximum security." Reid paused. "Still, the fact remains that he's a former convict. I don't think he'll come back to Rambling Rose, even to collect his things. But if he does, I want you to call me. My gut tells me he isn't involved in all of this, but I can't be one hundred percent certain. You should err on the side of caution where he's concerned."

Caitlyn bit her lip. A tree limb scraped the house's exterior as the oak outside her bedroom swayed in the evening breeze. She didn't want to talk about Manny anymore.

"You mentioned a second victim in the District," she recalled. Reid had been going to the crime scene when he had left her home that morning. "Who is she?"

"Another Jane Doe for now, but it fits the pattern."

"So there *is* a copycat." The words felt lodged in her throat.

"It's going to be okay. Just take the precautions we've discussed. I'll be in touch as soon as I know more, I promise."

"Reid? You left something here. A prescription medication—"

"I don't need it." He sounded polite but distant. "Good night, Caitlyn."

Just like that, he was gone. She replaced the phone in its handset and stared out the window into the black night. The limb scraped the house's siding again with a low, heavy rasp. Caitlyn glanced at the console on the bedroom wall, assuring herself that the repaired security system was active. Letting go of a breath, she drew her knees to her chest, willing away the nagging anxiety she felt. From inside her solitary bedroom, morning seemed about as far away as the moon.

Reid observed silently from the back of the room as Mitch laid the photos on the table in front of Joshua Cahill. Garbed in an orange prison jumpsuit that appeared two sizes too large for his thin frame, Joshua's dark eyes moved across the gruesome crime scene images. He wet his lips, frowning a bit.

"Someone's copying me?"

"Like you don't know," Mitch growled.

"I don't."

"Are you willing to take a lie detector test to validate that?"

Joshua pushed his scruffy bangs from his eyes, which had yet to leave the photos. He raised a tentative hand out to them.

"Don't touch," Mitch ordered. He leaned closer, his tone goading. "Nice, aren't they? This guy's stolen your act, Cahill. You're trapped in here while he's out having a good time. Know what I think? Maybe he's better at it than you."

Mitch pulled one of the photos closer, studying it. It was of the woman at Hains Point. "Just *look* at what he did to her. His work makes yours seem almost amateurish."

Joshua looked up then, his eyes slowly morphing into cold, black stones. His previously slumped shoulders squared a bit and his upper lip curled into a small smirk. Reid had witnessed the transformation before—in his myriad interviews with Joshua following his arrest, and in the psychological profile assessments following his conviction. He could turn on a dime from withdrawn, barely seeming capable of violence, to something bold and aggressive. It was as if a hardened, darker version of himself could overtake the more timid one at any time.

"But maybe I've got it wrong," Mitch admitted, scratching his head. "If you've been instructing him from behind bars, then the kills would be partly yours, right?"

"I told you. I don't know anything."

"Bullshit."

"I'll prove it. I'll take your stupid lie detector test. On one condition." His obsidian gaze moved to Reid. "*If* I can see my sister."

Reid crossed his arms over his chest, his jaw tightening. "Caitlyn's not coming here."

"But you could get her to. Couldn't you, Agent Novak?"

Mitch's back had been to Reid, but he turned in his chair to look at him, too.

"You can make her do just about anything, I bet. You got her to go through my things and steal from me. She turned her own brother in, all for you." He rotated his shoulder, touching the area where it met his clavicle. "It still hurts where you shot me—"

"Too damn bad."

"Maybe you got her to do some *other* things, too."

His suggestive tone made Reid's face grow hot. Instead of looking at Joshua—he wouldn't give him the satisfaction of letting him see his irritation—he focused on the barred window on the far side of the small room.

"Did she go down on you?" Joshua asked. "Caitlyn's got a real nice mouth."

Anger thickened Reid's voice. He still didn't look at him. "This is a waste of time. This asshole doesn't know anything."

With that, he strode out.

A few minutes later, Mitch caught up with him in the corridor. Reid ran a hand through his short hair. "You can use a lie detector test if you want. We can get a warrant. But it won't do any good. Cahill's a habitual liar. He'll fool the polygraph."

"Well, he knows how to push *your* buttons."

Reid said nothing. He looked at the heavy door separating them from Cahill.

"So, you witnessed the interview—what's your gut?" Mitch asked. "Does he know the copycat or not?"

Reid wished he knew. He had hoped to see something in Joshua's eyes when he viewed the photos. He'd expected some show of pride. If he was serving in the role of mentor to the second killer, Reid thought he might have seen that emotion. Unless Joshua was more in control of himself than anyone realized.

"It's still a possibility. Did you get the visitor list?"

Mitch nodded. "There's a minister from the Cahills' church who comes every few weeks, but the guy's in his seventies and half-crippled with arthritis. There's also a couple of women who show up regularly for visitation. Sick, huh? I guess they're erotic masochists who get off on the idea of Cahill torturing those women. Speaking of, he gets quite a bit of *fan mail,* which the warden is now screening. They're watching any and all postal mail and internet correspondence—what comes in as well as what he sends out."

"What about prison guards in maximum security?" Reid asked.

"We'll look into it."

They began walking toward the exit, stopping at the desk where Mitch had checked his gun. Handing over their clearance badges, they waited for the guard to open the cage door and let them out.

Maybe you got her to do some other things, too.

As the late morning sunlight greeted them outside the penitentiary, Reid felt another flare of anger. He was being baited, he knew, but it didn't keep him from seething inside.

11

At just before 1:00 p.m. on Wednesday, Farragut Square in downtown D.C. was bustling. Bicycle messengers congregated beneath the statue of the Union admiral, awaiting their next errand, while the business lunch crowd sat with brown bags on benches. Caitlyn traveled through the park, headed to a meeting for a nonprofit on whose board she still held a seat. It had turned out to be a beautiful fall afternoon, the air crisp and the sky bright blue, so she'd decided to walk instead of take a cab. She had arrived in town earlier that morning, checking into the nearby Montier Hotel in hopes of putting the past few days behind her.

With all the activity inside the park, she was reminded of the excitement of living in the nation's capital. Men in power suits were most likely brokering deals for or against some federal legislation, while tourists studied maps and snapped photos. A tattooed man in a skullcap strummed guitar and sang for a crowd. For most of her life, Caitlyn had been a part of the District's energy. She had been a senator's daughter—well connected, on the inside of it all. It seemed strange now to experience it merely as a visitor.

Although the stables were only an hour away, Caitlyn had opted to stay in the city for a day or two instead of driving back at the end of her meeting. Tomorrow morning she had an appointment with her financial advisor, and then afterward she would go to the adult care facility in Foggy Bottom, near George Washington University, to visit her mother. She also had a meeting about listing her family's Georgetown home for sale. But Caitlyn couldn't lie to herself; the overnight stay was about more than simple convenience. She considered it ironic that the District, the place from which she'd originally sought sanctuary, had become a temporary respite from her secluded life in the country.

At the crosswalk, she waited for the light to change so she could get across busy Seventeenth Street to the postmodern office building where the board meeting was being held. It was then that she saw the man. Tall and pale, with a receding hairline, he seemed to be staring directly at her. Pretty certain she didn't know him, she averted her gaze and crossed the street with the other pedestrians.

Reaching the building, Caitlyn checked her wristwatch. She was early, and considering the gorgeous day there was little point in going inside too soon. She took a seat on the ledge of a splashing fountain outside the marble and glass lobby, intent on soaking up some sun.

She spotted the man again.

He stood on the other side of the street, his hands stuffed into the pockets of his wrinkled trousers. His features were pinched, his gaze on her intense. A businessman bumped into him on the sidewalk, but he didn't break his stare. Their eyes locked for several heartbeats, until one of the metro buses pulled in front of the building, blocking her view. When it drove away a short time later in a cloud of black smoke, the man was gone.

Puzzled, she scanned the busy street looking for him. But it was as if he had vanished into thin air. Did she recognize him, after all? Something niggled at the back of her mind. She continued rifling through her mental Rolodex until her cell phone rang. She dug it from her purse and answered, expecting it to be Sophie.

"Caitlyn, it's Reid. I was just calling to check on you. Is everything all right?"

Several days had passed since the ruckus at the stables involving Manny Ruiz.

"I'm fine." She pushed away a few strands of hair the cool breeze had blown across her face. "I'm actually in the District for a couple of days on business. I'm staying at the Montier."

"Where are you now?"

Caitlyn squinted against the bright sunlight. "On Seventeenth Street at the Habersham Building, getting ready to go into a long and probably boring meeting."

There was a pause over the airwaves and for a second Caitlyn thought they had been disconnected. But then Reid spoke. "Have dinner with me tonight, Caitlyn? I'm sorry about how everything happened the other day. I can come by the hotel and pick you up."

The invitation surprised her. Caitlyn watched as a young couple strolled past, laughing and holding hands. "I'd like that."

"I'll pick you up at seven?"

Once they'd agreed to a time, Caitlyn closed the phone. *It's not a date,* she told herself. *He's only worried about me.* Still, Reid was under no obligation to take her to dinner. For all she knew he just wanted to show her more crime scene photos or discuss Manny again. But it hadn't sounded like a business arrangement.

It had sounded like a man asking a woman out.

"You saw Joshua?" Caitlyn placed her dinner fork on the edge of her plate. They were seated at Agava, a cozy Greek restaurant just off K Street that was within walking distance from the Montier Hotel. Reid had met her in the hotel lobby, dressed in a sports coat, khaki slacks and a deep blue dress shirt.

"Agent Tierney wanted to interview him about anything he might know about the copycat," he explained. "I went with him to analyze Joshua's reactions."

A small knot formed in her stomach. "What did you find out?"

"Not much. Tierney goaded him, trying to get him to brag about a mentoring role with the killer. He wasn't biting."

Caitlyn couldn't help but wonder how Joshua was

faring in a maximum-security prison—whether the psychiatrists or medication were helping to control his violent, impulsive thoughts. "I imagine Agent Tierney can be rather…intimidating."

"That's an understatement." Reid smiled faintly and took a sip from his water goblet before finishing the last of his *paidakia,* or grilled lamb chops. Although their conversation had shifted toward the investigation, until now they had talked mostly about other things—the urban nonprofit for which Caitlyn was in town, and the Rambling Rose equine therapy program. She'd expressed concern that losing Manny would be a disruption to what had become a pretty smooth operation. Manny had overseen the operational aspects of the stables and farm, leaving a large gap she feared wouldn't be easily filled. Already, she had placed an ad in the Middleburg newspaper.

"Do you ride?" Caitlyn asked after the waiter had removed their dinner dishes and given them a rundown on the evening's desserts.

"My uncle had a farm in East Tennessee," Reid told her. "Megan and I used to spend several weeks there every summer. We'd fish, ride horses and just generally goof around. It was a chance for the city kids to live in the country for a while." He shook his head in fond remembrance. "I really loved it there. But no, I haven't ridden competitively like you."

Caitlyn had taken an interest in horses from an early age and become an accomplished equestrienne. As a teen, her bedroom in her parents' Georgetown home had been filled with ribbons and trophies won for equitation and jumping. She'd even competed on the collegiate level for Sarah Lawrence, her alma mater.

"How'd you know about that?" she asked, surprised.

Reid didn't answer for several seconds. "When your brother was under investigation, it was my job to learn as much about him as possible, including his acquaintances and family. Your background came...up."

"Oh," Caitlyn said softly, embarrassed by her naïveté. She should have realized he'd been privy to such information. He'd no doubt kept some dossier that held the minute details of herself and her family. She wondered if that was how he had selected the restaurant—Agava was one of her favorites.

Her thoughts must have been reflected in her expression, because he said, "I didn't mean for tonight to be awkward, Caitlyn. I didn't even intend to talk about the case."

His gray eyes appeared intense in the table's soft candlelight, the dancing flame illuminating his handsome face.

"Then why *did* you ask me?"

"The truth is, I didn't plan to." He shrugged a little, his voice low. "But when you told me you were here in the District, I realized that I really wanted to see you. It was an impulse move."

His gaze held hers until the waiter's return. He carried a tray with their ordered desserts—baklava and a molten chocolate cake with fig ice cream.

"Yours looks delicious," Caitlyn noted, looking at the dense cake set in a brûlée dish.

"Would you like a bite?"

When she nodded, Reid dug his fork into the cake. Leaning across the small table, he held it out to her. Her fingers curled around his wrist as she helped him guide it into her mouth. The sensation of being fed by him caused a slow, disconcerting heat to unfurl in her stomach, mingling with the sensation of the rich chocolate melting on her tongue.

"Good?"

She nodded, swallowing and touching her napkin to her lips. Needing a distraction, she sipped from her cup of espresso.

Caitlyn chastised herself for her response to him. Was it really that long since she'd been with a man? Her feelings about Reid Novak were confusing…and becoming deeper despite the rational part of her mind warning her to stay unattached.

At the Montier Hotel, Reid escorted Caitlyn to her room. The elegant suite was decorated in shades of russet and gold. A Queen Anne sofa and love seat were arranged in front of a marble fireplace, and soaring Palladian windows gave views of the twinkling cityscape.

"I have a feeling this place definitely wouldn't be on the FBI's approved expenditure list," Reid commented wryly.

"It shouldn't be on mine these days, either, but I couldn't resist staying here again." Caitlyn placed her clutch purse on the coffee table and removed her pashmina wrap, draping it over the sofa's back. "When I was little, before we moved permanently to D.C., my family used to stay here. I was about six and I fell in love with the horse-drawn carriages and uniformed valets outside. It always seemed so magical to me, like staying in a palace."

At her wistful statement, Reid studied her, causing her to run a hand self-consciously through her hair. "I probably sound really spoiled to you, not to mention silly."

"You sound like someone who misses her family." His expression was sincere. "You've been through a lot, Caitlyn. You're very resilient. Most people wouldn't have the strength to start over like you have."

"I didn't have much choice. It was sink or swim, as they say." She smiled and tried to make the statement sound lighthearted, but realized she hadn't quite pulled it off.

"Caitlyn…" He shook his head in the pale glow of the table lamp. "You don't have to always act so brave. Not on my account."

"I do it for *me,* actually," she replied with honesty. "It's how I got through Joshua's arrest and the trial. All those reporters and their horrible newspaper articles. My father's death."

Sympathy reflected in his eyes. Reid stepped closer, until they stood just inches apart. Caitlyn realized her breathing had grown shallower. Gazing up into his face, she lightly touched his chest. Little goose bumps rose on her skin as his fingers skimmed her bare arms in response. She thought he might kiss her, but after several long moments he instead released a breath that sounded like regret and slowly dropped his hands. Caitlyn felt disappointment spread through her.

"I should get going," he said, voice hoarse.

She nodded. "Thank you for dinner. It was lovely."

As he reached the door, she stopped him. "Reid? Just a minute…"

She went to the bedroom and returned with his prescription medication. Caitlyn handed it to him. "I was planning to drop it off before I left town."

"Thanks." He accepted the vial and dropped it into his coat pocket, not meeting her eyes. Caitlyn touched his sleeve, halting his retreat. She had to know—the prescription had been on her mind since finding it in her guest bathroom. She'd considered bringing it up during dinner, but had decided to let it wait until they were alone.

"Are you ill?"

He shook his head. "No. Not anymore."

"I know Dr. Isrelsen. He's a neurologist. A neuro-surgeon, actually—"

"I had a brain tumor. A glioma," he confessed quietly. He touched his forehead with the index and middle fingers of his right hand. "In my frontal lobe."

His revelation shocked her. "Reid. I'm…so sorry—"

"I'm fine now," he assured her. "It was benign, but in a tricky location. I had surgery to remove it six months ago."

She searched his eyes. His mysterious absence from the FBI now made sense. "You must have been terrified."

"I got through it. *We* did, actually. My family and I."

"I'm glad." Caitlyn reached up, her fingers lightly caressing his temple. Reid briefly closed his eyes at her touch.

"Bolt your door behind me, Caitlyn," he said when she lowered her hand. He took a reluctant step back.

She nodded. With a final look at him, she closed the door and slid the bolt into place. Caitlyn remained in the suite's vestibule until she heard the chime that signaled the arrival of the elevator to take him downstairs. Then, walking to one of the windows, she stared out at the city lights. The realization that someone as strong and vital as Reid could also be vulnerable was deeply troubling to her...as were her unsteady emotions. There was little point in denying to herself that she wanted him. But who she was—and who he was—meant the cards were stacked so very high against them.

Caitlyn believed Reid understood that, too.

12

The man stood on the hotel plaza, gazing up at the illuminated exterior. He scanned each window, wondering which room was hers.

She was a honey-blonde, too. Just like his wife had been. He had gotten a good look at her today, at least until she noticed him and he had been forced to retreat back into the pulsating crowd.

The night had gotten colder, the relative warmth of the sunny fall afternoon disappearing as blue sky faded to evening. Pulling the thin jacket more tightly around his chest, he tried to ignore his feet that hurt from hours of following her around the District.

Seeking a distraction, he closed his eyes and concentrated on her cool beauty, thinking of her oval face with its delicate features and graceful ballerina's neck. But her image distorted until it became someone else entirely. Someone who was even more beautiful to him. He saw his wife—laughing at the beach on a summer weekend, helping their daughters wrap presents at Christmas. Cooing over the West Highland puppy he'd given her on their tenth anniversary. The memories wrapped around him until he felt dizzy with anger and need.

I'm so tired, he thought, grinding the heels of his hands against his closed eyes. He hadn't slept, hadn't been home in two days.

When he looked again, the valet under the hotel portico was holding open the glass doors, revealing the posh lobby and its sparkling chandeliers.

Reid Novak walked outside.

They had crossed paths before in the federal courtrooms—on business and on another more intensely personal matter. He stepped back into the shadows, watching as the FBI agent tipped the valet and drove off in an SUV. By all accounts, Novak was a good officer, fiercely intelligent and possessing a high moral character. Which made his involvement with her even more confusing.

He of all people had to understand she was tainted by evil, didn't he?

But when the man had trailed them from the restaurant back to the hotel, he'd noticed the way Novak's hand lingered against the small of her back. He felt a wave of hurt and betrayal.

Peering up again at the hotel facade, his eyes were drawn to a corner room on the third floor. Golden light emanated from its arched window, silhouetting the slender figure of a woman who looked out. He couldn't make out her face at this distance, but her hair was long and blond. His fingers curled tightly against his palms, his unkempt nails pressing half moons into his flesh. The unfairness of it nearly choked him.

"I want my wife back," he whispered into the darkness.

13

"Agent Novak." Hal Feingold tipped his pilsner glass toward Reid, who had entered the wood-paneled Ambassador Bar near Capitol Hill. "You saved me a trip."

"And how's that?" Reid took a stool at the bar next to the former reporter. He'd already been by Feingold's house and was told by his wife where to find him. Judging by the cell phone on the bar top and the fact that Feingold didn't seem surprised by his appearance, Reid guessed he'd been forewarned of his arrival.

"I'm working on a book about the Cahill family. As lead investigator on the Capital Killer case, you're on my interview list. You want a drink?" Feingold lifted his hand to signal the bartender.

"Not for me," Reid said.

"Suit yourself." Feingold shrugged thick shoulders under a tweed blazer. His balding pate reflected light from a wall-mounted television turned to C-SPAN. Accepting a refill from the bartender, he took a drink and wiped the foam from his mouth. "So how've you been,

Novak? I contacted the VCU offices a few weeks back and was told you were on medical leave. You've been ill?"

"I'm better now."

"But you're not on the job yet, are you? You're missing your firearm."

Feingold had hangdog eyes and the heavy jowls of a chronic drinker, but Reid knew his mind was sharp as a scalpel. He'd covered the crime beat for the *Washington Post* for nearly three decades before leaving to pursue a career as a true crime author.

Reid redirected the conversation. "I understand you've been trying to make contact with Caitlyn Cahill?"

"Having her cooperation on the book would be a bonus."

"She's not interested."

Feingold grinned. "What did she do? Make an official complaint? The Cahill name must still carry some weight if they're letting her use FBI agents as messenger boys. Or is that just what they have you doing until SAC Johnston lets you off the porch?"

Reaching for a dish of salted peanuts, he popped a handful into his mouth and chewed thoughtfully. "But as long as you're bringing it up, I'll tell you. I'm writing the book with or without Ms. Cahill's permission. I covered the Capital Killer investigation and her brother's trial, and I have five cardboard boxes full of notes that I don't plan to let go to waste."

"Caitlyn's been through enough. She doesn't need

to see a book about the worst part of her life on store shelves."

"And that's precisely what will make it a bestseller. The Cahills were Washington royalty before one of them turned into a hot, psychotic mess. But Ms. Cahill can relax—she's going to come out looking like the only sane one in the family. The only moral one, too." He crunched more peanuts, studying Reid with curiosity. "Why do you give a damn about Caitlyn Cahill, anyway? Her daddy nearly got you busted down to the Omaha field office, if I recall. There's nothing in Nebraska to investigate but cow wrangling, Agent."

Reid made no comment. Instead he said, "Caitlyn had a break-in at her home outside Middleburg a few nights ago. Nothing was stolen, although some files in her home office appeared to have been disturbed—"

"You think I'm breaking into homes now?"

"I think it's a possibility."

Feingold snorted. "Get back to me when you have some actual proof to back up that screwball theory."

"It's not unreasonable. You're the one writing a book about the Cahills."

"I'll use one of your phrases, Agent. No comment."

Reid massaged the back of his neck. He'd figured talking to Feingold wouldn't glean much information, but at least he could apply some subtle pressure about leaving Caitlyn alone. Slapping the flat of his hand on the bar to signal his intention to leave, he stood.

"So Ms. Cahill won't deign to give me an interview, and she sent in the Feds to make her point. Message received." Feingold stifled a belch with a closed fist. "But what about you, Novak? I've got my digital recorder right here if you want to tell me a little about your infamous run-ins with Braden Cahill. Otherwise, I'll just have to go with my third-party accounts—"

"See you, Feingold."

"You don't want to talk about the copycat?"

Reid looked at him. Feingold gave a knowing wink. "I heard the Bureau got an ID on the second vic this morning. Too bad I'm not in the newspaper business anymore. I'd give my left nut to be the reporter who breaks that story wide-open. Regardless, it's going to make a nice epilogue for my book. A new killer on the loose and all that."

Feingold still had contacts within law enforcement, apparently. Although the media had reported both murders, they hadn't yet been publicly connected, nor had the possibility of a copycat killer been released. Reid knew it would now only be a matter of time.

"How about if I keep my mouth shut in exchange for an interview?" Feingold suggested. "I hear Braden was a real son of a bitch. Wouldn't it make you feel good to unload? Tell your side of the story?"

"The man's dead. Forget it," Reid answered tightly.

"Good for you, Novak. Always the Boy Scout. Tell Ms. Cahill I'll be seeing her on the bookshelves."

Reid walked out of the bar with Feingold's phlegmy chortle in his ears.

Inside the graceful Georgetown home, images of Caitlyn's childhood flitted through her mind. She saw herself with Joshua, playing on the curved mahogany staircase, as well as the Christmas tree that graced the two-story foyer each year, decorated with crystal ornaments and plaid bows in honor of the family's Scottish ancestry. Under the wide, arched doorway leading into the study, she had posed for a college graduation photo with her father, his arm wrapped around her as he beamed with pride. Caitlyn stood alone in the same location now, feeling a bittersweet sadness wash over her.

The visit with her mother, Caroline, at the nursing home earlier that day had not gone well. Once again, her mother hadn't recognized her. The nursing staff had warned that her mother was having one of her *off* days, and that it was possible she wouldn't be responsive. Still, Caitlyn had sat with her, holding her hand and talking to her in hopes she might somehow be able to reach her. But Caroline had stared at her daughter with vague curiosity before pulling her fingers away and gazing off toward the hallway, as if she expected some other visitor who was yet to arrive.

She had looked frail and small in the lilac sateen pajamas Caitlyn had bought her, and far too young to be struggling with Alzheimer's, if that was indeed her affliction. Caitlyn couldn't be sure since the doctors had never fully confirmed the diagnosis. All she really knew was that her mother's mental state had begun to deteriorate when the FBI arrested her son. She had gone from vibrant D.C. socialite to a recluse who refused to leave the haven of her home, fearing the questioning reporters camped along their fashionable street.

Two days after Braden Cahill's stroke, Caroline had disappeared on her way home from the hospital. The District police had found her wandering the National Mall and unable to tell them her name or address. It was as if her mind had shattered right along with her family and social standing. Without those facets of her life, Caroline Cahill ceased to exist.

Caitlyn blamed herself.

She looked around the house that was cloaked in unbearable silence. White sheets now covered much of the remaining furnishings that would soon be auctioned off in an estate sale.

It had to be done. Caroline would never be coming home again, and the adult care facility where she now resided was costly. Caitlyn had found the nicest and most highly recommended center in the District, taking some comfort in the knowledge that at least her mother would still be in close proximity to her beloved George-town.

With a sigh of resignation, she climbed the stairs, stopping at the large window that overlooked the tree-lined, cobblestone street comprised of quaint shops and well-kept Federal, Georgian and Victorian townhomes. If the house sold soon, Caitlyn realized, she might never see this picturesque view again. But she couldn't live here, either—the memories would consume her. She gazed down onto the sidewalk, expecting to see the bobbing heads of passersby. Instead, what she saw was a man's face lifted up toward the window. He frowned in hard concentration, the deep lines bracketing his mouth, belying his relative youth. Recollection sent a slow shiver curling up her spine.

It wasn't just any man—it was the same one who had been watching her yesterday. Caitlyn took a step back, placing herself out of view. Curiosity and annoyance raced through her. Bolstering her courage, she hurried down to the main floor, her rapid footsteps echoing off the stairs. It was broad daylight—she would be safe enough. Throwing open the front door, she nearly let out a scream, not expecting the veranda to be occupied.

"Caitlyn?" Bliss Harper stood with her hand poised in midair, preparing to use the door's brass knocker.

"Bliss." Caitlyn sounded breathless.

"Am I...early?" Pushing her flaxen hair off her shoulder, she checked her Cartier wristwatch. "You looked surprised."

Caitlyn scanned the street behind Bliss, but no longer saw the man. "No—no. You're right on time."

The two women gave each other a meaningful hug. Bliss had gone to school with Caitlyn and was one of the few friends with whom she had kept in touch after Joshua's arrest and trial. Recently divorced, Bliss was now a Realtor specializing in estate homes, a lucrative profession for her since she traveled in the same circles with the people who could afford them. Caitlyn had contacted her last week about putting her family home on the market.

"You seem preoccupied," Bliss noted. "Should we reschedule?"

Caitlyn looked past Bliss and once again searched the street, but her mystery follower was definitely gone. She shook her head. "No. Let's do this now."

"It *is* a down market," Bliss reminded. She wrote notes in a leather-bound journal as they stood in one of the upstairs bedrooms. In a gentle voice she added, "And this house has a bad history, honey."

The listing price she'd recommended was well below what Caitlyn knew the home was worth. But she was also aware Joshua's infamy had cast a pall over it. Even though it wasn't his residence at the time of the murders, it was where he'd grown up. And the FBI had served a warrant to search the residence after Caitlyn had turned over the journals, giving them cause.

"This is one of the best-preserved Victorians on the street, not to mention the largest," she said quietly.

"We can up the asking price, Caitlyn. But be prepared to come down. Bad karma doesn't sell well." Bliss looked around the bedroom that had once belonged to Joshua, biting her lip. "Why don't we go back down to the dining room? We can spread the paperwork out on the table."

"You go ahead. I'll be down in a minute."

Once she was alone, Caitlyn took in the large room with its wood floors and wide bay window that offered a view of Montrose Park. An image of Joshua, around ten, sitting cross-legged on the upholstered window seat and reading a book, sprang into her head. She pictured his dark, intelligent eyes nearly obscured by his shaggy hair as he concentrated, a rainy afternoon visible through the window behind him. His child's voice became part of her memory as he read favored passages aloud. But that had been years before the schizophrenia diagnosis. Before the psychiatric evaluations and antipsychotic medications.

The room was unheated, and Caitlyn ran her hands over her arms as she studied the bookshelf still lined with Joshua's boyhood favorites. *The Hobbit, The Lord of the Rings, King Arthur and His Knights of the Round Table.* She removed one of the books to get a closer look at its front cover, then returned it to its resting place. Her eyes traveled over the antique writing desk where Joshua had done his homework. He had carved his name into its top, the childlike etching making her heart ache. Absently, Caitlyn opened one of the desk drawers. What she saw caused her breath to freeze inside her chest.

She removed the blond-haired Barbie doll, her heart beating rapidly. The doll was nude, its hands and ankles bound with pipe cleaners. Another pipe cleaner had been wrapped around its throat. Straight pins were buried deep into the rubberized pink flesh, inserted into the breasts and groin area. A red felt-tip marker had been used to simulate blood.

Her hands shook. Caitlyn placed the doll back inside the drawer and closed it with a hard shove.

Had Joshua done that when he was a child? Had it been here, waiting all this time for someone to find it?

If that were the case, Caitlyn was certain the police would have taken the doll during their search. Besides, the doll looked brand-new.

Someone else had been here and left it behind. Somehow, they had gotten inside. Feeling a flutter of anxiety, she thought of the man who had been watching her for the past two days.

14

After examining the doll, Reid placed it carefully in an evidence bag. He could see the distress in Caitlyn's eyes.

"I wasn't thinking. I shouldn't have touched it."

"It's okay," he said. "We'll take it to the lab and see if we can get any prints."

He had arrived at the Cahill home in Georgetown a short time after receiving Caitlyn's call. Reid remembered the house from the warranted search he'd led during the Capital Killer investigation, although its once elegant interior now appeared stark and barren. Caitlyn had been waiting for him downstairs with a real estate agent who was listing the house. They'd left her in the dining room, finishing up paperwork.

Reid watched as Caitlyn paced the bedroom before taking a seat on the bed's edge.

"Tell me about this man who's been following you."

"I saw him yesterday outside the Habersham Building, before I went into the board meeting. Then again this afternoon outside the house." Caitlyn ran a hand through her hair. "When I saw him from the window, I went downstairs. I was going outside after him, but Bliss was at the door. He slipped away."

Reid rubbed his jaw. "Confronting him wouldn't be smart, Caitlyn. Even on a busy street."

"I don't like being followed. And he didn't look dangerous—"

"A person's looks can be deceiving."

"You mean like Joshua?" She gazed at him.

Reid didn't look away. He thought of Cahill's slight build. "Exactly like Joshua."

He sat next to her. "Did this man try to approach you yesterday? When you were downtown?"

She shook her head. "Once he knew I'd seen him, he disappeared."

"Why didn't you mention him last night?"

"Because I wasn't sure…I thought yesterday he was maybe somebody I knew, or that he had me confused with someone. I didn't think too much of it until I saw him again today here."

"Could you describe him to a sketch artist?"

"I think so."

Caitlyn had already given him a basic physical description—tall and somewhat thin, with a receding blond hairline, approximately mid- to late-thirties.

"Are you okay?" Reid asked.

"The doll freaked me out."

"That's understandable." He looked around the room. "But I'm also talking about being *here.* And about the house being sold."

She placed her hands in her lap and released a soft sigh. "Selling it makes sense. My mother isn't going to be able to come back here, and my life is elsewhere now. It's painful, but I think letting go of this place could help me let go of…other things."

Reid knew she was thinking of the life she'd once had and the family she could never get back. It felt odd sitting beside her in Joshua Cahill's childhood bedroom. He reached for her hand in a gesture of support, his fingers briefly clasping hers until footsteps sounded farther down the hallway. Reid could tell by the heavy gait it was Mitch, whom he had called on his way over to alert him to what Caitlyn had found. He'd heard his voice earlier in the downstairs foyer, and Reid stood just before Mitch knocked on the door frame.

"It looks like someone gained entrance through a basement window," he said, looking at Caitlyn. "The lock's been jimmied—don't you have a security system for this palace?"

"I've had estate appraisers in and out over the past several weeks," she explained. "It's been easier to leave the alarm off."

"I'll need the names of anyone who's had access. We'll also need to schedule a tech to come in and dust." Walking farther into the room, Mitch picked up the evidence bag containing the doll. He raised an eyebrow. "Christ. Should we bring Ken in for questioning?"

"Where's Morehouse?" Reid asked.

"Still at the Roosevelt. You coming?"

"Go ahead. I'll call you later."

Once Mitch had left the bedroom, Caitlyn turned to Reid. Her eyes were questioning. "Why would someone break in here, just to leave a doll?"

He'd already considered this. "Breaking into the house probably helped with the unsub's fantasy of being Joshua—it made him feel closer. As far as the doll goes, he left it for shock effect. He knew the chances were good a family member would find it."

"By *family member,* you mean me," she clarified softly. "I'm really the only one left. I guess I should feel lucky it was a doll instead of a person."

Reid didn't respond, although he'd been thinking the same thing. Her hand pressed against her stomach, Caitlyn stood and went to stare blankly out the window. He didn't like seeing her scared but maybe the doll had opened her eyes to reality. She had to start taking precautions. If Reid were on active duty right now, he'd be pushing for a watch on her. But at the same time, he also realized the chances of getting it at this point would be small. The FBI had been hit with its own share of budget cuts, and VCU resources were scarce. Until a more direct threat was made, getting any protection assigned to her would be next to impossible.

Reid had something else to tell her. Something she needed to hear from him. "They got an ID on the second victim, Caitlyn. The woman at Hains Point."

She looked at him. "Who was she?"

"A tourist. Her name was Hannah Reece. She was in town with her fiancé. He was at a business meeting, so she went sightseeing alone. She never came back to the Roosevelt Hotel where they were staying. Agents Tierney and Morehouse spent most of the day talking to the fiancé, as well as the hotel staff—"

"But they don't have any leads."

Reid shook his head. Like the first victim, the body was clean, no physical DNA evidence left behind to run through the database in hopes of finding a match. He walked to the window to stand beside Caitlyn. Below, he could see Mitch climbing into his government-issue Crown Victoria. It pulled from the curb and disappeared down the street.

"We should probably go, too," Caitlyn said. As she picked up her purse from the bed, the cell phone inside it rang. Locating it, she flipped open its cover.

As soon as she answered, Reid saw the color drain from her face. She gripped the phone tightly.

"Joshua." Her voice trembled. "What do you want?"

"I want to talk to you, Caity. You *are* still my sister, right?"

Caitlyn's stomach twisted at her brother's voice. In all this time, she hadn't heard from him. Not once had he attempted to contact her. Her words were choked. "You haven't wanted to since your arrest. What's changed?"

"I miss you." He sounded sincere. "I understand now you did what you had to…to help me."

Caitlyn closed her eyes. She felt Reid's presence beside her.

"I'm doing a lot better. The doctors and the meds are helping this time. I want you to come see me."

"No," she whispered. "I can't."

"I know I can't make up for what I did to those women. But God, I'm so sorry. I think about it every day. And I think about you."

Her legs felt wobbly. Joshua was still talking, trying to convince her, when she relinquished the phone to Reid. His expression was stern.

"This is Agent Novak. If you try to make contact with Caitlyn again, I'll see to it your phone privileges are revoked." He closed the phone with a hard snap.

"He wants me to come see him," she said, upset. "After all this time."

"I don't think you should."

"He's still my brother. He says he's sorry for what he did—"

His hands gently grasping her upper arms, Reid forced her to look up into his face. His eyes were a steely gray. "Listen to me. No matter what he tells you, Joshua *hasn't* changed. He has no remorse. I've talked to him. I don't know what he wants with you, but it can't be good. I don't want you going to see him."

Caitlyn nodded, but she couldn't let go of the earnestness in Joshua's voice. *He called me. My serial killer brother contacted me from prison, asking to make amends.*

She wondered if there would ever be a day she would feel normal again.

15

Despite Reid's attempts to convince her otherwise, Caitlyn had returned to the Rambling Rose. He'd made it clear he didn't like her being so isolated, but the absence of Manny Ruiz meant there were additional responsibilities she had to attend to at the stables and farm. Not to mention, she had to find someone to fill the now-vacant manager position.

She had been back a full day—a long one spent in session with a therapist who was helping plan a new element of the equine program, and then later leading a group of inner-city children along the winding horse trail. Beyond that, Rob Treadwell had stopped by the stables without Sophie. Asking for Caitlyn's help in choosing a birthday present for his wife, he'd hung out in her office until she had run out of suggestions and been forced to mention how much work she had to do. By the time she had finished ordering supplies from the feed store, the late afternoon sun was fading. As Caitlyn reached the top of the long driveway to her house, she slowed the car. Manny waited for her on the front porch. He appeared hesitant, his big hands nervously twisting the John Deere baseball cap he normally wore.

Reid had instructed her to call him if Manny returned, and yet Caitlyn's gut told her to hear him out. Regardless of the prison record he'd kept hidden, Manny had been a model employee and an excellent manager. Didn't she at least owe him an opportunity to say whatever was on his mind?

"Please don't call the police, Caitlyn," he urged, coming closer as she opened the BMW's door. "I just want a chance to explain."

"About why you lied on your job application?"

His sun-worn features creased as he twisted the cap again. "I'm sorry about that. I know I should've been up front, but I didn't think you would hire me if you knew the truth."

"That doesn't make it right."

"I know. And I'm not makin' excuses—I *did* lie to you about my…background." He dug the toe of his dust-covered boot into the grass at the edge of the lawn. His brown eyes were sad. "But I wasn't lying about horses. I've been around 'em all my life. I grew up on a farm and I know how to make one work. We were getting things rolling out here, Caitlyn."

"We were," she agreed, feeling a twinge of melancholy for all they had accomplished. The wind blew her hair across her face, and she tucked it behind her ear. "Look, Manny. I still owe you for your last two weeks of work. I can give you that now, as well as a little extra to help you get started somewhere else…"

Manny looked crestfallen but didn't argue. Caitlyn went back to the car to retrieve her purse and the Rambling Rose checkbook, which she had brought home with her so she could work on paying bills after dinner. As Manny waited, she wrote out a check on the car's hood.

"Have you replaced me yet?" he asked.

"No, Manny. I have a feeling that's going to be hard to do."

"Did the FBI tell you what I went to prison for?" He'd come a few steps closer as Caitlyn tore the check from the large blue binder. She realized that she should feel some trepidation, but Manny just didn't provoke that reaction in her. She handed him the check.

"They said you kidnapped someone. And that you were also convicted of assault and battery."

He peered at her unflinchingly. "I beat the hell out of my ex-wife's boyfriend. I put him in the hospital—he was in critical condition for six days. I don't regret it, either."

The fierceness of his words surprised her, considering his usually soft-spoken nature. "What did he do?"

"He was hurting my six-year-old daughter, Maria. He broke her arm. My ex-wife covered for him, made up some story about Maria wrecking her bike. But I'd been seeing bruises on her for a while." A shadow passed over his face, his jaw hardening. "The bastard was *hitting* her. But every time I asked questions, I got a load of bull. So when she came to me with her arm in a cast, I went crazy. I caught up to the son of a bitch in a bar parking lot, and then I took Maria out of there. I don't call it kidnapping if it's your own child."

"You didn't have custody."

"No," he admitted.

"And you took her across the state line." A federal offense, Caitlyn knew.

He frowned, deepening the lines in his face. "I took her across *three* of 'em. We'd still be running if the police hadn't pulled us over for a busted taillight. I got into some trouble for forgin' checks, too, but we were broke and I had to keep my little girl fed and safe."

Empathy tugged at Caitlyn. Was she a fool to believe him? She hadn't asked Reid for the details of Manny's crimes, nor had he supplied them. Despite Manny's lie of omission on his employment application, she still held her belief that he was an otherwise honest man— his story seemed too heartfelt to have been conjured up for her benefit. In addition, for more than a year he'd had full access to the Rambling Rose's bank accounts and not a penny had been unaccounted for. Still, there had to have been a better way for him to help his daughter.

"Manny," she asked. "Couldn't you have gotten the police involved, or Child Protective Services?"

"I'm from a small town in South Texas," he confided. "My ex-wife's new boyfriend was the son of the town's mayor. His family owned the biggest factory around. I tried to get custody, and I tried to go through the proper channels. All it got me was fired from my job. I handled things the only other way I knew how."

Caitlyn heard the raw frustration in his voice.

"I have one more question. Did you know my brother?"

He shook his head. "We never met, I swear. I knew who he was, but he was in maximum security. I was in genpop. I know it looks suspicious, considerin' we were both at Springdale at the same time. But, Caitlyn, you have to know I would never hurt you."

"Where's Maria now?"

"Still with her mother, although the boyfriend's been gone for some time." Manny's eyes saddened. "I sent Maria some letters after I got out of prison, but I never heard back. She's not a little girl anymore. She's thirteen. She's probably embarrassed by her ex-con father."

Gazing across the lawn toward the low, stacked-stone wall, Caitlyn surveyed the acreage that made up her property. With the loss of fall leaves, she could just make out the Rambling Rose stables in the distance, including the big red barn with its high-pitched roof, paddocks and equestrian rings. She could also see the now-barren fields that in the summer grew organic vegetables that were sold to area restaurants. Manny had been a big part of the success she had managed so far.

"Caitlyn, if you could find a way to forgive me, to overlook my past, I'd be forever grateful." Manny's voice was hoarse. He stared at the ground. "I don't want to leave here."

Caitlyn released a small sigh.

"I don't want you to leave, either," she admitted.

"Just try to relax, Mr. Novak. This will take about forty-five minutes."

Reid lay on the conveyorlike table that moved him slowly into the core of the MRI machine. He'd had these screenings before; he knew the drill firsthand. And yet this time he felt a mild sense of panic as his head and shoulders were fed into the cavern's maw.

He'd had a few more headaches—the one last night severe enough to increase his anxiety over the routine scan, his last before being given a clean bill of health. Reid closed his eyes, pushing away the encroaching claustrophobia. The machine sounded like the inside of an engine, its loud knocks and pings increasing his discomfort. He realized his hands were clenched into fists and he uncurled his fingers as he willed his shallow breathing to deepen. *This scan will be clean, just like the others. Relax.*

Desperate for something to distract him from the curved roof of the MRI cylinder, Reid concentrated on Caitlyn and her situation. An image of her delicate features and wide, green eyes appeared in his mind.

Did she go down on you? Caitlyn's got a real nice mouth.

Cahill's provoking statements at the prison had struck a raw nerve. It also confirmed that he thought of Caitlyn as no different from any of the women he had tortured and destroyed. What he wanted with her exactly, Reid wasn't sure. But Cahill was a poison Caitlyn didn't need in her life. He'd damaged her enough already.

"Mr. Novak?"

His thoughts faded, his focus returning to the confined space of his metal coffin.

"I said, *doing okay, Mr. Novak?*" the female technician standing next to the machine repeated loudly enough to be heard above the mechanical roar. He could see only the lower portion of her floral-print smock through the open end of the cylinder.

Reid worked to find his voice. "I'm fine."

He wondered if she could even hear him.

Less than an hour later, he walked out of the MRI outpatient center. He'd been told the results would have to be interpreted by a neurologist, and that he would have them within a few business days. He had tried to get a read from the technician, but her face had been carefully composed, even blank.

Her eyes had avoided his, however, and that worried him.

16

A dreary grayness pervaded the Saturday Caitlyn had set aside for household chores. She had taken several boxes of old clothing to a Middleburg church accepting donations, then gone grocery shopping to replenish her refrigerator and pantry. By late afternoon, she'd finished some light housecleaning and was just settling onto the couch with a cup of tea and a book when the doorbell rang.

Peering through the front door's beveled-glass pane, she felt a surge of surprise. Caitlyn disarmed the security system and smoothed her hair as she opened the door to Reid. He had on jeans and a dark Henley shirt under his leather jacket.

"I thought I should check on you." His gray eyes reflected concern.

She tilted her head at him. "You could've just called."

"I did, actually. You didn't answer and I got a little worried."

"Oh." Caitlyn ran her hands over her upper arms.

She wore a thick, cable-knit sweater and a pair of black riding pants. "I was out running errands earlier. My cell phone was in the charger in the kitchen."

"You really shouldn't leave the house without your cell, especially considering things lately."

"You're right," she acknowledged, sheepish. She opened the door wider to give him entrance.

"I called the stables, too." He followed her inside. "The voice mail said it closed at three. When I couldn't reach you I decided to drive on out."

Caitlyn didn't like feeling that she had caused him any trouble—she had certainly done enough of that lately "I really am sorry. I'm sure you must have better things to do on a Saturday. But as long as you're here, I'm having some tea. Would you like some?"

Reid nodded. "That would be great. Thanks."

She left him in the living room, still a little puzzled about his visit. Certainly, if he was concerned for her welfare, he could have just contacted the Middleburg Police Department and had them send a squad car out for a safety check. Something else was bothering him, Caitlyn decided. It was evident in the tightness around his eyes and the hard set of his jaw.

When she returned to the living room with a china teapot and a second cup, she found him studying a grouping of silver-framed photos on the bookshelf. They were pictures of Caitlyn with her parents, in happier times. The ones including Joshua she had long since banished to a box in the attic, unable to face his image staring back at her on a daily basis.

"Where was this taken?" Reid asked. The snapshot was of Caitlyn with her father, both of them holding rifles as they stood side by side in a grassy field, a bright cerulean sky above them.

"Just a few miles down the road, actually. A family friend had a summer home out here, and my father used to take Joshua and me skeet shooting. I never cared for hunting game, but I loved the excitement of hitting those clay disks."

Caitlyn studied his profile as he replaced the photo. "Reid, is everything all right?"

He nodded, although his expression appeared shuttered. "Do you have anything in the gun safe upstairs besides shotguns?"

"There are a couple of handguns, too. Why?"

"I was on the way to the shooting range when I tried to reach you—my service gun's in the car." Reid slid his hands inside his pockets. "I'm going back to full duty soon. I need to requalify, and my exam's Thursday. You mentioned there was a shooting range set up on the property?"

Caitlyn looked past him out the window. The afternoon held a thick haze suggesting rain, but so far there hadn't been as much as a drizzle.

"It's in the woods. We can go by horseback," she told him. "It's pretty basic compared to what you're probably used to, but there're some targets that were left by the previous owner."

"You should get a jacket. And a gun."

* * *

As their horses traveled alongside each other, Caitlyn pointed out areas of interest along the wooded trail. She showed him the soaring, broad-limbed oak that was well over a century old, and the waterwheel that was once part of a working gristmill. It now sat half-buried in a rushing stream, its spokes worn smooth by water and the passage of time. Around them, the air held a damp chill that made their breath fog as they talked. Reid looked comfortable on the muscular dun Caitlyn had chosen for him, his strong fingers grasping the reins with ease and his body acclimating to the horse's easy canter. Her own horse, a dappled gray filly named Camilla, was more spirited than the other animal but Caitlyn guided her with a firm hand, keeping her under control.

They reached the clearing where the targets were located. A row of thin, metal plates were strung from wire in front of raised mounds of dirt.

"It's not fancy," Caitlyn said as she dismounted. "I'm sure the FBI offers better facilities."

"I prefer the fresh air." Reid squinted at the targets, which were about forty yards out. He'd already climbed down from his horse. "Do you come out here often?"

Caitlyn decided to tell him the truth. "Not until recently. But after what happened to Aggie and the break-in at my house I thought it might be time to brush up."

They walked the horses a good distance away from

the shooting area, ground tying them. The filly snorted and tossed her head. Caitlyn stroked her muzzle and spoke softly, putting the animal at ease.

"You gave me the tame one, didn't you?"

She grinned. "You're a better rider than I thought you'd be."

He pulled his handgun from the saddlebag of his horse. "*This* is more my comfort zone."

They took turns shooting at the plates, their guns' echoes reverberating like thunder along the hillside. Around them, the fall leaves were a cacophony of bright colors, burnt orange, sienna and golden brown. The air smelled of moist earth. Holding her own lightweight revolver in the proper safety position, Caitlyn watched Reid's stance as he aimed and fired at his target, his bullets piercing the plates with sharp pops. Her stomach knotted as her mind traveled back in time to two years earlier, placing him in a cold, dilapidated factory building at the edge of the Potomac.

"Have you ever shot anyone besides Joshua?" she asked quietly.

Reid didn't look at her, instead chambering another round. "I shot and killed a suspect who charged Agent Tierney with a knife. That was four years ago."

He aimed again, hitting his target in its center. Caitlyn moved to a lighter topic. "Well, the time away from the job doesn't appear to have hurt your accuracy."

"Your turn," Reid stated. He holstered his Glock in the clip he'd attached to his jeans. "Show me what you've got."

Caitlyn moved forward, concentrating on not jerking the trigger. She hit the first one, but missed on the second attempt.

"Line your hips with your target," Reid instructed from behind her. His body brushed against her backside, his hands touching her waist to correct her alignment.

Caitlyn fired again, missing.

"You were shooting better before."

Lowering her gun, she turned to him. He remained close, and she found herself looking up into the masculine planes of his face. His gray eyes were intense, their color like liquid steel ringed with inky black. His thick eyelashes were of the same midnight-dark tint.

"That's because you're making me nervous," she complained, her voice sounding a little shaky and hoarse. Caitlyn's eyes flicked to his mouth that had quirked up in a faint smile of amusement. There was no denying he was dead-on sexy. Compulsively, she licked her lips, her own mouth gone suddenly dry. Despite the coldness of the afternoon, the air felt heated around them.

As he stared at her, Reid's expression became serious, causing sensation to spiral inside her. He reached for her gun, slowly taking it and activating its safety. Then his free hand rose to touch her face, his thumb brushing across her full bottom lip. A fire raced through her. In the distance, she heard the soft whicker of one of the horses.

"Caitlyn," Reid whispered roughly.

His lashes lowered as he bent his head and kissed her,

his lips at once soft and firm on hers. Caitlyn grasped the open edges of his leather jacket, pulling him against her as their mouths melded together. She felt dazed, his kiss stirring a ravenous physical hunger.

Their contact broke only when the sky opened, unleashing fat, heavy raindrops that were like pellets of ice on her flushed skin.

"The mill house," she told him in a breathless rush. "Leave the horses under the trees. They'll be okay there."

Quickly gathering their belongings, Reid took Caitlyn's hand and they made a run toward the frame of the old mill house located near the streambed. The building itself was gutted out, but what remained of its roof provided some shelter from the downpour. Winded, laughing, they reached its shadowed haven.

"Are you cold?" he asked. His short, dark hair was spiky and soaked. He laid her gun and its carry bag on the ground.

She felt herself shiver. "I'm freezing."

Reid chuffed her upper arms with his hands. "Maybe outdoor target practice wasn't such a great idea."

His arms encircled her waist, pulling her into his heavy leather jacket, his body heat warming her. He felt hard and strong. Safe. For a short while, she rested her cheek against his chest, listening to the thudding of his heart. Then she looked up at him. Desire shone in his eyes. She pressed herself more fully to him, wanting to finish what they had started earlier.

He seemed to understand. Reid's mouth pressed

against hers again, this time more demanding. Caitlyn felt his hands tangling in her wet hair as he tilted her head back, deepening their kiss, his tongue parrying with hers. Instinctively, she rubbed against him, thrilling at the male hardness she felt through his jeans. He could have her right here, she thought wildly. Damn the cold and the rain. Her body felt hot and strangled by the confines of her clothing. Caitlyn half groaned into his mouth as Reid's fingers caressed her throat, her pulse pounding beneath his touch.

"I want you," she whispered against his lips. "I want you to…"

Caitlyn froze at the shift of shadows. The onslaught had darkened the afternoon, deepening the gray haze. She gasped. The man with the pale, receding hairline—the man who had been following her—stood in the corner of the ramshackle structure. He was wet and dressed in nothing but a thin, sodden windbreaker and dark pants. Reid turned, his hand on the holstered gun at his waist. But the man was already a step ahead, the barrel of the gun he held pointed directly at them.

"D-don't move, Agent Novak."

17

Reid took a subtle step forward, trying to place himself in front of Caitlyn.

"I—I said don't move!" The man appeared jittery. He remained in the shadows of the structure. Although Reid could barely make out his features, recognition tugged at him.

"Let's just relax," he suggested, slowly lifting his palms to show he wasn't going for his gun. "No one has to get hurt."

"Someone already got hurt." The man's voice was low and nearly inaudible, swallowed up in the pounding rain.

"You've been following me," Caitlyn said shakily. "What do you want?"

"I want…" His words faltered. "I want my wife back."

The gun's barrel trembled. His angular face and sharp chin flashed in Reid's memory. He'd lost a lot of weight, the drenched clothes enveloping his gaunt frame, but recognition hit him with a jolt.

David Hunter.

The brutal image of Julianne Hunter, sprawled on the floor of the decaying factory, appeared in Reid's mind. He'd first met her husband at the D.C. morgue, where he had offered his condolences and waited as a positive ID on the body was made. Throughout Joshua Cahill's trial, Hunter had sat red-eyed and silent in back of the courtroom, waiting for justice to be served. But the man now gripping the gun was a mere shell of who he'd once been. He looked disheveled, his thinning hair slicked down against his skull by the rain. His fevered gaze focused on Caitlyn.

"Your family destroyed my life! Julianne, she was everything to me, to my two girls..."

Caitlyn blinked. "I don't understand—"

"You don't know me? My wife? Your brother *murdered* her!"

Reid spoke. "She had nothing to do with your wife's death, Mr. Hunter."

"And why are you here with her? *Kissing* her?" Hunter waved the gun wildly. Spittle flew from his lips. "She should be your enemy, Agent Novak!"

"Your anger's misplaced," Reid said quietly. "Caitlyn's estranged from her brother. She helped in the investigation—"

"You look like her, you know." Hunter continued staring at Caitlyn. "She was blonde, pretty, like you... Why didn't he kill you?"

"I—I don't know," Caitlyn whispered.

"You knew what he was all along!"

She shook her head. "No! Please—"

"Your family protected him. You let him go on killing! Do you know what he did to those women? What he planned to do to Julianne if the FBI hadn't found them? Instead, he cut her throat!"

Reid blocked him from coming any closer. He could feel Caitlyn sodden and shivering behind him. If he had to, he would make a move for Hunter's weapon.

"Stop this now," he warned. "I'm not going to let you hurt her."

"I just want to understand why—"

"She can't help you."

"Get out of my way!"

Caitlyn screamed as Reid rushed the other man, knocking him backward and falling with him onto the ground. Hunter's arm struck the wet dirt, the gun discharging with a roar. He howled and kicked, fighting Reid for control.

Another male voice ordered, "That's enough!"

In his peripheral vision, Reid became aware of a fourth figure, holding a shotgun.

"I said that's enough!" A split second later, pieces of the mill house roof rained down on them as Manny Ruiz discharged the rifle into the air. Clad in a rain slicker and baseball cap, he cocked the weapon again and aimed its long barrel at Hunter.

"Give Agent Novak the gun! Now!"

There must have been some shred of sanity left in

Hunter's mind, because he stopped struggling enough for Reid to pin his arm to the ground and pry the firearm from his hand. Gaining control of the weapon, Reid pushed himself backward, panting and sitting on the wet, moss-covered ground.

"You okay, Caitlyn?"

"Y-yes," she answered Ruiz. Her eyes met Reid's, her face pale.

"Agent Novak?" Ruiz asked.

Reid ran a hand over his features and nodded, wondering what the hell was going on.

"So let's recap. You were out here on some kind of booty call—"

"I came out here to check on Caitlyn," Reid corrected Mitch. "She didn't answer her phone."

"Uh-huh. And you figured, hey, as long as I'm out here, why don't we go into the woods together and shoot guns?" They were back at the stables, the scent of rain mingling with the smell of hay and horses in the stables. It was nearing dark and still coming down outside. Water rushed from the high-pitched roofline, creating puddles in the packed earth underneath the gutter spouts.

Mitch continued his full-court press. "I mean, she *is* Braden Cahill's daughter. That NRA guns and glory stuff probably turns her on."

Reid ground his teeth. Mitch was obviously enjoying himself, but he was wet and cold and he'd had enough of his partner's smart-ass comments. Furthermore, he didn't like being questioned as though he were a civilian.

"I have to requalify on firearms. I had my service gun in the truck," he recounted with forced patience. "Caitlyn told me about the practice range on the other side of her property. If she's going to insist on living out here alone, she needs to be able to protect herself. So yeah, I suggested it. I wanted to see how well she could shoot."

Reid glanced toward Caitlyn, who stood with Ruiz at the far end of the stable's open-air instruction area, giving a statement to Sheriff Malcolm and Agent More-house. Her blond hair was wet and matted to her head, and she'd wrapped a wool blanket around herself to ward off the chill.

Following Reid's gaze, Mitch leaned against one of the horse stalls. "Well, she's not *entirely* alone. What I want to know is why Manny Ruiz is back here."

Reid had asked Caitlyn the same question while they'd waited for law enforcement to arrive. He didn't approve of her having an ex-con around—especially one out of Springdale Penitentiary. But he had to admit Ruiz had shown up at an opportune time, possibly saving both their lives.

"Caitlyn gave him his job back," he said with a shrug. "He made an appeal to her, and she decided to give him another chance. Apparently, he knows a lot about run-ning a working farm and stables."

"Or maybe she just has a soft spot for convicts." Mitch nodded toward the patrol car parked outside the stables, its lights flashing blue against the darkening sky. David Hunter sat in its backseat, handcuffed, his head bowed. "Who knows? Maybe when that guy gets done serving time for assaulting a federal officer, she'll hire him, too."

"He needs a mental evaluation."

"What he needs is a good, old-fashioned interrogation. I'm planning to reach down his throat and grab him by the balls, inside out," Mitch replied. "We might've found our copycat."

Reid pressed his lips together. Clearly, Julianne Hunter's murder had caused some psychotic break in her husband. Caitlyn herself had identified him as the man who'd been following her around the District. But whether he was guilty of anything else, Reid wasn't so sure.

"I don't like him for it."

"Look. The guy's been stalking her. Not to mention, he just threatened you *and* Ms. Cahill with a loaded gun. You want him to actually mutilate and strangle her before you'll buy in? He obviously came out here to harm her."

"The bloody footprints at the first crime scene," Reid recounted. "They were what, a size thirteen? Hunter might wear an eleven at most."

"So? Maybe those footprints aren't even the unsub's. Maybe some asshole contaminated the crime scene— like one of the Hispanic laborers."

"None of them had blood on their shoes."

"That doesn't mean one of them—like one without the proper documentation—didn't leave the scene before the cops got there. Hunter's been following Ms. Cahill, waiting for an opportunity, and he nearly killed you both. That makes him worth talking to about the murders." Mitch pushed off from the stall door. "Morehouse and I are taking custody of him. We're taking him back to D.C. tonight. You want in on this or not?"

Reid squeezed the bridge of his nose. "I want in."

"Good boy. Now before you bid a fond farewell to your ladylove, there's something else you need to know."

Reid looked at him, waiting for the proverbial other shoe to drop.

"Joshua Cahill is willing to give up another body. But he wants something in exchange."

Reid felt his lungs tighten. Although there were six confirmed victims of the Capital Killer, there had always been speculation about others. Five other women had gone missing during roughly the same time— blondes with good pedigrees who had mysteriously vanished from locations around the District.

Already fearing the answer, he asked, "What does he want?"

"A visit with his sister. Alone."

As much as Reid wanted the other bodies, he couldn't condone Caitlyn's involvement. "That's not going to happen."

Mitch sighed heavily. "You know what? As much as I need you back as my partner, I'm starting to think it won't work out."

"Damn it, Mitch—"

"You've *changed*. The Reid Novak I knew wouldn't put anything in front of closing a case. Especially not some spoiled socialite—"

"That's enough."

"Then tell me you'll deliver her to the Springdale Pen on Monday."

"What's going on?" Both men turned to find Caitlyn standing a few feet away, a questioning look on her face. How much had she heard? The horse blanket slipped a little from her slender shoulders, revealing her soaked sweater underneath. Her eyes locked with Reid's.

He released a breath.

"We need to talk."

_18_

"Are you arguing because of me?" Caitlyn asked as Reid closed her office door behind him. Despite her attempt to appear calm, she looked pale and as skittish as a colt. It was clear David Hunter had rattled her.

Reid rubbed the back of his neck, deciding to tell her the truth. "Agent Tierney thinks I've become too personally involved."

Her green eyes were uncertain. "Are you?"

"I think you know the answer to that, Caitlyn," he said in a low rasp. He'd had the stress of the MRI on his mind, and he had come up here craving the comfort of her presence. But Reid had allowed himself to get too caught up in his attraction to her, risking her life in the process. He'd been the one telling her to be careful and what had he done? He'd taken her out to an isolated area of her property. And instead of keeping himself on high alert, they'd been having a full-on make-out session. Letting things get out of hand.

"What occurred between us this afternoon was my

fault. I shouldn't have let it happen," he said. He hated the look of pain he saw on her features.

When she finally spoke, her eyes didn't quite meet his. "What was Agent Tierney saying about Springdale Penitentiary? Is there something I need to know?"

She had to be filled in on the situation. Caitlyn had heard too much of their conversation and besides, Reid knew Mitch was right. If they had to use her to get the locations of the other bodies, that was what they'd have to do. Giving some peace to the families was too important.

"There's been speculation Joshua is responsible for murders beyond the six he stood trial for. Five other women who disappeared. You're aware of that?"

"But there's no solid evidence. You weren't able to make any connection—"

"He's offered to give up one of the bodies, Caitlyn." Reid saw the impact of his words on her. She seemed to crumple in the knowledge that her brother was responsible for more deaths. He ran a hand through his damp hair and sighed. "He wants a meeting with you in exchange. Do you think you can do that?"

"Will you go with me?"

"I'll take you there. I'll be right outside the door, watching through the observation window. You'll be completely safe." He stepped closer. "But Joshua wants to see you alone. That's the deal."

She was still for a long moment, then nodded.

"I have to go back to D.C. We're taking Hunter into federal custody."

"That poor man."

"He pulled a gun on us," Reid reminded.

"He's out of his mind with grief. Can't you see that?"

He fell silent. His gut told him Hunter wasn't their copycat, but Mitch was right about that, too—his actions made him a viable suspect. At the least, he was guilty of stalking Caitlyn and threatening her with a lethal weapon. If Reid hadn't been there—if Ruiz hadn't shown up when he did—he wondered if she would be dead right now.

"Is there anyone you can stay with tonight, Caitlyn? I don't think you should be alone, not after what happened."

"Manny's a phone call away. He has a room upstairs." She looked upward, indicating a second floor to the stables.

"Someone *besides* Ruiz."

Caitlyn folded her arms over her chest. Reid's statement had clearly brought up some well of thought within her. "Why didn't you tell me Manny was imprisoned for beating up the man who was physically abusing his daughter?"

Reid felt heat rise under his skin. "It's still assault and battery. And kidnapping. He's still an ex-con who may or may not have known your brother. In my opinion, that's enough to keep him away from you."

"That's not your decision."

"No," he agreed, voice tight.

The damp sweater Caitlyn wore had lost its shape, stretching out over her fingertips and below her hips, engulfing her and making her look small and childlike. He could see the empathy shimmering in her eyes for Ruiz, and also for David Hunter. It wasn't fair someone with as good a heart as Caitlyn's had been shackled to Joshua Cahill for life. Without his infamy, she would no doubt be married by now, probably have a child or two and be living the privileged lifestyle her parents had intended for her.

But instead she was achingly alone. Reid recalled that she'd had a fiancé during the Capital Killer investigation, an up-and-coming senatorial aide with an Ivy League background. Their relationship had ended following Joshua's arrest. Reid had ruined that for her, too.

"You should go," she said softly.

Caitlyn stayed in the shower for what seemed like an eternity, using the hot spray to erase the chill from her body. She had escaped to the upstairs hall bathroom, leaving Sophie and Rob fretting in the living room about the man who'd confronted her in the woods at gunpoint. She wasn't sure who had called them, but they'd arrived just before the police cars pulled away from the stables. Reid's SUV and Agent Tierney's dark sedan had been in the rear of the convoy.

Finally, she turned off the shower, standing amid the lingering steam. She couldn't get Reid out of her mind. Not his kiss or the undeniable heat between them. Nor could she let go of his words later, when he'd told her things had gone too far.

He's right, Caitlyn. She reminded herself that any chance of something developing between them was a fool's dream.

Drying off with a towel, she wrapped herself in her soft, fleece bathrobe, then used the palm of her hand to wipe the fog from the bathroom mirror. Her reflection stared back at her, haunted and pale. Outside, rain beat against the window and the wind howled, reminding her of the cold, bleak night ahead of her.

When she emerged from the bathroom, she found Rob in the hallway. His presence upstairs surprised her. Caitlyn tightened the robe's belt around her waist and adjusted its shawl collar.

"Are you looking for me?"

"You've been up here for a while," he said, his big shoulders hunched and his hands shoved inside his pockets as he walked to her. "I thought I should come up and check on you. Make sure you're all right."

She tucked the damp curtain of her hair behind one ear. "Where's Sophie?"

"On the phone downstairs. Her sister in New York's been ill and she wanted to give her a call. She told you about Melanie, right?" Pausing, he pushed his wire-rimmed glasses higher on his nose. "The truth is, I really don't think you should be alone tonight, Caitlyn. Why don't you come back to the house with us—"

"Thank you. But I'd rather stay here." Rob and Sophie meant well, but she was tired and feeling more than a little depressed. Knowing how ungrateful she sounded, she tried to soften her words. "It's been a tough day, that's all."

He continued studying her. "The man who was here the other day when Sophie and I came by. He works for the FBI?"

She nodded faintly. "He does."

"He headed up the Capital Killer case." Rob said it more as a statement of fact than a question. "I thought I recognized him from the news conferences. Are the crazy things that have been going on around here tied to Joshua?"

Caitlyn was unsure how much to tell him. So far, the press hadn't reported on a copycat, but with two murders already committed, Reid had warned her it was only a matter of time. She focused on David Hunter.

"The man who confronted me in the woods is the widower of one of Joshua's victims," she explained. "His name is David Hunter. They think he was here to seek some kind of revenge on me."

"And you and the FBI agent were out alone together in the woods when this guy came after you?"

She felt a blush stain her cheeks. "How did you know that?"

"Manny Ruiz. He called Sophie and me, gave us a quick rundown and said we might want to come over. You don't harbor any ill will against the man who took down your brother?"

"Agent Novak was doing his job," Caitlyn said defensively. "And my brother *is* a serial murderer."

His curious eyes on her made her uncomfortable.

Lit by the soft hallway light, Rob's features appeared earnest as he took a step closer.

"Look, honey. I worry about you out here. Being all alone." He swallowed, his Adam's apple bobbing nervously. He laid a hand on Caitlyn's shoulder. "I just want you to know that I can be over here anytime you need me, *for anything*. In two shakes of a lamb's tail. To talk, or if you just need some company."

He bent his head and lowered his voice further. "You can call my cell instead of the house. We don't need to worry Sophie."

She nodded faintly, feeling awkward as Rob continued staring at her. Did he intend that as it sounded? His hand lingered on her shoulder, gently squeezing. From downstairs, she heard Sophie calling for them, announcing she'd made sandwiches and poured them all a glass of port. Rob dropped his hand and straightened.

"Coming, dear," he yelled back.

19

"Look who's here, my favorite son."

"I'm your only son, Dad," Reid responded as he walked into McCauley's Grill, dutifully playing along with his father's well-worn joke. A handful of Ben Novak's friends, all retired cops, chuckled and slapped Reid's back in greeting. They were gathered around a table cluttered with the remnants of bar food—wings, burgers and sweating mugs of dark beer.

Reid slid his gift into the pile of wrapped presents. He put a hand on his father's shoulder and spoke into his ear. "Sorry I'm late, Dad."

"You've missed the food, unless you want table scraps."

"That's okay. I'm not really hungry."

"Aren't you back on the job soon?" Leo Purcell, his father's former partner, interjected. He patted his own protruding belly. "You're looking too thin, Reid. Better bulk up—law enforcement's more intimidating with a few pounds on ya."

"That would be pounds of *muscle,* not fat," Ben quipped, giving Leo's paunch a poke with his elbow. "Besides, the Feds like their boys lean and mean. That way they look more *GQ* in their fancy suits."

Another round of laughter exploded inside the tavern, competing with the noise coming from a row of occupied pool tables and a jukebox playing an eighties Bob Seger song.

"At least he made it in time for cake," Megan acknowledged, giving her brother a look of feigned disapproval. She cleared a path through the men so Maddie and Isabelle could make their way to the table. The girls carried a sheet cake carefully between them that was decorated with glowing candles and a police shield made of gold fondant icing.

"Better get started—you've got some catching up to do," Cooper, Reid's brother-in-law, advised. He pressed a foamy beer mug into Reid's hand as the group broke into a rousing chorus of "Happy Birthday." Taking a sip, Reid watched as his father continued cutting up with his friends, an arm around each of his granddaughters.

"Way to go. You almost missed Dad's birthday," Megan said to Reid once the plates of cake had been passed around. She'd come over to where he stood at the edge of the crowd.

"Almost," Reid pointed out in his defense.

"Where were you?"

"We had an arrestee—"

"Have I mentioned you aren't supposed to be working yet?"

"I had a vested interest." He took a bite of the devil's food cake his sister had brought him. "The perp pulled a gun on me."

Megan's eyes widened. "Where?"

"In Middleburg."

"The case you're not supposed to be on, but are," she recalled. "What's the attraction up there, Reid? You're not even cleared for duty yet."

He sighed and set his paper plate on the bar behind them. He'd always trusted Megan, had told her things he probably shouldn't about the cases he worked. She often served as his confidante, the one he turned to when he needed a sounding board or perspective other than his own or Mitch's. She was also the first person he'd told after the doctors had diagnosed his brain tumor. They had gone to their father together to break the news.

"Okay, so don't tell me—"

"There's a tie-in to the Capital Killer case," he confided, his voice low. "It hasn't hit the news yet, but in all likelihood we've got a copycat. We have two victims already."

"Which is why they brought you back in early." Megan appeared worried. "God, Reid. The timing's horrible. You've been ill, and I know what the first case did to you."

He laughed weakly. "Killers don't give a damn about timing."

"So why were you in Middleburg?"

"Senator Cahill's daughter is involved. I was out at her place today."

"Cahill?" She frowned, shaking her head. "That's a name I'd hoped to never hear again. Not after what Braden Cahill did to you. Talk about an abuse of power. He nearly got you booted out of the FBI—"

"Senator Cahill's dead, Megan. And Caitlyn's not to blame for anything that happened."

"You're on a first-name basis with Braden Cahill's daughter?" Her brow furrowed as she processed this information. "And you were at her place when someone pulled a gun on you?"

"On both of us, actually."

Reid was relieved she didn't push for further details on his relationship with Caitlyn, or why exactly he had gone out there. Instead she asked, "Who was the guy?"

"The widower of Joshua Cahill's last victim. Mitch thinks he might be our unsub, but I don't agree. The guy's a mess psychologically. He never recovered from his wife's murder. He's unstable but my gut says he isn't a serial killer."

"What's going to happen to him?"

"We arrested him for assault with a deadly weapon. I just got back from the interrogation. He's being transferred to Washington Hospital for a full psych evaluation."

Reid looked across the room at their father, who stood in the doorway, bidding good-night to his old cronies. He felt a tug of emotion. Ben Novak looked good for his age and seemed to be in excellent health, but sixty was a milestone. Their mother would have been fifty-eight now. Reid felt Megan touch his arm. When he looked at her, he saw the anxiety in her eyes.

"I know you, Reid. There's something else. What is it?"

He used all of his self-control not to tell her more. And if he did, where would he even begin? What had happened with Caitlyn, the other details of the investigation, the headaches he'd been having and the results of the MRI he was waiting to receive—it all seemed too much to handle. Placing his hands on her shoulders, Reid looked into her eyes.

"Nothing, worrywart." He gave her a tight smile. "And now that the crowd's thinning, I'm going over to talk to the birthday boy."

"Thanks for coming, son."

Reid pulled his hands from his pockets, where he'd been warming them against the brisk night air outside McCauley's. "You know I wouldn't miss it, Dad. Sorry again for being late."

"Better late than never." Smiling, Ben enveloped his son in a bear hug. Reid embraced him back, his chest tightening as he felt his father's sturdy frame.

"Sure you're okay to drive home?" Reid queried.

"Are you asking if I'm piss-drunk?"

"You had a few."

Ben chuckled. "Relax. I'm entitled. Cooper and Megan are giving me a ride."

Reid nodded. The group had dwindled to just family,

and his sister and the others were still inside boxing up the leftover birthday cake. He waited with his father, making small talk until Cooper, Megan and the girls loaded into their Jeep Cherokee for the trip to Ben's condo and then back to Silver Spring.

Since weekend parking was scarce in the Adams Morgan neighborhood where Reid lived, he had opted for the D.C. Metrorail in lieu of driving. Reid walked the two blocks from the bar, then used his fare card to get into the station and went down the escalator. Checking his watch at the platform, he took a seat on one of the benches. The station wasn't nearly as full as during the workweek, but there were still handfuls of passengers strolling around, some with city maps marking them as obvious tourists. Above him, the station's skylight was filled with black night, and the sound of an approaching train rumbled inside the long tunnel. Reid glanced up at the flashing sign announcing its arrival; it wasn't his.

He people-watched as the group that was gathered on the platform waited for the doors to open, then bustled inside. The train was already fairly tight with passengers, and through the windows he could see the newer ones taking what was left of the available seats or gripping vinyl loops hanging from the ceiling to anchor them for the ride.

Reid felt electricity prickle his skin.

Julianne Hunter sat in the last seat, her blond hair half shielding her face. She wore the same prim, plaid skirt and white blouse as on the night in the abandoned factory, the collar bloodstained. In disbelief, Reid stood as she gazed back at him, a puzzled expression on her pretty features.

Julianne's face had haunted him for all these months since her death—he recognized it as easily as his own reflection. Reid made a run for the door as it began to slide closed but it shut a half second before he reached it. He banged on the Plexiglas window, causing passengers to turn in his direction.

The train began to move. Reid jogged alongside it, keeping his eyes on Julianne. She watched him with a mild curiosity, then returned her attention to a book she held open in her lap. Unwilling to let her go, he sprinted along the platform until the train finally outpaced him, barreling into the darkened corridor. Out of breath, Reid gulped air, his lungs squeezing. His heart felt as though it might slam out of his chest.

Doing his best to ignore the curious stares, he shouldered through the crowd and headed into the men's restroom. His hands trembled as he turned on the faucet in one of the basins and splashed cold water onto his face.

His head swam with confusion, a faint throbbing at its center that announced an impending headache. *Julianne was dead*—he had watched the life drain out of her. Her blood had coated his jacket as he fought to save her life. But despite what he had just seen, Reid didn't believe in doppelgangers or ghosts. He was too much of a realist for that.

The only explanation was something he desperately didn't want to face. Anxiety hit him like a hard blow in the chest. Perspiring, he waited in the bathroom for several minutes, trying to compose himself before going back out into the station.

20

Caitlyn waited outside the closed door in the corridor of Springdale Penitentiary. Dread pooled in her stomach, but she kept her shoulders rigid, vowing not to show weakness.

"It's going to be fine, Caitlyn," Reid reaffirmed, standing beside her. But the tense look around his eyes negated his words. "We've made no promises other than a private visit—five minutes, no more and no less. His wrists are shackled to the table. He won't be able to touch you."

Agent Tierney walked from where he had been conversing with a muscled prison guard, reminding Caitlyn of his presence, as well. "We'll be keeping an eye out through the observation window, Ms. Cahill. Remember our goal."

She released a tight breath. "To get a location on the remains."

"I don't like this." Whether Reid muttered the statement to himself or intended for someone else to hear it, Caitlyn wasn't sure. She'd met the two agents at the VCU offices in D.C., and they'd traveled together by car to the federal prison in Maryland. Reid had been pensive and brooding for most of the ride.

What occurred between us this afternoon was my fault. I shouldn't have let it happen.

Caitlyn recalled his regret about their kiss and felt her chest constrict all over again.

"Are you ready?" he asked.

When she gave a small nod, the guard moved to unlock the door. She walked inside the room on wobbly legs, her eyes meeting her brother's for the first time in two years. Physically, prison appeared to have changed Joshua little—he was thin and wiry, his raven hair still worn shaggy and hanging into his dark eyes. He had grown a goatee, making her wonder if it was an attempt to look tougher, more streetwise. The ugly, orange prison jumpsuit he wore clashed with his olive skin. It had a series of numbers printed on its front pocket.

"Hello, Caity." Joshua lifted his hand in a small wave, his movement restricted by the handcuffs attached to the table where he sat. "It's good to see you."

Caitlyn jumped involuntarily as the guard closed the door behind her, leaving them alone.

"Want a seat?"

Stiffly, she sat down across from him. Her mouth felt dry, and she realized her heart was racing. "How are you, Joshua?"

"I'm good." He rattled the handcuffs that tethered him and gave her a weak smile. "Considering."

His dark eyes darted over her, causing goose bumps to rise along her flesh. Caitlyn clenched her hands together in her lap, her whitened knuckles hidden from him by the tabletop.

"You haven't changed a bit."

"You're wrong," she whispered. "I have."

Solemn, he considered this. "I hope you've been able to get on with your life, at least."

Her chin rose slightly, although she didn't speak.

"I hear you're running an equine therapy program." He fidgeted in his chair. Was he as nervous as she? "It makes sense. I remember how you always loved your horses."

Caitlyn studied Joshua's mild features, trying to identify some monster lurking within him. Was it still there, or had the medication and psychiatrists finally managed to exorcise it? Reid firmly believed he hadn't changed.

"How's Mom?"

"She's...in a home now." When Joshua's forehead wrinkled in surprise, she added, "I had to put her there several months ago. Most likely she's in the advanced stages of Alzheimer's, although the specialists disagree on a diagnosis."

"I'm sorry." He looked genuinely sad. "I didn't know."

Whatever had claimed Caroline, Caitlyn knew one truth. Her brother's crimes were the catalyst.

"Mom's being well cared for," she said, tamping down the resentment she felt. "She's at the Vinings

Care Facility in Foggy Bottom. I'm selling the house in Georgetown to help pay for it."

He sighed. "I know how hard all this must have been on you, Caity."

"What about the families of the victims whose lives you took?" she asked quietly, unable to stop herself. "I'm sure it was much harder on them."

"I was sick." Joshua's eyes captured hers. "I have to live with what I did every day. And I'll pay for it the rest of my life. *No possibility of parole* means I'm never going to get out of here. Do you understand that? I need to at least have some absolution from you."

"You could have told me, Joshua." She stared down at her hands, trying to continue. "You could have told me about the...urges you were having. Maybe I could have—"

"Helped?"

Caitlyn looked at him.

"You saw my journal. What I fantasized about doing to women. What I *did* do to them, eventually. Do you really think you could've stopped me?"

"I—I don't know."

He gave a small, bitter laugh, shaking his head in seeming amusement. In a quiet voice he added, "I used to have the same fantasies about you."

The temperature inside the small room seemed to drop by twenty degrees. Caitlyn's breath came out in a little hiss as she stared at Joshua. His dark eyes had changed, appearing black and pupiless. "You were my muse, Caity. Didn't you know that?"

"Don't."

"You want to know the truth. I'm giving it to you."

Taking a breath, Caitlyn pushed on. "But you never… hurt me. You didn't try to kill me."

He glanced at the smoky window, then lowered his voice to a near whisper. "But I wanted to. So much. I used to jack off thinking about it. I'd imagine sneaking up on you when no one was home, tying you down and—"

Her chair scraped backward as Caitlyn stood, blood rushing in her ears. At nearly the same second, the door to the room flew open. Reid stalked inside, his eyes on Joshua. "Time's up."

Joshua smirked. "Not according to the clock on the wall, Agent Novak."

"I don't give a damn." Reid pulled at Caitlyn's arm. "Let's go."

"We're not done." Caitlyn's voice came out shakily. She would see this through. No matter what Joshua said to her, she wasn't leaving here without the information he'd promised. She wasn't going to have gone through this for nothing. Caitlyn's eyes locked with Reid's. "Give us two more minutes."

His features appeared strained, but he left the room again. Caitlyn turned back to Joshua. His eyebrows were raised in amusement.

"Novak's become your knight in shining armor, Caity. It was very *gallant,* the way he charged in here."

Caitlyn returned to her chair. She pushed a yellow

notepad and pen that lay on the table toward Joshua's shackled hands.

"Are you giving him any pussy?"

The vileness inside Joshua was clearer to her than it had ever been before. It was as if the quiet, reserved person she had known could be instantly drawn into the shadows, replaced at will by the disgusting creature in front of her. Reid was right. No medications, no doctors could ever drain the evil from inside him.

"Just give me the location—" she swallowed down her disgust "—of the remains of the other women you killed."

He blinked at her innocently. "Other women?"

"Don't play games."

A ghost smile appeared on his lips. Joshua reached for the pen, his handcuffs rattling against the restraint. "I only promised one. You want more, you'll have to come visit again."

As Caitlyn left the room, the prison guard moved past her, ready to take Joshua back to his cell. She clenched the paper tightly in her fingers. Reid and Agent Tierney waited for her in front of the smoked-glass window. Tierney appeared poised, his arms folded over his chest and his shirtsleeves rolled up to reveal sinewy forearms sprinkled with coarse hair. Reid was an altogether different matter, however. He looked stressed, and his eyes seemed to assess Caitlyn for some visible sign of damage. His face was flushed above the collar of his blue dress shirt. She realized it had taken every ounce of self-control he had to leave her alone with Joshua after the things he had no doubt heard him say to her through the room's intercom.

"Donna Faust is at Deep Creek Lake," she stated quietly, holding out the paper. "He drew a map to the location. It's pretty specific."

"That's helpful of him. If he isn't sending us on a wild-goose chase." Agent Tierney stepped forward and took it, studying the drawing.

Reid moved closer to her. "It's over now."

"It's not over and you know it." Caitlyn stared at him. "Not until he gives up the other bodies, however many there are. Those women need to be laid to rest."

"It's an hour from here to Deep Creek. We need to get out there." Agent Tierney folded the paper and stuffed it into the inside pocket of his suit jacket. "I'll have Morehouse meet us at the site with Forensics."

"I've got to go," Reid said to her. "I'll get someone to drive you back to the office."

"I'm going with you."

He shook his head. "No."

"I got you the victim's name and the body's location," Caitlyn implored. "I *need* to be there."

"I don't want you to—"

"Let her come," Agent Tierney interjected. He was looking at Reid, not Caitlyn, making her feel like an unwanted child who'd begged to tag along. "She can stay in the car."

Frowning, Reid ran a hand through his dark hair. His voice was low. "Let's go."

21

Deep Creek Lake was tucked into the autumn-hued mountains of western Maryland. Despite the brisk afternoon, sailboats glided along the crystalline waters. Caitlyn leaned against the front of Agent Tierney's Crown Victoria, shivering inside her wool coat. She watched as the closest of the boats slid past her with sails billowing before returning her attention to the grisly activity occurring a short distance away.

Forensic technicians were carefully excavating the sunken, brown earth in the location Joshua had described. The spot was about fifty feet back from a maintenance shed, at the edge of a wooded trail leading down to the shoreline. A clearly discernible *X* had been carved into the bark of a nearby oak, marking the spot where Joshua had supposedly buried Donna Faust's body. Reid and Agent Tierney stood with Agent Morehouse at the edge of the scene, their backs to Caitlyn.

"We've got something," one of the jumpsuited technicians called out, his voice raised in excitement. Anxiety tingling along her spine, Caitlyn left the sedan and moved closer. She saw several of the crime scene workers crouched at the edge of the shallow hole, using brushlike whisks to clear away loose dirt.

"Caitlyn." Reid gently caught her arm. "You were supposed to stay at the car."

She looked down at his hand on her coat sleeve. A latex glove, its tips smudged with dirt, encased his fingers. Caitlyn swallowed, realizing he'd been searching through the soil, as well. Looking for remnants of the woman Joshua had murdered.

"Go back to the car," he warned.

"I can take her back to the District," Agent Morehouse offered.

"She stays." Tierney peered at her, his large hands hooked into the gun belt at his waist. "I think she should get a firsthand look at her baby brother's work."

"Bone." A technician brushed at a series of grime-covered arches exposed in the dirt and decaying leaves. The man squinted up at the FBI agents and police surrounding the shallow grave. "Appears to be a rib cage, female, judging by the size."

He approximated an area about a foot higher, brushing at the dirt there, as well. "We've got a skull."

Caitlyn stared at the cap of rounded bone rising out of the dirt. She felt Reid's hand at the small of her back, and she realized her knees had gone weak. Pressing her fingers hard against her lips, she pushed away from him and forced herself to stand erect, watching as the rest of Donna Faust's skeleton was carefully and incrementally exposed. It had been more than two years since she'd been buried there, after Joshua had finished with her. There was nothing left of her but bones—no tissue, no putrid smell of decomposing flesh. Still, Caitlyn fought the urge to gag.

Another of the technicians sifted through the dirt with tweezers, extracting a hard, pink glob with leaves attached.

"Appears to be chewing gum." He dropped it into an evidence bag, then handed it off to continue his dig.

Caitlyn's throat tightened. The thought of Joshua chewing and snapping as he buried his victim, then spitting the gum wad into the makeshift grave after her, made her skin crawl.

"Probably contains Cahill's DNA," Agent Tierney muttered. Forensic cameras snapped at the exposed remains. "Not that we need it."

It was late afternoon by the time they rolled away from Deep Creek, leaving Forensics behind to close up the remaining details. Reid stared through the car's passenger window at the media vans gathered outside the park's entrance. Apparently word had leaked of a crime scene investigation at the usually placid recreational area, drawing news reporters like rotten food attracts flies.

He dropped the sun visor to conceal his face from the reporters they passed, and also to use its mirror to glimpse Caitlyn in the backseat. She sat huddled inside her coat with her hands clasped in her lap, her features drawn and pale. The wind had blown her honeyed hair for most of the afternoon so that it now hung in wild tangles. She peered out the window, her eyes clouded with pain and no doubt the ghastly recollection of Donna Faust's remains. Reid hadn't wanted to bring her out here, and he silently cursed Mitch for exposing Caitlyn to the full extent of her brother's violence.

I used to have the same fantasies about you... I'd imagine sneaking up on you when no one was home, tying you down and...

He wondered if Caitlyn was imagining herself in the shallow earth, another of Joshua's victims. Reid thought of the lewd, venomous words her brother had spewed at her in the stark confines of the prison interrogation room. Cahill had used her—he'd clearly gotten off on her shock and horror—and yet she'd steadfastly remained until he had given up the body's location as promised.

"I'm starving," Mitch announced from behind the wheel. He looked at Reid. "We're three hours away from D.C. I say we get away from all this hoopla and stop for a bite."

Reid nodded faintly. "Fine."

"There's a diner outside Swanton, right before the interstate exit. I've been there a time or two before." Mitch glanced at Caitlyn in the rearview mirror. "Or would a greasy spoon, cop hangout offend your culinary tastes, Ms. Cahill?"

"Give her a break, damn it," Reid muttered under his breath. "She's been through enough today."

Mitch fished his cell phone from his suit jacket to let Agent Morehouse, who was following in the car behind them, know of the planned stop.

The meal at the diner was eaten mostly in silence, save for the agents discussing a few specific aspects of the investigation. Caitlyn had ordered coffee and a grilled cheese sandwich, which Reid noticed she'd mostly picked at before leaving the congealed mess on the plate and excusing herself to the ladies' room. Not that he had eaten much himself. He hadn't slept well the night before, plagued by a headache and Julianne Hunter's image in the Metrorail haunting his dreams. Unfortunately, he had been unable to use the prescription sleeping pills, since he'd been due at the FBI offices early that morning for the drive to the penitentiary and didn't want to risk being groggy.

"Any news on Hunter?" Mitch asked, reaching for a ketchup bottle in a carousel at the edge of the table. He squeezed it, sending out a thick, red spurt across the fries on his plate.

"Not yet." Morehouse paused as he swallowed his last mouthful of a pastrami sandwich. "The psych evaluation should be completed tomorrow or Wednesday."

Mitch grunted, then turned to Reid. "When's your recertification on firearms?"

"I'm due at the range on Thursday."

"Good. It's about time you strapped on a gun again."

He popped another fry into his mouth. "Besides, you've been spending so much time working this case you might as well start getting full pay for it. How much time left on your leave?"

"Just this week." Reid thought of Julianne Hunter again and fought back the worry lacing through him.

Caitlyn returned to the table. Morehouse made a move to get up so she could slide back into the circular booth between him and Reid.

"It's okay," she said, halting him. She looked at no one in particular. "If you don't mind, I think I'll just wait in the car. I know you're all discussing…business."

Mitch twisted sideways and began digging in his pocket to hand her the keys.

"You know what?" Morehouse wadded his paper napkin and tossed it onto the vinyl tablecloth. "You're still eating and I need to get back to the District. Why don't I take Ms. Cahill with me?"

"I'd appreciate it, Agent Morehouse," Caitlyn said quietly. "Thank you."

Reid frowned. He didn't want Morehouse taking her back to D.C. In fact, what he wanted was to escort her directly to her car himself and make certain she was safely on her way back home. Hell, what he really wanted was a few minutes alone with her so they could talk privately for the first time that day.

He cradled the ceramic coffee mug he held between his palms, feeling what was left of its warmth. "Walk her all the way to her car, Morehouse, okay?"

"You got it. Good night."

Reid could have sworn he saw the younger agent blushing as he opened the door for Caitlyn and they went out together into the dusk. He returned his gaze to Mitch, who was studying the laminated menu with the focused concentration of a surgeon.

"I don't know about you," he said. "But I'm thinking of having the coconut cream pie."

22

She struggled against the cords binding her wrists and ankles, tried to scream through the thick cloth gag shoved into her mouth. The movement of shadows in the darkness told her Joshua was here. Hiding. Watching her. He moved slowly forward, moonlight falling onto his slim form.

"I brought you a gift, Caity." He held the mutilated Barbie doll, swinging it in front of her face by its long, blond hair. The straight pins inserted into its anatomy glimmered dully. "Don't you think she looks like you?"

She felt the dip of the mattress as he sat on its edge, his hands sinking roughly into her hair. "I do."

Caitlyn awoke, her chest heaving and her body slick with perspiration. The bedroom was quiet except for her own labored breathing. She pressed her hands over her face.

It was a dream, she told herself. Another one of her nightmares, brought on by seeing Joshua again and witnessing Donna Faust's remains being dug up from the ground. Still, Caitlyn pushed back the sheets and got out of bed, certain she wouldn't be able to reclaim sleep, at least not for a while.

Downstairs, she made a cup of herbal tea in the kitchen, turning on the small counter television set to keep her company and distract her thoughts. But Joshua loomed in her mind like a thug on a darkened street corner, waiting for her.

She couldn't help it, Caitlyn wanted to talk to Reid— she craved hearing his voice telling her things would be all right. She had nearly asked to speak to him in private at the diner, but Agent Tierney's intimidating presence had discouraged her, as did Reid's aloofness throughout most of the day. Returning to D.C. with Agent Morehouse, Caitlyn had engaged in small talk although she'd felt anything but social. Once they reached the VCU offices in Judiciary Square, he had dutifully accompanied her to her car, then stood watching until she pulled from the parking garage. On the drive back to Middleburg, Caitlyn had half expected Reid to call her cell and check on her, but the device sat mutely in her purse all the way home.

She jumped, spilling some of her tea into the saucer as the phone in the kitchen rang. Caitlyn looked at the wall clock, a black cat in silhouette with a swinging tail beating out the seconds. It was a little after 3:00 a.m. Steeling herself, she rose to answer it, her intuition telling her a call at this late hour could only be bad news.

"Hello?" No one responded, so she repeated the salutation. "Hello?"

"Ms. Cahill?" A woman's voice sounded hesitant. "This is Nurse Hillary at the Vinings Care Facility…"

Caitlyn's stomach sank.

"I'm calling about your mother, Caroline. I'm sorry to tell you this, but there's been an accident."

"What happened? Is she all right?"

"She got out of her room—we're really not sure how. The last time anyone checked on her was just after eleven when the night shift took over," the nurse explained in a nervous rush. "We started looking for her as soon as we realized she was missing—"

"Just tell me what happened."

"She fell down a flight of stairs in the emergency exit. We think she might've been there for several hours—"

"Oh, my God." Caitlyn closed her eyes, fear tightening her chest. "How badly is she hurt?"

"She's been taken to the E.R. at George Washington University Medical Center. I think you should go there." She hesitated again. "As soon as possible."

"Is she conscious?"

"I'm sorry…I'm not really sure."

Caitlyn hung up the phone, paralyzed by images of her mother and the vital woman she had been before the heartbreak and scandal of Joshua's arrest. Before her husband's fatal stroke.

Her mother was all she had left.

When she arrived in D.C., it was nearly four-thirty in the morning, dark outside and well before the business rush hour. As Caitlyn's car made the voyage over the Francis Scott Key Bridge heading into Georgetown, she barely noticed the stately, spired buildings of George Washington University rising up over the dark Potomac, or the iron moon that hung low in the sky. Her eyes burned from lack of sleep, but she felt wired and jittery, her only thought to talk to the medical staff and find out the severity of her mother's injuries.

She's going to be okay.

The affirmation repeated inside her head as she pulled into the hospital parking garage, her fingers tight on the steering wheel. She drove up three levels before finding a few vacant spots, then pulled the BMW into the first space and got out. Pressing the key fob to activate the car's security system, she heard its electronic chirp echo inside the concrete-and-steel structure. Caitlyn walked toward the elevators on the far side of the garage. She had dressed hastily in jeans, a loose sweater and jacket, and her boots thudded on the concrete floor. Although her path so far had been illuminated by fluorescent light panels in the garage's low ceiling, the elevator bay was dark, as if the lighting there had burned out. She stepped into the shadows, leaning forward to press the button.

Sudden awareness chilled her skin. She wasn't alone.

A male figure loomed in her peripheral vision. Caitlyn gasped, turning just in time to catch the blow across the side of her head. Stars exploded in front of her as she fell onto the hard concrete deck. She tried to scream, but the breath had been knocked from her and what emerged from her mouth sounded more like a mewling cry.

Caitlyn fought the pain inside her skull, trying to get a look at her attacker. But her vision was hazy, clouded and the man wore a ski mask. He made a grab for her, dragging her by her arms several feet across the garage floor. Caitlyn broke one hand free, closing it around her key chain that had fallen nearby and attempting to set off the panic button on its fob. She screamed in pain as the man stomped her hand under his heel, forcing her to let go.

She writhed in agony, crying out for help. He began dragging her again toward a white van parked nearby, its back door hanging open to reveal its darkened interior. The realization that he planned to abduct her was like a shot of adrenaline to her system. Caitlyn screamed louder and began kicking wildly, trying to tear free from her attacker's viselike grip. She cringed as the man drew his right hand into a fist and pulled it back, preparing to slug her again.

The elevator chime rang, the sound breaking through the madness. The man froze. He let go of Caitlyn, causing the back of her head to bounce against the concrete floor. The area around her tilted and spun as another white-hot flare shot through her skull.

She heard the elevator doors slide open, as well as the man's heavy footfalls as he made a run for the van. Caitlyn tried to sit up, wanting to call out for help to the couple who had emerged from the elevator, but a wave of dizziness washed over her. Her voice when it finally croaked out of her sounded as if she were at the far end of a tunnel.

"Help me...please."

The van's engine roared to life, its tires screeching as it sped away.

"Just lie still, miss." One of the two people, an elderly man with thick spectacles and gray hair, reached her. He squatted as best he could on the ground next to her, tentatively patting her shoulder. "My wife's calling the campus police."

Behind him, the woman talked excitedly into her cell phone. Caitlyn wanted to ask if they had gotten a license plate, but the words bouncing inside her head never quite formed on her lips. The side of her head felt sticky and warm, and her left hand had gone numb. The man dug into his coat pocket and removed a white handkerchief, folded into a neat square. She heard her own feeble groan as he pressed it against her temple.

"You're going to be fine, miss." He didn't sound all that convincing. His concerned expression wavered in front of her.

Caitlyn's world slowly faded to black.

23

Reid walked briskly across parking level three. Around him, evidence techs snapped photos of tire marks and splotches of dried blood. *Caitlyn's blood.* He'd received the call from Mitch a half hour ago.

He had broken every speed limit to get there.

"I don't understand," Morehouse said as he approached. He looked like a schoolboy expecting a reprimand from his teacher. "I walked her all the way to her car. I watched her get in, just like you said. I *saw* her drive off. She said she was going straight back to Middleburg."

Reid's mouth formed a grim line. "What time did you see her last?"

"About seven-thirty."

Through the open side of the garage, morning sunlight dappled the floor of the parking deck. He'd wanted to call her last night—in fact, he'd opened his cell phone on more than one occasion only to stare at its LCD panel before closing it again.

He thought he'd been doing the right thing. Taking a step back from Caitlyn. If he'd been the one to drive her back from Deep Creek Lake last night, would this have happened?

"Why would she lie to me about going home?" Morehouse asked.

"I don't know."

Reid turned upon hearing Mitch's low drawl. He'd entered the parking deck from the stairwell, where he was conversing with two policemen assigned to keep out civilians. He gave Reid a wave, motioning him over.

"She got a call, supposedly from a Nurse Hillary at the Vinings adult care facility where Caroline Cahill resides," Mitch said once Reid reached him. He dismissed the cops to go about their duties.

"You've talked to Caitlyn?"

"Yeah. She's pretty shaken up, understandably." Mitch scratched the side of his face. "The E.R. doc admitted her around five this morning. She's got a concussion and a messed up hand. They're still waiting on X-rays. She's a little dopey from the pain meds, but she did say the nurse told her that her mother had been hurt and was taken here for treatment. She drove back to D.C. in the middle of the night."

Reid frowned. "How's her mother?"

"That's the hell of it. I just called the Vinings facility—Caroline Cahill is fine. There was no accident involving her mother. Not to mention, there's no one on staff named Hillary."

Anger welled inside Reid. "She was lured here?"

"Looks that way."

"You should've called me sooner."

"I called you less than an hour after I found out. You're not officially on the case yet anyway," Mitch reminded.

It occurred to Reid that Caitlyn hadn't tried to get in touch with him. He wished she had. He could have been with her in the E.R. "Who contacted the police?"

"An elderly couple. They must've spooked the perp when they got off the elevator."

"Can they give a description?"

"Unfortunately, no. The assailant had already gotten into his vehicle by the time they noticed Ms. Cahill on the ground. He took off like a bat out of hell in a nondescript white van with dark windows parked right about there." Mitch pointed out a nearby space. "No lettering or signage on the vehicle. They didn't get even a partial number off the plate. If you want to talk to them, they're still in the E.R. waiting room. I had to get them to some chairs."

Reid looked at the metal elevator doors, about twenty yards away. Unlike the other fluorescent lights in the shadowy garage, the one that lit the elevator bay appeared to be out of operation.

"He took out the lights," he noted. "What about security cameras?"

"I'm going downstairs to look at the tape now. Want to come?"

What he wanted was to see Caitlyn. But instead, Reid gave a small nod.

* * *

The poor lighting made the digital recording dark and grainy, but what Reid *could* see sickened him. He sat forward in his chair, watching as the slender form he knew to be Caitlyn was attacked. The man was large, but other than that he appeared as only a darkened mass coming at her out of the shadows. He wore a black bomber-style jacket and black pants, and a ski mask concealed his face.

Reid's gut wrenched. Even after Caitlyn was dragged out of camera range, he could still hear her cries. When the tape showed the elderly couple emerging from the elevator, he got up and paced the small room.

"Do you want me to back it up?" A member of the hospital security staff held the remote. He looked at the two agents expectantly.

"Yeah," Mitch said, studying the freeze-frame of the screen. "And we're going to need you to make us a copy."

Reid looked away as the scene restarted. Despite his training telling him that he needed to view and re-view the footage, he didn't think he could take it again. Besides, the video appeared to be useless. Other than the size of the attacker, not much else was discernible. Not even his race. Reid doubted the lab techs would be able to increase the video resolution enough to make any real difference.

"How often do you patrol the parking garage?" Reid asked the hospital guard.

"We have a golf cart that goes through on the half hour."

"Which means the guy either planned well or got lucky," Mitch commented. "Do you have a camera on the garage exit?"

Reid knew what he was thinking—that maybe they'd be able to get a license plate off the van. He waited tensely as the guard fiddled with the remote again, shuffling through digital images of the garage until he got to the ones on the main floor. He rewound until the white van approached the steel arm of the automated attendant's booth. Reid's stomach sank as the van's rear came into view. The license plate had been removed.

The door to the private hospital room was half-closed. Reid knocked tentatively and went inside. Caitlyn appeared pale against the blue hospital linens, her blond hair spread across her pillow. Already he could see the shadowed bruise on her temple where the man had struck her.

Although she didn't speak, her reddened eyes met his as he came closer. Her left hand was pillowed in an inflatable cast, and the normally slender fingers that peeked out of it appeared puffy and bluish.

"Is it broken?" he asked hoarsely.

"Severe bruise." Her lips were dry, and Reid could see the dilation in her pupils that nearly overtook the vivid green of her irises. Whether it was from the pain medication she'd been given or the concussion, he wasn't sure.

"I got a suture, too." Weakly, she pointed to her hairline with her good hand. Reid flinched inwardly at the dried blood still matting her hair around the wound.

Sitting in the chair beside her, Reid shook his head. "Caitlyn..."

"I should've been more careful. My caller ID said 'unknown,' not Vinings Care Facility." Her voice thickened. "I just got so scared about Mom—I wasn't thinking."

The fact that a woman had lured Caitlyn to the parking garage meant *someone* knew who the unsub was, Reid thought. It also meant there was a possibility he had an accomplice.

"Agent Tierney already checked," he told her. "The call was made from a disposable cell phone. It's untraceable."

Reid laid his hand on Caitlyn's forearm. He could feel her pulse under her skin, and he thanked God for the elderly couple that for some reason had been leaving the hospital in the very early morning hours. If they hadn't been there—if they'd arrived even a minute later—it could have been too late.

"Caitlyn," Reid said gently. "The man who tried to abduct you...he's probably our copycat."

And he intended for you to be his next victim. Reid couldn't bring himself to say it aloud, but he could tell by Caitlyn's unsurprised expression she'd already made the realization, as well.

"I'm going to see about getting a security detail at your house."

He half expected Caitlyn to argue with him, but she gave a faint nod of agreement. This had all gone too far. But things would have to change now—Caitlyn's connection to the case was no longer some vague hunch he had based on a piece of jewelry found at a crime scene. The killer had lured her to the parking garage with the intent of taking her.

"I wanted to call you last night," Caitlyn said quietly. "After seeing Joshua yesterday...after digging up that poor woman..."

And yet she hadn't. He cursed himself for not being there for her.

"I want to see my mother," she whispered.

"I'll take you as soon as you're discharged. For now you just need to rest."

After a short while, her eyelids drifted closed and her breathing slowed. Rubbing a hand over his face, Reid tried to get control over his own careening emotions. He remained there, struggling not to drown in the heavy tide of his thoughts, until a nurse rolled a blood pressure cart into the room. Reid rose from the chair and went into the hallway just as Mitch walked into the corridor.

"You want to tell me this was just coincidence?" he asked sharply, pointing to Caitlyn's room. "You think the intention wasn't for her to have ended up as victim number three?"

Mitch raised a hand to stop him. "I'm not arguing with you. But I need to make a correction. Ms. Cahill would have been victim number *four*."

Reid felt a spiraling dread.

"I just got a call, which is why I came looking for you. Two calls, actually. First off, we've got another body."

He'd barely had time to absorb the information when Mitch made his second announcement. "The second call was from the psych ward at Washington Hospital. David Hunter escaped last night."

24

A cold drizzle had begun to fall. Reid watched somberly as the nude female corpse was zipped inside a black body bag and loaded onto a gurney. It had been there for days, apparently, lying amid the garbage in a Dumpster behind a K Street restaurant. A homeless person who'd been rooting through the bin had found the body, and Reid wondered how the stench had gone unnoticed for so long.

Mitch was talking to the man now, a gaunt junkie with café-au-lait skin and unwashed hair. His partner held in one latex-gloved hand the cellophane evidence bag. It contained the chess pawn that had been wedged inside the victim's mouth. Two workers with the M.E.'s office rolled the gurney past and loaded it into a van.

Walking to where Reid stood, Mitch jerked his thumb toward the homeless man. "He wants to know if there's a reward for calling 911."

He handed the evidence bag to Forensics, then turned up the collar of his jacket against the rain and looked around. "Where the hell did Morehouse go with my umbrella?"

On the drive over, they'd spoken briefly by phone to the administrator at the psych ward from which David Hunter had escaped. The details of exactly *how* he had eluded the hospital staff were still sketchy, but his disappearance hadn't been discovered until early that morning.

"We're lucky—thanks to the District's stretched resources, the garbage hasn't been picked up yet. Based on decomposition, the body's been here at least a week," Mitch said. "Hunter was arrested just four days ago—do the math. Not to mention, his breakout sometime last night puts him in the running for the attack on Ms. Cahill."

"The man on the surveillance tape's too big."

"What's Hunter? Six foot?" Mitch pointed out. "He's on the thin side, but with the heavy jacket and mask the guy's wearing and the bad-to-no lighting, it could be him. I don't think we should overlook the basic rules of means, motive and opportunity."

"It's not him," Reid said quietly.

"I forgot. Hunter doesn't fit your psychological profile."

Morehouse cleared his throat, letting them know he was approaching. He looked at Mitch. "We need to go to the morgue with the Jane Doe—"

"You do it." He tossed him his car keys. "I've got bigger fish to fry. And give me my umbrella."

"Bigger fish?" Reid asked once the younger agent

had relinquished the black umbrella and headed in the direction of the sedan, his shoulders hunched against the increasing downpour.

"You've got your intuitions and so do I. I'm going to see this Dr. Abrams at the hospital and try to figure out how Hunter could slip away without anyone noticing." Mitch nodded toward the SUV. "Want to give me a ride?"

Reid's cell phone rang. He flipped it open, his stomach tightening as he saw the call's source. But instead of answering, he replaced the phone in his jacket pocket. "I'll go with you."

As they walked toward the vehicle, Mitch asked, "How long are they keeping Ms. Cahill?"

"A couple of nights, I'd guess."

"She didn't look good."

Reid climbed into the driver's side of the SUV. "No."

Once they'd pulled from the alleyway, he said, "We need to get protection for her."

"We can try, but resources are tight. The Feds have had job cuts along with everybody else."

"She's in trouble. Whoever attempted to abduct her is going to try again." Reid looked at Mitch. "I'll call SAC Johnston, extend my leave another few weeks and stay with her myself if I have to."

"Let's not jump the gun. I'll see what I can do."

Caitlyn's hospital room had darkened with the falling evening, and silvered raindrops trailed along the window glass. For most of the day, she'd been drowsy, the pain medication providing a measure of anesthesia against her thoughts. But she assumed the physician had begun tapering her dosage, since her mind was now growing clearer and with that clarity came anxiety and memories she couldn't stop—of a man wearing all black, his face concealed by a ski mask. Caitlyn nudged the mobile tray that held her uneaten dinner away from the bed. She reached for the television remote, hoping to find something that might distract her from her thoughts.

"Let me clear that, hon." A pleasant-faced hospital worker in floral-print scrubs came through the door. She smiled brightly. "How are you feeling?"

Caitlyn put the television speaker on Mute. "I'm… fine. Thank you."

"You're looking a little better. How's the head?"

"It hurts," she admitted.

"I'll bring you some acetaminophen as soon as I come back through."

"Do you know when the doctor will be making rounds?" Caitlyn asked as the woman covered the plastic food tray with its top and began rolling it toward the door. Despite how she felt, she desperately hoped to be discharged in the morning. She hated the antiseptic hospital smells and the constant threat of needles.

"Dr. Singh should be by sometime in the morning, but his schedule varies." She gave Caitlyn a sympathetic look. "I'll be right back with the meds."

Once the woman left, Caitlyn looked back up at the television screen. The six o'clock news was on, and a female journalist stood in front of an alley. Police crime scene tape crisscrossed its entrance, and the blue light bar of a patrol car flashed in the background.

The hair on Caitlyn's nape stood up as she saw the caption across the bottom of the screen.

Capital Killer Copycat.

She searched for the television remote lost in the bed's sheets. Finding it, she clicked on the volume button with a sense of dread.

"...believed to be the third victim. Preliminary forensics estimate the body had been concealed in a Dumpster here for the past week. Although the Federal Bureau of Investigation and District Police are not releasing the details, certain aspects of the crime scene suggest a copycat may indeed be at large..."

The throb inside her head grew a little more insistent, drowning out the reporter's monologue. The killer had claimed a third victim. She absently twisted the sheets with her uninjured hand.

"I was hoping to tell you first." Reid stood in the doorway, his leather jacket and his dark hair damp from the rain. He came into the room and sat in the chair beside her bed. "The copycat story broke this afternoon. They'll probably release the newest victim's identity soon. Her name was Sherry Halston. She was a D.C. events planner."

Caitlyn felt sick thinking about it. "Do the press know about the attack on me yet?"

"So far it hasn't been reported by any of the media outlets. But if it comes out, they're undoubtedly going to make a connection." Reid's gray eyes were filled with concern. "There's something else I need to tell you, Caitlyn. David Hunter escaped last night from the hospital psych ward."

25

"Hello, Mom," Caitlyn said softly, her chest tightening as her mother looked at her with no sign of recognition on her unlined, still-pretty face. A fashion magazine open in her lap, Caroline sat on a chintz sofa in one of the Vinings common rooms. Behind her, a wide picture window framed by raw-silk curtains provided a view into the facility's well-tended gardens.

Moving closer, Caitlyn sank onto the adjacent wing chair, carefully adjusting the sling that held her arm against her chest to protect her badly bruised hand. Her fingers were stiff and swollen, and the dull throb of her headache lingered. Caitlyn wore the same clothes she'd had on yesterday morning when she'd rushed to the District, thinking her mother had been hurt. She had come directly from the hospital as soon as they discharged her, needing to see for herself that her mother was really all right.

Caitlyn's eyes met Reid's, who stood inside the doorway but hadn't come any closer. "This is a friend of mine, Mom. Reid Novak?"

She wondered if the name might cause some flash of memory inside Caroline's weakened mind, that perhaps the sheer duress that had once been attached to the name *Novak* might cause some reaction—anger, hostility— to rise inside her. But Caroline simply blinked at Reid, studying him for a few moments before returning her gaze to Caitlyn.

"And who are you?" she asked, puzzled.

Caitlyn's face burned. "I'm your daughter. It's me. Caitlyn."

Caroline tucked a few stands of her hair behind one ear, nodding thoughtfully. Its pale color—lighter than Caitlyn's—held only a touch of gray. Even then, the color was an attractive, lush silver.

"Do you live in the District?"

"No." Caitlyn shook her head. "Not anymore."

"There's a soiree next month. It's invitation-only— the First Lady's Fire and Ice Ball. I'm picking out a gown." Caroline bent her head in concentration as she flipped slowly through the magazine she held. She stopped at a page with its top corner dog-eared and placed her finger on a photo of a statuesque model in an ice-blue evening gown. "I like this one. What do you think?"

Caitlyn knew there was no ball, and if there were, Senator Cahill's widow would not be on the guest list. Still, she looked into Caroline's eyes and smiled. "You'd be beautiful in it."

"I...don't know you," her mother admitted. "Do you work here?"

When Caitlyn stared up at Reid, the pain she felt was reflected on his features. He held her gaze for several long moments, and the sympathy and guilt emanating from his eyes was almost more than she could bear. Caitlyn took a breath. She moved to the sofa to sit next to her mother and continued studying the magazine. When she looked up again, Reid had disappeared into the hallway.

"It was a good visit," Caitlyn said quietly as they walked out to Reid's vehicle. He held the lobby's glass door open for her, his hand on the small of her back as he guided her down stone steps that led to a patio with wrought-iron benches and a gurgling fountain. Caitlyn took the steps slowly, still feeling stiff from the attack.

"She's worse sometimes?" he asked.

"She was talking today. Sometimes she doesn't respond at all. She just stares right through you like she's a million miles away."

"Does she ever remember who you are?"

Caitlyn shook her head. "No."

He stopped walking. Reid touched her arm through the sling. "I'm sorry, Caitlyn. I know I had a hand in what happened to her."

She said with honesty, "You're not to blame. You were doing your job."

The afternoon wind was brisk, and Caitlyn shivered a little. Reid took off his leather jacket and placed it around her shoulders. The heat from his body was still inside the garment, and she allowed herself to take comfort in its warmth. The visits with her mother always left her feeling blue. She stared out over the facility's grounds, focusing on the rustle of leaves in the fall wind and the slightly overcast afternoon sky.

"How are you feeling?" Reid asked, apparently attuned to her mood.

"Sore. My head still hurts a little."

Caitlyn knew the hospital security tape hadn't been able to reveal much about her attacker—at least no more than she'd been able to make out herself in the darkness. He was still a faceless but menacing threat. It had all happened so fast and she had done everything wrong. She hadn't fought back well enough, hadn't made a grab to unmask him.

She was lucky to be alive.

"Are you taking me back to my car?" Caitlyn asked as Reid helped her into his SUV—an awkward process due to her injured hand. He had driven her to the Vinings Care Facility to visit her mother, so her car remained in the parking garage at the medical center. Her stomach knotted at the thought of returning to the place where the attack had occurred.

"Actually, we're going to my apartment."

The announcement was not entirely unexpected. Reid had made it clear he didn't think she should return home until he had some kind of security worked out.

"What am I going to do? Spend the night there?"

"One night. Maybe two. And it's not the first time we've slept under the same roof."

"I could get a hotel room."

He peered at her. "You're not in great shape, Caitlyn. I'm still trying to figure out how you coerced the doctor into signing your discharge papers so soon. I doubt you can even drive a car right now with your hand, not to mention dress or bathe yourself."

As he reached across her lap, pulling the shoulder belt across her chest and fastening it, he was undeniably close. Reid smelled clean, like a masculine soap, and Caitlyn was aware of her own rumpled appearance. He straightened, standing outside the car with his right hand on the SUV's roof.

"I'd go back with you to Middleburg tonight, but I have firearms recertification tomorrow. It makes more sense for you to stay with me instead of the other way around."

Caitlyn remained silent, unable to find a point for argument. Manny wasn't even at the Rambling Rose, since she had insisted he take the week to go visit his daughter, Maria. Other than the day workers, she would be completely alone. She could call the Treadwells, but after the strange incident with Rob in the hallway outside her bedroom, she wasn't sure that she would feel comfortable staying in their home. She had seen Rob's number come up, three times on her cell phone since then, although he had failed to leave any message when she hadn't answered. She wondered again if she had misconstrued his overture. Maybe he was just genuinely trying to be helpful, and he'd suggested calling his cell instead of the house so as to not worry Sophie with all the things going on. Caitlyn knew how high-strung Sophie could be.

She chewed her lip thoughtfully as Reid closed her door. *I'll only stay today and tonight,* she conceded silently. *Manny's out of town and I need to get back to the stables.* Once they reached Reid's apartment, she would call out there and make sure things were running okay with just the therapy instructors and stable hands.

"I'm going to need a change of clothes," she said as Reid got into the driver's side.

He started the engine. "We'll stop at the mall."

What the hell had happened to her?

Hal Feingold hunkered in his new Lexus coupe, his eyes on the SUV that had just pulled away from the curb. He'd been sitting across the street from the adult care facility as Reid Novak escorted Caitlyn Cahill along the sidewalk. The FBI agent had taken every excuse he could to touch her, Hal noted cynically. Her arm had been in a sling and even from a distance he could see the bruise shadowing her right temple.

Was it a car accident? Something else? Activating his digital recorder, he spoke into it, preparing a note for his assistant. "Run a check to see if Caitlyn Cahill comes up in any police reports over the past forty-eight hours."

Tossing the recorder onto a copy of the *Washington Post* that lay on the passenger seat, he drummed his pudgy fingers on the car's leather steering wheel in thought. A worker at the Vinings facility had tipped him off, letting him know Caitlyn was there visiting her mother. His intention, plain and simple, had been to ambush her outside the place and get her to agree to an interview. Even more, he wanted to gain her cooperation, win her blessing over his book. His publisher was insisting that her involvement would bring in greater sales. Hal's mouth twisted. Apparently, what a pretty, former socialite had to say held more interest for readers than a veteran crime journalist.

But he reminded himself that Caitlyn wasn't just any former socialite. She'd been at the center of the Capital Killer case, her family dethroned by the revelation of her brother's dirty little secret. In many ways, she'd been the tipping point in bringing Joshua Cahill down.

His publisher was right, Hal admitted to himself. Her story was the one readers would want.

But his plans had been bushwhacked by Novak's unanticipated presence. The way he'd helped her into his car, carefully buckling her seat belt for her—well, it had been downright tender. And it suggested more than a professional acquaintance. Hal remembered his recent confrontation with Novak in the bar.

The plot thickens, he thought with a contemplative grunt. His curiosity was piqued. He pondered again how Caitlyn Cahill had ended up looking like she'd come off the losing end of a bar fight. Maybe one of her horses had thrown her, but Hal had a feeling it was something more. Was Novak with her as some sort of bodyguard? And how well *did* they know each other?

His paunch pressing against the steering wheel column, Hal leaned forward to start the coupe's engine. It purred like a cat. He'd bought the car with part of his advance on the book. The *Post*'s headline on the seat next to him briefly caught his attention, causing his lips to tug upward in a grin: FBI Fears D.C. May Have Capital Killer Copycat on Its Hands.

He knew one thing—the timing couldn't have been better.

26

Caitlyn held her cell phone as she sat on the couch in Reid's apartment. She'd checked her voice mail at the stables to find several messages from the D.C. press, all requesting a statement about the emergence of a second Capital Killer. The reporters wanted a sound bite from her about someone emulating Joshua's crimes. If they knew she had very nearly been a victim of the copycat herself, they'd no doubt be camped out at the Rambling Rose gates. Publicity like that could shut down her program, she realized. Caitlyn sighed inwardly. Even without Hal Feingold's book, it was starting all over again.

She looked around the small yet well-furnished apartment. At least here she had a safe haven. But Caitlyn knew she would have to go back soon. Without Manny there, the stables needed her, and she needed to put some distance between herself and Reid. Being near him like this made it too easy to depend on him—something that would only cause them both trouble and hurt.

"How was your nap?" he called from the kitchen over a clatter of pots and pans.

"Refreshing," Caitlyn replied, deciding not to tell him about the messages just yet. She stood, stretching briefly to test the soreness of her muscles. After they'd stopped at a Target so Caitlyn could purchase a few necessities, a toothbrush and underwear among them, she'd fallen asleep on the couch. She came into the kitchen, enticed by the aroma of something on the stove. Her stomach growled and she realized that she hadn't eaten in hours.

Reid wore faded jeans and a long-sleeved, white T-shirt. He stood at the stove, stirring a large pot with a wooden spoon.

"Chicken chili," he announced. "Nothing fancy, but it's pretty good."

"It smells great."

He held the wooden spoon to his lips, gently blowing on its contents, then offered it to Caitlyn for a taste. It was reminiscent of him feeding her dessert that night at Agava.

"Delicious," she said around the spicy mouthful. She fanned her mouth. "And hot."

"It'll be ready soon. We're just waiting on the bread." Reid wiped his hands on a dishtowel as his gaze traveled over her. "The sweats are a little big, but they'll do."

Caitlyn wore a pair of Reid's sweatpants and a gray sweat jacket with the University of Virginia printed across its front in bold maroon letters. The sleeves had been turned up to accommodate her smaller frame. She had managed to dress herself, although it had taken close to a half hour and Reid's help in zipping up the jacket. She blushed, recalling that he had briefly seen her bare stomach and bra as he provided assistance.

"Reid," she began hesitantly. "I want to thank you for…everything. For letting me stay here tonight, and for taking me to visit Mom today."

He lifted a beer from the counter and took a sip. "We're hoping to have some kind of security in place at your home soon. I'm waiting to hear."

Caitlyn nodded, wondering if he would be glad to have her off his hands. He looked handsome—sexy—in the comforts of his own kitchen, cooking a meal. Even with his job, it seemed odd he wasn't in a serious relationship. *For all I know, maybe he is,* she thought. Maybe there was a girlfriend he had failed to mention—one who'd be unhappy about Caitlyn even being here. If that were the case, she'd be even less pleased about their heated kiss at her farm. She did her best to push away the mental image of herself in Reid's arms. His kiss had broken through the wall she'd built around herself and the numbness she'd existed in for too long. But its aftermath had also wedged a tension between them. They had both taken a step back and realized the inappropriateness of their attraction to one another.

Things had simply gone too far.

Caitlyn walked to the desk where Reid apparently paid his bills and handled other housekeeping tasks. Above it, a window provided a view of the lively Adams Morgan neighborhood. Small, white lights decorated trees lining the sidewalk and an ethnic restaurant—a place cleverly and suggestively called Thai Me Up—was located across the street. Its name flashed on the glass of its storefront in neon letters. Next to it, a dark-windowed establishment appeared to be a bar. A man and woman stood to the left of the door, entangled in a heated make-out session under the shadow of the building's awning. Caitlyn watched guiltily for several seconds before moving her gaze back to the desktop with its neat stacks of bills and mail. Reid's cell phone lay next to a notepad bearing his handwriting.

Dr. Isrelsen, test results.

There was a number to call.

Caitlyn frowned. Reid was tumor-free, he'd told her that himself. She wondered if it had simply been a follow-up visit, a final pronouncement of his good health. But physicians usually just left news like that in a voice mail message, didn't they? It was news of the other variety they wanted to discuss in person.

"Dinner's ready."

Caitlyn turned as Reid set two earthenware bowls on the table next to a basket of bread.

"I'd offer you a beer but with the medication you're taking…"

"Water's good," she murmured, studying his face. His even features gave no indication of anything wrong. He pulled out a chair for her and helped her settle into it with her sling.

"How long do you have to wear that?" he asked, sitting at the other side of the table once he'd filled a glass with ice water and placed it in front of her.

"A couple of days, to keep me from jarring it. Then I can just wear the brace the hospital gave me." Caitlyn lifted the spoon to her mouth, grateful again the injured hand wasn't her right one. "Regardless, it's going to be difficult mucking out stalls for a while."

She chewed and swallowed. "This really is delicious."

"Good," he said. "You need to eat, Caitlyn. You've lost weight."

Caitlyn gathered her courage. "Reid, are you sure you're all right? I mean, the stress of all this must be weighing on you, too, and I know you're recovering—"

"I'm fine." He moved the chili in his bowl around with his spoon. "I'm recertifying on firearms at 8:00 a.m. tomorrow. And I start back to work officially on Monday."

Caitlyn wanted to ask about the note she had seen but didn't want him to think she'd been snooping. She let the matter drop for now.

They were clearing away the dishes when a knock sounded at the door.

"Are you expecting anyone?" Caitlyn asked.

"No. Wait here." Moving to the desk, Reid extracted a gun box from one of the lower drawers. He removed his firearm and then peered carefully between the window blinds. Caitlyn saw his shoulders visibly relax.

"Who is it?"

"My sister." He opened the door and an attractive woman with dark hair the same color and texture as Reid's bustled inside, bringing in with her the noise from the busy street below.

"Megan. What are you doing here?"

"Nice greeting," she said, eyeing the gun in his hand with an arched eyebrow. "Cooper and the kids are in the car. We're going to that Mexican restaurant the girls like, the one with the mariachi band? I thought you might want to join us."

"Why didn't you call?"

"I did and got your voice mail. Maybe you should try answering once in—" She stopped, spotting Caitlyn who stood behind the island that separated the kitchen from the living area. "Oh...you've got company."

Reid scrubbed a hand through his hair. "Megan, this is Caitlyn Cahill."

"I know who she is." Although she wasn't rude, her voice held a distinct coolness. Not that Caitlyn could blame her, not after what her father had done to Reid in order to waylay the investigation into Joshua. Caitlyn detected an instant protectiveness in Megan's eyes.

"Hello," Caitlyn said quietly. She walked closer, joining them.

"We just ate, actually." Reid laid the gun on the desk and indicated the kitchen where dishes were still being rinsed and placed in the dishwasher.

"God. What happened to you?" Megan's gaze swept over Caitlyn's sling and the ugly bruise on her right temple. Caitlyn looked at Reid, who rubbed his forehead with the index finger of his right hand.

"Megan..."

"I was attacked in a parking garage two mornings ago," Caitlyn answered truthfully. "I just got out of the hospital."

Megan turned to Reid. "This is tied to the copycat, isn't it? It's been all over the news, which is exactly why I came over here."

"And the truth comes out." Reid released an exasperated breath. "Now it makes sense why you drove all the way from Silver Spring on a Wednesday night for fish tacos. You were checking up on me."

"Don't you think someone should?" She lowered her voice, although Caitlyn could still hear her clearly. "That case nearly destroyed you, and it's all coming back again. Dad said he left you a message, too."

"Give me a break, Megan. Dad understands the job. You should, too."

Caitlyn bit her lip in silence. She could tell Reid was irritated with his sister, but what she also saw was a close, caring sibling relationship, one that made her yearn for a normal family.

Reid placed his hands on his sister's shoulders, gently turning her around and guiding her toward the door. "Go have dinner. Tell the girls I said hello. Cooper, too."

His cell phone rang. He walked over to check its screen. "It's Mitch. I need to take this. Good night, Megan."

He went into the bedroom, leaving Caitlyn and

Megan alone. Reid's sister remained at the door, her hand on the knob, although she hadn't yet opened it. Caitlyn didn't look away from her evaluating gaze.

"The media doesn't know about the attack on me," Caitlyn said hesitantly, breaking the tense silence. "Reid...the FBI...they're hoping to keep it out of the news."

"They're protecting you. Don't you find that a little ironic?"

Caitlyn's reply was soft. "I do."

The two women continued staring at each other until Reid emerged from the bedroom. He picked up his jacket from the arm of the couch. "Megan, what are the chances of you, Cooper and the girls staying here for about forty-five minutes? I need to take care of something—"

"That's not necessary," Caitlyn interrupted. "I'm perfectly fine by myself."

"Megan?" Reid asked again. He'd moved to the security box to place his weapon inside it, then locked it and returned it to the drawer. "If you guys can't wait for dinner, there's about a half ton of chicken chili leftovers in the fridge."

Megan sighed and pulled her cell phone from her purse. "I'll tell Cooper to look for a parking spot."

"Tell him he can have mine." His eyes met Caitlyn's briefly, and then he disappeared through the door.

Where was he going? Caitlyn carefully shifted her hand in the sling and wondered how she would get through the next forty-five minutes.

"Reid's taken a personal interest in you," Megan acknowledged, her gray eyes narrowing fractionally. Caitlyn had seen Reid use that same tactic before to express his disbelief over something. The family resemblance between them was remarkable.

"After everything the Cahills put him through, what I'd like to know is why," she said.

"I'm part of his job."

"He's not on the job right now. Supposedly."

Caitlyn took a small breath. She understood her hostility, *she did*.

"Well, as long as you plan to interrogate me, maybe you could do it while I take a shower?" She indicated her injured hand. "The truth is, I could really use some female assistance."

27

"Are you still in touch with your brother?"

Caitlyn heard Megan's question through the noise of the running water. Her shower completed, she reached for the faucet handle and turned it off, standing briefly in the heavy steam cloud before answering.

"No. At least, not until recently." She accepted the large towel Megan held out to her through the closed shower curtain. "Reid took me to Springdale Penitentiary to talk to him a few days ago."

"Why?"

"Because Joshua killed other women, apparently. More than those he went to prison for." Caitlyn tried not to think of what Joshua had said to her, about her being his muse and the things he'd wanted to do to her. She slid back the shower curtain, the striped towel held in front of her for modesty. "He promised to give up the location of the remains only if I would come see him."

Shock was evident on Megan's features. She sat on

the edge of the vanity, sipping a beer she'd commandeered from Reid's refrigerator. "Did he?"

"He gave up one. I'll have to see him again to get the others."

"How many others?"

"They're not sure."

"I can't imagine," Megan admitted.

"You don't have to," she replied. "Your brother is a good man."

Water dripped from her hair, making a soft plunking sound on the molded plastic shower floor. Megan eyed her silently over the top of her beer bottle. Then she stood and placed the bottle next to the sink and helped Caitlyn into Reid's terry cloth robe. Caitlyn used her good hand to blot her shoulder-length hair with the towel. Even in the steamed mirror, the bruise on her temple was visible.

"How did you get into the sweats earlier?" Megan asked, frowning as she watched Caitlyn's slow, careful movements that reflected the soreness she felt. "Did Reid—"

She shook her head. "I mostly managed it myself, but it took forever. I appreciate the help."

"That was *really* none of my business," Megan said, sounding embarrassed. She seemed to be loosening up a little. "Reid's the law enforcement officer in the family, but I've been told I'm the real interrogator. He'd strangle me if he knew I'd asked you..."

She stopped speaking, realizing her faux pas. Caitlyn

knew what she was thinking—Joshua had strangled his victims.

"I'm sorry, I didn't mean that."

"It's okay. I'm used to it."

Megan had introduced Caitlyn to her family—albeit coolly—before they had gone into the bathroom together. They'd decided to wait and have dinner at the Mexican restaurant, so Megan's husband and daughters were now in the living room, watching a sitcom on the flat-screen television. The younger of the girls was talking excitedly about her day at school, her voice carrying through the door panel.

"Maddie and Isabelle are adorable," Caitlyn said, changing the subject.

"They're a handful," Megan conceded. "But totally worth it."

"I'm sure."

She watched as Caitlyn ran a brush through her wet hair.

"I know you…helped…in the Capital Killer case. That you turned over evidence to prove your brother's guilt." Megan shook her head. "And I also know that I shouldn't be angry with you about the investigation, but I can't help it."

Her gray eyes were so similar to Reid's and just as direct. "Your father put Reid through hell, you know. He nearly lost his position at the VCU, everything he's worked for over the past nine years."

"I know," Caitlyn said quietly. Pain and regret weighed on her.

"Reid's been ill."

"I know that, too."

"He's better now, but it doesn't keep me from being overprotective." Megan sighed as she tugged pensively at the beer's label, peeling it from the bottle. "Our mother died of a brain tumor when Reid and I were just kids. It made us pretty close."

Caitlyn thought of the note she'd found in Reid's handwriting. Anxiety fluttered inside her, but she didn't bring it up. She hadn't known his mother had died from the same illness—something that must have made the diagnosis more terrifying for all of them.

"Sometimes I think the Capital Killer investigation caused the tumor to grow in his head." Megan shrugged. "Pretty crazy, I know. But he took the investigation so personally. Every victim got to him. I'm worried about it happening again."

Her eyes seemed to say, *and I'm afraid you're the reason he's involved this time.*

"Reid takes his work seriously. It's an important job."

Megan nodded. "He's good at what he does—he's great actually, according to his superiors. He has more commendations than any other agent his age. But he doesn't have what our dad calls 'cool detachment.'"

And that was exactly what made Reid different, Caitlyn thought. It was what separated him from men like Mitch Tierney, who treated suspects and victims with an almost equal cynicism. But at the same time, she knew it must be hard to see what they saw and not become hardened by it. That tough, protective shell was also a necessity.

"The brain tumor Reid had," she asked, "was it hereditary?"

"You know how squirrelly doctors can be about things like that." Megan sat the now-empty bottle on the vanity and wiped her hands on her skirt. "It was the same type. Reid was lucky, though. His was benign and operable. Still, it was a major surgery. The recuperation was pretty bad."

"He told me how fortunate he was to have you," Caitlyn said. She thought it was something his sister should know.

Megan bowed her head. "Did you know he had a fiancée?"

The pang Caitlyn felt surprised her. "What happened?"

"They met after the Capital Killer case. They started dating and then moved in together before getting engaged. Andrea broke things off…after they found the tumor. She couldn't handle the thought of Reid being incapacitated, or even dying, if the surgery failed."

"How terrible," Caitlyn murmured. She wondered how someone who claimed to love Reid could have deserted him when he needed her most. The question left her lips before she'd even realized it. "Does he still have feelings for her?"

"I don't think so. I know they haven't been in touch."

"Why are you telling me this?"

"Because Reid's been through a lot. He doesn't need

to get hurt again." The two women stared at each other for several meaningful seconds. Then Megan took a step toward the door. "I'm going to go check on the girls. I'll be back in a minute to help you get dressed."

She left Caitlyn alone with her thoughts. Her mind traveled to her own fiancé who had broken up with her after Joshua's arrest. The losses were something she and Reid had in common.

Reid stood beside Mitch in the foyer of the Cahills' Georgetown mansion, listening as the Bureau's blood-spatter specialist gave a rundown on the scene. Lucy Kim's black hair appeared glossy underneath the lights of the crystal chandelier.

"Medium velocity impact spatter indicates blunt force trauma, consistent with the blood pool on the carpet." Lucy indicated the dark, congealing stain on the Oriental rug, then led them to the curved staircase with its carved mahogany rail. "The bloodstain on the wall is a transfer, most likely made by the victim's hand."

Reid studied the gruesome smear on the elegant fleur-de-lis wallpaper. "She was trying to get away."

"She made it as far as the stairs, which is where it appears the perpetrator hit her again. Judging by the dryness of the stains, I'd estimate it happened five to six hours ago." Lucy pushed her stylish, horn-rimmed glasses higher on her nose. "My team will be done soon. Any questions?"

"Yeah," Mitch said, giving her a wolfish grin. "When are we going out, doll?"

Lucy smiled sweetly. "When hell freezes over, Agent Tierney."

She walked past him, her designer high heels clicking on the Italian marble flooring. "And by the way, nice cologne."

Once Lucy was out of earshot, Mitch looked at Reid. "You think my aftershave's too strong?"

"A little," he admitted.

"Damn. It's new." Mitch sniffed the lapel of his jacket, testing it out for himself. "I had a date. Or at least I did until I got a call from the D.C. police."

The residence was a hive of activity, with evidence techs scurrying about and policemen blocking the front entrance.

"Who discovered the blood?" Reid asked.

"The real estate agency Bliss Harper works for sent someone over here after she didn't report back to her office this afternoon. She'd said she was coming by to take photos of the interior for a sales flyer." Mitch peeled the latex gloves from his hands and tossed them into a brass umbrella stand. "Instead of Ms. Harper, they found this mess. The blood's presumably hers, since she's nowhere to be found."

"Someone went by her home? Checked with her family and friends?"

"No one's seen her since lunchtime today. And she's not answering her cell phone. Everyone says it's out of the ordinary for her."

Reid stared up at the chandelier. The foyer was brightly lit so Forensics could do its job. Through the window, he noticed a news van had pulled onto the street outside. "Any sign of a weapon?"

"No weapon, no body. Uniforms did a grid search of the premises." Mitch adjusted his shoulder holster. "She was attacked and, judging by the blood, injured. The unsub probably dragged her into a vehicle out back. The service entrance is secluded. There's an overgrown hedge back there taller than me."

"Bludgeoning wasn't part of Joshua Cahill's M.O."

"No. Maybe the copycat is adding a few twists of his own."

"Or she fought back." Reid felt tension knot the muscles in his neck. "Things didn't go according to plan."

He didn't look forward to telling Caitlyn about the likely abduction of her friend, or the fact that it had taken place at her family home. But based on the news van's arrival, the story would be on the ten o'clock news. Hopefully, he'd have a chance to talk to her before she saw it on TV.

"All I know is this—Hunter's still out there somewhere. And he's been seen outside the residence before, by Caitlyn Cahill herself," Mitch pointed out. "Let's just consider for a second that he came back here, hoping to confront Ms. Cahill again. Instead he ran into Bliss Harper. Another attractive blonde."

Reid had to admit the scenario made sense. Still, the picture was incomplete. "To our knowledge, Hunter doesn't own a white van like the one used in the attempted abduction on Caitlyn."

"Maybe he jacked it. Or bought it hot off the street."

Reid thought for a moment. "What did the evaluating doctors tell you about Hunter?"

"They never got a chance to complete the full psychological review before he escaped, but he's clearly disturbed."

"Enough to be capable of murder?"

"I couldn't get them to go that far."

"Any word on protection for Caitlyn yet?"

Mitch shook his head. "Not yet. Where is she, anyway?"

Reid didn't want Mitch to know she was staying at his apartment. Instead he said, "With Megan and her family."

It wasn't a total lie, he rationalized. At the moment, she *was* with them. Reid only hoped Megan hadn't taken the opportunity to rake Caitlyn over the coals. She'd been through enough already. "I've got to get back. Thanks for the call."

Mitch walked him to the door. "No problem. I figured you'd want to see this firsthand. Hey, you okay?"

"I'm fine," Reid lied.

"You've got your firearms recertification in the morning, right?"

"At eight o'clock."

"Good luck." Mitch jerked his head toward Agent Morehouse, who was talking to one of the uniforms on the other side of the room. He'd been called to the scene from his home, apparently, and was wearing dark warm-ups that made him look like the center on a high school basketball team.

"I'll be losing an errand boy, but gaining my real partner back," Mitch said.

Once outside, Reid went down the steps and past the news van, ignoring the reporter who called out to him asking for a comment on whatever was going on inside the house. It wasn't hard, since his mind was on other things. Things that actually went beyond the current investigation, or even Caitlyn.

The first voice mail message had been left on his cell yesterday. The second one, this morning.

It's important you contact us, Mr. Novak. We'd like to make an appointment for you with Dr. Isrelsen at your earliest convenience. It's about the results of your MRI.

Reid had been using the events of the past two days as a distraction. But if the worst were true, it was something he couldn't run from forever.

28

When Reid returned to his apartment, Caitlyn appeared to have recently showered, her hair still damp and her skin pleasantly flushed. She sat on the couch between Maddie and Isabelle, wearing the simple cotton pajamas she'd purchased earlier that day. At his arrival, Megan stood and announced, "Okay, girls. Uncle Reid's back. Get your things. Let's go have dinner."

"Thanks for staying," he said to Megan as she began gathering her troops.

"Everything okay?"

"Yeah." Reid nodded, although his eyes fell on Caitlyn, who was helping Isabelle shove her collection of spiral notebooks and stickers into her Hello Kitty backpack. The time with his nieces appeared to have relaxed her some, and he dreaded telling her about the latest turn of events.

"Good to meet you, Caitlyn," Cooper said as he held his older daughter's coat out for her to slide her arms into.

"You, too."

Reid didn't miss the look that passed between Megan and Caitlyn. It made him think they'd actually talked while he was away instead of staying in their opposite corners like prizefighters waiting for the bell to sound. At least Caitlyn looked none the worse for wear. He owed Megan for not coming down on her too hard.

"Thanks for the help," Caitlyn said as Megan turned to leave.

His sister nodded. Reid lowered his head to allow her to place a kiss against his cheek. "Take care, big brother."

He gave her a hug, grateful for her presence in his life. Once the group was gone, Reid refocused his attention on Caitlyn. She'd remained on the couch with her feet tucked underneath her.

"Did you have to leave because of the case?" she asked.

He sighed heavily, removing his leather jacket and laying it on the wing chair Cooper had vacated. "Agent Tierney asked me to come to the scene of an abduction."

He saw her shoulders tense underneath her pajama top, her green eyes searching his. Reid walked to the couch and sat beside her.

"An abduction? The copycat's taken someone else?"

"It occurred at your Georgetown residence, Caitlyn."

It took just seconds for her to realize the victim's identity. Her lips parted and horror filled her eyes. "Oh, God. Bliss?"

"Ms. Harper told her real estate office she was going

by the house to take some photos earlier today. She never reported back in, and she failed to show up for an evening appointment. Her office sent someone to the house looking for her a couple of hours ago."

"But you said 'abduction.'" Caitlyn grasped at hope. "That means there's no body. Isn't it possible that—"

"It's obvious there was a struggle. There's…significant blood at the scene."

Closing her eyes, she shook her head. "No."

"This isn't your fault—"

"You don't understand." Her voice trembled. "I *hired* Bliss to sell the house. If I hadn't contracted her, she wouldn't have been there. She wouldn't be…"

She was unable to finish the sentence. Reid gently pulled her into his arms.

"I can't believe…Bliss," she murmured brokenly. "We've known each other since grade school. I was a bridesmaid in her wedding. And now because of me…"

Reid rocked with her. He smelled the scent of his shampoo in her hair. "Don't blame yourself, Caitlyn. This guy is a sociopath."

"He knew I was still in the city." Her words were muffled against his chest. "He was hoping to find me there instead. Don't tell me you don't think that."

He couldn't disagree. "The D.C. police have an APB out for her. She could still be alive."

"But for how long?" She looked up at him then, tears glistening in her eyes. "And what's happening to her right now?"

Reid eased them both back against the sofa cushions.

She cried herself out as he held her. After a long while, he finally felt her body relax and her breathing become slower and steadier, indicating she had fallen asleep. But Reid didn't want to wake her. Instead, he sat silently, watching the television Megan and her family had left on after their departure. He tried to get interested in the detective show storyline, but his mind was scattered in different directions—Bliss Harper and the copycat investigation, his own questionable health. Caitlyn felt small and boneless in his arms, and Reid admitted to himself that having her here was a comfort. In knowing that she was safe for now, at least.

In knowing he wasn't alone.

Caitlyn awoke with a start in the unfamiliar bedroom. It took several moments to remember where she was, although she didn't quite recall ever climbing into bed. The last thing she remembered was…

Bliss.

Reality hit her like a tidal wave, causing her heart to ache and simultaneously pound inside her chest. Was Bliss dead already? Or was she being tortured at this very moment? Caitlyn looked around the shadowed room, hearing only her shallow breathing and an alarm clock ticking on the nightstand. A faint memory now danced at the edge of her mind, one of Reid tucking her into bed and kissing her forehead. He'd told her everything would be all right. But she didn't feel that way. Instead what she felt was an incredible helplessness.

She couldn't go back to sleep.

Pushing away the covers, Caitlyn got out of bed and carefully felt her way down the short, unlit hallway that led into the apartment's living room. What she expected to find was Reid, lying on the sofa with one of the bed pillows tucked under his head, sleeping. But the couch was empty. Only a crumpled blanket indicated anyone had been there. As her eyes continued adjusting, she made out his tall form. He was in the kitchen, leaning against the counter with his head in his hands.

She went to him. "Reid?"

His skin felt clammy where she touched him. She could see the brush of his black lashes against his cheeks, his eyes closed in pain.

"Reid, please answer me!"

"I'm…okay." His voice sounded weak. "It's just a headache."

Caitlyn wondered how long he'd been like this. "Where is your medication?"

"I've already taken it," he said quietly. "Go back to bed, Caitlyn."

"You need to lie down."

Slowly, she coaxed him to the sofa, then guided him down onto it. Once he had stretched out, she went into the bathroom and ran cool water onto a washcloth. Gently, she placed it over his eyes, studying his tightened features as he seemed to fight some internal menace. Sitting on the edge of the cushion, she waited in silence beside him, watching for nearly twenty minutes until his frame finally began to release some of its tension. After another interval of time he lifted the washcloth from his eyes and ran it over his face.

"Better?"

He nodded faintly. "Yeah."

"Something's wrong."

His eyes remained closed. "I'm fine."

"You're *not* fine," Caitlyn argued. "I saw the message on the notepad, Reid. Dr. Isrelsen's office called about some test results."

He paused, swallowed. "I'm having some residual pain, that's all. My last MRI was clean."

"I want to believe that," she said softly.

Reid gazed at her, his eyes glassy and fevered. "Believe it, Caitlyn. I don't want you to worry about anything else right now—"

"I do worry," she whispered. "I'm worried about you."

He reached for her uninjured hand.

"Everything's going to be okay," he assured her for the second time that night. "It's just a headache, that's all. Nothing more. I'm back on duty in a few days. And I swear to you I'm going to catch this bastard if it's the last thing I do—"

"Sssh," she urged. It was just a saying, she knew, but it still frightened her. "Just rest, all right?"

Caitlyn threaded her fingers through his damp hair. His entire body was hot, perspiring.

"Come lie down with me," she suggested. "You're too big for the couch to be comfortable. I just want you to get some sleep."

"Caitlyn..." He said her name on a weary sigh.

"Let me take care of you." She stood, waiting until he pushed himself up from the couch. The migraine or whatever he'd experienced seemed to have receded. Still, he appeared spent, wrung out. How long had the pain ravaged him before she'd found him? A half hour? More? As Reid walked to the bedroom, Caitlyn stopped in the bathroom and refreshed the damp cloth. When she reached him, he was already lying on the mattress on his back, still dressed in the jeans and T-shirt he'd had on the previous evening.

Caitlyn placed the cloth over his eyes and was rewarded with a murmur of thanks. Then she lay down beside him, resting her head in the crook of his shoulder. In less than two minutes, he was asleep. As her fingers stroked his broad chest, Caitlyn stared into the darkness.

Did she believe him about the headache? She wanted to, desperately. Still, what she'd witnessed didn't seem normal, and the message from the neurologist was especially troubling. A seed of worry germinated inside her. Her mind raced with questions. How long had he been experiencing these headaches? Who was he hiding them from—his family, the Bureau...himself?

The possible answers, she realized, scared her more than the copycat.

29

Squinting through safety glasses at the target in front of him, Reid fired off another series of careful shots. The squeeze of the trigger, the repeated kick of the Glock in his hands, the explosive sound of each discharge—they were reminders of his training days at Quantico. With an electronic whir, the wire-strung cardboard target moved back another twenty-five feet.

"Fire!" the instructor called from behind him.

Pop. Pop. Pop. Pop.

"Halt!"

The smell of gunpowder burned his nose as Reid engaged the gun's safety. The target moved toward him once again. Even before the instructor stepped into the partitioned space to take it off the line, Reid could see from the visible holes that he'd done well. The silhouetted figure of a man had distinctive marks at the head, shoulder and chest.

"You've still got it, Novak," the instructor commented. He initialed the target and placed it in a drawer underneath his stand. "The time away didn't hurt you any."

Removing his glasses and protective earmuffs, Reid felt relief—relief that he'd easily passed the first part of the firearms recertification, and even more important, that the loud noises hadn't caused another headache. He hadn't been able to identify a cause. Sound? Stress? Whatever it was, he hated that Caitlyn had witnessed one of his more severe bouts last night. And that he'd lied to her about the message from Dr. Isrelsen.

Reid holstered his firearm. He felt strong today—his vision was clear, and there were no signs of the tremors he'd experienced in his hands before the brain tumor had been diagnosed. Didn't that mean something? He just needed to make the call to Dr. Isrelsen, find out what the hell was going on. *He knew that.*

Soon.

His mind heavy as he exited the FBI firing range, he ran into Mitch, who had apparently been watching from behind the shooting platform.

"Not bad," Mitch commented as he removed his own protective headset. "Exactly how much practicing have you been doing?"

"Some."

"You bona fide yet?"

"Not yet," Reid said as they walked from the facility and into the sun-filled parking lot. His SUV stood out among the sea of sedate, dark sedans—government-issued vehicles. "I've still got the course to go."

The obstacle course was a miniature-scale city street

with human figures that popped up in random locations without warning. Some were intended to be armed criminals, some civilians. The course was meant to gauge reaction time and how well an agent could assess threat levels under pressure.

"Any update on Bliss Harper?" he asked.

Mitch shook his head. "Morehouse is with the family now. I've been up most of the night working on leads with the task force, but it's all been a dead end so far. I just wanted to drop by and check on you. I'm considering going back to the office and crashing in one of the cots in the back room."

He fished his sunglasses from the inside pocket of his suit coat and put them on. "Look, Reid. I've got some news you're probably not going to like."

"About what?"

"SAC Johnston called this morning. The Bureau's refusing security detail for Ms. Cahill."

Reid released a breath. In some ways, he wasn't entirely surprised considering how stretched FBI resources were right now. "Even with the attack on her two days ago?"

"There's no direct evidence linking the attack to the serial murder investigation," Mitch said. "For all they know, it could have been a random attempted robbery or rape."

"Right." Reid's tone was sarcastic. "Random victims aren't lured by a phone call."

"You're preaching to the choir," Mitch said. "Unfortunately, the supposed lack of evidence wasn't enough to keep the media from speculating about the attack. I got a call last night from a reporter at the *Post,* asking about the incident in the parking garage. I told him no comment, of course. But I'm amazed they hadn't caught wind of it before now."

"What about the surveillance on Hunter's residence?" Reid asked. Mitch had accompanied him to where the Explorer was parked.

"That we have, sort of," Mitch said. "Since he's considered a fugitive from the law, the D.C. police have a plainclothes stationed in the neighborhood. No sign of him so far, though. From what I understand, his home's about to go into foreclosure. It's a nice place, too—big house, upscale neighborhood. But the lawn's a mess. Overgrown grass and weeds. The homeowners association's up in arms about it. They've left a half-dozen citations on the front door."

Reid frowned as he opened his vehicle. The poorly maintained home was an apt metaphor for David Hunter's deteriorating life. After the loss of his wife, he had lost the will to care for it, for anything. "Were you able to get a search warrant for the house?"

"Not yet. The judge is being a real son of a bitch about probable cause. The unofficial word is that he knows Hunter from his days as a prosecuting attorney and he's sympathetic. We're trying to get it in front of someone else." Mitch shoved his hands into his pockets. "Jesus, I'm starving. Got any lunch plans?"

Reid checked his watch. "It's nine-fifteen."

"Okay, breakfast."

"I don't have time," Reid said. "I've got the second part of the exam in a half hour—I'm on my way to the course now—and afterward I have some things to take care of."

"Guess I'm eating alone then, but no problem. Glad you're back, man." Mitch turned and walked toward his own car.

Glad you're back, man.

Was he back? It all depended on what Dr. Isrelsen had to tell him.

"Caitlyn, it's me." Reid knocked as he stood outside his apartment door. He'd given her strict instructions not to open it for anyone else. Soon, he heard the slide of the lock and then the turn of the dead bolt.

She stood in front of him, already dressed. He wondered how long it had taken her to manage that feat on her own. He also noticed the sling that was supposed to stabilize her injured hand was missing. Reid felt it was too soon, but didn't want to criticize. Instead, she was wearing only the brace they'd picked up at the hospital pharmacy the day before.

As he closed the door behind him, she asked, "How did it go?"

"I passed."

"How are you feeling?"

"I'm fine, Caitlyn," Reid reassured. He removed his gun and holster clip and laid them on the desk near the kitchen, suspecting he was about to be questioned.

"Last night was an isolated incident. You don't need to worry."

"Isolated? Meaning it hasn't happened before?" Her eyes searched his as she waited for a response. Reid wanted to give her solace, but he wasn't sure what to say. He didn't want to lie to her further.

"Were you able to sleep after I left?"

"Not really. I watched TV. Bliss's abduction is all over the news." She added somberly, "So am I."

Reid followed her gaze to the television set. Although the network was currently airing a commercial, he guessed the local stations were having a field day with the story, especially since the abduction had taken place at the Cahill residence. Something like that was an obvious tie-in to the original Capital Killer case.

"Is there any update on Bliss?"

"I'm sorry, Caitlyn. No."

She bit her lip. But she seemed to fight her way through her emotion, instead turning toward the kitchen. "I made some coffee and toast. I hope you don't mind."

"That's fine. You could have made some eggs, too."

"I wasn't that hungry," she admitted. "Would you like coffee?"

"That would be great."

Her hair had been pulled behind her head in a loose, messy bun. Reid's heart lifted a little when he saw the hair clip she'd used.

"Hello Kitty?" he asked.

"What? Oh." Handing him a cup of coffee, Caitlyn

absently touched the back of her hair. "Isabelle must have left it. And since I currently have the manual dexterity of a six-year-old, I was able to use it."

Reid took a sip of coffee. The hair clip seemed to have broken the solemn mood a little, until the string of commercials on the television ended and a female reporter began talking about the abduction. An image of a blonde, smiling Bliss Harper, taken on a sunny beach somewhere, appeared behind her.

"*...In a possibly related story, authorities confirm that Caitlyn Cahill, daughter of the late Senator Braden Cahill, was assaulted two mornings ago inside a parking deck at George Washington University Medical Center. Law enforcement won't verify whether the attack on Ms. Cahill is related to the copycat investigation. Caitlyn Cahill played a prominent role in helping bring her brother, Joshua Edward Cahill, to justice for the murders of six women in the D.C. area two years ago. Ms. Cahill was released from the hospital yesterday morning....*"

"I'm going back home," Caitlyn said. "Right away."

"Caitlyn—"

"This isn't up for discussion. News like this is going to affect the therapy program. I need to be there to show everyone it's business as usual. I've worked too hard to let things fall apart. If you're dead set on having a bunch of FBI agents camped out there, fine."

Reid released a breath. He might as well tell her the rest of it. "We didn't get approval for the security detail. The Bureau denied the request."

Caitlyn frowned, busying herself with folding a dish towel she'd left on the counter.

"I know you're scared, Caitlyn. You have a right to be. You can stay here."

Her eyes met his. "I can't. I have to get back."

"You'll be unprotected—"

"I don't care." She moved toward the bedroom. "I'm going to get my things together. If you can just drive me to my car—"

Reid caught her arm, causing her to look up at him. Her eyes were wide, haunted. He'd been about to give her a stern lecture, but it died on his lips.

"Manny will be back from his trip on Sunday," she said, trying to sound businesslike. "He can help with security. And I know very well how to use a gun."

"Caitlyn," Reid murmured. Her bravery both impressed and scared the hell out of him. He toyed with a strand of her blond hair that had escaped the confines of the clasp. "Counting today, I have four days before I'm officially back to work. If you want to go home, all right. But I'm going with you. I don't want you out there alone."

30

Caitlyn watched from inside the stables as Reid spoke with the reporter who'd brazenly appeared from a news van that had traveled up the dirt road. Although she couldn't hear what he was saying, she had seen him flash his shield at the beginning of the discussion. Reid wore jeans, a flannel shirt and hiking boots, his gun holstered at his hip.

She'd be lying if she said she wasn't glad to have him here. Even if it were only for a few days.

Caitlyn hadn't taken her pain medication so that she could drive her own car back from the District despite her injured hand. Reid had followed in his SUV. When they'd arrived, things were exactly as she had predicted. Several reporters were roaming the stables, and flustered therapists had delayed sessions due to the disruption. Reid had quickly escorted the media out, warning them not to pass beyond the front gates at the stables' main entrance. Caitlyn breathed a sigh of relief as the reporter he was currently talking to got back into the van. Within moments, it made a sharp U-turn and disappeared down the road.

Reid's eyes met hers, his gaze watchful. She turned as a shaggy-haired, adolescent male approached.

"The horses should have been brushed at noon." Aaron Fleming held both a dandy brush and currycomb. He spoke in a monotone, his eyes glued to the ground. "We should use long, sweeping strokes that follow the direction the hair grows. It's important to start on one side and then move around to the other side from the front…"

Caitlyn listened patiently as he continued a one-sided discussion on the various steps for brushing down a horse. He fidgeted as he spoke, his body weight shifting from one foot to the other.

"You're right, Aaron, we're late getting started with the grooming. Maybe in the meantime you can check the brushes and make sure they're all clean and ready to use?"

He gave a faint shrug that looked like indifference, but Caitlyn knew he'd follow her instructions to the letter. "What happened to your hand and face?"

"I fell," she said simply, leaving out the details.

"That's Aaron," she told Reid, who joined her once the teen headed in the direction of the tack room. "He has Asperger's. There's a group here on Tuesdays and Thursdays. We have a really amazing therapist who specializes in the disorder."

"Working with the horses helps?"

"It builds personal interaction, since Asperger's

children often lack basic social skills and can be very remote. The occupational therapy is also good for stress management."

Reid nodded thoughtfully. He seemed to be taking in the busy stable area, which had begun to settle down to business as usual once the media circus had dispersed. The Asperger's group was gathering around a docile, sable-coated horse named Romeo, petting him and feeding him slices of apple. Outside in the equestrian ring, a therapist was showing children from an urban program how to properly mount and dismount a horse.

"How many horses do you have?" Reid asked.

"There're eighteen used in the therapy program— over half of them are rescue horses." Caitlyn felt a pang as she realized she'd subtracted her beloved Aggie from the total. Aggie's stall remained empty, its gate closed, and someone had placed a wreath of daisies on the gate. The flowers had been there for a while, and were drooping and brown. "I also have two that aren't used in the program. They're a bit high-spirited."

"They're for you."

She nodded. "I rode one of them the day we had target practice."

Her mind flashed on an image of Reid holding her in the rain and kissing her.

"Reid," she began uncertainly. "You should go back to D.C. tonight. Maybe you can help with Bliss's abduction. I feel guilty having you here watching over me instead."

"There's a half dozen other Bureau agents and a

police task force assigned to the kidnapping," he told her. "I'm keeping in touch with Agent Tierney by cell phone. For now, the best thing I can do is shoestring some type of security for you out here before I go back on active duty. I'm going to talk to Chief Malcolm later today, to see if he can spare a unit to sit in front of your home in the evenings."

Caitlyn took a tight breath. "Okay."

"You trust Manny Ruiz."

It was a statement—not a question, she realized. "Yes."

"I'll talk to him when he returns on Sunday. Before I leave."

She watched as he walked to one of the stalls that contained the horse he had ridden previously. He called it over by name, smiling as the animal nudged his hands and pockets, looking for treats. Reid patted its long neck.

"Easy, girl," he spoke softly. "I've got nothing for you, but I'll see what I can find."

He really was a beautiful man, Caitlyn thought, watching Reid's gentle ministration. The recollection of him clutching his head in pain had stuck with her, and the possibility he might be ill again was something she found hard to face. Caitlyn said a silent prayer he was telling her the truth, that there really was no reason for her concern. She admitted to herself that despite whatever had happened last night, he seemed perfectly all right now.

"There's a call for you, *señorita*," one of the stable

hands, a Hispanic man in his early twenties, said as he passed by her, hauling a heavy leather saddle.

"Thanks, Pablo. Do you know who it is?"

"No, ma'am."

Caitlyn figured the call was from a reporter. It wouldn't take her long to say "no comment." She looked at Reid again, who was now in conversation with one of the therapy instructors. Leaving the stalls, she walked past the hay storage room and down the hallway to her office. A note was attached to the door and she took it down. It was a message from Rob Treadwell, letting her know he had come by. She sighed inwardly, wondering how long the note had been there, and went inside. Line two blinked insistently on the phone console on her desk.

"This is Caitlyn Cahill."

"Hello, Caity." The unexpected sound of Joshua's voice caused a jolt of electricity to pass through her. "When are you coming to see me? I thought you'd want me to draw you another map."

She could tell by his caustic tone that it was the *other* Joshua who was speaking, the one who overshadowed any glimmer of the boy she had once known. It took everything Caitlyn had not to slam the phone back onto the console. She swallowed her revulsion. "I—I'll be back out soon. I promise."

"This weekend?"

"No. That isn't possible."

"Can we talk some now, then?"

She closed her eyes. "I don't think so—"

"I miss you, Caity," he wheedled. "Give me five minutes. Then when you come visit, I'll give you two bodies instead of one. A twofer." He laughed. "That sounds like a good deal, doesn't it?"

Caitlyn halfway hoped Reid would walk into her office, take the phone from her and tell Joshua to go to hell. But instead, she reached over and closed the door with a soft snap. Pulling out her desk chair, she sank onto it. She had to do this.

"All right," she said wearily. "What do you want to talk about?"

"Bliss." He lowered his voice. "I've been thinking about her all day. About what's probably happening to her right now. If he's really like me, what he's *doing* to her—"

"How do you know about Bliss?"

"There *are* televisions in prison, Caity. I know about the attack on you, too."

"Joshua, listen to me." She grasped the receiver more tightly. "Do you know who took Bliss? Where she is?"

She could practically hear him shrug. "Sorry. I don't have a clue."

"You knew Bliss! We all grew up together. If there's anything you know that could help find her—"

"Bliss was a snotty, spoiled bitch. I hope he *enjoys* her." He must have been able to gauge Caitlyn's reaction, because he added, "We're only a minute into this. If you hang up on me now, you're back to one body."

Caitlyn passed a trembling hand over her eyes. "I'm still here."

As Joshua talked, she watched the clock on her desk, counting down the seconds until his time had elapsed. Then she wordlessly disconnected the phone, feeling a chilling numbness wrap around her. She'd listened as Joshua described in vivid, grotesque detail the things that were very likely happening to Bliss at that very moment. The same things he'd done to each of his victims, and that he'd fantasized about doing to her. His words had been low and hoarse. At the end of the conversation, the hitch in his breathing and a last, hard grunt told her he'd been masturbating.

She felt dirty, sick.

A knock sounded at the door. Reid leaned inside. "I was looking for you. One of the hands said you had a call…"

He stared at Caitlyn. "Who was it?"

"Joshua. He offered to give up two bodies the next time I…visited."

Reid came closer. His eyes were the color of cold, gray steel. "In exchange for what?"

"For letting him describe to me what's probably happening to Bliss."

He sighed angrily. "I'm sorry."

"I'm not. If it gets this nightmare over with sooner—"

She startled as a child's piercing scream came from somewhere outside the stables. Reid ran toward the sound with Caitlyn behind him.

Children scattered as they reached the outdoors. One of the quarter horses, a black gelding named Midnight, was reared up on its hind legs a hundred or so feet from the stables at the edge of the trail. A girl of about ten clung desperately to the animal's saddle. One of the female therapists was smacking at something on the ground with a long stick. Caitlyn gasped at the large copperhead amid the dust the horse's hooves had kicked up.

"Don't!" she called, rushing forward. Reid got there first and reached for the horse's bridle, trying to pull it back down on all fours. For a heartbeat, Caitlyn feared he would be trampled. The snake struck his boot. He managed to back the horse away and pass the reins off to Caitlyn, who pulled it toward the stable area with her uninjured hand.

"Get back," Reid yelled at the therapist. He took aim with his gun and shot. The snake's head exploded, although its serpentine body continued to flop and twist for several seconds before becoming motionless.

Caitlyn helped the crying girl off the horse, then sent her over to the therapist who'd been poking at the snake. She led the child away, her arm around the girl's shoulders. Caitlyn spoke softly to the gelding, stroking his flank until he seemed to calm.

"Are you okay?" Caitlyn asked as Reid holstered his gun and walked to her. His jeans and boots were covered in dust.

He nodded. "Thank God for thick boots."

Still, Caitlyn felt a disquiet spread through her, although whether it was due to the snake or Joshua's phone call she wasn't sure. She had never seen a snake in such close proximity to the busy stables before, and she felt foolish for thinking it was some kind of omen. The stable hands and program participants were talking excitedly, and a few of the bolder teenagers had moved forward to get a closer look at the copperhead's decimated remains.

"Caitlyn." Reid's voice recaptured her attention. "Did Joshua give any indication he had personal knowledge into Ms. Harper's abduction?"

She shook her head. "He claims to have just heard about it on the news."

"I'll let Agent Tierney know he contacted you. It might be worth sending an agent out to speak with him."

"You?" she asked.

"I don't know. That's Mitch's call. He's the lead on the investigation."

"If you go out there, I want to go, too. I want to find the victims for their families." Caitlyn tried to keep the emotion from her voice. "There's nothing I can do for Bliss, but I can…help them."

Reid didn't reply, but his fingers briefly covered hers on the horse's flank.

Caitlyn peered at the group now crowding around the dead snake. She thought of her brother, her mind flitting between images of Joshua in his prison uniform, her faceless attacker in the hospital parking deck, and the striking copperhead. To her, the three evils seemed to run together until they were one and the same.

31

Reid stared out the living room window as dusk settled over the farmhouse like a thick, gray blanket. Looking past the driveway, the forest of trees was already dark and blurred, making him realize all over again how truly isolated Caitlyn was out here.

He'd spent the latter part of the afternoon at the Middleburg Police Department, filling Ed Malcolm in on the situation and attempting to enlist his help. Like most small townships, Middleburg had only a handful of law enforcement officers, but at least the police chief had agreed to have a squad car conduct drive-throughs on the Rambling Rose property several times each night. He'd feel better if Caitlyn would agree to a temporary move back to the District. But at the same time, Reid understood her need to be out here—near her work and away from the tragedy of her past. He'd simply have to rely on Ruiz.

He turned from the window as she came down the staircase. Caitlyn wore a jersey skirt and soft, scoop-necked top—clothing he imagined was easier for her to get in and out of, considering her injured hand.

"You're not wearing your brace," he noted.

"I took it off to shower. It makes my skin itch. I'll be careful."

"Ready to eat?"

She sighed. "It was thoughtful of you to get takeout while you were in town, but I'm still not very hungry."

"You need food, Caitlyn," Reid admonished. He coaxed her into the dining room that was separated from the kitchen by a large butler's pantry. On the table, foam packaging held generous portions of linguine with clam sauce and a meat ravioli. There were also yeasty Italian rolls dusted with grated Parmesan.

"I didn't know any of the restaurants around here. Ed Malcolm recommended the place."

"DeLucci's is perfect. Thank you." She walked to the wine cabinet near the French doors and extracted a bottle of merlot. "Could you open this?"

Reid took the wine and corkscrew opener she handed him, expertly popping open the bottle in a few deft moves.

"Looks like a good bottle." He poured a small amount into each of the two balloon goblets Caitlyn had set out.

"It is. I have some nice wines from the local vineyards but this one came from my father's collection. The Georgetown house has a wine cellar. I brought the best bottles with me—there's no point in wasting good wine."

She grew silent, and Reid wondered if she was thinking of Bliss again and what had happened inside her family residence the day before. When he'd returned from town, using the key and security pass code Caitlyn had given him to get inside, she had already gone up to shower. But the living room television was on and turned to a news station. Clearly, she'd been searching for the latest information on her friend's abduction.

Caitlyn accepted the glass Reid handed her. Self-consciously, she ran a hand through her damp hair. "You must be tired of seeing me like this. My hair wet and no makeup."

"I think you look perfect."

In the room's subdued lighting, her green eyes appeared mossy and gold-flecked, her skin porcelain. Reid sampled his wine. He was no connoisseur, but even he could admire its velvet texture and slightly peppery taste. He pulled out a chair for her and they sat at the dining table.

As they ate, Reid steered their conversation away from the investigation. Instead, they talked of the equine therapy program and the organic garden Caitlyn grew from spring until fall. Apparently, selling the produce—as well as hormone-free beef and chicken—to some of the upscale restaurants in the Northern Virginia countryside had become a fairly profitable sideline.

"I guess I was hungrier than I thought," Caitlyn admitted as she finished off the plate of linguine Reid had dished out for her. "Or maybe it's just the company. I appreciate not being alone tonight."

Reid reached across the table, his fingers lightly

clasping hers. He wanted to ease the sadness he saw in her eyes. After a few moments, she gently withdrew her hand.

"Would you like more wine?"

"Thanks, but I'd better pass." Although he wasn't officially working, he intended to stay alert. "You should have some, though."

He picked up the bottle and refilled Caitlyn's glass. In another life, they would probably never know each other, he realized. She had been part of the D.C. political elite, the power brokers, while Reid was in many ways a public servant, called to serve and protect.

"What are you thinking?" she asked.

"Just that the one good thing that's come out of all this is seeing you again." Reid felt the need to be honest with her. "I never forgot you, Caitlyn. Not your beauty or your bravery. You made an impression on me."

She bowed her head, toying with her fork at the edge of her plate before speaking.

"I was attracted to you during the first investigation," she confessed. "I had a fiancé, but I still felt something…"

She stared into the crimson liquid in her goblet, not looking at him. "I wonder sometimes if I gave in to you—if I helped find evidence against Joshua—only because of that attraction."

"Caitlyn," he murmured, pausing until she raised her eyes to his. "I think you would have done the right thing, regardless. You're a good person. I've seen that. I *do* see that."

Her lips parted slightly, and her gaze was soft. The forged-bronze chandelier over the dining table cast golden highlights onto her hair. Spending the past few days with her, Reid believed he had almost gotten used to her physical presence. But at that moment he felt charmed by her all over again. After several seconds, she slowly scooted back her chair. "I should get things cleaned up."

Reid stood the same time she did. "Let me help."

"It's okay. You picked up the food, you should…" Caitlyn stopped speaking as he stepped closer, until they stood mere inches apart. Taking the plate she held and returning it to the table, he placed his fingers under her chin and lifted her face to his. Her chest rose and fell with her shallow breathing.

She lowered her lashes as Reid slowly bent his head, his mouth tentatively touching hers. The kiss began sweetly, chastely, then deepened as she slid her palms up his chest, her arms looping around his neck. He moved his hands to the slight curve of her hips, pulling her closer to him.

He needed her, needed this. Caitlyn's small, round breasts pressed against his chest as his mouth tasted hers more deeply. The wine on her lips and tongue was a heady sensation. If they went much further, he feared there would be no going back.

Breaking their kiss, Reid cupped the delicate curve of her jaw. She looked breathlessly up at him, her pupils large and dilated, her still-damp hair framing her face. Who he was and who she was didn't matter to him in that moment. Reid walked her backward with deliberate steps, until the small of her back pressed against the granite counter of the butler's pantry.

"Reid," she whispered unsteadily, his name a gentle yearning on her lips. His mouth came down on hers again, this time firmer and more demanding as he lifted her easily onto the edge of the counter. Her legs slid apart, making room for him so they were pressed more intimately together. His heart thudded as his hands slid under her skirt, pushing it higher as he grazed the silken skin of her thighs.

God, he wanted her. Caitlyn's head fell back as Reid's lips moved to the slender column of her throat. His hands grew bolder and he skimmed the lace edge of her panties, slipping a finger under the elastic. He was rewarded with Caitlyn's soft moan of approval. She was wet, hot. Her fingers kneaded his shoulders, then caressed the back of his neck.

"We should go upstairs," she murmured, panting against his ear. "We should—"

The doorbell rang, followed by a series of raps on the front door. Caitlyn froze as Reid groaned, pressing his forehead against her collarbone. He tried to bring his breathing under control.

"Caitlyn, honey?" The doorbell chimed again as a male voice called from the porch. "I'm here to check on you. Let me in."

"It's my neighbor, Rob Treadwell," Caitlyn said. "My car's outside. If I don't answer—"

Reid had left his SUV at the stables.

He sighed and backed away from her. His legs felt a little wobbly. He went into the kitchen to calm himself as Caitlyn scooted down from the counter, smoothed her skirt and went to the foyer. In the kitchen, he ran cold water into the basin and splashed it onto his face, then plucked a paper towel from a holder. With a deep breath, he picked up his holstered gun from the table and clipped it back onto the waist of his jeans before returning.

"I heard about the abduction at the house in Georgetown. And about the attack on you," he overheard the man say. He was tall and large-boned, with salt-and-pepper hair and wire-rimmed glasses. Reid recalled seeing him once before on an earlier visit.

"They're saying there's a copycat. Sophie was a wreck when she couldn't get you on your cell phone."

"I'm sorry," Caitlyn responded. "I haven't been up to returning calls just yet. Please tell her not to worry."

"I've been trying to reach you, too, sweetheart." He stepped closer and laid a hand on her shoulder, then slid it down to her upper arm. Caitlyn stiffened a little. She turned as Reid made himself known. Her skin was attractively flushed, and her lips appeared slightly swollen from their kisses.

"Rob, this is Agent Novak with the FBI. Reid, my neighbor, Robert Treadwell."

The man appeared surprised by Reid's presence, but he quickly recovered and moved forward to shake hands. "I didn't realize you had company, Caitlyn. Or is this official business?"

"I'm staying at the farm for a couple of days, until we can get some security worked out for Ms. Cahill," Reid explained.

"So you're her bodyguard?"

"Something like that."

Rob placed his hands in his trouser pockets and gave him an evaluating gaze. "I have to admit I recognized you from the Capital Killer investigation, Agent Novak. The original one, of course. I followed it closely. But I haven't heard your name in any of the news reports on the copycat case so far. Instead there's been a…" He snapped his fingers, searching for the name.

"Agent Tierney," Reid supplied. "He was part of the first investigation, as well."

"But you're not the *lead* this time? That is the proper terminology, isn't it?"

"Rob," Caitlyn chided gently.

He gave a small laugh. "You'll have to forgive me. I'm naturally inquisitive and all this cops and serial-killer stuff fascinates me. My wife's always teasing me about watching the true crime channel."

"Where *is* Sophie?" Caitlyn asked.

"She's at home. I was on my way back from a business meeting in the District and thought I should stop by to check on the place. I didn't expect to see the lights on and your car outside."

"Thank you for checking, but I'm really fine," Caitlyn said. Her voice sounded a bit strained. "Please tell Sophie I'll call her soon."

"She's going to want you to come for dinner." He

patted Caitlyn's arm. "And we won't take no for an answer the next time."

He bid good-night to them both, then left through the foyer. Caitlyn locked the front door after he'd left the porch. They stood in silence until they heard Rob's vehicle start up and disappear down the driveway.

"Interesting guy," Reid said.

"They've been good neighbors. Rob's a very successful architect and Sophie writes children's books."

"But they're not good neighbors now?"

"Why do you say that?"

Reid shrugged, observing the rigidity in her shoulders and the way she'd crossed her slender arms over her chest. "You just seem a little tense around him, that's all."

Caitlyn hesitated, as if deciding what to say. "I'm not sure, but I think he might've made a pass at me last week."

"You're not sure?"

"Maybe I misread his signals and he really is just being protective of me. But since then, I haven't felt comfortable. His wife is a good friend of mine."

Reid didn't ask for specifics. He could see Caitlyn's concern was genuine, and he'd noted that the way the man touched her seemed overly familiar. He made a mental note to check into Treadwell through the FBI database, just to be sure there wasn't anything in his background. Regardless, his unexpected arrival seemed to have thrown water on the fire that had been nearly out of control between Caitlyn and himself.

Maybe it was for the best, he rationalized despite the disappointment he felt. Caitlyn had mentioned her fiancé—the one who'd ended things with her during the first Capital Killer debacle. Reid had been engaged for a while, too. But Andrea had faded from the picture when he became ill. If there was a chance he was sick again, he didn't need to bring Caitlyn into something like that. He had a feeling if they truly came together, it wouldn't be a one-night stand. Caitlyn wouldn't let him down.

Caitlyn went into the bathroom to prepare for bed, unable to stop thinking about what had happened earlier. Her mind was preoccupied with the way Reid had touched her and her white-hot response to him that so clearly illuminated her need.

Neither of them had brought up their romantic interlude, however. Once Rob was gone, Reid had built a fire in the stacked-stone hearth, then left Caitlyn to watch television while he made some phone calls in the kitchen. When he returned, he had kept a careful distance, sitting in the wing chair instead of on the couch beside her.

She wondered if he again regretted what had happened.

At least she'd been with him a solid twelve hours and there had been no recurrence of the debilitating headache she'd witnessed the previous night. She had planned to talk to him about it again, hoping the time spent together would encourage him to open up to her.

If there *was* anything to open up to her about. Caitlyn stared at herself in the mirror, unsure. Then she picked up the hand brace from the vanity and sat on the toilet's closed lid, balancing the cumbersome device on her thighs so she could attach the Velcro straps.

The noise coming from somewhere inside the room was barely audible—a faint, mechanical whirring sound. Caitlyn looked around, wondering what it was. But it just as quickly disappeared. She stood with a sigh, moving back to the vanity to brush her teeth, but stopped in midstep. There it was again.

Whir.

What was that noise? It seemed vaguely familiar, but she still couldn't place it inside the confines of the bathroom. Had it always been there? Usually she had running water in the sink or shower, as well as a small CD player she used to listen to jazz. Tonight, she had turned it off, not wanting anything else to compete with the thoughts running rampant inside her head.

When she moved to the linen closet for a clean hand towel, she heard the sound once more. Her curiosity piqued, she crouched on the hardwood floor, realizing it was coming from the air vent. As she peered between the metal bars of the Victorian-style grate, the whirring started again.

She saw something round. A cylinder. Something glass?

Inside the closet, she located a small toolbox she kept there for minor repairs. She knelt on the floor again, using her uninjured hand to loosen the grate screws with a small screwdriver. As she worked, she didn't hear the sound again. Finally, the last of the four screws dropped out and Caitlyn removed the iron grate.

With a shock, she realized why she'd recognized the sound. The lens of a video camera stared back at her, the whirring noise its autofocus.

Caitlyn let herself out of the bathroom. She hurried down the hall and knocked on Reid's bedroom door, which was closed although the light inside was still on. "Reid?"

"Coming," he said. A moment later he opened the door, wearing jeans but nothing else. She'd apparently caught him as he'd been undressing for bed. His broad chest was toned and sprinkled with a light dusting of dark hair.

"What's wrong?" he asked, seeing her face.

"Please, come take a look."

He followed her, and Caitlyn realized he had picked up his gun, not that it would do any good against the thing she was about to show him.

"What is it?"

"Down there." She pointed at the open, black hole where the grate had been.

Reid moved closer, staring down into the space. She heard him curse. He turned to look at her, his features hard.

Caitlyn wrapped her arms around herself. Not even the intrusive reporters during the first investigation had made her feel so invaded. Exposed.

"Someone's been watching me," she said.

32

Bliss Harper writhed in a vain attempt to loosen her binds. Cold fear kept her trying, although her skin was raw and bleeding where she had repeatedly yanked at the tight cording.

He would be back soon.

Helpless tears formed in her eyes, clogging her throat and nearly suffocating her. The gag in her mouth was wet with her own saliva. She knew from her dull head-ache and dizziness that the stickiness on her head was matted blood.

How long had she been here? Time to her had lost all meaning, each second an eternity as she lay bound on the dirty, bloodstained mattress.

She vaguely recalled him standing in the darkened recesses of Braden Cahill's library. She'd felt terror—then relief—as she recognized him. He'd given her a good excuse for being there. At first, they'd talked about how Caitlyn was faring, but all the while she'd gotten an increasing feeling something was wrong. When he'd gotten too close, too friendly, Bliss had known it for certain.

For a brief moment, she'd thought she might be able to talk her way out of things. Distract him long enough to run away, flee from the house or lock herself in the bathroom and use her cell to dial 911. But when he struck he'd been surprisingly quick. To her credit, she hadn't gone down without a fight.

Where was she? In some basement? It was dark and cold, and smelled of mildew.

He had raped her repeatedly. Choked her with an electrical cord while he was on top of her. Burned her with cigarettes. The wounds hurt, throbbed…

A muffled, terrified sob escaped her. She closed her eyes, trying to regain control over her fear. She *would* survive. She had lived through a disastrous marriage, a bitter divorce, started over on her career for…this? Too many people considered her soft because of her privileged upbringing, but she had proved her resilience. This wouldn't be the way it would end. Someone would find her, they had to.

The ceiling creaked overhead, causing perspiration to break out over her nude body. Heavy footsteps sounded. *Oh, God. He's back.* Bile rose in her throat, her stomach clenching as she felt herself being pulled into the undertow of absolute panic. Bliss struggled frantically, feeling the sharp bite of the cords on her wrists and ankles.

He came down the wood staircase. She saw his shadow lurking in the darkness of the windowless space, next to a washer and dryer. For a long time he stood there, motionless. Watching her. She tried to scream—beg—anything, but the thick gag in her mouth curtailed the sound.

Finally he snapped on the light switch, illuminating the cinder-block room with a single, bare bulb that hung from a cord above her. Bliss blinked at the monster who stood in the doorway. He held a large knife.

"Miss me?" he asked.

33

Reid stood in the living room with Cal Bernard, one of the Bureau's computer specialists. Behind them, pale morning sunlight filtered through the lace curtains covering the large picture window.

"Thanks for coming all the way out here, especially on a Friday," Reid said.

Cal had black hair pulled into a short ponytail and a well-trimmed beard. He took a sip of his coffee. "As a favor to you? No problem, Reid. I just wish I'd been able to tell you something more definitive. It's going to be hard to find out who was on the other end of that connection."

"But not impossible?"

"As soon as he realized you were on to him, the connection disappeared. Your voyeur went through over two-dozen chained proxy servers, including several outside the country. It's a pretty elaborate setup—whoever the guy is, he's a real computer geek." Cal snorted. "Maybe the Bureau should recruit him."

Reid squeezed the bridge of his nose, his eyes burning from lack of sleep. He knew enough about computer forensics to understand Cal was talking about an advanced form of anonymous IP surfing. He didn't have a lot of hope they would be able to find the origination point.

Finishing his coffee, Cal picked up his laptop bag. "Give me a few days and I'll see what I can do."

Reid walked him to the door, then watched as he got into his vehicle and disappeared down the road. When he turned around, Caitlyn stood on the staircase, barefoot and wearing a robe over her nightgown.

"Did you get any sleep?" he asked.

"A little. I've mostly been watching television in my room. I was trying to keep out of your way."

She went into the kitchen. He found her there, pouring a cup of coffee from the pot that had been made nearly three hours earlier when Cal had arrived before daybreak. She took a sip and frowned, then dumped the remainder of the coffee into the sink and started over with fresh beans. He waited until the noise of the coffee grinder died down before speaking again.

"How are you?"

"I'm pretty creeped out," she admitted.

"That's understandable. We've been through the whole house. There are no other cameras."

The information didn't appear to settle her. "Are you going to be able to find whoever put it there?"

"Cal is going to try. He's one of the best."

For a time, they stood in silence with the glub and

hiss of the coffeemaker the only sound between them, and then Caitlyn asked, "Do you think it was Joshua's copycat?"

He sighed. "I don't know, Caitlyn. There's always the possibility it's unrelated. Just someone random who gets a thrill watching..."

He didn't complete his sentence, he didn't have to. The look on Caitlyn's face made it clear she was thinking the same thing he was—someone who got off on watching women in the shower, in various stages of undress. Even watching them do...other things.

Caitlyn leaned against the butcher-block counter. Her blond hair was bed-tousled and he could see the top of her white cotton nightgown peeking out from the V of her robe. On anyone else he might have considered the gown prim, but on her it appeared romantic and sweet.

"I was wondering if whoever broke in here a couple of weeks ago did it to place the camera."

"That makes sense," he acknowledged. It was something he'd already considered. "Especially since nothing seems to have been taken. Maybe the point of the break-in was to leave something *behind,* instead."

But at the same time, they had no idea how long the camera had actually been there.

Caitlyn shook her head. "I just can't believe I didn't notice something like that. When I think about how many times I've been in there, not knowing, I feel like a fool."

"Hey." He stepped closer. "No one expects to be watched in the privacy of their own home."

"Where is the camera now?"

"I sent it with Cal. The lab will dust it for fingerprints and use the serial number to see if they can track it to a purchaser."

The truth was, Reid was angry about the webcam. Angrier than he wanted Caitlyn to know. If it was the copycat who'd planted it, it meant the son of a bitch had been inside the house. It was a terrifying thought. But if he'd gone to that amount of effort, why not just use the opportunity to take Caitlyn as his victim?

"I want you to write down the names of any men who've had access to the house over the past six months. Anyone you can think of. Don't try to decide for yourself if they could have done it. Let me work through the list."

She nodded, gazing at the coffee carafe, which was now over halfway full. "I'll do it at the stable office this morning. It's Friday, so there's a lot going on. I need to get down there soon."

"I'll go with you."

Concern appeared in her eyes. "You must be exhausted. Why don't you stay here and sleep for a few hours, then come down?"

"That's not a bad idea," he admitted with a sigh. He'd been too wired to even catch an hour of sleep while he'd been waiting for Cal to arrive. Instead, Reid had stayed in the living room for most of the night, grappling with the idea that someone had been watching Caitlyn in the most compromising of situations. If it wasn't the unsub, it could have been anyone—a repairman who'd come in

after the break-in, even one of her employees. There was
no accounting for the perversions of otherwise normal
men.

One thing was for certain. If the hidden camera
wasn't directly linked to the copycat investigation, it
was yet another traumatic event Caitlyn was being
forced to deal with.

"Some of these are going to have to be discarded.
They've got mold," Caitlyn told the worker as she examined the bales of hay grass and alfalfa that had been
brought into the storage room for feed.

"Yes, ma'am."

"We also need to reorder the sweet feed concentrate.
We're going to be out in another week." She ticked off
the other items the stables required, including a special
mineral salt lick the vet had recommended as a supple-
ment. Supplies normally fell under Manny's responsibilities, but she didn't want to wait for his return.

"You want the whole grain mixed with molasses this
time?"

"Yes. Thank you, Rus." Caitlyn looked over the remaining bales, pointing out a few more bad ones. It was
just after 10:00 a.m. and the stables were bustling. Children and adolescents were gathered into groups around
the horse stalls or in the classroom area for practical instruction. Already, Caitlyn had helped with participant
sign-in, ordered box lunches for those who were staying
past noon, and applied medication to the hooves of a

thoroughbred that appeared to be in the early stages of a thrush infection.

While all the tasks were necessary, they also gave her something to focus on besides her current situation. The discovery of the video camera had been unsettling, and she didn't want to think about who it was who'd been watching her or for how long. Distracted and tense, Caitlyn found herself at the last stall, which housed one of the horses that was not part of the therapy program. The white-faced, chestnut thoroughbred named Sampson was a sleek, powerful animal built for speed. It whinnied and stamped its hooves in recognition as Caitlyn entered the enclosed space. For a time, she cooed and petted the horse. She needed a release, she realized as she ran her hand over its silky mane.

The woods near the stables called to her.

One of the workers helped her to saddle and bridle the horse. Caitlyn disregarded the man's worried gaze and polite suggestion that riding such a spirited animal with her injured hand might not be a good idea. Within moments she and Sampson were out of the stables and arena, starting off at a brisk trot. On the trail, Caitlyn expertly guided the horse around a group of other riders, leaving their lighthearted conversation behind her. The beginner's trail was out in the open, running alongside the fenced paddocks and farmland, but the more experienced riders often took the more rugged, scenic path through the woods.

At the fork dividing the two trails, Caitlyn traveled into the trees, in the direction of the shooting targets she'd used with Reid not long ago. She lengthened Sampson's stride, trying to lose herself in the beat of his hooves on the hard earth and the flash of fall colors overhead. Sunlight reached as best it could through the orange-and-gold-leaf canopy, dappling the ground below her. Caitlyn leaned closer to the horse, making her body nearly one with it. She urged Sampson to go faster, squeezing his sides with her legs. Joshua, Bliss, the webcam—all of it seemed to whirl around inside her head. Frustration and a helpless anger gnawed at her insides.

A half-fallen tree lay propped on a low, stone wall near a creek bed a hundred or so yards ahead of them. It must have gone down with the recent rain but had not yet been reported by the other riders. For several seconds, Caitlyn considered her options—slowing to a canter and going off the trail around it, or jumping the fallen tree.

Sampson was an accomplished jumper. So was she. But the partially downed tree was at a high, odd angle and the creek bank appeared muddy and slick. Despite this knowledge, Caitlyn felt an uncommon reckless-ness. *The need for speed.* Pushing Sampson on, they continued their mad gallop. As she neared the trunk, however, she realized its incline was even steeper than she first thought. Apprehension glided through her.

Still, she kept going.

Reid witnessed Caitlyn's approach. Borrowing one of the horses from the stables, he'd taken a shortcut through the beginner's trail, somehow knowing instinctively where she was headed. He nearly called out to her, but her name died inside his throat, fearing he might create a lethal distraction.

He wasn't a horseman, but even he could see the daredevil foolishness of the jump she was about to make. Caitlyn looked wild, beautiful, her blond hair flying behind her.

Jesus. Was she trying to kill herself?

His lungs froze as the horse arched upward and sailed gracefully over the massive trunk. Its rear hooves barely cleared the uneven obstacle—seemingly by millimeters—and then it landed on the other side of the soft creek bed, sending mud and water flying. But the ride hadn't stopped. The horse continued onward in a blur of chestnut and billowing black mane.

"Caitlyn!"

Reid kicked at his own horse's sides, setting off after them. He called her name several more times, nearly having his head taken off by a low-lying tree branch, before he saw her look back. Momentarily, she slowed the horse's pace, then came to a halt on the leaf-strewn trail in front of him. Reid was off his horse before it had even come to a full stop. He stalked forward, half assisting and half pulling Caitlyn off the panting animal's back.

"Damn it, Caitlyn. What the hell?" He caught her arms and gave her a small shake, scared by what he had just seen. It was then that he noticed how upset she appeared. "What's wrong?"

"Nothing."

"Do you realize how dangerous that was? What if—"

"I can handle myself."

Still, he felt her body tremble a little under the heavy sweater she wore.

"You could've broken your neck."

"I'm sorry," she said finally. "You're right. It was a stupid thing to do. I could've hurt Sampson."

"It's not the horse I'm worried about."

Behind them, their animals snorted, clomping their hooves on the forest ground. Reid studied her. She wanted to seem strong, but it was clear the stress of the past week was beginning to wear on her. Caitlyn had gone out to the forest to be alone, to ride off her anger or whatever else she felt.

"What are you doing out here?" she asked, taking a step back from him and wiping a fleck of mud from her face with the cuff of her sweater.

"I came looking for you. They told me at the stables you'd gone out riding by yourself. That's not a good idea right now." He nodded back toward the half-fallen tree, not yet ready to let it go. "Neither is trying to jump that."

She pressed her lips together. Reid noticed how she cradled her hand inside the brace and he hoped she hadn't reinjured it during the jump.

"Are you hurt?"

"No." She shook her head. Reid wondered if she was telling the truth. He released a tense breath and gazed into the tree boughs over their heads. He didn't want to leave her, but it was why he'd come out after her.

"What is it?" she asked, apparently sensing that he had something on his mind.

"Manny Ruiz is at the stables. He came back a couple of days early."

Her tone was cautious. "That's…good."

Reid paused. "I have to get back to the District. Tonight. Mitch just called. He needs me there for a briefing. I'm going to be starting back to duty this weekend."

Her face paled. "What is it?"

"I'm sorry, Caitlyn. They found Bliss."

34

As Reid and Caitlyn approached the stables, she saw Manny waiting for them by the schooling ring used for horse training. A dark-haired, teenage girl stood with him.

"You okay, Caitlyn?" he asked as she and Reid dismounted. His concerned gaze lingered on her bruised temple. "Agent Novak told me about what happened in the hospital parking garage."

"I'm fine," Caitlyn assured him, even though she felt shattered inside. She suspected Manny had also been informed of her friend's murder.

Reid took Sampson's reins and led both their horses into the stable. On their ride back from the woods, he'd told her that Bliss's body had been discovered that morning, dumped beneath an interstate overpass just outside of D.C. Caitlyn tried to tamp down the pain and guilt she felt. She'd been preparing herself, but she realized now a small part of her had been holding out hope that Bliss would be found alive.

"Caitlyn, this is my daughter, Maria," Manny said. The teenager mumbled a shy greeting, her eyes flicking briefly upward to Caitlyn's before returning to the packed dirt.

"It's nice to meet you, Maria." She did her best to appear welcoming.

"If it's all right, Maria's going to be staying with me for a while."

"Of course." Caitlyn thought of the apartment over the stables. It had only a small living area, an efficiency kitchen and single bedroom. "But do you think you'll have enough room?"

"The couch unfolds into a bed. We'll do just fine."

Caitlyn knew from a previous conversation with Manny that Maria was thirteen. The girl was thin, with dark hair and sad, chocolate eyes. Manny had gone to Texas to reunite with his daughter, but Caitlyn hadn't expected him to return with her. She thought of him running away with Maria once before and hoped this time she was here with her mother's permission.

"I'd like to have a word with you, Ruiz," Reid said upon returning. "Maybe we should go into Caitlyn's office."

"Okay…" Manny sounded hesitant.

"You're not in any trouble," Caitlyn told him quietly.

He lifted his ball cap from his head and ran a hand through his thick hair before settling it back into place. Once the men walked away, Caitlyn placed her hand on Maria's shoulder. "Maybe I can show you around while they're inside. If Manny hasn't already?"

"No, ma'am."

"Call me Caitlyn, okay? Do you like horses?"

"I love them." A spark of interest lit her eyes.

Caitlyn watched as Reid and Manny disappeared into the stables. She was all too aware the topic of conversation would be her safety, and what Manny could do to help protect her in Reid's absence.

"I'm sorry I have to leave."

"Don't be. I understand."

They were back at the farmhouse, having returned there after the stables closed for the afternoon. Reid had already been upstairs to pack, and his duffel bag now sat in the living room. His slate-gray eyes held worry. "I know the news about Bliss Harper has hit you pretty hard."

She wrapped her arms around herself, determined to hide her feelings. "You're needed in the city. Probably much more than I need you. I'm just grateful for the time you've been here."

"Manny coming back a couple of days early was good timing," Reid said as he picked up the duffel, slung its strap over his shoulder and walked to where she stood. "He and his daughter will be staying with you in the evenings. There will also be a patrol unit doing a check on the grounds several times each night."

She nodded, thinking that at least Manny and Maria would have more room in her house than in the cramped apartment over the stables.

"This is important, Caitlyn. I don't want you going

out alone. You stay here or you take someone with you. And definitely no more going into the woods by yourself. Promise me."

"I promise," she agreed, then asked the question that had been on her mind. "Has Bliss's family been notified?"

"It hasn't made the news yet, which probably means they're still notifying next of kin before releasing the victim's identity."

Caitlyn bowed her head. She thought of Bliss's mother and father, her two siblings. How many slumber parties and birthday events had she been to at the Harper household growing up? She and Bliss had been roommates at equine camp during the summers. They had been in ballet recitals together. Now she was…gone.

"This isn't your fault," he reminded.

She wanted to believe him, but couldn't. "I'm going to the funeral, Reid. I'll be coming back to D.C. next week."

He frowned. "I think it would be better if you didn't."

She understood his reservations. The funeral would be a media frenzy, and having the sister of the original Capital Killer in attendance would only add fuel to the fire. Worse, she didn't know how the Harper family would react to seeing her. William Harper was a well-respected appellate judge. He and his wife had been close friends with Caitlyn's parents, but they were also among the many people who'd broken ties with her family after Joshua's arrest. Only Bliss had stayed in contact with Caitlyn, and this was what it had gotten her.

Even if Reid told her not to blame herself, she feared the Harper family would. Still, she had to be there for Bliss. To say goodbye.

"I have to go," she said. "You understand that, don't you?"

Finally, he gave a small nod. "As soon as the funeral's scheduled, we'll make arrangements."

Caitlyn felt her heart ache. It seemed to her the world was moving too fast, and growing more insane with each passing hour.

Reid moved to the door. She could hear the solemn ticking of the grandfather clock in the foyer behind him.

"Set the alarm and open it only for Manny and his daughter. They'll be here before dark." His eyes held hers. "Take care, Caitlyn."

The fluorescent lighting inside the conference room cast a pall over Mitch's blunt features. For the past forty-five minutes, he'd been briefing members of the joint D.C. police and FBI task force on the latest details of the investigation. More than twenty law enforcement personnel had been called in for the Friday night meeting. Reid leaned against the far wall near the window, his arms crossed over his chest. On a display board behind Mitch and SAC Johnston were blown-up photos of the four women who had been killed, including Bliss Harper. There was also a grainy black-and-white image of the van seen leaving the hospital parking deck following Caitlyn's attack.

"Take one and pass the others down," Mitch instructed the room as Agent Morehouse stepped forward and handed the stack of photocopied sheets to a police detective in the front row. "The man in the photo is David Hunter. Caucasian male, mid-thirties, six foot, receding hairline. He escaped a psychiatric hold at Washington Hospital earlier this week."

"This is our guy?" the detective asked.

"He's only a person of interest at this point," Mitch clarified. "But he is wanted for assaulting a federal officer. He should be considered mentally unstable and has been known to carry a weapon, so approach with caution. His photo's been circulated to local news outlets, as well."

Reid listened as Mitch fielded several other questions, including one about talking to the media.

"Tell any reporter to get in touch with SAC Johnston, Agent Novak or myself. For anyone else, your reply is 'no comment.' I'm dead serious about no more leaks."

Another hand went up. "Do we have a profile of the killer, or should we just be looking for Hunter?"

"Agent Novak?" Mitch yielded the floor and Reid walked to the front of the room.

"Our data's preliminary, but more than likely we're looking for a white male, mid-thirties to early forties, unremarkable physical appearance, although he's strong enough to overpower a woman and relocate the body postmortem," Reid said, starting with the physical assessment. He moved into the intellectual and psychological aspects. "We think he has at least a four-year university degree and is gainfully employed, possibly even in a position of power or authority. He may be congenial, but masking a deep-seated anger toward women."

"You think?" A uniform gave a snorting laugh.

Reid looked at him. "The bottom line is we're not looking for a lowlife here. The unsub is probably white collar, no criminal record and well integrated into society. In all likelihood, the victims don't perceive him as an immediate threat. In fact, they may have initially felt safe around him."

"Has the copycat been in contact with Joshua Cahill?" The question came from an agent in the back of the room.

"We considered that early on, but to our knowledge, no," Mitch supplied. "Cahill's correspondence and visitations are being monitored. We've also looked into the prison guards working the wing where Cahill is being kept, but they've all turned up clean."

"Is that all, Agent Tierney?" SAC Johnston asked when the questions ebbed.

Mitch responded in the affirmative, and Johnston moved to the center of the briefing table. The room's fluorescent lighting reflected off his bald head, and he placed his hands on his hips, revealing muscular forearms. "As many of you are aware, Bliss Harper—the latest victim—is the daughter of William H. Harper, a high court appellate judge. The pressure is going to rise on arresting a suspect—let's make it happen soon. One more thing. Those of you who helped canvas the area where Ms. Harper's body was found need to report to Agent Morehouse in room three."

As the group dispersed, several of the Bureau's field agents greeted Reid, welcoming him back. He shook hands and exchanged pleasantries, then began helping Mitch pack up the photos and other items from the investigation.

"How'd I do?" Mitch asked.

"You were solid," Reid told him, meaning it.

"SAC Johnston would probably prefer you take over as lead."

"If Johnston wanted that, trust me, he would've said so." Reid briefly examined the series of cellophane bags that held the chess pawns—now four of them—as well as the Tiffany horseshoe charm that had been used to identify the first victim found in the row house. Mitch saw him looking at the charm.

"Speaking of horse country, how's Ms. Cahill?"

Reid had told him about the call Caitlyn had received from Joshua, and about the web camera hidden inside her home. He put the items in a labeled cardboard box, which would have to be returned to the evidence room. "She's upset about Bliss Harper. They were close friends."

"Did you work out any local protection for her?"

"I've got the Middleburg Police conducting drive-bys and Manny Ruiz staying at her house."

Mitch shook his head. "From convict to crusader."

"Without Bureau approval for a security detail, I don't have much choice. But Caitlyn trusts him. I'm starting to, as well."

"You ask me, a leopard doesn't change its spots. Once a con, always a con." Mitch tossed the remaining flyers with Hunter's photo on them into a wastebasket. "I'm on my way to the morgue. The M.E. just got permission from the Harper family to perform the autopsy. Judge Harper's a VIP, so they're not waiting until Monday."

Reid drew in a tight breath. Bliss's photo lay on top of the items he'd placed inside the evidence box. It stared out at him.

"I'll go with you," he said.

35

Caitlyn returned downstairs once she'd gotten Maria settled into one of the guest rooms. The teenager had been thrilled by the four-poster bed and homey patchwork quilt with eyelet ruffle, and Caitlyn had left her listening to her iPod. As she walked into the kitchen, she found Manny nursing a cup of coffee.

"I have a gun safe," she mentioned, noticing his shotgun that leaned against the wall next to the fridge. "Or do you anticipate needing that?"

Manny smiled. "Hopefully not. But I like to be prepared."

"Is this decaf?"

When he nodded, she poured a cup for herself and sat down across from him.

"How are you doing, Caitlyn?" he asked.

She shrugged, trying to count how many times she'd been asked that question over the past few days. Searching for a change of subject, she said, "I guess you heard about the copperhead outside the stables."

"I heard your FBI agent blew it away." He chuckled. "Some of the handlers couldn't wait to tell me. There hasn't been that much drama around here since…"

He fell silent, and Caitlyn realized he'd almost mentioned Aggie, or possibly his detainment by law enforcement.

"Sorry, Caitlyn."

"It's okay." She took a sip of coffee, thinking of the past few weeks. "There's been a lot of activity around here lately. So much for the quiet country life."

He nodded in stoic agreement. Caitlyn decided to take the opportunity of their being alone together to broach the topic of his daughter.

"Maria seems like a very sweet girl. And I want you to know she's welcome here, Manny, for as long as you need. But I didn't realize you were planning to bring her back with you."

"The truth is, I wasn't." The lines bracketing his mouth deepened. "Her mother's having some issues. Turns out she's got a new boyfriend, and it doesn't look like Maria's too wanted in the picture right now. In fact, Selma asked if I'd let her stay with me for a while."

Caitlyn wondered if Maria knew her mother had wanted a break. "For how long?"

"She says a few weeks or a month. But I'm guessing longer."

"Then she should probably be registered for school."

"I'm figuring that, too. I just didn't want to overwhelm her with too much all at once. I was also wondering if her mother might change her mind. Start missin' her, you know?"

"How does Maria feel about all this?"

"I'm surprised she agreed to come back with me," he admitted. "She barely knows me, and the things she's probably heard about me from her mother can't be good. It makes me wonder if things are still that bad for her with Selma."

He shook his head. "I'd hoped Selma had grown up, started thinkin' of her child first instead of just herself. But I guess not. It's funny that seven years ago she had me put in jail for taking Maria away. Now she wants me to take her off her hands. I'm glad to have her—it gives me a chance to get to know my little girl again. But I'm worried about her."

"If there's anything I can do, Manny."

He seemed to consider her offer. "If I enroll her in school, I might need your help gettin' her some clothes. It's warm back in Texas and the weather's already turning cold here. I don't know much about fashion, never mind what teenage girls like to wear."

"I'd be happy to help." Caitlyn thought it might be fun to take Maria shopping. "I also have a few things here she might like—some jackets and sweaters?"

"That'd be nice."

"Let's take one day at a time," she suggested. "But if it looks like Maria might be more of a…permanent addition, we might want to consider moving the two of you to an apartment in Middleburg. It would be closer to the school and you'd have more room. If you're worried about rent, we can discuss an increase in your pay."

"Caitlyn." Manny laid his sun-weathered hand over hers on the table. Gratitude shone in his dark eyes. "I want you to know how much I appreciate everything you've done for me. Hiring me and giving me another chance, even when you had good reason not to. I'm sorry about your friend. And I'm prayin' they catch this psycho so your life can get back to normal."

"Thank you," she said softly.

"So…you and this Agent Novak?"

Surprised, Caitlyn's eyes flew to Manny's. His were filled with quiet amusement.

"I didn't mean to make you blush, Caitlyn." He regarded her over the rim of his cup. "It's just that the two of you seem…close. If I overstepped my bounds—"

"You haven't, Manny. But Reid and I…" Words failed her, and Caitlyn shook her head, unsure of what to say. They were friends, definitely, quite possibly something more. The care between them was clear, as was the deep physical attraction. But she truly didn't know where she stood with him. Once the investigation was closed, she wondered if Reid would fade from her life again.

"He's a good man. Even if he did interrogate me like a son of a bitch."

She couldn't help but smile at Manny's comment. Caitlyn clasped her coffee cup in both hands, feeling its heat seep into her palms.

"It's just that the timing isn't right for us." Her eyes grew serious. "Maybe it never will be."

"Timing is overrated. You ask me, you don't let it stand in the way of being happy with someone." Manny stood, placing his hand on her shoulder. Then he rinsed his cup in the sink and set it upside down in the dish drainer. Picking up the shotgun, he bid her good-night. Momentarily, she heard his heavy footsteps climbing the stairs.

Caitlyn wondered what Reid was doing now. Whether the FBI was even one step closer to finding Bliss's killer. She had hoped he would call her that evening to update her, but she knew about the task force meeting and suspected he had his hands full.

Getting up from the table, she peered through the kitchen window into the darkness and glimpsed a vehicle pulling away outside. But it wasn't a Middleburg Police squad car. Instead, it was the Treadwells' station wagon that disappeared into the copse of trees as it headed back down to the main road. She had spoken to Sophie earlier by phone and she hadn't mentioned coming over. Caitlyn's guess was that it was Rob, dropping in again to check on her. He must have noted Manny's truck in the driveway and decided not to come inside.

She thought of his recent overfamiliarity with her and felt glad he'd changed his mind.

Reid stood with Mitch a few feet from the stainless steel counter that held Bliss Harper's corpse. Dr. Ketel, one of a half-dozen medical examiners for the District of Columbia, was conducting the external review of the body. Bespectacled, with thinning gray hair, he spoke into the recorder that hung over the table. "Three lacerations found on the right breast, two on the left, the latter including a near excise of the nipple."

His gloved hands explored the lacerations. "Incisions are two to three inches in length, approximately one-half inch deep…"

The verbal description continued. A body block had already been used to position the corpse for autopsy. Reid knew what would come next—the Y-incision that would open the body cavity in order to observe any irregularities or indicators as to cause of death. Not that it was necessary, he thought grimly. The blackened ligature marks encircling the throat made it clear she'd been strangled. Still, all deaths where homicide was evident or suspected required that an autopsy be performed.

"…the body bears a series of marks, approximately one-fourth inch in diameter, traveling up the inside of the right forearm. They appear to be cigarette burns," Dr. Ketel observed in an unemotional monotone. "Similar, additional marks are present on the torso and thighs…"

Despite the low temperature inside the suite, Reid felt hot in his suit, his dress shirt and tie confining. Anger and repulsion churned inside him and he looked briefly away. The body was a mess, telling the story of the agony the woman had endured. Cuts, burns and bruises covered her pale skin, as offensive as graffiti on a church wall. Whoever their killer was, he was starting to take the abuse further.

"He's escalating," Reid murmured to Mitch, who gave a focused nod of agreement.

"...multiple ligature marks indicate the victim was choked repeatedly prior to a full asphyxiation and crushing of the trachea..."

The antiseptic-laced air, combined with the faint scent of Mitch's musky aftershave, made him feel slightly nauseous. He left the room, needing a moment to pull himself together.

Toughen up, he thought critically, pacing the windowless basement corridor. But the realization that the body on the table was a friend of Caitlyn's—that she'd been abducted from a place Caitlyn still visited—made the autopsy harder to take than if it had just been a random victim. He didn't want to feel that way; all victims mattered. But Bliss Harper had affected him in particular, made it seem all too real how easily Caitlyn could be the one lying on that table instead.

He had been gone a few minutes when the door to the autopsy room opened and Mitch stepped outside. "Jesus, Novak. You're acting greener than Morehouse."

Reid rubbed his forehead with the second and third fingers of his right hand. "Sorry. I guess I've been away longer than I realized. Did I miss anything?"

"The external's over. Victim was raped, but no semen. Vaginal bruising indicates he got rough. Ketel also thinks there was penetration with a foreign object."

Reid nodded. He expected Mitch to give him hell, but to his surprise he let the opportunity pass.

"You all right?"

"Yeah."

"Take your time, okay? After this is over, maybe you and I should go have that beer. I can bring you up to speed, give you more detail than we were able to cover in the briefing."

A high-pitched, electronic buzzing noise came from inside the autopsy suite. Reid knew from experience it was the bone saw Dr. Ketel was using to open the chest cavity. Mitch gave him a last, concerned look and returned to the room.

A persistent thought ran through his mind. If the killer was escalating, he'd also want the thrill with increasing frequency.

He would abduct another woman soon.

36

The medication wasn't helping this time.

Reid slid down his bathroom wall, feeling the cold chill of the ceramic tile against his bare back. Reaching the floor, he rested his head in his hands. The throb was insistent—a deep, repeated knife-jab inside his skull, like some kind of animal trying to claw its way out.

Only a few hours had passed since he had left Mitch at the bar. He'd woken in bed, aware of the faint auras around the furniture and door frame as he stumbled to the bathroom, barely making it to the toilet before vomiting. Dizzy, he decided to stay put until the pain subsided. *If it did this time.* The pain was worse, its duration longer than two nights ago when Caitlyn had discovered him.

Another pulsating stab blurred his vision, squeezing his lungs and stealing his breath. He scrubbed angrily at the tear that slipped down his face.

If the tumor had returned…

Megan and Cooper, his father, Isabelle and Maddie—

if he were ill again, all their lives would be turned upside down, put on hold as they cared for him just as they had six months ago. He would have to take another medical leave of absence and he wasn't sure his career would survive it a second time. But even more important, the unsub would still be out there, inflicting violence and death. And Caitlyn would still be in his sights. The killer had already gotten to her once—he couldn't let it happen again.

Keeping his eyes closed, he battled the pain.

At the same time, Reid knew he was playing a dangerous game. He understood that with a growing certainty. He had been in denial, continuing to ignore the repeated messages from the neurologist's office. Leaning his head back against the tiles, he bargained with God for just a little more time.

But he would have to make a decision soon.

The Wednesday afternoon was rainy and gray, befitting the somber occasion. Caitlyn stood at the edge of mourners with Reid beside her. Rain dripped from the rim of the umbrella he held over their heads, and their combined breath fogged in the biting cold.

Wet-eyed, Caitlyn listened as the minister spoke from behind the carved-wood, pewter-trimmed coffin, a massive spray of red roses on its top. He talked of Bliss, her zest for life and the people she loved, as well as the tragic circumstances of her death. Caitlyn felt the gazes of the other mourners shift to her from time to time, and she heard their faint whispers that drifted in the chilled air around her. She clung to Reid's forearm, absorbing his strength. At times she thought he was the only thing keeping her upright.

Elaborate mausoleums and gravestones dotted the hillside in Saint John Cemetery, some of them more than two hundred years old. Stone angels, cherubs and Madonnas commingled among whitewashed, Gothic crosses. The freshly dug hole where Bliss would be laid to rest seemed in stark contrast to their ancient beauty.

"Earth to earth, ashes to ashes, dust to dust," the minister intoned. "In sure and certain hope of the resurrection into eternal life…"

Caitlyn's heart tore as a sob came from the front row where the family sat in folding chairs, protected from the rain by a funeral home tarp. Bliss's mother, Meredith, was crying, her head bowed. Judge Harper was beside her, his arm encircling her shoulders.

The minister gave a signal and the casket slowly lowered into the ground. Then one by one, each family member rose and threw a symbolic handful of dirt over the coffin while a woman sang "The Lord's Prayer" in a soaring a cappella soprano. As Felicity, the youngest of the Harper siblings, reclaimed her seat, her eyes met Caitlyn's through the crowd. A mix of grief and hatred shone on her face. Caitlyn felt new tears threaten, and then Reid's hand against the small of her back. She wanted to press her face against the lapels of his dark trench coat, gather it in her hands to anchor herself to him. But instead, she squared her shoulders and looked straight ahead.

The crowd began to disperse. Still holding the umbrella over her head, Reid turned Caitlyn in the direction of his SUV, which was parked under the orange burst of an oak along the road leading into the cemetery. The rain had increased, the late afternoon fog growing thicker, and the mourners began moving like a swelling tide toward their cars. Caitlyn glanced around, seeing Agents Tierney and Morehouse as they surveyed the masses. Reid had told her the FBI would have a presence at the service, since oftentimes the perpetrator would attend such an event in order to witness the suffering of those impacted by his crime. It was yet another way for him to enjoy the pain of others.

She felt a shiver rise inside her that had nothing to do with the cold.

As they neared the vehicle, Caitlyn heard a male voice call her name. Judge William Harper approached. He was an imposing man, tall, with silver hair and shoulders as broad as a linebacker. His black suit was streaked with rain.

"Judge Harper—"

"How dare you come here," he spat.

Caitlyn felt as if the ground were crumbling beneath her. "Bliss was my friend. I—I just wanted to—"

"You got her killed!" He shoved a finger under her nose, his wild, grief-stricken eyes narrowing under bushy eyebrows. "It should have been you! The newspaper said the killer was looking for *you* in that house."

"That's enough. Walk away," Reid warned, his voice

low and controlled. He subtly indicated the Department of Justice shield he wore on his belt.

The judge sneered. "You think I give a damn about that, son? Do you know who I am?"

"You're grieving, Judge Harper. I'm sorry for your loss. But the last thing you want to do is make a scene here."

He glared at Reid, then cut his gaze back to Caitlyn. The words were thick in his throat. "I told my Bliss not to take the listing—that place, your family—they're cursed. It should have been *you,* Caitlyn. I hope you live with that knowledge every day."

As he pivoted on his heel and strode back toward his family, Caitlyn remained frozen. Her lungs felt like stone. She couldn't breathe. The faces that passed her held looks of curiosity, accusation, or both. From under the funeral tarp she could hear Meredith Harper's high-pitched wail of grief.

"We're going," Reid murmured. His face was flushed. Caitlyn realized his hands were on her, coaxing her to move forward. She was only now aware of the tears flowing from her eyes.

As he helped her into the SUV, a starburst of light exploded in front of her face.

"Get out of here," Reid snapped at the photographer. The media had been instructed not to go beyond the cemetery gates, to give the family and mourners some respect. But at least one of them had dared to venture inside.

"Does it feel like déjà vu, Ms. Cahill?" the man

called, his camera concealing the upper portion of his face. "The first Capital Killer was your brother—do you know this one personally, too?"

Caitlyn stood openmouthed as Agent Morehouse appeared, grabbing the photographer by the arm and ushering him away. Once she was situated inside the vehicle, Reid closed the passenger door, then jogged around to the other side. But he stopped as Agent Tierney approached. She waited, rain streaking the SUV's windshield and beating on its roof as Reid and his partner spoke. She couldn't hear their words through the onslaught.

Her recuperating hand ached in the damp cold.

"What's going on?" Caitlyn asked when Reid finally entered the vehicle.

"Agent Tierney received a tip on David Hunter's whereabouts." Reid started the engine, but he was unable to pull from the curb due to the mourners still leaving the graveside. The SUV's heater blew out lukewarm air. He looked at her, sympathy reflected on his even features. Even with the protection of the umbrella, his dark hair had gotten damp, and his pale blue dress shirt and silk tie under his trench coat were splotched with water. His intense gray eyes were the same color as the darkening late afternoon.

"You're shaking." He turned the heater up a notch.

"What are you going to do?"

"We're going to check it out." He gazed into his rearview mirror, and Caitlyn knew he was looking at Agent

Tierney's dark sedan, which was parked behind them with its lights on.

"My father lives a few miles from here," Reid told her. "I'm going to drop you off at his place for a while. You can't be safer than with a retired cop."

Caitlyn wanted to protest, but she knew Reid wouldn't leave her alone. At his instruction, Manny had driven her to the District earlier that day, handing her over to Reid so he could get back to the stables and farm. After escorting her to the funeral, the plan was that Reid would drive her back home. She was being treated like a captive, and it was a feeling she didn't like.

"I don't want to intrude on your father," she said quietly.

"Don't worry about it. He'll probably make you have a beer with him and play cards."

As the flow of mourners passing in front of the SUV finally subsided, Reid pulled onto the road. Caitlyn dropped the sun visor and used its lighted mirror to examine herself. Her hair hung in limp strands around her face, framing her teary eyes. The bruise on her temple had faded somewhat, but it was still an ugly patch of pale yellow and green.

"Do you really think David Hunter is the copycat?"

Reid didn't look at her. He was concentrating on avoiding the cameramen and reporters who were outside Saint John Cemetery. They stood in the pouring rain, wearing slickers and setting up their equipment in preparation for the five o'clock news.

"My gut says no," he said. "But we'd be remiss not to bring him in if we can."

They passed through the heavy ironwork gates, just one among a long line of cars leaving the cemetery. He added, "Regardless of his guilt or innocence in the murders, Hunter's still an established threat—to himself and to others, Caitlyn. Especially to you."

37

"David Hunter!" Mitch rapped on the motel room door, then stepped to the left so that an exterior concrete wall protected his body. He held his gun in his right hand, its barrel pointing down. "FBI. Open up!"

Reid and Morehouse stood on the opposite side of the entrance, guns drawn, as well. When they received no response from inside the room, Reid nodded to the Indian motel manager who stood farther down the second-floor breezeway. He came nervously forward and unlocked the door.

"Go," Reid told him. Once the manager hurried away, Mitch swung open the door, moved back and Reid rushed inside, scanning the space with his gun poised in front of him. Mitch and Morehouse followed closely behind. The room was as rundown as the motel's exterior, with a frayed bedspread and cheap art prints in plastic frames. The few pieces of furniture were scarred and littered with liquor bottles.

But there was no sign of Hunter.

Reid proceeded to the bathroom, reaching around the door frame to turn on the light. He peered carefully inside.

"Clear," he called in a hollow voice, holstering his weapon. Incredulous, he looked around the cramped, closetlike room. Photos of Julianne Hunter covered nearly every inch of space—the walls, vanity mirror, even the mildewed shower stall. They were ordinary photos from a life lived, snapshots of birthday parties, beach trips, baby showers. Reid swallowed hard, his mouth dry.

This time Julianne was no hallucination, but something achingly real.

Driven from his home, David Hunter had built a shrine to his wife here, a place where he could be alone with her memory. An eight-by-ten-inch photo had been positioned in the center of the mirror. It was a family portrait of the couple with their two small daughters. The fact that Julianne's life had been reduced to a series of photos, now taped to a bathroom wall in a seedy motel room, was unspeakably tragic. Reid felt guilt wrap around him, his mind returning to the dilapidated factory building where his momentary hesitation had cost the young mother her life. He saw her, crumpling to the battered floor as crimson spurted from the deep gash in her throat.

"Christ, look at this," Mitch uttered, joining Reid in staring into the small space.

"Is that his wife?" Morehouse asked from behind

them. He hadn't been assigned a new partner yet, and for now was still tagging along.

Mitch holstered his gun. "It's not Britney Spears."

They all turned, hearing a noise. The motel manager stood near the bed. Apparently sensing nothing big was going down, he'd gotten braver.

"When's the last time you saw Hunter?" Mitch asked him, reentering the room.

"Maybe last night," he replied in a heavy accent. "He hasn't paid in two days."

"I wouldn't pay for this roach trap, either," Mitch grumbled once Morehouse had taken the manager down to his office to get a statement.

Reid went back into the makeshift shrine. He continued studying the photos, attempting to get inside Hunter's mind. Where was he now? Aimlessly roaming the dangerous streets of southeast D.C.? Or in Middleburg near Caitlyn's home, plotting another confrontation? The manager had claimed he'd seen Hunter only on foot—no car and no white van.

He checked the vanity drawers. They were empty. Reid lifted the lid off the toilet tank. A knife was submerged in the water.

"Mitch," he called over his shoulder. "You're going to want to see this."

The knife was something he hadn't expected, and he wondered if the M.E. would be able to match it to cuts on the victims' bodies. He'd accused Mitch of having tunnel vision—of being interested in only one possible suspect—but for the first time Reid grappled with the idea that maybe it was he who'd been wrong.

"Me first, Novak. Get out here."

Mitch stood next to the bed. He held a necklace, which he'd picked up, using the tip of a ballpoint pen. A white topaz stone swung from a thin, gold chain.

"It was in the drawer of the nightstand. Want to wager whether this belongs to Bliss Harper?"

"It could have been his wife's," Reid said.

"One way to find out. We see if the Harper family can identify it. If not them, then one of the other victims' families."

Ugly, vinyl-lined curtains had concealed the room's picture window, but someone—probably Morehouse—had pushed them back to gain an unobstructed view of the breezeway. It was still difficult to see outside, since the rainy night and the room's air conditioner had joined forces to create condensation on the glass. Reid walked closer, using his palm to wipe through the fog enough to see. Outside, the motel's red neon sign blinked, the last two letters in its name burned out. His heart skipped a small beat.

David Hunter stood at the edge of the parking lot, his haggard features lit by the sign's intermittent glow. He stared up at his occupied room.

"He's outside!" Reid sprinted down the breezeway and took the concrete steps two at a time to the ground level. He ran across the rain-slick parking lot, looking for Hunter. But there was no sign of him, no echo of his footsteps running away—only the slap of raindrops on asphalt. Reid turned, searching for the most likely route. Above him, Mitch barreled down the stairs.

The hotel and the building next to it created a darkened alleyway.

"You sure you saw him?" Mitch was breathing heavily as he crossed the parking lot.

"Yeah. I'll take the alley." Reid pointed to the street. "You go that way."

As he reached the narrow strip between the two buildings, he heard Mitch in the parking lot, calling on his cell phone to alert patrol units in the area. Reid moved cautiously forward. At the far end of the alley, he could see an opening, most likely onto Georgia Avenue. The alley was filled with garbage bins, stacks of cardboard boxes—lots of places for someone being hunted to hide. Keeping his gun in front of him with both hands, Reid kept going, his eyes searching the darkened crevices. When he reached the end, he met up with Mitch, who had come down the busy street running parallel to the motel.

"Nothing, goddamn it," Mitch muttered. He wiped water from his face. Police sirens wailed in the urban area around them, broadening the search.

Reid shoved his rain-soaked hair from his forehead. His breath fogged in the chilly air. He'd seen David Hunter—it wasn't another hallucination. It had been *him,* staring up at the hotel room.

Unless he made it to the Metrorail station, he had to be somewhere nearby.

* * *

Caitlyn sat up in the comfortable easy chair at the sound of the doorbell. Covered by a knitted afghan, she'd been watching late-night television with Reid's father.

"Stay here, Caitlyn." Ben Novak rose, picking up the pistol that had been placed on the bookshelf next to family photos. He stepped into the condo's foyer. A few seconds later, she heard Reid's voice as the two men conversed in low tones.

When he entered the living room, Reid appeared tired and wet, his trench coat and the suit underneath it sodden. Caitlyn was aware it was well after 11:00 p.m.

"Want me to get you some dry clothes, son?" Ben asked. He was a kind man, silver-haired, with the same gray eyes as Reid. Despite her last name being Cahill, he had made Caitlyn feel welcome, feeding her dinner and keeping up small talk for most of the evening.

"No, thanks, Dad. We're going to go ahead and leave. We'll let you get to bed."

"You want a bite to eat first? There's leftovers. Caitlyn and I had pork chops and potatoes."

Reid forced a weak smile. "I'm not very hungry."

"Did you find him?" Caitlyn asked. She stood from the chair, smoothing the black dress she'd had on since the funeral, and slipped back into her shoes.

"No." Reid sounded beaten down. "We were close, but he got away."

Ben had gone to retrieve Caitlyn's coat from the closet, and he helped her into it.

"Thank you for everything, Ben," Caitlyn said, meaning it.

"Take care, Caitlyn. You've been good company for an old man."

"You're far from old." She touched his arm.

"Your father's charming," she said to Reid once they'd left the condo.

"I'm not sure the criminals he put away as a vice detective would think so."

Caitlyn placed her hands inside her coat pockets to keep them warm. "I expected him to be…gruffer. I guess I was worried he'd have some preconceived notions about me."

"Like Megan?"

She didn't respond. Reid guided her around a rain puddle on the sidewalk. "Do you recall Bliss ever wearing a white topaz necklace?"

"No. But I didn't see her that often. Why?"

"We found one in Hunter's hotel room."

"Oh," she said softly, understanding the implication. She knew of Joshua's penchant for taking souvenirs— personal items from his victims that he had kept as mementos. It was likely the copycat did the same thing.

"We found a knife, too." He rubbed his forehead. "As well as a shrine to his dead wife."

He opened the passenger door to the vehicle for her. The rain had faded into a gentle mist, and it clung to his dark hair. A streetlight was nearby, making the tension in his features visible to her. She noticed again the small lines of fatigue around his eyes and realized how long the day had been for him.

Caitlyn's lips parted slightly as he slowly lifted his hand to her cheek. His fingers were cool, and she nearly shivered at his touch. She stopped breathing altogether as he lowered his head and kissed her, sending a slow heat spreading through her body. He pressed his forehead against hers.

"I need you," he whispered.

38

She removed her coat as soon as they entered his apartment. Reid closed the door behind them and locked it, his mouth finding hers.

On the drive from his father's condo, silence had lingered between them even though they'd kept their fingers intertwined on the SUV's armrest. Caitlyn had broken the quiet only to call Manny, speaking to him briefly and telling him she wouldn't be home that night.

She sighed as Reid's lips moved lower, tracing along her throat. Her head dipped back, giving him access to the wild beat of her pulse. His hands cupped her bottom, then moved to her back, playing along her spine until they found the dress's zipper.

Reid hadn't lied—his need for her was palpable, the concentration on his face intense as if he were trying to use her to distance himself from whatever was haunting him. Bliss's murder? The guilt he felt over David Hunter's mental collapse? Caitlyn gulped air, her thoughts becoming jumbled as she heard the zipper's metallic rasp and felt cool air against her back. The reason didn't matter, she realized. She needed him just as much.

Caitlyn pushed at the shoulders of his wet trench coat. It dropped to the floor, his suit jacket following. Removing his gun still inside its holster, he laid it on the end table next to the couch. She worked at the knot of his tie as he peeled the black wool dress from her upper body. Their ragged breathing was the only sound in the room as his hands molded to the round curves of her breasts, his fingers teasing her hardened nipples through her bra's sheer netting and black lace. Caitlyn pulled the now-loose tie from his neck, her suddenly clumsy fingers struggling with the buttons of his dress shirt. Even the white T-shirt he wore underneath it was damp with the evening's rain.

"In the bedroom," he instructed hoarsely, walking her slowly backward, his hand at her nape. He caught her when she stumbled in her black heels. Passing through the door frame, she ditched the shoes. At the bed, Reid pushed the dress down over the gentle swell of her hips. The garment pooled at her feet. Her panty hose came next.

"God, Caitlyn." His words were a low rumble, his eyes drinking her in. Her core felt liquid, hot, as his mouth slaked over hers.

She tugged the T-shirt from the waist of his suit pants, and he broke their kiss long enough to pull it over his head. Caitlyn ran her palms greedily over him, reveling in the feel of his skin over the hard, flat muscles of his abdomen. It was clear he'd been working out in preparation for his return to duty. His shoulders were broad and strong, and she felt the tension he'd been holding in them release as her fingers caressed and kneaded. Caitlyn pressed her lips against the center of his chest, the sparse hair there tickling her cheeks.

His hands framed her face, tilting it up so his mouth could taste hers again. Reid's tongue explored, his lips gently bruising, demanding all she could give him and more. Caitlyn felt his fingers at her backbone, undoing the clasp of her bra. The flimsy undergarment fell from between them and she gasped at the skin on skin contact.

Shakily, she worked at his belt until his hands replaced her own. Reid's face was flushed, his dark lashes forming half moons against his cheeks as he completed the task; his shoes, socks and pants joining Caitlyn's clothing in a crumpled pile.

Her breath left her as he guided her backward onto the bed, his body levering over hers. His arousal was hard and insistent between her thighs. Caitlyn rubbed against him, wild with the need to be filled by him. She was wet, the center of her body throbbing.

Caitlyn moaned softly as Reid's mouth moved to her breasts. He sampled her, sucking at her nipples. Erotic sensations overrode all rational thought as his teeth gently abraded the sensitive peaks. Her hands were in his dark hair, clinging, pulling him to her.

"Reid." She said his name like a whispered prayer. "I can't wait anymore…please."

Within seconds they were both completely nude. Reid paused, his eyes gazing into hers. She saw in them a mix of desire and yearning, commingled with yet another emotion she couldn't quite define. Caitlyn trailed her fingers across his cheekbone, his lips, memorizing his face by sight and touch. The light stubble on his jaw sent an erotic thrill through her. He kissed her once more before entering her with a single, hard stroke. She cried out with the shock of it, bringing her legs around his hips, opening herself wider. She wanted to be impaled by him, consumed.

"Ah, God, Caitlyn," Reid muttered. His mouth found hers again as he began to move inside her. The hot friction he created was a sweet torture. Their bodies fit perfectly together, each thrust making Caitlyn feel that much more strongly connected to him.

The tension inside her built, until she breathlessly called out his name. Reid silenced her with his lips, his hand slipping between the mattress and her lower back, lifting her higher, arching her until he was even more deeply inside her. Their union was meaningful, desperate, as if neither of them would ever experience it again.

She'd gone too long without having a man make love to her, Caitlyn realized. But at the same time she knew from the moment Reid had entered her life again, there had been no one else she wanted to fill that void. Her attraction to him had begun during those first, dark days of the investigation into her brother. In the two years that had passed, she was aware that it was his face she imagined above hers, his body she fantasized about during all those nights alone.

Reid's thrusts grew more urgent. As he continued pumping into her, Caitlyn felt herself tighten and spasm around his hard length. The stunning orgasm splintered her into what felt like a thousand pieces, creating a chain reaction that caused Reid to cry out. With a last, hard stroke, he reached his own release, burying his face against her shoulder.

This was what it should be like.

After several long moments, after his breathing had returned to normal, Reid raised his head and kissed her. His lips lingered against hers, then moved gently to her bruised temple, her eyelids. Her hand slipped through his dark hair.

"Caitlyn," he murmured, searching her eyes. She wanted to stay like this forever, to remain joined to him in the physical sense. But after a short while he withdrew and slowly rolled onto his side, pulling her with him so she remained tucked against his body. His heart thudded under her ear. She felt warm. Safe. Spent.

And she wondered where they would go from here.

Although he'd been quiet, she knew Reid remained awake. His fingers lightly stroked her from midthigh to the side of her breast, sending small shivers along her skin. She tried to push away the inkling that something was wrong.

I need you. His admission echoed inside her heart.

"What is it, Reid?" she asked softly in the darkness, needing him to open up to her.

But he simply hushed her, kissing the top of her head and holding her even more tightly.

Reid stared into the grainy darkness long after Caitlyn's body had relaxed against his, her breathing slowing and deepening as she fell asleep in his arms. Maybe he was being selfish, but he had needed her here with him tonight.

More than anything, he had needed to feel alive.

Bliss Harper's funeral had rocked him more than he had realized. He couldn't shake the vision of himself lying in that rose-covered coffin. Of his family and Caitlyn at some cold, rainy grave site, grieving for him. In a few short months, a year, that could *be* him.

He was falling in love with Caitlyn and he didn't want to leave her.

But he wasn't even fighting to stay with her.

He watched as she shifted away from him in her sleep, lying on her stomach so that her face was obscured by the mass of honey-blond hair that spilled across his pillow. The curve of her lower back and rounded buttocks was exposed, her long legs tangled in his bed sheets. The gentle swell of one breast appeared milky-white in the pale glow of the streetlight outside his bedroom.

Reid ran his finger along the fine arch of her shoulder blade. He smiled faintly, aware of the desire she created in him.

Whatever it was—whatever news Dr. Isrelsen had to tell him—he had to face it, and he couldn't put it off any longer. As much as he feared the scan results, they were merely a harbinger of the things going on inside his head. If the worst were true, if the tumor was back, there was only one certainty. Without treatment, he would grow sicker, maybe even die.

He knew his family wouldn't want to lose him. Nor would Caitlyn, he believed.

If I'm ill again, just keep her safe.

She protested sleepily as he gathered her back into his arms, needing to keep the warm silk of her skin against his body. Resolution settled over him. Tomorrow, he would call and make the appointment. He would deal with whatever he had to.

The sterling silver flask was engraved with Hal Feingold's initials. It had been a going-away gift from the newspaper, given to him on his last day of work. At times, Hal admitted he missed the thrill of the investigative reporter's hunt—meeting unnamed sources in seedy bars, following leads, conducting surveillance. Hunkered inside his Lexus across from Reid Novak's apartment, he was reminded of the good old days.

Hal tipped the flask and took another sip of the aged, triple malt Scotch. He felt its delicious, slow burn down his throat and into his gut. It was exactly the kind of night in which one needed fortification. It was rainy, cold—hell, it had been that kind of day. He'd attended the graveside service for Bliss Harper, standing discreetly for more than an hour among the throngs of mourners as the skies poured down. But he hadn't been there to pay his respects to the Harper family, not really.

Instead, his focus had been on Caitlyn Cahill.

An idea had been taking seed inside Hal's head for several days now. One that was time-tested and could be described in two little words.

Sex sells.

He'd seen her with Reid Novak for the first time outside her mother's nursing facility, then again today at the funeral. Novak had once again been protective and attentive to her. Overly so. There was a sense of real familiarity between them. A single question had become his latest obsession. Was it possible they had carried on an affair during the first Capital Killer investigation?

If not, one thing was for certain; they were having one now. He'd had to call in a favor to get Novak's home address, but a few hours waiting outside his apartment had confirmed his hunch.

He'd seen them kissing in the feeble glow of the streetlight. Caitlyn had clung to him as he unlocked the door. The interior lights had never even come on. Hal felt aroused at the idea of what was going on inside. He took another sip from the flask, his mind whirling with dirty possibilities. This new angle—a sexual relationship between the sister of the Capital Killer and the man who'd been tasked with bringing him down—could add the scandal and spice to help his book ascend the coveted bestseller list.

At the least, the revelation could force Caitlyn Cahill's cooperation. He wondered what information she might share with him in order to keep her liaison with Novak out of the book. Blackmail would be so much easier than breaking into her house as he'd done a while back. He'd been looking for a journal—anything—that might give him personal insight into the Cahill family's difficulties, but it had been a dry haul. Not to mention a crazy stunt on his part. Hal smiled to himself. Never let it be said he wasn't willing to go out on a limb for a good story.

Figuring he'd seen all he was going to, he had one last nip, returned the flask to his coat pocket and prepared to start the car's engine. But his hand froze on the ignition switch.

A man emerged from the shadows near the stairs leading up to the apartment. How long had he been there? Hal watched, curious, as he climbed the steps. He stood outside the door as if he were trying to eavesdrop.

As if he were considering a home invasion.

The man's back was to him. He bent to place something on the doormat. Reaching to the glove box, Hal fumbled for the pair of tiny binoculars he kept there. It took only a few seconds to focus the lenses and see what it was.

He felt the coarse hair on the back of his neck rise.

He knew enough about the investigation—had enough insider information—to understand the significance. Hal found himself breathing hard, his lungs squeezing from the thrill. He'd felt nothing like it since his early days as a reporter.

In all likelihood, he was watching the copycat leave a message behind.

The man turned and for the first time Hal realized he was wearing a ski mask. No wonder his face had been indiscernible in the shadows. Looking around, he skulked back down the steps and moved quickly to the end of the short block, turning the corner into the alley.

On impulse, Hal opened his car door, leaving it ajar. Gathering his courage, he slid his girth from behind the steering wheel and followed the man's path.

If the copycat was parked in the alley, it might be possible to covertly get a look at his car tags when he drove past. *He could do this, just like the old days.* Hal imagined the credibility boost—the media attention— he'd get for helping the FBI crack the serial murder case. Moving stealthily around the street corner in pursuit, he tried to control his galloping heart rate. He tugged at his necktie, the exercise and excitement almost too much.

There was a vehicle idling in the fire lane. It was farther down and a large, green metal Dumpster mostly hid it from view. Hal could hear the low purr of its engine. He went more deeply into the alley's dark recesses, keeping carefully out of sight as his hand dove into his coat pocket for his ever-present recorder. When the car drove past, he'd capture the tag number and— boom—Katie Couric would be asking for an exclusive interview.

In a hushed whisper, he noted the time. Forty-seven

minutes past midnight. He began describing the car, the ink-black alley, planning to use it all in his book.

By the time Hal sensed the man's presence behind him, it was too late. He felt the cord as it dropped around his fleshy throat. There was no time to scream. The cord tightened instantly, cutting off his windpipe. The recorder clattered to the ground as he grabbed for his neck, trying frantically to loosen the makeshift garrote. The man was tall and strong, nearly lifting Hal out of his shoes. His arms flailed and his stubby legs thrashed. Warm urine flowed down his pant legs.

He fought until his body grew sluggish. The man grunted and strained as he pulled the cord ever tighter.

Hal felt his heart explode.

When he hit the rain-slick asphalt thirty seconds later, he was already dead.

39

Noise from outside broke into Reid's sleep. He sat up, rubbing his hands over his face. A glance at the clock told him it was still early morning.

"What is it?" Caitlyn asked groggily from beside him.

He rose and went to the window. The blue lights of squad cars—four of them—cut through the darkness and reflected off the wet street below.

"Something's happening. Stay here." He located jeans, sneakers and a fleece pullover, got dressed and headed to the front of the apartment, grabbing his gun and shield. Opening the door, he froze in its frame. Five perfectly aligned chess pawns sat on his doormat. The pieces were details not released to the press, which meant in all likelihood the unsub had left them.

He'd been here, within feet of them.

Reid glanced around the chaos on the street, his breath fogging in the chilly air. Was he still nearby somewhere, watching to get his reaction? But he saw no one looking his way. Uniformed officers were talking, redirecting cars. The activity had been going on for a while. An unmarked sedan with a blue light on its dashboard was double-parked against the curb, indicating a detective was also on the scene.

What the hell was happening? He would have to deal with the chess pieces later. Reid carefully sidestepped them and locked the door to his apartment, then jogged down the steps toward the officers. He held up his shield. "What's going on?"

"Dead body in the alley, Agent," one of the uniforms told him.

Already, a police barricade was being set up in front of the alley that separated his apartment building from a two-unit structure housing a German bakery and a dry cleaner. Turning the corner, Reid saw a jumpsuited evidence tech taking photos of a body sprawled on the asphalt. He moved closer, another jolt of surprise hitting him as he recognized Hal Feingold's paunchy form.

"Who are you?" A stern-faced man in a trench coat wanted to know. He wore a gold detective's badge on a chain around his neck.

"Agent Novak. FBI. I live over there." Reid nodded toward his building. "I know who this guy is—"

"So do we. His name's Harold Feingold. The wallet's still on the body. Which means it wasn't a robbery."

Reid filled him in. "Feingold's a former reporter for the *Post*—he's been writing a book about a case I handled a couple of years back."

Recognition dawned on the detective. "The Capital Killer investigation, right?"

He reached out his hand and Reid shook it.

"Detective Vecchio. D.C. Homicide. We're still waiting on the M.E.'s office." He placed his hands on his hips over his gun belt. "So, Agent Novak. Feingold was writing a tell-all about the case that basically made you famous and he's found dead next door to your residence. You think this has anything to do with you?"

"I think it has more to do with the case I'm working now." Reid noted the heavy ligature marks on Feingold's neck. His eyes were open, his mouth gaping and tongue protruding.

"The copycat case." Vecchio peered at the body. "But I thought the vics were all women."

Reid voiced the theory forming inside his head. "My guess is Feingold was in the wrong place at the wrong time. He probably had me under surveillance, doing research for his book. Both he and the copycat were lurking outside my apartment and this is how it ended."

The detective's eyebrows lifted. "That's some coincidence."

"The unsub left a gift on my doorstep sometime last night, so he was in the same proximity. Feingold might've made him. Strangulation fits the killer's M.O."

"We can't get a body temp until the M.E. arrives, but based on the lack of rigor mortis, I'm guessing he's been dead no more than three or four hours," Vecchio said. "A bakery worker comes in to heat the ovens at five-thirty. He found the guy."

A uniform called Vecchio away, leaving Reid alone with the forensics photographer and the body. The camera flashed repeatedly, lighting up the alley's dark confines. Reid's chest tightened. He didn't care for Feingold, but he didn't want him dead, either. He also hated the thought that he'd let his guard down. That the killer had gotten so close. He'd been distracted last night by his need for Caitlyn and his own personal dilemma.

Another camera flash illuminated the concrete near the body. Seeing a small object on the ground, Reid borrowed an evidence bag and carefully scooped it up. The jagged piece of plastic was marked with the logo of an electronics manufacturer. Reid thought of the digital recorder Feingold always carried—it was the same brand. Unless the device had been tossed into the Dumpster, it appeared that whoever killed him had confiscated it.

When Vecchio returned, Reid alerted him to the missing recorder. He talked with the detective for a few more minutes, then walked back to his apartment. The chess pieces were still there, lined up like soldiers guarding the entrance. But the door was half-open, and Caitlyn stood in the threshold with her arms wrapped around herself. She wore Reid's bathrobe, her face made pale by the streetlight.

"He was here, wasn't he?"

Reid nodded, wishing he could diminish the fear in her eyes.

"The chess pawns," she noted quietly. "There are five of them, but only four victims so far."

He didn't respond. He'd been thinking the same

thing. His guess was that the killer had wanted him to feel vulnerable, to be aware of how close he'd gotten to Caitlyn.

"We may be able to lift prints off the pieces." Reid reached into his jeans pocket for the extra evidence bag he'd taken. He had already informed Detective Vecchio that the scene now had federal jurisdiction. "I've got to make some calls. You need to go back inside."

"What are all the police here for?" Caitlyn pressed. "What's going on?"

He could hear the buzz of the cops' voices, as well as the honk of a car horn from an impatient commuter who was waiting to be routed around the disorder. The predawn sky had begun to lighten, revealing low-lying gray clouds.

"There was a murder last night in the alley. Hal Feingold. He's dead."

Caitlyn appeared shocked. She shook her head, her blond hair swaying. "I don't understand."

"More than likely, he trailed us here, but ran into the unsub." Reid thought again of who else besides Feingold might have been watching them last night. An image of David Hunter confronting them in the woods ran through his mind.

"The family confirmed it belongs to Bliss Harper." Mitch pulled the evidence bag containing the necklace from his suit pocket and dropped it onto his desk. "Even you have to admit this makes Hunter look damn good for it."

Listening, Reid stared out the office window, his arms crossed over his chest. The view hadn't changed since his leave of absence—the same brick high-rises with tinted windows, the same sliver-thin glimpse of the park and busy urban street several stories below.

"What about the security cameras at the Metrorail?" he asked.

"Morehouse went through the digital footage last night. He was at it until after two. If Hunter used the train to leave the motel area, he wasn't caught on camera." Mitch joined him at the window. "You want to give me your take on what went down at your place?"

The two men had talked earlier by phone, but their conversation had been brief since Mitch was at the Harper household getting an ID on the necklace. Reid had quickly told him about Hal Feingold and the chess pawns, which he had already taken to the evidence room along with the plastic fragment from the digital recorder. The one thing he hadn't mentioned was Caitlyn's presence.

"Feingold was strangled outside my apartment sometime between midnight and 3:00 a.m. When I went out this morning to see why the cops were there, I found the chess pawns at my door." Reid recounted his theory about Feingold witnessing something that had gotten him killed.

Mitch frowned. "Well, the unsub knows where you live. Don't you see that as a threat?"

"I can take care of myself." He was going to have to tell him, he realized. Caitlyn's safety was more important than saving himself a lecture on Bureau protocol. "I think we need to request security for Caitlyn again."

"No means no, Reid. Why would they reconsider—"

"Because she was at my apartment last night. I think she's the real reason the unsub was there."

"She was there *all* night?"

Reid understood the implication. He gave a faint nod. "I think the chess pawns were a direct threat to her, not me. He wanted me to know how close he'd been able to get to her."

"Where is she now?"

"On her way back to Middleburg. Manny Ruiz drove into the city this morning to pick her up."

Mitch's gaze was hard. "Other than the fact that you're screwing Cahill's sister, which I already figured, is there anything else you need to tell me?"

"What do you mean?"

Mitch paced a few steps away, scrubbing a hand through his sandy hair before turning back to face him. He appeared frustrated. "At the bar the other night, you seemed...off. Distracted. Like you weren't even listening to me."

Reid sighed. "Mitch—"

He tapped his own forehead with a blunt finger, not finished. "It's like when they started messing with your brain, trying to get out that goddamn tumor, *it changed you*. This stuff with Caitlyn Cahill, even the way you acted at the Harper autopsy. You're not in the game, buddy. Are you sure you even want to come back? You need to talk to me and tell me what's going on with you."

Reid bowed his head. They'd been partnered for nearly nine years. He had wanted to know first what he was dealing with, but it wasn't fair to keep Mitch in the dark.

"The neurologist wants to talk to me about the results from my last MRI," he said quietly. "I'm having headaches again…bad ones. Something's wrong."

"Reid," Mitch uttered, surprised. "How long's this been going on?"

"For a few weeks."

"Have you spoken to Johnston about this?"

"No. And I don't plan to until I know what the problem is. The same goes for my family. Maybe it's not as bad as I think."

Mitch laid a hand on his shoulder. "Listen, if you want to blow the rest of the day off, I'll cover for you—"

"I'd rather be at work. I've been gone for too long. And I want this case closed." Reid focused on the files spread across the credenza in their shared office. Crime scene photos, court depositions and interview transcripts from the original Capital Killer case were stacked on the left, material from the current investigation on the right. "My neurology appointment's scheduled for tomorrow morning. Let's just go from there, all right?"

He tried to ignore Mitch's concerned stare. His cell phone rang. Reid dug it from his suit pocket and answered. Going to his desk, he used a pen to jot information from the caller onto a yellow notepad. The conversation took less than a minute. When he hung up, he said, "That was Cal Bernard."

"The computer forensics guy?"

"There's someone else besides Hunter on our radar." Reid walked to the door. "The webcam hidden in Caitlyn's house—Bernard just traced it to one of her neighbors."

40

Absently, Caitlyn wiped down the butcher-block counter in her kitchen. She had attempted to make herself a late lunch—a bowl of soup and a sandwich—before going to the stables, but she'd ended up putting most of it back into the refrigerator. She didn't feel like eating, her mind elsewhere. Making love with Reid had been more intense than anything she'd ever experienced. She had slept dreamlessly, peacefully in his arms, until morning brought with it the blue flash of police lights through their bedroom window.

The return to reality had been harsh.

She thought of the intrusive reporter. Hal Feingold was dead, and, based on the chess pawns, at the hands of the copycat who had been right outside Reid's apartment. The body count had risen again. Caitlyn closed her eyes, attempting to ease her frayed nerves.

She had wanted to stay with Reid that morning, but he'd rightfully shifted into FBI mode and taken control of the crime scene. For more than an hour, she had waited inside his apartment for Manny to arrive and escort her home. As she'd climbed into the passenger side of the Rambling Rose pickup truck, she had glimpsed Reid on the mist-grayed street. He'd been in discussion with a trench-coated man who was also in law enforcement, judging by his authoritative stance and gun belt. Reid's eyes had met hers only briefly before Manny spirited her away.

Outside her house, the previously cloudy day had begun to brighten. She heard the muffled voices of Manny and Maria, and Caitlyn looked out the window to see them unloading chrysanthemums from the pickup's bed. Maria had shyly mentioned her love of flowers and asked if she could work on the garden in back of the farmhouse. Caitlyn had given her free rein, even suggesting Manny take her to the nursery in Middleburg.

Dressed in riding breeches and a lightweight turtleneck, she retrieved her leather-bound organizer which sat on top of a newspaper Manny had left spread out across the table. She noticed he'd circled several listings for furnished apartments in town. As she read through their descriptions, the telephone rang. A look at caller ID told her it wasn't Reid as she hoped. Instead, the name *Treadwell, Robert* appeared on-screen. Caitlyn sighed and considered not answering, but finally picked it up. Based on the number displayed, the call was coming from the house and not Rob's cell phone.

"Hello?"

"Caitlyn?" It was Sophie on the other end of the line. Her voice trembled. "I need your help."

"What's wrong?"

"The FBI and police are here. They've got a search warrant for the house. They're taking Rob's computer! I—I don't know what to do!"

Her grip on the phone tightened. Caitlyn attempted to process what Sophie had just told her, her mind leaping ahead. Was it possible Rob was behind the hidden webcam, or was this about something else entirely? She ran a hand over her forehead, trying to calm herself.

"Sophie, listen to me," she said above the other woman's frightened whimpers. "Is Rob there?"

"He's out of town. They're in his office. They're going through everything! What's going on, Caitlyn? I heard them mention your name!"

Her heart sank.

"Hold on. I'll be there as soon as I can." She disconnected the phone and stared blankly into the hallway. Despite the overtures he'd made to her recently, it seemed unthinkable that Rob was the one who'd invaded her privacy. That Sophie's husband was the one who had been watching her. She felt disgusted. At the same time, another, even worse thought entered her mind. She and Reid had talked about the possibility that whoever placed the camera could also be the person responsible for the murders. Could Rob be Joshua's copycat?

No. For Sophie's sake, she wouldn't allow her thoughts to go there.

Caitlyn pushed the sequence of buttons on the security console so she could exit the house without setting off the alarm. Right now, she had to get to Sophie. Try to explain things to her. But she had no idea what she was going to say that wouldn't tear her friend's world apart.

"This could all be another mistake, couldn't it?" Caitlyn said to Reid, her voice low. He'd ushered her into the sunroom to gain some privacy from the FBI agents and police officers filtering through the Treadwells' sprawling, Georgian-style home. "I mean, you were wrong about Manny—"

"Computer forensics is very specific, Caitlyn. And Treadwell's had repeated access to your house." Reid stood with his hands on his hips. Despite his even tone, tension seemed to emanate from his body. "I expect what we find on his computer will corroborate our tech's findings."

"What would he be charged with?"

"At the least? Burglary of a habitation, possibly felony eavesdropping and harassment. And that's if we can't tie him to the serial murder investigation."

"God," Caitlyn uttered, feeling sick. "Where's Sophie?"

"In the living room."

She started to move past him, but Reid placed his hand on her forearm.

"What are you doing here?" he asked gently.

"Sophie's my friend. She called me. She needs my help."

Frowning, he ran a hand through his hair. His gray eyes had darkened. "This guy was watching you without your consent. Try to remember that."

He stopped speaking as Agent Tierney walked past them, heading in the direction of the house's expansive kitchen. Once he was out of earshot, Reid ordered, "Go home, Caitlyn. Now. Your presence is inappropriate."

"I can't do that—"

"How do you think she's going to react to you when she finds out her husband's been spying on you?" He didn't wait for her answer, instead supplying it himself. "She's going to be angry and hurt, and she'll probably treat you like it was your fault."

Through the sunroom's heavy glass panes, Caitlyn could see Rob and Sophie's swimming pool, now covered by a tarp for the fall and winter. The outdoor rattan furniture wore similar cloaks, as well. Compared to the summer months, the flagstone patio appeared bleak and barren. She bit her lip, knowing Reid was probably right about Sophie blaming her. Still, she couldn't deny her call for help. The two of them were supposed to have lunch together the next day—Sophie was going to pick her up. Caitlyn couldn't believe this was happening.

"Just let me talk to her for a few minutes, all right? Then I'll go. I won't get in your way."

"Where's Ruiz?"

"I sent him to the stables. He wanted to come with

me, but it's only a three-mile drive and the middle of the afternoon. I told him I'd be fine."

"Those weren't my instructions."

Her chin lifted fractionally. "He isn't your employee."

Caitlyn stared at him, wishing this hadn't been their first conversation after what had happened between them last night. Reid released a labored breath, then nodded his consent. "Fine. Go talk to her."

Traveling down the hallway, Caitlyn felt hollowed out inside. She tried to keep in her head what Reid had pointed out to her—that Rob had done something terribly wrong. But the rationale was lost in her sympathy for Sophie. None of this was her doing.

"Sophie?" Caitlyn said gently as she reached the opening into the living room. Sophie sat on the floral sofa, silhouetted against the room's floor-to-ceiling windows that were covered by ice-blue silk drapes and gauzy sheers. She clutched a crumpled tissue, dabbing her eyes.

"They're accusing Rob of spying on you."

So she already knew. Caitlyn sank onto the sofa next to her.

"What proof do they have?" Sophie asked.

Caitlyn swallowed hard, forcing the explanation out. "There was a web camera hidden in my upstairs bathroom. The FBI's computer specialist traced the connection…it went back to Rob's computer here in the house."

"That's a lie. They're wrong!"

Sophie shook her head, sniffling. Caitlyn reached for her hand, but the other woman snatched it away.

"Rob said you have a crush on him. That you came on to him and he turned you down, so he thinks you devised this whole scheme to get even."

The accusation stung and Caitlyn felt her face grow hot. She had to defend herself. "He's lying to you, Sophie. I would never do that to you or him. When did he tell you this?"

Sophie's mascara had smudged, and a blackened trail of tears marred her cheeks. "When I called and told him the FBI and police were here. Right after I called you."

"It's not true! He's been calling me and coming by—"

"Because he's been worried about you! That's all!" She picked at the frayed tissue, leaving lint on her brown corduroy skirt. "I heard those FBI men talking. They're trying to tie my Rob to those murders, too! Why are you doing this to us, Caity?"

The nickname made Caitlyn's stomach clench. "I'm not doing *anything*—"

Sophie's voice shook, its volume rising. "We've always been so good to you! Even when everyone else around here was whispering behind your back, we befriended you. We felt sorry for you!"

"Please calm down—"

"I've changed my mind." Sophie squared her shoulders but still looked devastated. "I don't need you here. I want you to leave."

"Sophie—"

"Get out!"

Caitlyn stood stiffly. Sophie's choked sobs were like arrows being thrown at her back as she retreated to the foyer. Reaching the open front door, she went through it and drew in a large gulp of crisp, fall air. Her heart ached for Sophie but it also hurt that her friend had so quickly believed the worst of her. She jumped at the sound of Reid's voice.

"Caitlyn."

She didn't turn to face him, not wanting him to see the humiliation in her eyes. Not wanting him to know exactly how right he'd been. Who was she kidding? He had probably heard Sophie screaming at her anyway.

"Caitlyn," Reid repeated, his tone less harsh this time. As she dug her keys from her purse, he said, "Let me drive you home."

"I got myself here. I can get myself back."

When she didn't turn around, he walked to face her, putting himself between her and her car.

"I'm sorry," he said simply.

"You tried to warn me." She located her keys, but her uncooperative fingers dropped them on the stone walkway. Reid bent and picked them up, handing them to her. His eyes reflected her pain, and Caitlyn had to look away. She focused on the assortment of dark government sedans and squad cars parked along the house's circular drive.

"What happens next?" she asked.

"The Loudoun County D.A. will have to bring any charges relating to the webcam. The Bureau just wants to interview him regarding his interest in you and any connection he might have had to the dead women. Did he know Bliss Harper?"

Caitlyn felt dread constrict her throat. She had to tell him. "He met her at my house this past summer. I…I had a small dinner party and Bliss came out for it."

Reid squinted across the house's wide lawn. An elaborate, tiered fountain was in its center, surrounded by sedum and mounds of red and purple winter pansies. A brick and wrought-iron fence gave the residence privacy from the road.

"Treadwell's not answering his cell," he said. "He's checked out of his hotel in Atlanta. He was supposed to be there all week. He never made it to his business appointment this afternoon, either."

Caitlyn realized the implication. Sophie's call had warned him. "Maybe he hasn't disappeared. Maybe he's just trying to figure out what to do."

"Maybe," Reid agreed quietly, but he didn't look convinced.

41

Reid spoke with Megan on his cell phone as he stared out the darkened window of his apartment. "Tell Maddie I'm sorry I couldn't be there. Give her a kiss for me, okay?"

He said good-night, regretting he had missed his niece's dance recital. His hand rose to clasp the back of his neck, massaging the tense muscles he found there. The day had been a long one. It was already after 10:00 p.m. and he still wore his dress shirt and suit pants, although he had discarded the jacket and tie upon arriving at home fifteen minutes earlier.

His mind felt heavy, overloaded. Robert Treadwell, David Hunter, his appointment with Dr. Isrelsen set for eight the next morning—it all weighed on him. Reid was all too aware his life moving forward could be determined by what a fatherly, middle-aged man in a white lab coat had to tell him.

Moving aimlessly into the kitchen, he stared into the refrigerator's contents but ended up extracting only a beer. Reid leaned back against the counter and tried to fight the worry pooling inside him. He'd placed his cell phone nearby. He stared at it, needing more than anything to hear Caitlyn's voice. Finally giving in, he retrieved the device and located her number in its storage.

She answered on the second ring, her tone carrying relief. "Reid. I'm so glad you called. I wanted to apologize."

He absently pressed the amber beer bottle against his closed eyes, its chill soothing. "For what?"

"For coming to Rob and Sophie's house today. I know that I put you in a bad position."

"I understand why you did it. It's okay." He realized she was probably upset, still worried about what Sophie Treadwell was going through.

"Is there anything new?" she asked. "About Rob?"

Reid sighed, unsure of how much he should tell her. But the truth was, he hadn't been playing by the books for a while now, not where Caitlyn was concerned.

"Agent Tierney and I got a call from Treadwell's attorney in Georgetown. He won't tell us where Treadwell is—he claims he doesn't know—but he's promising to deliver him to the Middleburg Police by Monday. He's probably trying to talk Treadwell into turning himself in before he's considered a fugitive."

"Do you think he's in the District?"

"I have no idea." Reid really didn't want to bring up the webcam but he figured she might as well know all of it. "Our computer specialist went through Treadwell's

PC back at the lab. You're not the only woman he's been spying on, Caitlyn. We found digital footage of others. A couple of them appear to be in their homes, another one in a public bathroom, maybe inside an office complex."

"The women…" Her voice wavered a little. "Are any of them victims of the copycat?"

"No." If they were, it would make it a slam dunk to link Treadwell to the murders. But at the moment, all they knew for certain was that he was a deviant who'd been illegally taping women. The link between Treadwell, Caitlyn and Bliss Harper was promising, but it wasn't any proof. Not like the incriminating evidence found in Hunter's hotel room. Still, in Reid's opinion Treadwell fit the profile much better than David Hunter.

Either way, both men were still out there somewhere.

"Are Ruiz and his daughter there with you tonight?" he asked.

"Yes."

Reid nodded to himself. "Good."

"Manny found a furnished, two-bedroom apartment in Middleburg today. It looks like Maria will be staying for a while and the apartment over the stables is really too small," she told him. "He put the first month's rent down to hold it, but they won't move in until after…"

Her voice trailed off, and Reid understood what she was thinking. It was probably difficult for her to imagine any of this would ever be over.

"I just can't stop thinking about Sophie," she confessed. "I know she doesn't want to see me and I don't plan to approach her again, but she's all alone right now."

"We found some other things in Treadwell's home office today. Hard-core pornography and some pretty extreme S&M videos. They were in a locked drawer of his desk."

"I don't believe this," she said quietly.

Reid had seen a portion of one of the DVDs and it had been particularly disturbing. A woman tied down and being gang raped and sodomized, although it was obvious from the bad acting that it had been staged for the camera. The DVDs weren't illegal, but they were another indicator of Treadwell's unhealthy prurient interests.

"How are you holding up, Caitlyn?" he asked. She met his question with a sigh.

"I wish you were here," she replied softly.

Reid swallowed. He thought of what he would be facing tomorrow. "Me, too."

He wanted to tell her, share the burden he carried. But he didn't want to worry Caitlyn until he knew exactly what he was dealing with, and how bad it was. Part of him realized that if he received the worst news tomorrow, he should break things off with her. It would be the right thing to do.

Reid just wasn't certain he would be strong enough.

Police squad cars sat in front of the two-story brick colonial in the upscale, Bethesda neighborhood. His heart heavy, Reid parked across the street, flashed his shield at the uniforms standing guard and waded across the weed-filled lawn still wet with morning dew. He ignored the huddle of neighbors on a nearby driveway, holding coffee mugs as they spoke in low tones to one another. The house's soft gray brick and black shutters were out of sync with the overgrown shrubs, and a real estate sign now announced the property as Bank Owned. Entering the foyer, he noticed the homeowners' association citations still taped to the door.

He'd gotten the voice mail from Mitch after leaving Dr. Isrelsen's office and had come directly over.

"Where's the body?" he asked a uniform standing in the hallway.

"In back, Agent."

Mitch's deep voice came from the house's rear. Reid followed the sound of it, arriving in a sun-filled kitchen with granite countertops and top-of-the-line appliances.

"I got here as soon as I could," he said to his partner, who stood in the midst of forensics technicians and workers from the M.E.'s office going about their jobs.

David Hunter slumped over a maple wood table, a nearly empty bottle of gin nearby. Blood pooled beneath him. His right arm hung downward, fingers pointing toward the .357 Magnum that lay on the Mexican tile floor. Reid's chest tightened. He took a step closer, saw the massive exit wound on the left side of the skull.

"A squad car conducted a drive-by and saw a light on," Mitch said. "This is what they found. The blood spatter expert confirms the pattern is on target with a suicide. They're estimating time of death was four to six hours ago."

A ballistics technician moved around them, measuring the bullet's trajectory from Hunter's head to where it was buried in the plaster wall a few feet away. Brain matter speckled the cheerful wallpaper.

"You might want to see this," Mitch added.

Reid accepted a pair of latex gloves, snapped them on and took the bloodstained paper held out to him. The statement on it was written in a loose scrawl.

I wanted to understand what made him do it. I thought something about it would feel good. It did for a while.

I'm no better than him.

"We can have our specialist compare the note against samples of Hunter's handwriting." Mitch's eyes returned to the corpse. "But I think we have our copycat."

Reid said nothing. Instead, he stared out through the sliding glass doors, looking at a swing set in the fenced-in backyard. The grass was unmowed and stood nearly a foot high, and a flowerbed held the brown skeletons of summer plants.

"What?" Mitch asked, lowering his voice. "We've got what's tantamount to a written confession, jewelry belonging to the last victim in his possession—not to mention a knife that might've been used in the murders."

"You're right," Reid agreed.

"Then why don't you look satisfied?"

He released a long breath. David Hunter was unstable and capable of taking his own life, certainly, but despite all the evidence, something kept whispering to Reid that he wasn't their killer. Ever since the visit to Hunter's hotel room, he'd been attempting to convince himself of the man's guilt. But try as he might, something still just didn't *fit*. He recalled how the man had confronted Caitlyn and him in the woods. Hunter had trembled and wavered, made accusations, but he hadn't pulled the trigger. He lacked the certainty of someone who had killed before, who was doing it for pleasure.

"I still want to talk to Treadwell," he said before walking from the kitchen.

Grappling with his thoughts, Reid found himself inside the home's den. The room had two walls of windows, and built-in bookcases framed a brick fireplace over which hung a painting of a field of red poppies. An area rug covered warm hardwood floors. The furniture was casual, a plaid, overstuffed couch and matching wing chairs in an intimate arrangement. Reid imagined the Hunters gathering here, watching television— mother, father and two little girls.

That family no longer existed.

Still wearing gloves, he picked up a framed family photo from an end table. He felt gutted out by guilt. No matter how you looked at it, his inability to stop Julianne Hunter's murder two years earlier had kicked off a tragic chain of events. Reid wondered about the Hunters' children, how they were faring being raised by their maternal grandparents and whether they even remembered their mother. They had both been so young at the time of her death. Megan had once told him she thought his job ate at him, had actually caused the tumor to grow inside his head. He'd laughed at her then. Now he wasn't so sure.

Reid turned as Mitch cleared his throat, sending his thoughts scattering.

"What are you thinking?"

"The garage doors are open," Reid said. "There's no white van."

"He could've dumped it. Besides, Treadwell doesn't own one, either." Mitch came farther into the room. "What are you driving at, Reid? That someone set Hunter up?"

"I don't know," he admitted.

"Here's the scenario the way I see it—Julianne Hunter's death caused a psychotic meltdown in her husband, and he began mimicking the killer who murdered her. But ultimately, he couldn't handle the guilt. So he came back here—to his home, the place that held every good memory of his wife and family, to blow his brains out."

Reid nodded faintly, still looking at the family photo he'd replaced on the end table.

Mitch gave a resigned sigh. "But, hey, if you still want to talk to Treadwell on Monday, then that's what we'll do. *If* his lawyer produces him. How did your appointment go this morning?"

"They cancelled it after I got to the office. The doctor was called away on an emergency. It's been moved to next week."

"You okay?"

"Yeah."

Mitch's gaze was discerning. He stared at Reid for several long seconds, until one of the police officers called him back to the kitchen.

The lie tasted bitter in Reid's mouth, but he wasn't ready to discuss his meeting with Dr. Isrelsen, or his diagnosis.

He was still trying to come to terms with it himself.

42

The bluish haze of dusk had deepened outside the stables. From her office window, Caitlyn noticed that only a few vehicles remained in the parking lot. Manny was still here, she knew, closing things up for the evening although she hadn't seen him in over an hour. Ever since the televised news conference, she'd sequestered herself, still trying to process the information that David Hunter was dead.

The small TV on the metal filing cabinet remained on, but she had placed its volume on Mute once the station returned to its regular programming. Agent Tierney had acted as FBI spokesperson, updating the public on the latest turn of events. He'd stated that Hunter, a prime suspect in the investigation, had been found that morning, dead from a self-inflicted gunshot wound. Evidence at the scene indicated he was the copycat.

Caitlyn realized she should feel relief—if David Hunter was the killer, it meant her nightmare was over. It also meant Rob was guilty only of the illegal video tapings, something far less worse for Sophie to deal with than murder. Still, she couldn't stop thinking about the tragedy of Hunter's life and that Joshua was ultimately responsible.

Something else bothered her. On more than one occasion, Reid had voiced his doubt to her about Hunter's culpability. Had he been wrong?

The crunch of gravel outside caused Caitlyn to look up. Reid's Explorer pulled into the parking lot. She had seen him only briefly on television. He'd remained in the background at the news conference, the camera's focus on him fleeting. Not wanting to wait for him to find her, she headed past the tack room and down the hallway, meeting him at the stables' entrance.

"Reid?" Horses neighed in their line of stalls. "What are you doing here?"

"I…wanted to see you. You heard about David Hunter?"

"I watched the news conference. We've gotten calls from reporters, but I've been letting them go to voice mail." Stepping closer, she looked into his eyes and saw the disquiet there. Something was on his mind. "Do you want to go into my office?"

Once she'd closed the door behind them, Caitlyn waited for him to speak. He had taken time to change, since he now wore jeans and a gray, V-necked sweater instead of the suit and tie she'd seen him in on television.

"To your knowledge, does Treadwell have familiarity with guns?"

She nodded, puzzled. "He's president of the local foxhunting club, and he's won awards for marksmanship. Why? I thought the Bureau had proof Hunter was the copycat."

Reid ran a hand over his dark hair. "Both the Bureau and D.A.'s office are ready to close the investigation based on the suicide note Hunter left behind. The handwriting is his. But some things don't add up to me. As disturbed as he was, I just don't see him copying the actions of the man who took his wife."

"So you still think Rob is a suspect?"

I'm not sure what I think right now." Tensely, he stared out the window into the encroaching darkness. "We're still planning to question him on Monday if he turns himself in to the Middleburg Police, although I think Mitch is just humoring me with the interview. And for now Treadwell's still MIA."

Shaking his head, he said softly, "I don't know. Maybe I'm way off base and it *was* Hunter all along."

His expression was troubled. She'd never seen him appear so lost. Caitlyn moved closer and touched his arm. "What is it, Reid? Is there something else?"

He took a measured breath, finally turning to face her. "I had an appointment with Dr. Isrelsen this morning. It was about the results of my last MRI. You've been right about the headaches. There's another tumor."

"Oh, God," she whispered. Caitlyn wrapped her arms around his neck and embraced him. His face felt hot against her cheek.

"I thought about not telling you." He paused, swallowing. "But I...just..."

Her heart twisted as his words trailed off.

Reid sat on the sofa with Caitlyn in her living room. The coffee on the table in front of him remained untouched as he filled her in on the little he knew so far.

The last MRI had shown a small mass inside his skull, which most likely was causing the severe headaches. He'd had a neurologic exam that morning, and more tests were scheduled for the following week.

"Dr. Isrelsen said there's no reason to think it isn't another glioma. It's in a different location this time—it may have been there all along." Reid toyed with Caitlyn's fingers as he spoke, his voice low. "Once I have the other tests they'll know more, including whether it's benign or malignant, and whether it's operable."

Caitlyn listened somberly. They had taken her car back to the farmhouse, leaving Reid's SUV at the stables. Despite the fire crackling and hissing in the hearth in front of them, she felt chilled to the bone.

"The first tumor was benign *and* treatable," she stressed. "This one will be, too."

It had to be.

Reid sighed heavily. "Even so, it would mean more surgery and recuperation time. I missed months of work. I don't know if my career will survive another lengthy medical leave."

"What matters is *you,* Reid. Not your job."

He ran a hand over his mouth, shaking his head. "The last surgery was…hard. Not just on me but my family."

"I'll be there with you this time, too," Caitlyn promised.

Reid bowed his head. After a moment he rose from the couch, moving to the fireplace where he placed his hand on the mantel and stared into the dance of red-and-orange flames. He must have sensed her presence behind him, because he said, "It's my fight. I shouldn't involve you in this."

Caitlyn moved beside him. His profile remained still. "I *want* to be involved."

"I feel like I'm right back where I started."

"You're not. And I'm not going anywhere." Her words were heartfelt. "Whatever happens, we'll fight this."

Reid looked at her and slipped a hand through her hair, his fingers sifting through the long strands. Then he wrapped his arm around her shoulders, pulling her closer.

"I'm in love with you, Caitlyn," he said quietly. "And I want a chance for us to be together."

She offered a soft smile. "I want that, too. I love you, too."

The pressure of his lips against hers was a comfort they could bring to one another. Caitlyn felt the solidness of his body. Their embrace was broken only by the insistent shrill of Reid's cell phone. With an apologetic look, he pulled it from his pocket and glanced at the screen.

"It's Mitch. I have to take this." He opened the phone's cover.

Caitlyn watched as he morphed into Bureau mode. Picking up his coffee cup, she went into the kitchen to give him privacy. Except for Reid's voice, the house was quiet. Manny and Maria had left a short while earlier, intending to spend some time at their new apartment since Reid was with her. Alone, Caitlyn allowed herself to feel the fear that had been welling inside her. A part of her had suspected the return of his illness all along, but it hadn't lessened the shock. After what Reid had already been through, it all seemed so unfair. She said a silent prayer the tumor would be more easily treatable this time. And if not, that she could make this go-round somehow easier for him, be his strength.

Whatever happens, we'll fight this. Caitlyn thought of Reid's fiancée who had left him when he had needed her most. That would never be her. Despite her worry, her heart lifted at the words they'd exchanged. A mist of tears blurred her vision. But Caitlyn wiped them quickly away as she heard Reid wrapping up his call.

"Do you have to go back?" she asked when he arrived in the doorway.

"Mitch wanted me to go out for a beer. He doesn't know about my diagnosis yet, and as far as he's concerned, the investigation's winding down. He's in a celebratory mood." Reid shrugged as he stepped into the kitchen. "I told him I was going to Cooper's game with Megan and the girls. He coaches high school football. The Silver Spring Wildcats."

Caitlyn placed the dish towel she'd been holding on the counter. "So you're staying tonight?"

He moved closer and ran his hands over her upper arms.

"I'd like to, Caitlyn," he admitted.

"I can call Manny. Tell him he's got the night off."

"They won't mind?"

She shook her head. She wanted to be with him, too. He needed her support right now. "No. I'm sure of it."

Reid slowly tipped her face up to his. Caitlyn sighed, her hands sliding over his chest. David Hunter and Rob Treadwell, the investigation—all of it paled as she looked into his eyes.

That night, their lovemaking was less urgent, but no less meaningful. They took their time undressing each other, savoring one another's bodies and finding a slow, perfect rhythm. Each thrust inside her brought Caitlyn closer to the realization of how deeply she cared for him.

After Reid had fallen asleep, she lay in bed next to him. The curtains inside her bedroom were open, and silver moonlight caressed his skin. Watching him, she vowed the warmth of his body and his steady breathing were things she would never take for granted, if they could somehow overcome this latest obstacle placed in their path.

Caitlyn joined him in slumber, her fingers intertwined with his.

43

Reid opened his eyes in the darkness. The faint sound had awakened him, and he strained his ears, listening for it again. The farmhouse was old and no doubt had its share of mysterious creaks and groans, but this one was recognizable to him.

The squeak of hardwood floorboards had come from downstairs.

His gaze moved to the security console on the bedroom wall. Its panel was dark. Dead. Apprehension traveled over his skin. Caitlyn stirred as he got out of bed.

"Stay here," he whispered. She sat up, her eyes widening in the shadows as she, too, heard the noise on the floor below. Reid slid into his jeans and retrieved his Glock. As he checked the gun, his voice remained low. "Is there any chance it could be Manny?"

She shook her head. She'd climbed out of bed and was tying the sash of her robe around her waist. "He'd never come back in the middle of the night. Not without calling first."

Nor would Manny knock out the security system. Reid picked up the phone's receiver on the nightstand. No connection. His heart beat harder. "Where's your cell?"

Her face paled. "It's charging in the kitchen."

He'd left his phone downstairs, as well. She followed Reid to the door, but he stopped her from going farther. "Do you have a gun nearby?"

"In my dresser bureau. I've been keeping one there for a while now."

"Good. Close the door behind me and lock it."

"I'm going, too—"

"No, Caitlyn." Their eyes held, until he sensed her agreement. She touched his arm with chilled fingers, then reluctantly closed the door. He waited to hear its lock turning before moving cautiously down the unlit hallway with his gun in front of him. Reaching the landing, Reid paused, listening for another sound. But it was quiet now except for the steady, baritone tick of the grandfather clock in the entry hall.

Taking a tense breath, he began traveling slowly down the staircase with his back against the beadboard wall. He scanned the living room but saw nothing in the dark except furniture and the glow of dying embers in the hearth. The next place to check was the dining room and beyond that, the kitchen and mudroom.

Leaving the staircase and turning the corner, Reid's gaze swept the large dining area. His stomach flip-flopped. One of the French doors leading onto the wrap-around porch stood partially open, and a breeze from outside caused its bottom to rasp against the aged pine-wood floor. Going over, he checked the door and saw that its lock had been broken. But the room itself appeared empty. With watchful steps, he retreated and began traveling down the long corridor toward the kitchen.

He made a quick check of the powder room and came back into the hallway. Reid heard the gun's roar, felt the spray of plaster inches from his head. He spun, aiming and firing at the shadowed figure who had appeared from somewhere behind him. He wore a ski mask.

The man dove into the dining room. His adrenaline spiking, Reid pressed himself against the wall with his gun poised, waiting. Had he hit him? From the floor above, he could hear Caitlyn frantically calling his name.

"I'm with the FBI!" Reid yelled into the darkness. "Put your weapon down and come out now!"

There was no response. Chances were if the intruder wasn't down, he'd run back outside through the open door. Steeling himself, Reid inched forward. He took a breath and cut sharply into the shadowed room the intruder had entered, prepared to shoot again.

The French door moved with another nighttime gust. Wind chimes clattered wildly on the porch.

A barely audible creak sent electricity through him. He turned, at that same moment seeing the flash of a gun muzzle. The explosion sounded like cannon fire, the bullet's force knocking Reid to the floor. His right arm felt heavy, numb. The figure stepped from the closet behind the butler's pantry, the black mask concealing his face except for his mouth and eyes.

Reid tried to suck in air, but his lungs refused to respond. He was bleeding from the wound in his upper biceps. Where was his gun? He searched the dark floor. Seeing it a few feet away, he tried to reach for it but his fingers wouldn't cooperate.

The man stared down at him, gun pointed. Reid tried to push himself up against the wall, his heart hammering as he awaited the trigger's squeeze. But the next gunfire came from outside the room. The man flinched as the windowed doors of the butler's pantry shattered behind him, raining down glass. He took off through the open door.

"Reid!" Caitlyn ran into the room, dropping to her knees beside him. She held a small derringer. "Oh, God!"

"I'm…okay." He squeezed his eyes closed, covering the hole in his arm with his opposite hand. The numbness was rapidly giving way to a screaming pain and warm blood leaked from between his fingers. The acrid odor of gunpowder laced the air.

"You've been shot—"

"Caitlyn, listen to me." He clenched his teeth, trying to keep focus. "Go…see where he went."

She rose and looked out the open door as a car engine started in the distance. "He parked in the woods—I can see his taillights. He's…leaving."

"Can you see the vehicle?"

"There're too many trees."

Reid's gut had been right—David Hunter might be dead, but the threat still existed. Treadwell's image loomed in his head.

Caitlyn went swiftly into the kitchen, returning with her cell phone and a stack of dish towels. Her face chalky, she made the call to 911, then helped him sit up more fully against the wall. As she pressed the towels over the wound, he groaned in response to the white-hot wave of pain.

"I'm sorry," she whispered.

"Hey," he murmured, trying to calm her. But despite his best effort, he heard the weakness in his own voice. "I think it went through my arm. It hurts like hell but it's going to be all right."

The wet, crimson stain on the towels was growing, however. His body shivered, and Reid hoped he wouldn't faint from blood loss or go into shock. He didn't want to scare Caitlyn like that. Her hands trembled as she held the dish towels in place.

"The man who attacked me in the parking garage. He wore a ski mask, too."

He nodded, swallowing. "I know."

"This means you were right about David Hunter."

His thoughts were growing fuzzier. His upper arm felt as though it were on fire, burning where the bullet had traveled through him. Caitlyn smoothed his damp hair back.

"Your forehead's cut." The laceration stung as she used another towel to wipe blood from his hairline. She shook her head. "It's probably from the broken glass. I—I tried to hit him."

"You did great," Reid whispered. He worked to breathe through the pain. His bare shoulder and chest were sticky with blood, the coppery smell of it making his stomach clench. "Just keep talking to me, okay?"

"You're bleeding a lot. Stay with me—the ambulance and police are on their way."

The fear on her face kept his eyelids from closing. He fought the growing drowsiness that would bring with it release from the agony shredding his limb.

"Rob helped install the new security system," Caitlyn said in recollection. "After the break-in a few weeks back. He recommended the system and came out with the technician to install it. He…wanted to help me out."

The wail of sirens sounded in the distance, moving closer.

"Just a few more minutes, Reid. Hold on, *please*…" Her voice sounded as if it were a half mile away. He struggled to stay alert, but the darkness had begun to tug harder at him.

It slowly won.

44

"It was a clean shot. Through and through," Agent Tierney said to Caitlyn as he reentered the surgical waiting room. He'd used his DOJ shield to solicit information on Reid's condition. "The bullet missed bone but nicked the brachial artery. He's damn lucky he didn't bleed out."

She nodded, relief threading through her. The foam cup of coffee she held had long since turned cold. "Thank you for finding out."

Tierney's large frame filled the chair beside her. She had contacted him as soon as the ambulance she'd ridden in with Reid arrived at the regional hospital in Leesburg.

"I just spoke to SAC Johnston by phone," he said. "What about Reid's family? Have they been notified?"

She rubbed her forehead tiredly. "He woke up in the ambulance and asked me not to call them unless it was bad. I haven't been sure what to do."

"They've been through a lot with his tumor scare.

I can understand him not wanting to worry them. Still, I think they need to know. You want me to call?"

Caitlyn wore jeans and a thin, merino wool sweater, the first things she could find in her closet once Reid had left her locked inside her bedroom. The sweater was now blotched with rusty stains. *Reid's blood.* She shivered a little in the hospital's artificial coolness. The place smelled like antiseptic and sickness.

"No. I'll do it," she said. He had been injured at her home, protecting her. She owed Megan and Ben that much.

"You want to tell me what happened?"

Caitlyn had already recounted the event to the Middleburg police officer who'd arrived at the E.R. behind the ambulance, but she prepared to run through it again. She sat the coffee cup next to a stack of ancient magazines and tucked a few pale strands of hair behind her ear. "We heard someone downstairs—"

"Where were you and Agent Novak?"

"We were in my bedroom." Her face grew warm with the admission. "It was a little before midnight. The security system and phones were knocked out, too. Reid went to investigate. I heard shots and I got scared, so I came down with my gun. Reid was on the floor in the dining room. The man was standing over him. He had on a ski mask."

She closed her eyes at the unwanted recollection. "I fired."

"Did you hit him?"

"I don't think so. He ran out the door."

"What about the vehicle?"

She shook her head. "I'm sorry."

"I talked to Reid by phone around six-thirty last night. He said he was going to his brother-in-law's high school football game." He gave Caitlyn an evaluating gaze. "I guess he had a change of plans."

She was certain her blush had deepened. If Agent Tierney hadn't known about Reid and her before, he did now.

He'd been shot. Caitlyn still couldn't believe what had happened. Only a few hours earlier, she'd thought their most imminent threat was the new tumor discovered inside Reid's head. And now he was lying in a hospital with a gunshot wound. It all seemed like some sort of bad dream. She recalled him telling her that Agent Tierney didn't know about his diagnosis yet. Regardless, it wasn't her place to tell him.

"Reid didn't believe David Hunter was the copycat," she said quietly.

"I'm aware of that." Tierney appeared weary himself, the room's harsh fluorescent lighting emphasizing the dark circles under his eyes. "And based on what went down at your home tonight, it looks like he might be right. Do you think the intruder could've been Treadwell?"

Caitlyn ran her hands over the thighs of her jeans in contemplation. "I don't know. He was the right size, but I can't be certain."

He grunted and rubbed a hand over his jaw. "At this point, the only thing I feel sure about is that the investigation isn't over. The police are conducting a sweep of the area around your property. They have surveillance on Treadwell's home but he hasn't come back there."

Their conversation briefly halted as an orderly in green scrubs strode past the waiting room, pushing an EKG cart. One of its wheels needed oiling and it squeaked noisily down the hallway. Overhead, the intercom system paged a physician to the E.R.

"Reid and I have been partnered for almost nine years," he stated once the sound had faded. He appeared pensive instead of his usual gruff self. "That's a hell of a lot longer than either of my marriages. We make a good team, Ms. Cahill."

"He's told me that, too." She added gently, "And you really should start calling me Caitlyn."

He stretched out his legs. "Maybe. But you should keep calling me Agent Tierney. Even my mother does. Everyone but Reid, actually."

Caitlyn smiled faintly at his joke, then dug into her bag, searching for her cell phone. "If you'll excuse me, I'm going to step into the hall and call Reid's sister."

"It'll take them an hour or more to get here. They're in Silver Spring, and they'll probably have to find someone to stay with the girls. Why don't I give you a ride home?"

She shook her head. "I'm staying here."

"He's in recovery—the nurse said it would be a while before he's moved to a room." He looked pointedly at Caitlyn's bloodstained sweater. "And I'm thinking when his family arrives, you might not want to be wearing *that*."

Her lips parted in realization. He was right—she couldn't face Ben or Megan looking like this. It would only frighten them further.

"I'm going to your house anyway. Now that I know Reid's out of the woods, I need to take control of the crime scene from the local boys." Agent Tierney stifled a yawn with his fist as he stood. "You can make the call from the car. After you've changed, I'll have a cop escort you back. With all the hell breaking loose around here, you don't need to be out alone."

"All right."

"I'm going by the men's room. I'll meet you downstairs."

Gathering her things, Caitlyn stopped at the nurses' station, leaving her cell number in case Reid's condition changed before she returned.

They stopped at a convenience store outside Leesburg for gas. As Agent Tierney pumped and went inside to pay, Caitlyn remained in the car, her mind still on her brief conversation with Reid's sister. They had spoken for less than a minute, with Caitlyn quickly explaining what had happened, where Reid was and that he was going to be all right. Megan had promised to be there as soon as she could and then disconnected the phone. She hadn't seemed angry or accusatory, just scared. Not that Caitlyn could blame her.

Without the heater running, the sedan's interior had

turned cool. Placing her cell phone on the car seat, she rubbed her hands over her upper arms as she gazed at Tierney through the store's window. He stood in line behind a woman with a fussy child on her hip, waiting for his turn at the register. Caitlyn willed the woman to hurry and complete her purchase, wanting to get home to change so she could return to the hospital. She breathed a sigh of relief when he finally pushed through the plate-glass doors, stuffing what appeared to be a pack of cigarettes into the pocket of his suit coat.

"Did you see that?" he asked, scowling as he slid into the driver's side. He closed the door and shrugged into his seat belt. "Why would anyone have a kid out at this hour?"

Caitlyn shook her head in agreement.

They pulled back onto the highway and headed toward Middleburg. Conversation waned between them, with Tierney seeming to concentrate on his driving. Her hands in her lap, Caitlyn watched the occasional approach of headlights on cars headed in the opposite direction. A few minutes later, an intersection light ahead of them turned yellow. Tierney began to slow the vehicle, which until then had been traveling at a rather accelerated speed.

"Freaking lights," he muttered, braking harder as it switched to red. As the car came to a stop, inertia caused Caitlyn's phone to slip from the leather seat onto the floorboard.

"My cell." Undoing her seat belt, she reached down, feeling around for it in the darkness. Her fingers closed around a thin rectangular object. Caitlyn sat up. She held a digital tape recorder, although its casing was cracked and a chunk of plastic was missing from one side.

"There's a lot of junk sliding around down there. I'm always losing things—it's like the Bermuda Triangle," he commented. "Mind putting that in the glove box for me?"

Caitlyn did as requested and then finally located her phone, which she placed inside her purse this time. She refastened her seat belt just as the car rolled forward again. Tierney clicked on the radio and searched for a station, finally drumming his fingers on the steering wheel in time to an old, eighties Pat Benatar song.

He sang along with the chorus in an off-key baritone. Caitlyn felt uncomfortable. She never knew how to react to people who enjoyed singing aloud, and she wondered vaguely if he ever did it in the car with Reid. Thankfully, the exit toward her house was just ahead.

"Turn right at the sign," she said, uncertain as to how familiar he was with the area. He gave a curt nod of acknowledgment. But when they reached the turnoff point, the car remained on the same path.

"I...I think we missed it."

He didn't respond. They passed by a lit billboard, and Caitlyn caught a second-long flash of his profile before it disappeared again into shadow. He'd stopped singing, his face stern and unreadable.

"Agent Tierney, did you hear me?"

"I heard you," he replied in a calm tone. His fingers curled more tightly around the steering wheel. "There's been a change of plans, Caity."

45

Reid awoke, feeling groggy and disoriented. Within seconds, Megan's face came into soft focus above his bed. She leaned over him, her dark hair silhouetted by the light from a television mounted to a pale blue wall.

"Reid?" Relief flooded her features. He tried to rub at his blurry vision, but something restricted his movement.

"Be careful. You're hooked to an IV." Gently, she lowered his hand to the sheets.

He heard his own raspy voice. "What are they giving me?"

"Fluids and antibiotics. Probably a painkiller. You were *shot*, Reid. Do you even remember that? The doctor said there might be some memory gaps. You lost a lot of blood."

He struggled to think. He had been at Caitlyn's—he'd gone to the stables after the news conference, wanting to be with her after receiving his MRI results. A faint recollection of making love to her, and then of someone being in her house, pierced the fog inside his head. "I'm back in the District?"

"No. You're in the regional hospital in Leesburg. You have a through and through to your upper arm. And you need to rest." She frowned worriedly. "It could've been much worse. They said the bullet nicked an artery. How do you feel?"

"Like hell," he whispered.

She laid her fingers over his forearm. "It's hard seeing you like this again—in a hospital bed."

Reid closed his eyes and swallowed, thinking of the new diagnosis he would eventually have to share with her. But now wasn't the time. His bandaged arm throbbed as he searched for the panel that would raise the mattress to an upright position. He realized who was missing.

"Where's Caitlyn?"

"You shouldn't be sitting up just yet—"

"Megan, is she here?"

"**She**'s here somewhere, I'm sure. Just relax, okay? She's the one who called to tell me what happened and where you were. Cooper and I have only been here a little while. Dad's on his way—Cooper's waiting for him in the lobby."

Reid released a breath. If Caitlyn had contacted Megan, it was a good sign she was okay. Still, he wanted her nearby. After what had happened, it was clear she needed protection more than ever. "Will you find her for me?"

"All right. But keep your voice down." Megan indicated the curtain dividing the room. "You have a room-mate."

Once she'd left, Reid tried to summon up exactly what had happened at Caitlyn's house. The shadowy image of a man standing over him was disconcerting. He concentrated on the vague picture he had of him, recalling his size and the dark ski mask concealing his features. Had it been Treadwell? Caitlyn had fired on the intruder, causing him to flee.

There was something else he needed to remember, something about the dining room, but it lingered at the edges of his still-drugged brain.

"I can't find her, but it's a big hospital," Megan said when she returned several minutes later. "Don't worry. She left her cell phone number at the nurses' station and asked to be contacted if your condition changed."

"Give me your phone, Meg."

She fished it from her shoulder bag and handed it to him. Reid called Caitlyn's cell but it went directly to voice mail. It wasn't like her to not be here with him, especially considering the circumstances. He worked through the possibilities—that she was somewhere inside the hospital, in a restricted area that didn't allow cellular phones. Or she was being interviewed by law enforcement off-site. It was even possible she'd retreated to give his family some space. Reid left a message, asking her to call him in his hospital room.

He phoned Mitch next. His partner answered on the second ring. "Tierney."

"Mitch, it's me."

He sounded surprised. "I didn't recognize the number. You're awake already."

"Yeah." Reid squeezed the bridge of his nose. "Where are you?"

"I'm at Ms. Cahill's residence in Middleburg." Reid heard conversation and noise through the phone in the background. "The place is a mess—bullet fragments in plaster, broken glass all over the dining room, not to mention a nice bloodstain on what I imagine are vintage hardwood floors. Is that *yours,* buddy?"

"Is Caitlyn with you?"

"Hold on a second." Mitch barked out a warning about evidence contamination, then returned to the conversation. "Christ. Some of these country-mouse cops act like they've never worked a crime scene—"

"Mitch, listen to me. Have you seen Caitlyn tonight?"

"Yeah, sure," he said. "She was at the hospital. She's the one who called me."

"Where did you see her last?"

"In the third-floor waiting room outside surgery. I sat with her until I had to leave to come over here."

"How long ago was that?"

"About an hour ago, I guess."

"I can't find her and she's not answering her cell."

"She's there somewhere," Mitch assured him. "She was pretty worn-out—maybe she's in the cafeteria getting coffee. Besides, cell reception is piss-poor in areas of the hospital. I couldn't get a call out myself."

He lowered his voice. "By the way, Johnston's here. He's on his way there next. You should be prepared to explain why you were at her house overnight, since there's no official security detail."

At the moment, SAC Johnston was the last thing Reid was worried about.

"Hey," Mitch said, "Is your family there yet?"

Reid's hand twisted the bedsheets, frustration and worry bearing down on him. "Yeah."

"That's good. Look, I've got some questions for you about what happened here. I hate to admit it, but you might be right about Treadwell. That he set Hunter up." Mitch pulled away from the phone again, talking to someone about a chain of custody issue. Then he said, "Look, Reid, I've got to go. I'm going to get this scene closed down and go home and grab a few hours of sleep. I'll talk to you in the morning when your head's clear."

"I need you to find Caitlyn—"

"And I'm telling you, she's there at the hospital. Get some rest, okay?"

The phone went dead. Reid looked at Megan. She sat bleary-eyed and yawning in a vinyl-padded chair, her gaze on a television infomercial, about the only thing airing at 4:00 a.m. Reid felt a wave of guilt. Still fighting the sedative effects of the medication, he laid his head on the pillow, again running through the possibilities of where Caitlyn could be.

She had to turn up soon.

Some time later, he opened his eyes, startled and angry with himself that he'd dozed off. He didn't know which was worse—the soreness radiating through his arm and shoulder or the fuzzy cloud the drugs had put him in. Megan was gone but an orderly was in the room, emptying the wastebaskets. The aroma of the man's spicy aftershave wafted in the air. The scent jogged Reid's subconscious, causing him to remember the thing that had been eluding his grasp. There had been a recognizable scent in the dining room, mingling with the acrid odor of gunpowder.

Cologne.

The orderly walked out, taking the bagged trash with him.

Reid dismissed the eccentric thought, chalking up the recollection of Mitch's musky aftershave to confusion from the blood loss, or even the tumor jumbling memories inside his head. A glance at the room's round-faced wall clock told him another thirty minutes had elapsed. Still no sign of Caitlyn. Where was she?

Hoping to convince him to look for her, Reid called Mitch again using Megan's cell, but this time he didn't answer.

A note in Megan's handwriting lay on the nightstand next to the bed. He picked it up.

You were sleeping and we didn't want to wake you. We're in the cafeteria having coffee. Call us on Dad's cell and we'll come back up.

She'd drawn a smiley face at the end of the note. Her car keys were also there, lying next to a sweating water pitcher and a stack of disposable cups.

He had to find Caitlyn. But the problem was that he had no idea where to look for her. Despite all the assurances, his gut told him she wasn't at the hospital, and he had a growing sense that something was wrong. Reid sat up and dropped his legs over the side of the bed, waiting a few moments for the dizziness to subside. Wincing slightly, he pulled the IV needle from the back of his hand.

He would locate Caitlyn, make sure she was safe, then return.

Standing, he stepped to the room's vanity. A cabinet held the jeans he'd been wearing when he had been brought into the E.R. With some difficulty, he put them on. But he had neither shoes nor a shirt. Reid looked at the sleeping form in the bed on the other side of the curtain—a male, probably in his early to mid-forties. He quietly shuffled through the man's belongings that were placed neatly in a separate compartment. A pair of brown loafers appeared to be about the right fit. There was also a flannel, button-down shirt—a size too big—which could be helpful due to the thick bandage wrapped around his biceps. Reid pulled off the hospital gown. His arm stiff and aching with the effort, he put the shirt on and then slid his feet into the loafers.

Picking up Megan's cell and car keys, he walked to the door and looked into the empty corridor. Quietly, he moved down the hall, taking the stairwell to reduce the chance of running into the floor nurses or his family. He'd made it halfway through the hospital's marble and glass lobby when someone called his name.

"Agent Novak?"

A Middleburg policeman came toward him. "I'm Officer Cusick—we met before? At the Treadwell house?"

The man was young and fresh-faced. If not for the uniform, Reid would have guessed him to be a college student. "Right...Cusick."

"I bet you're hurting," he noted, glancing at Reid's injured arm. "I'm surprised they discharged you already. You were bleeding pretty good when you got to the E.R."

"You were here?"

"I answered the call at the Cahill house. Chief Malcolm sent me here to get a statement from Ms. Cahill. I followed the ambulance over." He grinned. "I'm dating one of the nurses, so I've been hanging out. Playing a little hooky, you know? I should be getting back before they have my ass—"

"You talked to Caitlyn Cahill tonight?" Reid asked.

"Yeah. While you were in surgery."

"How long ago?"

"It's been a while." The officer peered at him. "If you don't mind me saying, Agent Novak, you look a little pale. Maybe you should sit down—"

"Have you seen her since? It's important."

He wedged his hands just above his gun belt, thinking. "You know, I *did* see her again."

The officer indicated a wood bench next to the information desk. "My girlfriend was on break, and she and I were sitting right over there. Ms. Cahill was with that big guy. You know him—he's another FBI agent. I recognized him from the Treadwell house. That and he was packing heat. That kind of thing tends to get my attention in a public building."

"Agent Tierney?"

"That's him."

Reid had an unsettling feeling. Mitch had claimed he'd last seen Caitlyn in the surgical waiting room upstairs. The next question felt foreign and unexpected coming out of his mouth. He barely believed he was asking it aloud.

"Did you notice if Ms. Cahill left with Agent Tierney?"

Officer Cusick nodded. "Sure did. They went right through those doors into the parking lot."

46

Reid pushed through the glass doors, exiting the hospital. By the time he located Megan and Cooper's Jeep Cherokee among the rows of vehicles, he was perspiring, his body shaking from exertion. Climbing inside the vehicle, he took a minute, closed his eyes and rested his head against the back of the driver's seat.

He wasn't losing his mind. He *did* have reason for his disturbing thoughts. Mitch hadn't told the truth about where he'd last seen Caitlyn, and he now had an eyewitness who saw them leave the building together. Reid considered the possibility they'd gone their separate ways outside, or that the rookie officer was just plain wrong. Regardless, something was definitely out of whack. He grappled with the idea that the cologne scent in the dining room had been real. Starting the engine, Reid tried again to visualize the shooter's eyes as they peered at him through the mask's slits. Rattled and uncertain, he rubbed a hand over his face.

This was crazy. This was *Mitch* he was thinking about.

In the meantime, Caitlyn had vanished. Pulling from the parking lot, he tried to ignore the stiffness and throbbing in his right arm. Not sure what else to do, he began driving toward Middleburg, hoping Mitch might still be at the scene. At least then he could confront him, try to figure out what was really going on.

It was less than fifteen miles to Caitlyn's home. Reid took the highway at a high rate of speed even though he was without his driver's license or DOJ shield. As he drove, the spin cycle of his mind kept kicking out thoughts.

Speaking of ice queens, how's Ms. Cahill?

He recalled a previous conversation with Mitch. They'd been in a bar, early in the investigation. Mitch had referred to Caitlyn as an *ice queen*. It was a term Joshua Cahill had used repeatedly to describe his victims during the psychological interviews Reid had conducted. He hadn't reflected on it until now. Was it merely a coincidence Mitch had used the same description?

He knew he was grasping at straws.

Still, on impulse, he called information and got the number to the Springdale Penitentiary. It took several minutes to reach someone capable of helping at the early morning hour, but he finally succeeded.

"Agent Novak?" a guard with a heavy Baltimore accent said through the phone. "You say you need someone to go through visitor logs for prisoner 86213? Joshua Edward Cahill?"

"I'm looking for a specific visitor. FBI Special Agent Mitchell Tierney."

"Well, I can see he was here yesterday," the man noted after a few seconds. "His name's on the registry."

Reid's mouth went dry. "What time?"

"He signed in at five-fifteen, back out just before six."

Mitch had gone to see Cahill immediately after the news conference. Why? It was a visit he hadn't mentioned to Reid. It occurred to him that, although they'd been monitoring Cahill's communications and visitors since the copycat's emergence, they hadn't been looking at Bureau personnel. And Mitch had been in charge of the surveillance.

"I need you to look back over the past few months and tell me how frequently Agent Tierney's been there."

"Each log is only good for that week, Agent. I'll have to get into the records room to look at the old ones. I can call you back."

"Please do it as quickly as possible," Reid said. He gave him Megan's cell number and closed the phone as he made the turn up the wooded road leading to Caitlyn's home. When he pulled onto the driveway in front of the farmhouse, a Middleburg Police patrol car was the only vehicle there besides Caitlyn's BMW. Fortunately, the officer standing guard on the porch recognized him.

"How long ago did Agent Tierney leave?" Reid asked as he got out of the Cherokee and approached.

"About twenty minutes ago," the officer said. He was balding and middle-aged with a slight paunch under his dark uniform.

"Was he alone?"

"I'm pretty sure." He looked at Reid curiously. "You okay, Agent Novak? Shouldn't you be in the hospital?"

"Discharged," Reid muttered. Was it possible Mitch had stashed Caitlyn somewhere while he made himself present at the crime scene? He envisioned her bound and gagged in the trunk of his government-issued car, his chest squeezing at the image. He stepped onto the porch. "I've got to get inside to get my badge and gun."

"Your weapon was taken into evidence. Agent Tierney has your shield."

"I need in anyway."

The officer nodded, letting him pass. Reid lifted the crime scene tape and ducked under, feeling the flash of pain in his arm and shoulder with the movement. He went upstairs to Caitlyn's office. To his relief, the combination to the gun safe was still inside the desk, written on a slip of paper. Reid opened the safe and removed a handgun and some bullets. He slipped the weapon into the waistband of his jeans, concealing it beneath his oversize shirt. As he passed through the living room, he picked up his cell phone, in case Caitlyn tried to contact him on it.

In case the absurd path of his thoughts was wrong.

He prayed to God it was.

Reid had just started up the Cherokee when the twin orbs of headlights emerged from the wooded road. The Rambling Rose pickup truck roared up the drive. Reid braked and lowered his window as the two vehicles met.

"I was up early and heard on the television about the shooting. A federal agent," Manny Ruiz said above the growl of the truck's engine. "I thought it was you."

"Caitlyn's disappeared. Has she contacted you?"

He shook his head, his forehead creasing with worry. "I tried callin' the house and her cell phone, but she never answered. That's why I came over. What can I do?"

Reid advised him to look anywhere Caitlyn might be. "Check the stables as well as the woods. Do you have a gun with you?"

"My double-barrel. That's all I need."

"If you see anything that looks unusual, call me and then get in touch with the local police."

Ruiz gave a quick nod. As Reid started back down the wooded road, Megan's cell rang. He glanced at the screen and saw that the incoming call was from his father. It looked as though his absence from the hospital had been discovered. Reid felt bad about it, but didn't answer. A few seconds later, the phone shrilled again. This time the screen read *Springdale Federal Penitentiary.*

"Agent Tierney's been visiting Cahill two or three times a week," the guard told him. "I've got his signatures right here in the logs."

"For how long?"

"Every page I'm looking on has him registered. I'd say for the last several months."

Reid accelerated the vehicle. Mitch had never mentioned the visits to him. Why would he be going to see Cahill so often? And why did the visits start a few months ago? He felt a sinking sensation in his stomach. The timing coincided with Mitch's divorce. He'd been bitter. Angry. Had it triggered something inside him? He tried to imagine Mitch forming some sort of twisted bond with Joshua Cahill. If that were the case, both men had been conning him, starting with the prison interview two weeks ago.

"Have the visits been recorded?" Reid knew it was standard protocol.

"There's a note here about that," the guard said. "Agent Tierney enacted a strict embargo. No digital recordings. It was just he and the prisoner, alone. Cahill gave permission for it."

Reid ended the call. If Mitch had Caitlyn, if he was the one responsible for the killings...

He didn't want to think about what could be happening right now.

Reaching the end of the tree-lined drive, Reid pulled back onto the main road. The white-painted Rambling Rose sign appeared behind him in his rearview mirror, swinging faintly in the early morning breeze. He made two more calls. One was to put out an APB for Mitch's Crown Victoria. The other was to Agent Jimmy Morehouse.

So far, the copycat had killed all his victims inside D.C. Reid didn't see a reason he would deviate.

Reaching the interstate exit, he headed toward the District.

Caitlyn heard the approach of a car outside her prison. Her heart beat a rapid staccato inside her chest. She was cold, swathed in darkness, and she'd lost sensation in her hands some time ago due to the tight binding on her wrists and ankles.

The cramped shed was filled with gardening equipment—a mower and chainsaw, a Peg-Board from which hung various shovels and rakes. Caitlyn lay on her side, the rough plywood floor scratching her cheek. How long she'd been here, she wasn't sure. Vaguely, she recalled Agent Tierney reaching across the car seat, slamming her head against the passenger window hard enough to crack the glass. The rest of her memory was wrapped in shadow and fog.

She heard the death of the car engine. Nearly hyperventilating, Caitlyn tried to breathe through the thick cloth gag in her mouth. Her lungs begged for air. Footsteps moved closer, and she prayed someone had found her.

God. Please.

The door to the closetlike space opened. Caitlyn blinked at the shadowed form staring down at her. Her heart jolted as she heard the deep, familiar voice.

"Told you I'd be back. After I took care of business."

Tierney hoisted her up as if she were weightless, carrying her toward the waiting sedan. Over his shoulder she saw the metal-and-wood storage unit where he had hidden her. It sat a hundred or so feet off the rural road. Less than ten miles from Caitlyn's own house. She had passed by it dozens of times, barely noticing. Above her, stars winked in a black velvet night.

"Your brother's a real son of a bitch, did you know that?"

She cried for help, but the gag stifled the sound. The trunk was open, its black metal mouth waiting to swallow her.

47

Tall leyland cypresses flanked the rear of the Georgetown house, concealing the Crown Victoria from the street.

"Walk." Tierney had untied Caitlyn's ankles, and he followed behind her, prodding her between the shoulder blades with the barrel of his gun. Fallen leaves crackled under her feet. Her head ached and she felt dizzy and unsteady.

"Is the alarm on?" He punctuated the question with a sharp gun jab into her spine.

Caitlyn shook her head, her mouth still gagged and her hands bound uselessly in front of her. They climbed the short flight of stairs onto the covered service porch. Tierney came around to face her. He stood close, his hot breath fanning her face. The scent of his musky cologne was strong.

"You better not be lying to me." He had gone through her purse and taken her keys, and he poked and jiggled each of them in the lock until he found the right one.

Pushing the door open with a soft creak, he shoved Caitlyn inside ahead of him. They continued walking in darkness, passing through the gourmet kitchen with its black-and-white tiled floor and down the long, wainscoted hallway.

"This isn't my usual place," he confided, his hand at her nape as he propelled her forward. She could feel his body heat and the bump of the duffel bag he carried against the small of her back. "It was Joshua's idea."

Caitlyn felt a cold chill.

They reached the two-story entrance hall, the elegant vestibule now seeming foreign and sinister. The unlit crystal chandelier floated like an apparition above their heads, and the arched entrance to her father's library appeared dark and foreboding. The Palladian window facing the street let in only a feeble amount of moonlight, but it was enough to see the rusty swipe of Bliss's bloody handprint still on the wall. Caitlyn closed her eyes in a vain attempt to block out the image of her friend being attacked here.

Her heart raced with the probability she would be next.

All this time, the copycat had been hiding in plain sight. The dichotomy of good and evil, of being the man chasing monsters and the monster itself was nearly more than her mind could process. Tierney had always seemed indomitable, and she wondered how Joshua had managed to infiltrate his psyche, his soul.

"Upstairs." She felt the thrust of the gun again at her back. At the bottom of the curved staircase, Caitlyn froze. The second floor would limit any opportunity she had for escape. Her legs felt wooden and unable to move. The gag muffled her cry as Tierney sank his hand into her hair, snapping her head back until it rested against his hard chest.

"Get up the goddamn steps now," he ordered, his mouth at her ear. "Or we'll get things started right here."

Somehow, she found the strength to do as she was told. Reaching the landing, Caitlyn panted heavily, fighting to take in air through the thick cotton pushing against her tongue. Bile rose in her throat as Tierney cupped the curve of her bottom, squeezing hard.

"The room in back, *Caity*. You know which one, don't you? I'm going to fulfill *his* fantasy."

He pushed her toward Joshua's old bedroom. Panic fell over her as she thought of the doll she'd found there—the pipe cleaner that had been wrapped around its neck, the straight pins inserted into its nude, rubberized body.

Entering the room, she glimpsed the streetlamps in Montrose Park. Their light cast a pale glow over the remnants of Joshua's childhood. A mobile of the solar system hung from the ceiling, gently twirling. Nothing seemed real. She wondered what this would do to Reid—finding out his partner was responsible for her death, and the deaths of the others. Or would he ever know? She prayed there had been security cameras at the hospital, and that they had captured her leaving with him.

Even so, for her it would be too late.

Holstering his gun, Tierney dropped the duffel bag onto Joshua's desk. He snapped on a pair of latex gloves as Caitlyn's eyes followed his movements. The bag's metal zipper rasped. He removed what appeared to be a folded square of plastic sheeting and unfurled it into the air. She winced as he arranged it over the bed. Caitlyn felt lightheaded. The sheeting would act as a drop cloth.

"You should thank me, sweetheart. More blood will only make the resale value worse." Despite his dark attempt at humor, his expression remained stony. Hateful. "I don't want to leave any of my DNA around here. Police training counts for something, right?"

As he loomed closer, Caitlyn shrank against the wall, her wrists working against the tight binds cutting into her skin.

"It's your fault, you know." Angrily, he jabbed a hard finger into her sternum. "I didn't want to shoot him. I had to or he would've chased me outside. He would've seen my car."

He raked a big hand through his coarse hair, pacing a few steps away before returning to glare at her. "He wasn't supposed to even be there tonight. He lied to me—he said he was going to a football game! It was supposed to be you and that worthless con, Ruiz. Reid's car wasn't even at your place. How was I supposed to know?"

His laugh sounded bitter. "But I guess that's what I get for making a deal with the devil, right?"

Roughly, he grabbed her jaw with hard fingers, dragging her face closer to his.

"Let's get one thing straight. Joshua's the reason you're here. I'd decided to leave you alone, did you know that? It was too risky with my partner hanging around you like a dog after a bitch in heat."

Tierney's pale eyes appeared bloodshot, and up close his skin was sallow and porous. "I had it all set up! Hunter was the perfect fall guy— I could end it right there, go back to my old life..."

His upper lip curled into a snarl, and Caitlyn felt spittle from his mouth land on her cheek. "But your fucking brother wasn't having any of it! He called me after the news conference, threatening to tell everything if I didn't carry out *his plan*. He wasn't ready to let me end it without you. So here we are..."

His index finger trailed down her neck, going lower and lingering between her breasts. Tierney smirked, enjoying the violent trembling she could no longer control. Then he returned to the duffel bag and fished inside it.

"Luckily, your neighbor has given me a new prime suspect, which I'm going to need after tonight." Extracting a small video camera from the bag, he placed it on a tripod on the desk and aimed it toward the plastic-covered bed. He peered through the viewfinder, making sure of the correct placement. "You know what a snuff film is, right?"

Caitlyn's mind reeled. Tierney had framed David Hunter, had probably staged his suicide. And now he was planning to set up Rob Treadwell for her death.

He chuckled. "Don't worry, I don't plan to film this. I'm not that crass. I just want it to look like *someone* did. And who do you think will be at the top of the FBI's suspect list? Treadwell's been getting off filming women, including you—so why not make it look like he's into torture and murder, too? We already know from his DVD collection that he likes it rough and kinky."

Her heart dropped into her stomach as Tierney extracted more binding and a knife from the duffel. The knife's steel flashed in the moonlight. Caitlyn wanted to try to flee, but his hulking form blocked the door to the hallway. His eyes glittered.

"It's time to have a little fun, Caity." He lunged forward, grabbing her arm. The gag muffling her cries, Caitlyn fought him, using her bound hands to pound at his chest. With a low grunt, he struck her face hard with his open palm, knocking her backward onto the bed. Stunned, she felt the coppery taste of blood in her mouth. He was on top of her in a flash, his body levering over her.

"If it makes you feel better, I'll make sure Treadwell pays for the mess he's going to make of you."

Her lungs froze as he seized her hands and sliced through the cording with the knife. But just as quickly he wrenched her right wrist up to the headboard, preparing to tie it to the bedpost. Caitlyn jerked her right knee upward as hard as she could, catching him in the groin. Tierney roared in pain, rolling off the bed and cupping his genitals.

"Fucking whore!"

She scrambled to the other side of the mattress. She couldn't escape—his bent-over, writhing form remained between her and the room's only exit. The closet offered the only protection. She ran inside it, sliding the door closed with a bang and holding onto its latch from the inside. Sobbing, she worked the gag from her mouth, dropping the knotted cloth around her neck. Her skin prickled as she heard his footsteps.

"You're only making it worse for yourself, *Caity,*" Tierney warned through the door. "You're going to get an extra burn, an extra cut for every minute you defy me—"

He tried to yank the door open, then gave it a forceful kick that jarred her hands. The door shuddered, its panel cracking. Still holding on to the latch with one hand, she felt frantically around the closet's blackened interior with the other, searching for something, anything, to use as a weapon. Blindly, her fingers traveled over long-forgotten sneakers, boxes of board games, a tennis racket...

"I'm going to rip you apart!" His deep voice vibrated with fury. He kicked at the door again, deepening the crack in the wood. "I'm going to find out why my partner can't get enough of your tight little—"

He tore the shattered door from its track, sending it crashing to the floor. Caitlyn screamed as he reached into the closet, grabbing a fistful of her sweater and dragging her out. She swung the baseball bat she'd found. Tierney raised his arm to ward off the blow but it hit him squarely on the forearm. He bellowed, curses spewing from his mouth.

Caitlyn swung again. This time the bat glanced off the side of his head as he ducked. But it was enough to send him toppling backward onto the broken door.

She darted past him and down the hallway, screaming for help and running to the staircase. As she reached the landing, the mahogany railing exploded next to her.

"Stop there," Mitch warned. "Or I'll put you down now."

Caitlyn turned to face him, panting and unable to catch her breath. He stood less than a dozen feet away, his gun trained on her. Crimson trailed down the side of his head where she had hit him, dripping onto his shirt collar. His chest heaved.

"Drop the bat. Throw it over the railing. Now!"

Blood rushed in her ears. Mitch staggered closer with the gun trained on her face. Numb with terror, Caitlyn did as she was told, heaving the bat over the splintered banister. Its crash echoed as it bounced off the antique table in the foyer below. Her only hope was that someone had heard the gunshot and reported it. She felt faint. Her legs would no longer hold her, and she sank onto the hallway's carpeted runner, holding her reinjured hand.

"You're going to suffer for this." Tierney gripped her so tightly she heard the bones crunch in her wrist. Dragging her on the floor by one arm, he headed back down the corridor.

Back to Joshua's bedroom.

48

"I don't think anyone's home." Morehouse sounded tinny and distant through the cell phone. "There's no light on inside and his car's not here."

Reid gripped the steering wheel harder, disappointment filling him. He was still on I-66 headed back toward the District. He had sent Morehouse to Mitch's Arlington neighborhood, since the agent lived in the same general area and could be there before him.

"I need you to go around the house, look into the windows—"

"Agent Novak?" Morehouse's voice held disbelief. "You're sure about this?"

"Pretty sure," he said quietly, although the conviction sat in his stomach like a block of lead, heavy and unsettling. The scant number of other cars on the highway appeared motionless as he moved past them at a high rate of speed. "You've worked with him for the past six months. What do you think?"

"No. I mean, I don't know...maybe," Morehouse conceded nervously. He seemed winded and Reid guessed he was already conducting a check around the exterior of the modest, ranch-style residence. The house had been left to Mitch by his parents and was the only thing he'd managed to keep in the divorce.

"Him leaving the hospital with Ms. Cahill and lying to you about it, all the unrecorded visits to her brother—it's weird," Morehouse admitted. "He's got some anger management issues, and he doesn't seem to like women much. Not as *people,* anyway. But he's a federal agent…"

The sky overhead was still dark, and Reid could see the reflective glow of city lights ahead of him. His mind spun with ideas of where Mitch could be, where he might have taken Caitlyn. The possibility she was being hurt at that very moment tore into him like a dull knife.

"Agent Novak?"

Lost in the private hell of his thoughts, he'd nearly forgotten Morehouse was still on the line. "Do you see something?"

"I'm in the backyard. There's a vehicle inside a detached garage. It's between the two houses so I'm not sure which one it belongs to. The door's padlocked, but the vehicle's got a tarp over it." His voice grew pinched. "It's dark inside but I can see a little through the window. I…I think it might be a white van."

Reid felt blood rush through his veins. "Get inside the house. You have exigent circumstances—you don't need a warrant."

"But no one's here—"

"As far as the courts are concerned, you don't know that for certain," Reid emphasized. "Caitlyn's in grave danger and something inside could help us figure out where he might have taken her. Morehouse, use the opportunity. We don't have time to go through the legal channels."

"All right. I'll call you back."

Reid disconnected the phone. A sign announcing the Arlington exit appeared in front of him. He had planned to get off there, but there was no point now. Morehouse could cover the residence without him, and the time he had left to find Caitlyn alive was leaking away like water from a cracked vase. He rubbed a hand over his eyes, aware of the dull throb beginning inside his head.

He drove past the exit and headed farther into the District.

As he drove, Reid tried to control his anxiety and think clearly. Caitlyn would be special to Cahill—he would want Mitch to take her to a special location. The dilapidated factory on the Potomac in Southwest Washington would have been a strong possibility if it hadn't been razed a year earlier. But there was another place. Thinking of the mutilated doll, his foot pressed harder on the car's accelerator.

He was going on raw instinct. If he was wrong, the lost time could be devastating.

Passing over the Francis Scott Key Bridge a short time later, the river's choppy waters below him were dark. Reid considered calling the cops and sending a unit to the Georgetown home, but he feared the wail of sirens closing in might cause Mitch to panic, to move things along faster. If he and Caitlyn were even there at all.

As he took Wisconsin Avenue toward Montrose Park, his cell phone sent out an electronic shrill. "Novak."

"There's no one here," Morehouse confirmed, excitement spiking his words. "But the basement, it's set up like some kind of torture chamber. There's a blood-stained mattress on the floor, ropes—"

"Get Forensics out there. Document everything." Reid heard the tremor in his own voice. A blackness washed over him. He wiped a hand over his mouth and felt his heart pound at the image of Caitlyn being tied down, being tortured and raped by the man Reid had trusted with his life. He struck the steering wheel with his fist, causing a flare of pain to shoot up his injured arm.

Goddamn it, Mitch.

Self-recrimination churned inside him. He should have known, should've seen signs that Mitch was experiencing some kind of psychological break. Just because Reid had been ill, distracted—it was no excuse. Nor was the fact that Mitch was smart enough to mask any suspect behavior around those most likely to pick up on it.

He had planted the knife and jewelry in David Hunter's hotel room. And although the handwriting on Hunter's suicide note appeared genuine, Mitch had probably forced him to write it, then administered the fatal shot to his skull. As a trained law enforcement officer, he understood bullet trajectory, blood spatter and other forensic sciences. He would know how to make it look like a self-inflicted wound. But if he'd gone to all the trouble of setting Hunter up for the murders, why take another victim now?

It didn't make sense.

Reid ignored the faint auras appearing around the wrought-iron streetlamps as he reached the outskirts of Montrose Park. His vehicle sped past the waterfront and woodlands before making the turn onto the affluent residential block. The Cahills' stately house stood wrapped in shadows. The interior was equally dark, with no light coming from the main level or the dormered windows on the top floor. Boxwood hedges and an elaborate ironwork fence framed the home's front yard.

Caitlyn had to be here. If Reid was wrong, if he had wasted precious time...

He drove past, parking farther down the tree-lined street. His right arm felt stiff as he exited the Cherokee and circled back on foot to the cobblestone walkway leading to the house's rear. Keeping close to the home's side, he scanned the backyard with its brick courtyard and lush veil of climbing ivy. The jut of a metal bumper was almost entirely concealed by the large cypresses at the property's boundary. Reid moved closer, his heart thumping.

Mitch's sedan sat in the narrow back alley.

The pain inside his head grew more persistent,

spreading its tentacles through his brain. For a moment, Reid closed his eyes, fighting his own internal battle. Then he called for backup. But he wouldn't wait to go inside. His best shot was to get to Caitlyn before all hell broke loose. Trying the back door, he felt its easy give. He entered quietly, moving into the kitchen and down the hall with his gun poised in front of him. Adrenaline coursed through his body. The chilling sound he heard caused perspiration to pop out on his forehead.

Caitlyn's muffled screams floated down to him from upstairs.

49

By sheer force of will, Reid resisted the urge to charge toward Caitlyn's cries. He kept his pace slow and careful, letting his gun lead the way into the shadowed foyer. Still, the wrenching sound of her stifled sobs felt like a physical assault.

A baseball bat lay in the entryway's center. Passing the bloody handprint still visible on the wall, he tried to shut out the gruesome image of Mitch using the bat on Caitlyn, bludgeoning her like he did Bliss Harper. At least her screams meant she was still alive. Cautiously, Reid began moving up the curved staircase, his eyes searching the landing above him.

Halfway up, Caitlyn's muffled cries died.

He felt a surge of dread. Each creak on the stairs seemed to resonate through the large house, announcing his arrival. Reaching the second floor, Reid glimpsed the entrance to Joshua's bedroom. It yawned at the end of the long corridor, waiting for him like an open, black mouth.

The silence was the tell; things were too quiet. *Too still*. He clenched his weapon harder. His presence was known.

"Mitch?" he called finally into the darkness, voice hoarse. "We need to talk."

In his current condition, he knew that he was no match for his partner's strength and size. His body trembled from the blood loss, compounded by the ever-encroaching drumbeat inside his skull. He called out again, but again received no response. Drawing closer to the bedroom, he saw that a window had been opened. White sheers fluttered ghostlike in the nighttime breeze. A rush of chilled air met his face.

Reid stepped inside, his heart somersaulting. Caitlyn lay on the bed, her wrists tied to the spindled headboard, her mouth gagged. She wore only her bra and panties. Abject terror sliced through him as he made out the electrical cording wrapped around her throat. Her eyes were closed, thick lashes resting against her pale cheeks. He couldn't see her chest moving.

He kept his gun raised as his gaze swung quickly around the room. But only wisps of musky cologne and the faint odor of cigarettes remained. The roof sloped gently outside the open window. There was a possibility Mitch had escaped to the ground below.

His hands shook as he checked for Caitlyn's pulse, his fingers pressing against the slender column of her neck as he removed the cording restricting her airway. Relief flooded through him—her pulse was thready but still there.

"Caitlyn," he whispered, touching her face. She felt cold. Her eyelids fluttered, then went still again. Reid worked the cloth gag from her mouth. Pressing his mouth over hers, he created a seal and blew air into her lungs. She responded, coughing weakly.

"Breathe."

She struggled to take in air on her own, wheezing with the effort. Anger roiled inside him as he saw the inside of her right forearm. Weeping, circular burns pocked her soft flesh. The plastic sheeting underneath her made it clear Mitch had only gotten started. Reid's arrival had forced him to jump ahead in his plans. He'd been strangling her with the electrical cording, *killing her,* which was why her sobs had ceased.

A video camera sat on the desk, facing the bed. Reid stroked her hair, taking solace in the rise and fall of her chest as he continued urging her to breathe.

He had to get her out of here. Now. Placing his gun on the bed next to Caitlyn, he began working at the tight cording abrading her wrists. She coughed again, moaning softly as he freed her of the first restraint. He rubbed circulation back into her hand.

"Stay with me, Caitlyn. You're okay—"

"He's still here." Her voice was raspy, barely audible. "Reid, he's still here..."

A sixth sense tickled the back of his neck. Seizing his gun, he turned toward the door in time to see Mitch's shrouded form pass along the hall and disappear into darkness. He glanced at Caitlyn. Her breathing remained ragged but she was inhaling and exhaling. Help would be here in a matter of minutes.

He couldn't allow him to escape.

Reid moved into the hall, the nose of his gun making a sweeping arc across the open doors of the other rooms as he watched for human movement within the shadows. His nerve endings thrummed. Reaching the splintered railing on the landing, he scanned the staircase and foyer below. Had Mitch gone downstairs?

He felt the sudden charge of electricity in the air around him. Reid spun instinctively, his gun raised.

"Hey, partner," Mitch said quietly. He stood hidden by a tall armoire, his own weapon aimed at Reid's heart. He stepped slowly forward, his face illuminated by the moonlight seeping inside. His mouth was a grim line, his eyes flat. Feral. As if he had subsumed Joshua's evil. The man looking at Reid was his partner, but wasn't.

Reid tightened his grip on the Glock. "This is over, Mitch."

"Looks that way," he conceded. "I guess Johnston's golden boy finally figured it out. What gave me away?"

The hair on the right side of his skull was matted with blood, and rusty stains were visible on the open collar of his dress shirt. It appeared as though Caitlyn had put up a good fight.

"Why?" Reid asked hoarsely. "Why do this?"

Mitch raised his big shoulders in a shrug. "I wanted to know what it was like, I guess. Having that kind of power, that kind of control."

Disbelief coiled inside him. He couldn't understand

how Mitch had fallen so far. "You should've talked to someone about what you were feeling. What we do... the violence...there's a lot of pressure—"

Mitch laughed bitterly, white teeth flashing in the darkness. "But you'd never consider something like that, would you? Taking a walk on the dark side? You and I have different appetites, Reid. *Different needs.*"

"We're not that different—"

"You sure about that? When you were on medical leave, I reopened the psych interviews with Cahill. I was intrigued. We talked a lot about the women, about what he did to them, and why. I realized I *understood* him..."

Mitch's face had settled into hard lines. He licked his lips, his voice lowering. "I kept looking at his drawings, reading through his journals with every little thing described in detail. Jesus, they excited me—"

Reid felt disgust. "You're ill, Mitch."

"Maybe," he acknowledged. "Like they say, maybe I lost my *moral compass.* Fell into the abyss or whatever the hell you want to call it. But that kind of impulse—it can't be created. It was always in me, right?"

"I don't believe that."

Mitch gave a small, chilling smile in response. Reid saw something evil move behind his eyes.

"At first, I just fantasized about doing the things that little freak had done. I thought it would be enough for me, but I realized I wanted more. I killed that horse, thinking of Caitlyn and knowing she would see it. Cahill suggested it as a warm-up," he said, unremorseful. "He also picked out the first one—Allison Murrell, a stuck-up socialite who liked to get her drink on. It was a piece of cake to scoop her out of that bar parking lot in Middleburg. One less drunk bitch in the world."

"And the others?"

"They were *my* choice." Mitch thumped his chest, revealing something akin to pride. "Including Bliss Harper. I met her right here in this house, remember? Caitlyn called us out here about the doll. *My doll,* actually. I talked to Harper after you went upstairs. Good-looking woman. I thought we might have something in common with both of us being recently divorced. I suggested we get a drink but the ice queen turned me down cold—she thought she was too good for me."

He made a snorting sound. "I knew I'd catch her here alone, eventually."

Reid felt his jaw tighten. His headache had worsened and he had to focus to keep talking. "What about Caitlyn? Was she your choice, too?"

"Cahill wanted her. He'd been after me to take her once I perfected my skills. But the truth is, I'd decided to skip her. Things were getting too hot, especially after the near miss in the parking deck. Harper was going to be my last one. I wanted to quit before I got caught."

"You left the pawns at my door—"

"To prove I was just as good as you!" Mitch snapped. His face reddened with anger. "I was right under your nose. You're Johnston's top profiler and you still couldn't see it! No one could! But that fat-ass reporter almost made me."

He cursed vilely, a vein in his forehead bulging. "I came *so close*. I had Hunter all locked down for the murders—I was done—and then *fucking Cahill* calls me from prison, ordering me to take his sister or he'd rat me out. He gave me twenty-four hours."

His eyes bored into Reid's. "You weren't supposed to be at her house."

Reid worked to steady his grip on the gun, aware of the blood that had begun seeping through his shirt-sleeve. Mitch noticed it, as well. He lifted an eyebrow.

"Looks like you popped a suture, buddy. Sure you're going to be able to keep holding that thing?"

"For as long as I have to," Reid answered, throat tight. Their guns remained pointed at one another as police sirens punctured the night, moving into the Georgetown neighborhood. For several moments, Mitch listened to their keening wail. He appeared haggard and depleted.

"I'm not going to jail."

"You don't have a choice."

He chuckled faintly. "You're as weak as a kitten, Reid. I could take you down now. One blow to that arm and you'd bleed out on the floor before anyone could help you."

"You've had two chances to kill me tonight—at Cait-lyn's and right here. You didn't take them." It was true. Mitch could have fatally shot him at either location. Both times, he'd had the vantage point. Reid's injured arm shook with exertion. "Even if you get past me, we know who you are now. There's no going back."

His face grew hot with emotion, his voice roughening. Reid felt the loss of his partner, as well as a sharp betrayal. "Did you really think you could just *quit,* Mitch? That you could kill these women, pin the murders on someone else and just return to your old life? You need help—"

They realized they were no longer alone. Caitlyn stood at the other end of the hallway, her hand pressed against her bare stomach. She'd managed to free herself, although one cord still hung from her slender wrist. In the moonlight, she looked like a pale goddess, her blond hair tousled and her eyes wide and frightened. A line of purplish bruising encircled her throat.

"I'm not going to jail," Mitch repeated. He shook his head, his eyes reddening. The sirens had gotten louder, the squad cars turning onto the street. "You know I can't go to prison. That's no place for a cop."

Blue lights flashed through the windows, staining his skin. He took his gun barrel off Reid, slowly and deliberately moving it toward Caitlyn. Reid felt his heart pound.

"Mitch," he warned. "Don't do it."

"If you think Julianne Hunter haunts you—"

"Mitch!" He caught the subtle change in his stance, the fractional move of his finger in preparation against the trigger. There was no time to respond otherwise. The kick of the gun shot pain up Reid's arm as noise exploded. Mitch lurched backward, hitting the armoire and leaving a trail of red down its front as he slid to the floor like an oversize rag doll. He lay half-propped against the furniture's heavy, balled feet. Gunpowder and the metallic smell of blood mingled in the air.

Reid felt his lungs constrict. He couldn't breathe. He stepped forward and kicked Mitch's gun away with his foot, then knelt next to him. Blood bloomed like a large, red corsage in the center of the heavier man's chest.

"Mitch…" He placed his hand on his shoulder. Mitch gasped and coughed as he attempted to draw in air. Bright, pink bubbles formed on his lips. He stared at Reid.

"Knew…you could do it, partner," he whispered. Life drained from his eyes.

Reid felt for a pulse, then bowed his head. The phrase *suicide by cop* flashed through his mind. He passed a hand over Mitch's face, closing his eyelids. A few inches from the body, a white chess piece—the queen—lay on its side. He picked it up, clenching it tightly in his palm. The pain in his head magnified. It felt like a scalpel inside his skull, blurring his vision. He sensed Caitlyn's presence nearby.

"You're bleeding," she murmured, voice croaky. He was vaguely conscious of the warm, sticky wetness now soaking more heavily through the sleeve of the borrowed shirt. He felt dizzy and wasn't sure he could stand.

She went into the closest room and pulled a coverlet from the bed, wrapping it around herself. Returning, Caitlyn sank onto the runner behind Reid. She put her arms around his back, pressing her cheek against his shoulder. He felt her body shudder against his. They remained together in silence as below them, a police SWAT team burst through the front door.

50

One Month Later

Agent Morehouse stood with Caitlyn inside Springdale Penitentiary.

"Sure you're okay to go in?" he asked. She nodded, noting the garland that had been strung around the door frame of a visitor break room. The plastic greenery was the only sign of the approaching holiday. Someone inside the room was making microwave popcorn and its slightly scorched smell wafted in the air.

"I can go in with you—I mean, if you'd rather not see him alone," he offered as they walked past a row of chairs. A sign on the wall outlined Visitation Rules in black print. To their left, a large, windowed space revealed prisoners meeting with their families in a supervised area.

"Thanks," Caitlyn said, avoiding the concern in his eyes. "But I can do this. I've done it before."

They stopped at a finger-smudged Plexiglas wall,

behind which sat a burly, uniformed prison guard. Caitlyn knew that beyond this point was the maximum-security area. Both she and Morehouse presented ID and signed the registry, and the FBI agent checked his gun before they went through a metal detection booth that fed into a windowless hallway. A second guard waited for them near a door at the end of the corridor. He had been leaning against the wall, but as they approached he straightened, waiting for a signal from Morehouse that she was ready to go inside.

"Let's get this over with." Caitlyn's voice sounded calm, masking the sea of feelings she carried. Morehouse gave a small nod and the guard unlocked the door.

"Mind your manners, Cahill," he ordered brusquely as Caitlyn entered. She waited for the door to close behind her with a metal snap before she took the seat across from Joshua. She placed a small, digital recorder on the weathered tabletop between them.

"Merry Christmas, Caity. I was starting to think you weren't coming."

"I said I'd be here. It's just taken some…time."

Joshua wore an oversize jumpsuit over his thin frame. His handcuffed wrists were shackled to the table. Other than the fact that his ebony hair was slightly longer, he looked exactly as he had when she'd seen him nearly six weeks earlier. On that visit, Reid and Agent Tierney had accompanied her.

"I understand. You've been through *a lot* since we talked last, haven't you?" Joshua shook his head in commiseration, although a faint gleam was visible in his dark eyes. "I heard about that nasty business with Tierney. Who knew?"

Her shoulders rigid, Caitlyn reminded herself she hadn't come here to confront Joshua about his role in what had happened to her. She kept her tone impersonal. "I want the names of the women and where to find their remains. You promised two, remember?"

"You'll get them, but I want to talk first." He leaned slightly forward in his chair, his handcuffs clanking against the restraint bar.

"How *are* you holding up, Caity? From what I hear, if it weren't for Agent Novak you'd have ended up like that Barbie doll Tierney was so fond of." He smirked, his gaze shifting to the window that Morehouse and the guard were using to supervise their visitation. "Speaking of Novak, where is he? It's strange he'd let you come all alone and unprotected. Unless Richie Cunningham out there is supposed to do the job."

Tamping down her emotion, Caitlyn glanced pointedly at his shackled wrists. "I don't need protection from you."

He tossed his shaggy hair from his eyes.

"I'm very busy, Joshua. Are you going to give me what I came for, or not?"

"Relax." He lowered his voice. "But I want something from *you* first. I want to see them."

"I don't know what you're—"

"The scars." His eyes fell to the long sleeves of her cashmere sweater. Caitlyn felt her heart beat faster.

"C'mon," he urged quietly. "I know Tierney got at least that far."

Her throat ached with revulsion. A hard knock sounded on the door. Morehouse came into the room, his hands on his hips as he directed a warning glare at Joshua.

"It's all right," she said, composing herself. She turned in her chair to face the agent, holding his gaze until he reluctantly retreated from the room.

"So how about it, Caity?" Joshua continued once they were alone again. "What if I sweeten the pot? I'll give up *another* girl—that would make three. All for a little look-see."

She swallowed hard. "How many...more are there?"

"Including the two I already promised? Four."

"I want all four. And I want the names and locations *first*." Caitlyn fought the rising hatred inside her. "Then I'll...show you what you want."

He shook his head. "I don't think so. If I give them all up now, how will I get you back here? I look forward to your visits."

Caitlyn wanted this nightmare over, wanted the cancer that was Joshua severed from her life, once and for all. She would do what she had to in order to gain closure for the families of the women her brother had murdered. Her fingers traced the raised scars on the inside of her forearm through the soft cashmere, aware that Joshua's dark eyes followed her movement.

"Tierney told me they were a...*gift*," she finally said in a quiet, frayed voice. "From you."

His tongue darted out, moistening his lips. "Did they hurt, Caity? Those sweet kisses?"

She gave a tight nod, her stomach knotting at his inhaled hiss of pleasure.

"Tell me what it felt like?"

"Give me the names and locations. All of them. Then I'll share...everything." She forced herself to breathe, to meet his heated gaze. Her words were measured. "I'll tell you about each burn. About the cord he wrapped around my throat. I'll talk about it for as long as you want...if you give me what *I* want first."

Joshua studied her, a mix of doubt and need on his face. His breathing had quickened and his pupils were dilated, merging with the inky-black of his irises. She waited, disgust nearly choking her as he finally nodded in agreement.

Caitlyn's hand shook as she started the digital recorder. Then in a hushed, dreamlike monotone, he began naming the murdered women and the locations where their remains could be found.

"Amber Lynette Brickell...she's in the Anacostia First High Reservoir at the second mile marker. I weighted her body down with cinder blocks...Collette Susan Goodman...dumped in a plastic bag in the Fairfax County landfill...Kirstin Ann Mertz...buried on farmland off route 50 outside Aldie, under a weeping willow tree..."

When he had finished delivering up all four, she stopped the recording. Joshua looked at her expectantly, his obsidian eyes like dark, shimmering pools. Caitlyn realized she was perspiring, her nape damp and her skin clammy under her clothes.

"That's all of them," he murmured. His gaze returned to her sweater sleeve. "Now it's your turn. Show and tell, sis."

Caitlyn placed the strap of her purse over her shoulder, then took the recorder from the table. Joshua snapped up his head as she stood.

"We had a deal—"

"Go to hell," she whispered. "I hope you rot in here."

"Caity? Caity!" The handcuffs clanked against metal, the table rocking as he leaped to his feet. "You promised! You bitch!"

She walked to the door. The guard entered the room, his hand on his weapon as Caitlyn slipped past. She gave Morehouse the recorder without looking at him. Her back straight, she went down the hallway, ripping the guest badge from around her neck. Joshua's screamed curses echoed in her wake.

The darkening sky had begun to spit snow, the first of the season. Reid watched as Caitlyn's BMW pulled onto the drive in front of the farmhouse. He'd been working on his laptop, waiting for her arrival and trying to talk himself out of being angry with her. Jimmy Morehouse had called a short while earlier, divulging the truth about where she had actually been that afternoon.

He'd said he thought Reid needed to know.

With a sigh, he rubbed a hand over his jaw as she

killed the car's headlights. Caitlyn sat in the vehicle for several long moments before finally getting out and coming onto the porch.

"You got a tree," she said, appearing surprised as she entered. She dropped her purse and keys onto the foyer table. Shrugging out of her coat, she came into the living room to survey the large Douglas fir.

"Since you're having my family here on Saturday, I thought you should have one. Manny helped me cut it down. We hauled it here in the truck."

When she gave him a worried look, he added, "I needed the exercise, Caitlyn. And I got the go-ahead from the doctor three days ago."

"You're right," she admitted. "I'm being overprotective."

In more ways than one. Reid wondered again why she hadn't taken him with her to Springdale Penitentiary.

Caitlyn walked to where he stood. She touched his chest in an affectionate gesture, causing some of his upset to evaporate. Reid was intensely fortunate, he knew. The second tumor he had been diagnosed with was benign, and in a location treatable this time through stereotactic radiosurgery, also known as gamma knife radiation therapy. Compared to the vastly more invasive brain surgery he'd undergone the first time, the procedure had been minimal. He hadn't even needed to shave his head. Reid was scheduled to officially return to work following the Christmas holiday, which was just a little over a week away. He'd been staying at the farmhouse at Caitlyn's invitation as he recuperated. It had given them a chance to get to know one another better, as well.

"I haven't actually had a tree yet—in the house, I mean. My first Christmas here, I just couldn't work up the holiday spirit." Her green eyes were soft as she gazed at him. "But this year, I feel like I have something to celebrate."

"*We* have something to celebrate." Reid bent his head and brushed his lips over hers. "How did the Christmas shopping go?"

"Fine," she said, sounding artificially upbeat. She stepped away to retrieve the coat she'd laid on the couch and went to hang it in the closet.

"Where are the presents?"

"In the trunk."

"I'll get them for you."

"No." Caitlyn halted him. "There're some gifts for you in there. I don't want you to see them—"

"I'll just bring the bags in," he offered, pressing the issue. "I'm a big boy. I won't peek, I promise."

"Really, let's just leave them there until morning."

Reid crossed his arms over his chest, deciding to end their charade. He gave her an evaluating gaze. "I can tell when you're lying, Caitlyn. Your cheeks get all pink. And I already know you haven't been anywhere near a shopping mall today."

Her blush deepened. Reid realized what he felt wasn't anger but concern. "Morehouse called me. He told me you went to see Joshua."

"I had to," she admitted. "He owed me the locations of the other women. I got all four of them."

"He told me that, too. Excavation teams are going to search for the bodies starting tomorrow if the weather doesn't interfere. I'm planning to take part. It was my case and I need to be there."

Caitlyn's only response was a faint nod. He realized how hard it must have been for her to see Joshua, knowing her brother had blackmailed Mitch into abducting her, and that his intent had been for her to suffer a horrible death at his hands. Although he understood her motive in going to visit him, it was something Reid would never have wanted her to do alone. He thought of the cigarette burns that had left scars on her porcelain skin. They were a painful reminder of the nightmare she would most likely carry with her forever. He tried to console himself with the knowledge that he had managed to stop Mitch before Caitlyn had been raped, tortured further, even killed. But sometimes that knowledge wasn't enough.

"I wish you would've let me come with you," he said.

"I know. It's just that I know you've been struggling…"

She didn't have to say about what. The revelation that his partner was behind the copycat killings had been a lot to handle. Alternately, Reid felt hurt, angry and even responsible because he had failed to pick up on Mitch's illness. And that was what he was calling it. An illness. There was simply no other explanation for his downward spiral.

I wanted to see what it was like, to understand what made him do it. I thought something about it would feel good. It did for a while.

I'm no better than him.

Reid thought often of the suicide note left behind by David Hunter, aware Mitch had coerced him into writing it. He had probably dictated it to him, word for word. Reid believed its contents had come from some still-sane portion of Mitch's brain, one that felt shame and remorse. In the note, he hadn't been speaking for Hunter, but himself.

Ultimately, Mitch had committed a form of suicide, even though it was Reid who had pulled the trigger. He looked at Caitlyn and felt his heart tug. Mitch had left him with no other choice.

"Did you get to see your mother today, at least?" he asked.

She absently touched a brown pinecone still attached to one of the tree branches. The entire room had begun to take on a fragrant evergreen scent. "Before I saw Joshua. She wasn't talking much today."

Reid heard the tinge of melancholy in her voice. He moved to stand behind her, his hands caressing her shoulders. Caitlyn had lost so much. Family. Friends. Rob Treadwell had been arraigned by the Loudoun County D.A.'s office two weeks earlier on charges relating to the illegal videotaping, and the Treadwells' home now had a real estate sign on its front lawn. The local gossip was that Sophie had left her husband and moved back to upstate New York where she was from. Caitlyn hadn't heard from her.

"The woman who called me that night, about Mom," she recalled, turning to him. "The one pretending to be a nurse so I would come to the hospital? Who do you think she was?"

"Maybe someone Mitch was seeing," Reid guessed. "He probably told her she was helping with some kind of sting to bring in a suspect."

"Do you think she could've ended up as one of his victims? Someone we don't even know about yet?"

It was a sobering thought. "I hope not."

Caitlyn noticed his laptop as it switched to screen saver mode. It sat on the walnut coffee table, nestled between an earthenware mug and a stack of files from the copycat investigation. Reid had been going through them, looking for some sign of Mitch's unraveling he might have missed.

"You've been working today?" she asked.

"Just catching up on some email." He wanted to tell her, to hopefully make her part of his decision. "SAC Johnston contacted me about writing a paper for the FBI training academy at Quantico. About the Capital Killer investigation, as well as the copycat case and the discovery that a federal agent was behind the murders. He thinks it could be a good psychological study on the pressures of the job and the realities of dealing with violent criminal behavior on a daily basis. If the paper turns out well, there's a possibility I could teach a course."

"What do you want to do?"

"Writing the paper might be cathartic. And Mitch... he's someone we're going to be studying for a long time." With a sigh, Reid thought of the famous Nietzsche quote, the one about he who fights monsters taking care not to become a monster himself.

"I just don't want you to take on too much, too soon—"

Gently, he lifted her chin with his fingers and stared into her eyes. "There's no need to protect me, Caitlyn. And I'm dealing with Mitch."

Her slender fingers curled around his wrist. "I know you are. We both are, actually."

"I really do love you," he whispered.

He lowered his head to hers, their mouths melding as Caitlyn looped her arms around his neck. He pulled her closer. Reid reveled in the feel of her body against his, and he loved the realization that he had become familiar with every soft curve of her.

"There's something in the kitchen for you," he said once his lips had left hers.

She gave him a curious look, then walked from the room.

When he reached the kitchen, he found Caitlyn gazing at the small, rectangular box wrapped in silver holiday paper.

"Is this a Christmas present?" she asked, holding the box as she turned to face him.

"Just an early one."

With a small release of breath, she sank onto a chair

at the kitchen table and tore away the paper. Inside was a small diamond pendant on a delicate, white gold chain.

"It's beautiful."

"It's a thank-you for letting me stay here," he teased. "Megan helped me pick it out."

Taking the necklace from the box, she carried it over to Reid and he helped her put it on, securing the clasp at her nape.

He owed her so much. Caitlyn was the reason he'd been willing to submit to whatever treatment was required to make him well again. She was why he had stopped running from the possible harsh reality of it, the fear. He'd been expecting the worst, had been prepared for it, but the gamma knife option was something he hadn't considered open to him. He prayed this time he would stay healthy. He wanted to live a full life.

She turned to face him, the small diamond glimmering in the shallow hollow of her throat.

"Having you here is gift enough, Reid." Her voice was soft.

He cupped her delicate jawline, his thumbs stroking her pale cheeks. They had been talking about the possibility of making their current arrangement more permanent. He had to admit he was enjoying the quiet, country life. Middleburg was peaceful, with its quaint antiques shops and traffic circles, or *roundabouts,* inside the town limits. It was a respite from the violence he saw almost daily in his job. He would need to keep his apartment in the District for practicality, but the idea of staying out here with Caitlyn, waking up beside her in the mornings whenever he could, was tremendously appealing to him. She belonged out here with her horse stables and equine therapy program, but she could keep some things at his place in D.C., as well.

"I know once you start back to work this would be a long commute—"

"We'll work something out. I want to be with you, Caitlyn." He added, "But what I really want to know is whether you're ready for the Novak family onslaught."

Caitlyn had invited all of them out for a weekend at the stables. The snowfall would make for a breathtaking holiday setting. Ben and the girls would be staying in the spare guest rooms, while Megan and Cooper had booked a suite in town at the nearby Red Fox Inn, a historic bed-and-breakfast. Caitlyn was planning a big, family-style dinner. She'd asked Manny and Maria to come, as well.

"I can't wait to take Isabelle and Maddie on their first horse ride," she said, smiling. "Megan says it's all they've talked about."

He wanted to share his family with her, too. Try somehow to make up for the one she no longer had. Caitlyn and Megan had begun a friendship, and it was clear his father and nieces were wild about her already. Reid was falling more deeply in love with her each day.

"We could decorate the tree," she suggested, looking again at the giant, bare fir. "I have some lights and ornaments from the house in Georgetown. They're in boxes in the attic. I'll go get them."

She turned, but he caught her hand.

"I'm thankful for every day I have with you," he said solemnly. "Caitlyn, we both know my health is still tentative—"

She hushed him, placing her fingers against his lips. "Dr. Isrelsen believes your prognosis is excellent. He says the tumor is responding extremely well to the treatment. It's going away. Everything's going to be okay, Reid. I can feel it in my heart."

He embraced her and she settled her head against his shoulder. There was no certainty about what tomorrow might bring. No one truly had that. He thought of his parents and his mother's illness that had separated them. He also thought of David and Julianne Hunter. But he and Caitlyn had right now. The headaches were gone. He felt healthy and whole.

"We don't have to decorate the tree this very minute, do we?"

She looked up at him. "Did you have something else in mind?"

"Maybe dinner." He slowly kissed her mouth and then murmured, "Maybe something else."

"I like how you think."

Reid closed his eyes and breathed in the fresh, clean scent of her hair. Having her in his arms felt right. Being here for *her* felt right, too. Tragedy and unspeakable violence had caused their lives to intersect once again, but this time he wasn't going to let her go. He wasn't going to walk away. She was the one good thing that had come from all this. Fat, white flakes were now falling outside and Reid counted his blessings as they drifted past the picture window.

They belonged together.

* * * * *